Flint

Paul Eddy

HEADLINE
FEATURE

First published in 2000
by HEADLINE BOOK PUBLISHING

First published in paperback in 2001
by HEADLINE BOOK PUBLISHING

10 9 8 7 6 5 4 3 2 1

ISBN 0 7472 6424 4

Typeset by Avon Dataset Ltd, Bidford-on-Avon, Warks

Printed and bound in Great Britain by
Mackays of Chatham plc, Chatham, Kent

HEADLINE BOOK PUBLISHING
A division of Hodder Headline
338 Euston Road
London NW1 3BH

www.headline.co.uk
www.hodderheadline.com

In memory of Julien Bourdonnec
1978–1999

one

Grace Flint has a device smaller than a packet of cigarettes that she can hide in your car, or on your boat or plane – even, if it suits her, in your briefcase – that will track your precise location for the next six months.

Unless the batteries give out, or the satellite goes on the blink.

Grace Flint has a microphone the size of a shirt button, connected to a transmitter as thin as a credit card, that will relay any foolish admissions you might make to her from around the corner, or across the city, or from just about any place on earth.

Unless the lower atmosphere is dirty, or the transmitter spikes, or something else goes wrong; things that the tech boys don't like to talk about.

And even when the technology works, it can be totally irrelevant.

Grace Flint is in the stairwell of a multistorey car park in Belgravia, with the microphone taped to the underside

of her left breast and the transmitter high up inside her
left thigh, secure in the knowledge that the back-up teams
are only yards away, listening to every word, waiting for
the first sign of trouble, unaware that between her and
them is a steel-lined door installed by the right-thinking
management of the garage to deter theft and vandalism
at night, but which, on this particular day, someone has
neglected to unlock.

'I don't want to talk to your friends,' says Frank
Harling to Clayton Buller, apropos of nothing. 'Know
who they are? They're the law.'

Watch their eyes, the instructors at Hendon used to
say. *Don't listen to what they're saying because they're
lying, just like you're lying. Watch their eyes.*

But she can't see Clayton Buller's eyes because of the
dark glasses he wears, and DI Pendle doesn't seem to be
alarmed. Besides, in this heart-stopping moment, she
wants to believe that Frank Harling is only trying it on,
that he can't possibly know the truth of his assertion.

'You're paranoid,' snorts Buller. 'You think I didn't
check them out?'

'Oh, did you?' says Harling, his voice now loaded
with contempt. 'Trust me, dickhead. They're the filth.'

*If the subject makes any sudden move, assume it is
hostile and react immediately*, but Buller's move isn't
sudden; it is slow and even graceful for a big man. He
leans over and reaches down into the depths of his
lawyer's case and suddenly the neurotransmitters in
Flint's brain are passing frantic messages about a gun.

Afterwards, Flint will not be sure if she saw the gun

or heard it first. There is a lot she will not be sure about at the subsequent inquiry. The individual details will be clear enough, each one perpetually etched upon her memory. It is their precise sequence that will evade her.

Pete Pendle has begun to react when the sound of the first explosion fills the stairwell, stunning her with its intensity. It is still resonating when the second explosion comes and then the third. Pendle is pushed backwards by the impact of the first bullet but the stairwell is narrow and with his back against the wall he and Buller are still no more than four feet apart. She will remember his body jerking as the second and third bullets entered his chest, as though he were being shaken by some unseen hand, and she will tell the inquiry it was after the second shot, though it may have been the third, that the spray of blood erupted from his mouth. She will remember very clearly that its colour was a brilliant scarlet and that when it reached her it was warm.

She too has her back to the wall, on the other side of the stairwell, and she sinks down onto her haunches when Buller turns the gun on her. She recognises it immediately as a nine-millimetre Browning, though the inquiry will incline to the view that she probably learned that fact subsequently. She will not recall closing her eyes or covering her face with her hands as she waits for Buller to kill her.

That he does not do so will be easily explained, to the satisfaction of the inquiry, by the fact that the fourth bullet jams in the clip, and Flint loses count of how many times he works the slide in an attempt to clear it.

She is by now aware of too many other sounds and impressions. She is aware of DI Pendle's laboured efforts to breathe. From too far away she hears the raised voices of increasingly desperate men and the pounding of solid objects against a steel-lined door. She hears Frank Harling say, in his unmistakable south London cadence, 'Finish it, Buller. For fuck's sake, get it done.'

Above all she is aware of the grunted exertions of a seriously overweight lawyer from Beverly Hills who is now standing over her beating on her skull with the butt of his otherwise impotent Browning.

She will concede she must have put her hands over her head, for both her thumbs and seven of her fingers are broken. What she will vividly recollect, however, is falling onto her back and feeling the weight of Buller as he comes down on top of her. She feels his elbow in her throat and his manicured fingernails gouging into her skin as he seeks to gain a firmer grip on the fabric of her blouse and bra and rip them away. Absurdly she thinks he is going to rape her but having exposed her breasts, and having found the microphone he is looking for, he gets to his feet. She hears him say, 'Bitch, bitch, bitch,' over and over, and then the real pain begins.

He leans against the wall to maintain his balance while he methodically stamps her chest with the heel of one of his handmade Italian boots. Perhaps out of some irrational impulse he is trying to destroy the microphone as if by doing so he can erase the evidence it has collected. He only succeeds in driving it deep into her abdominal wall.

Then he goes to work on her face, the heel of his boot
raining down blows on her with the indifferent brutality
of a jackhammer. She loses consciousness – though not
for long if her recollections are accurate. She will recall
for the inquiry lying in the stairwell like a broken doll,
tasting her own blood and the gritty enamel of her
shattered teeth, smelling her own urine, listening to the
sound of footsteps running up the stairs, listening to Pete
Pendle die.

Clayton Buller did not get far. Perhaps the realisation
that he had just killed one British police officer and
stamped the face of another into pulp was too much for
a heart already overtaxed by the strain of his excessive
weight and a three-pack-a-day cigarette habit. In any
event, it gave out. They found him in Elizabeth Street,
dead behind the wheel of his Hertz car that came to rest
in the interior of what had been, until his arrival, a
fashionable boutique.

But they did not find Frank Harling, either on that
day or in the course of one of the most intensive
manhunts ever mounted by the Major Crimes Task
Group. Detective Inspector Pete Pendle had been as
popular with his men as any supervisor is likely to be,
and they did not take kindly to his murder, or their own
failure to prevent it. And any and all of those detectives
who saw Grace Flint's shattered face, or heard descriptions of it, wanted to get their hands on Clayton Buller
and, having been denied that gratification by his death,
they transferred their anger to Frank Harling.

Righteous anger that churned their stomachs for, after all, it was Harling who had provoked and encouraged the mayhem.

They're the law, said with utter certainty. *Finish it, Buller*, an incitement to murder if ever there was one.

And it was Harling who had rendered the back-up teams helpless by arranging for the door to the stairwell to remain locked, or so the police strongly suspected. How that was achieved, and how Harling knew he was walking into a police trap were gnawing questions that ate at their collective consciousness like a canker.

So every favour owed Major Crimes was called in. Throughout Metropolitan London, and then the south of England, and then the length and breadth of the country, every police force was enjoined into the hunt. Every port and airport was placed on full alert, and it seemed safe to assume that if Harling left the country he did not do so by any means of public transportation, unless under a convincing and ingenious disguise. Nor, if he remained in Britain, did he, or anyone fitting his description, check into any hotel or boarding house or squat, nor did he take refuge in any sanctuary known to any of the countless police informants who, coaxed by threats or sometimes reckless promises, did their best to please their masters.

No, Frank Harling simply vanished and remained invisible. They raided his house in Virginia Water and in it they found evidence of four different identities he had employed. They found the wife from whom he was separated – or rather the woman who thought she was his wife, though they were obliged to tell her that Frank Harling was, among other things, a bigamist. Through her they found his modest office in Surbiton, rented in the name of UniFi Consulting, and evidence of one-hundred and eighty-two bank accounts he had maintained, each one in the name of a different and obscure corporation, through which vast amounts of money had passed. They also found a Compaq personal computer holding on its hard disk some two gigabytes of encrypted data. Major Crimes pulled another favour, and the computer experts at the FBI laboratory in Washington said they were confident they could find the key that would decrypt Frank Harling's secrets. But in the course of first copying the contents of the hard disk – a seemingly sensible precaution – they triggered the hidden program that irrevocably destroyed them. Like the man, Harling's secrets ceased to exist.

Eventually they gave up the hunt, if not in spirit then in actuality, because they did not know where else to look. They did not admit that to Grace Flint, however, for her doctors considered it important to her recovery and even her sanity that she continue to believe that Frank Harling would be found.

It took them almost a year to rebuild her shattered face. The photographs that record the progress of their painful work (painful for her, that is) are not pretty. In the interim her husband, Jamie, left her. He said that was because he could neither understand nor accept her determination to return to Major Crimes once she had recovered, a determination that never wavered. One day, not long after she had endured yet another session under the surgeon's knife, he took a mirror from her dressing table and thrust it in front of her face to reflect the livid scars and the bruising under her eyes. 'Look at yourself, Grace,' he said, as though she didn't know how she looked. 'I can't stand this. I simply can't take it.'

He packed some of his things and left their flat, pretending it was only temporary; a breathing space, he said. It was a month before she discovered he was living in Pimlico with a woman named Caroline. Caroline, it transpired, had a child who was already one year old; a son that Jamie had fathered.

Still on sick leave, she went to the small village and the Georgian farmhouse where she had grown up, to where she knew at least the physical scars would heal.

Her father called her 'Amazing Grace'. In the depths of the night, he might pray that she would never again be the bait on the end of Major Crime's hook but Dr John Flint did not believe it was his place to tell his daughter what to do. Though he had never understood where her instincts came from – certainly not from him – he saw it as his duty and his pleasure to love her for what she was.

In the wholly unquestioning climate he provided, Grace slowly mended. When she was not in hospital for further bouts of reconstructive surgery, she worked in his operating theatre where the patients paid no mind to her disfigurement.

'You know, Gracie, you'd make a hell of a good vet,'

her father told her, but that was the nearest he ever came to voicing his deep dread.

II

To the inquiry board that exonerated her of any blame for the death of DI Pendle; to the doctors and psychiatrists and the grey men from Human Resources who sceptically evaluated her fitness to return to work; to the instructors at Hendon where she was sent for retraining, who seemed determined to break her; to the new supervisor who replaced Pendle, though not in the affections of his men; to her fellow officers who welcomed her back to Major Crimes with a standing ovation, but who could not look her in the eye; most of all to herself, Grace Flint insisted that Clayton Buller had broken only her bones and her teeth, not her spirit.

It was not true.

The physicians had performed a near-miracle. They rebuilt her jaw and implanted plinths and crowns to replace the teeth that Buller's boot had shattered. Slowly, they reconstructed her nose and her cheekbones and then other surgeons with other skills covered up the traces with dexterous grafts of skin. When they had finished they had sculpted a mask, a replica that was every bit as beautiful as the original, and more enduring. 'You'll look like this when you're fifty,' she was told and though vanity was not one of her sins she took some consolation in that.

But no one repaired the hidden damage because she would not admit that any had occurred.

She was fine, she said. It was not true.

The truth was that Grace Flint, who had once positively enjoyed the involuntary tightening of her stomach muscles and the acute awareness of her own senses every time she went out there alone pretending to be somebody or something she wasn't, now lived in terror of working in the void.

Until Buller did his work, she had been a highly effective undercover operative because she did not look like one. Depending on the circumstances, and the selection she made from her wardrobe, she could be anybody she chose. She was a high-class tart working a private club in the City where some of the wilder currency-exchange dealers were prone to letting their hair down. She was a continuity girl for the BBC drama department with a sick mother to support who, for a fat fee, was willing to fly down to the Cayman Islands carrying money for the Cali cartel. Once, God help her, she was a Provo's girlfriend looking to buy a case-load of rocket-propelled grenades from a Chilean arms dealer in Miami. Or, as Clayton Buller had thought until Frank Harling disabused him, she was a no-nonsense investment banker operating out of Zurich, willing to launder a couple of hundred million dollars that the Internal Revenue Service didn't know about.

She liked weaving her complex webs of deceit and she was good at it. She liked being on the edge, and the heady feeling of euphoria when the risk of her own exposure was over. Above all, she liked watching their eyes as it first occurred to them that she was not, as they had thought, their victim or their customer or their accomplice, but the instrument of their ruin.

Not any more. The breezy confidence with which she got through the days at Major Crimes was as artificial as her face. At night, alone in her small north London flat, she lay in the dark waiting for the dreams that, more often than not, would take her to the capital of her private hell; a Pandemonium that usually resembled a stairwell in Belgravia.

She came to look forward to the nights when migraine headaches would rob her of the ability to think of anything but the tightening steel band around her head; when, after the nausea finally came, she would fall into an exhausted sleep too deep for dreams.

Her colleagues in Major Crimes knew, of course, though they pretended not to. Perhaps they did not comprehend the sheer depth of her fear but they certainly knew that Grace Flint could never work undercover again. They gave her informants to run, they sent her out on surveillance, they made her an indispensable part of every back-up team and they took her along on every bust. And, when even that seemed too much to ask, they sent her to the United States – out of harm's way, as they saw it – to a desk job at the British Consulate in Miami, where she became Major

Crimes' liaison to the Federal Crimes Joint Task Force.

Nobody dreamed of asking Flint to step out once more into the abyss – until Cutter came along.

Was Cutter mad? Did he set out to make or break Flint, or, as his enemies prefer, was he simply too vainglorious to care? Even now, after all that has passed and despite all the evidence at Harry Cohen's disposal, it is not a question he can answer.

III

Thomas Breslin sits plump and comfortable on an L-shaped sofa upholstered in white leather. The sofa occupies a good proportion of the palatial living room of the Alhambra Suite, the most deluxe accommodation offered by the Buccaneer Hotel in Miami's Coconut Grove. Beside him sits his wife, though she is surely much too young to be the original Mrs Breslin.

They are a handsome couple, expensively dressed, he in an azure-blue silk shirt with tiny pearl buttons and white linen trousers, she in a crimson silk pant suit that reveals all but the top few inches of her slender legs. Breslin allows the fingers of his left hand to trace idle patterns on the inside of her thighs. It is a gesture that says 'She's mine.' Mr Breslin gives the impression that ownership is an important concept to him.

They had arrived at Miami International Airport that afternoon from New Orleans – if you believe the flight plan filed by the pilot of the Learjet that supposedly brought them to Florida. They were met at the airport by two young men who looked as though they spent a lot of time in the gym. They both wore linen jackets that were cut modishly loose, under which they might conceal any manner of things. They did not carry the Breslins' luggage themselves, preferring to keep their hands free, but they made very sure that the skycaps loaded each and every piece into the trunk of the white limousine that awaited the Breslins directly outside the terminal. They entered the car only after the Breslins were safely on board. Vigilant is the adjective that best describes them.

The Breslins did not check into the Buccaneer Hotel; they simply arrived. The beaming day manager, obviously welcoming back valued customers, met them in the hotel atrium and led them directly to the elevator that was reserved exclusively for the occupants of the Alhambra Suite. The two young men travelled with the Breslins in the elevator, as did their luggage. There was never any question of it being otherwise.

Finishing touches were still being made to prepare the suite, which displeased Breslin, though he did concede that the arrangements had been made at very short notice. Nevertheless, he remained impatient until the work was done. He had visitors coming.

There were three of them and they arrived at the hotel precisely on time. They hurried through the atrium lobby, only to be kept waiting at reception while the clerk used the phone to confirm that Mr Breslin was indeed expecting them. A bellboy punched in the three-digit code without which the doors to the Alhambra Suite's elevator would not open.

In one of the deep alcoves of the lobby, a man put

down a newspaper he had not been reading and said, apparently to himself, 'Alpha four. Rykov and two unknowns. On their way.'

Aldus Cutter allowed his hand to stray to the very top of Grace Flint's thigh which he patted. 'Fix us a drink will you, honey?'

You do not have to do this, Grace. You do not have to be in this room with these people, pretending to be some scumbag's whore. You can end this now. You can say, 'Back in a moment, honey,' and you can walk into the bedroom and out onto the fire escape and not come back. This is Cutter's operation and his responsibility – and he has no bloody right to put you in this position. You've paid your dues. You do not have to do this. Grace, listen: YOU DO NOT HAVE TO DO THIS.

But of course she has to do it. What choice does she have?

When Aldus Cutter called her to the headquarters of the Federal Crimes Joint Task Force in North Miami that morning, and told her 'Rykov's taken the bait,' and told her 'He's going to sell us eighty-million dollars' worth of counterfeit one-hundred dollar bills' – exquisitely manufactured by Lebanese forgers in Beirut; when Cutter said, 'He wants to meet Mr Big. That's me. You're Mrs Big. You get to wear the wire,' what could she have said?

Could she have told Aldus Cutter that she did not feel well, that her period was due, that she felt a migraine coming on? Or could she have told the most senior special agent of the FBI she had ever encountered, 'Mr Cutter, I just cannot hack this. I can no longer do what an undercover copper is supposed to do because Clayton Buller put his boot in my face'; should she, in other words, have admitted to Aldus Cutter what she could not admit to herself?

Whatever the prudent course, she had not taken it.

'Why me?' she said, trying to sound normal; trying to disregard the tumult inside her head.

'Because you're supposed to be good at this, Flint. It's what you do. Right?' She didn't respond and Cutter continued, 'It's time to get back in the saddle.'

'Excuse me?'

'When you've taken a fall you need to get back up there. Longer you leave it, the harder it gets.'

'Right.'

When Cutter then said, 'Got something to wear that'll make you look like a big shot's woman?' she'd replied with a lightness she did not feel: 'Well, a big shot's much younger woman,' and that had won her a rueful smile.

'You'll be fine, pilgrim,' Cutter said, and she'd chosen not to argue with him.

At least it had proved unnecessary for her to wear a wire. Despite the gloomy predictions of the tech boys, Aleksei Rykov had not balked at the invitation to meet Thomas Breslin in the privacy of his hotel suite and thus they had been spoiled for choice as to where to conceal their devices.

'What'll it be, Aleksei?' she says, walking over to the bar. Rykov dismisses her offer of a drink with a flick of his hand. He has not yet addressed a word to her, and doesn't seem inclined to do so.

She seems not to notice. She also ignores the four other men in the room on the grounds that Tommy Breslin's wife does not concern herself with the comfort of the hired help. 'Honey?' she says.

'The usual.'

Thanks a lot, Cutter. How am I supposed to know what you drink? She makes him a vodka martini, and one for herself, and loads his glass with olives, speared on a cocktail stick that is topped with a paper parasol bearing the designer motif of the Buccaneer Hotel.

'There you go, sweetheart, wet and sweet, just as you like it.' Cutter gives Rykov a broad, lascivious grin. Rykov does not respond, even when Mrs Breslin sits down next to him on the sofa and curls her legs in his direction.

She pretends to sip her drink, watching him watching Cutter. There is no script and there has been little time to rehearse. Her role is whatever she chooses to make it.

So here we go, she thinks to herself. To Aleksei Rykov, who wishes to be regarded as a significant player in the counterfeit currency business, she says breezily, 'So, Aleksei, are you gonna piss or are you gonna get off the pot?'

Thomas Breslin does not exist. He is entirely a figment of the imagination of Aldus Cutter and the other architects of Operation Harvest.

Yet in New Orleans, as Rykov's hoods have easily established, Tommy Breslin is a man to be reckoned with. There is not a snitch for the FBI in New Orleans who has not been offered generous compensation for information about Breslin, and that fact by itself has enhanced his reputation. The DEA, the ATF, the Secret Service, the IRS and the Louisiana State Narcotics Task Force have all asked questions of their own about Breslin. Thus his legend has grown exponentially, and among the denizens of the underworld there is now certainty that Tommy Breslin, a man they have never met, is a major factor in gambling, prostitution and narcotics in their city. He is also believed to be Mob connected; not main Mob, not with a name like Breslin, but Mob connected nevertheless. Given the scope of his activities, and the rise of his reputation in the city's criminal milieu, he has to be.

And dealing in counterfeit bills is another activity of the Breslin empire, so the story goes, hence the interest of the Secret Service. So far it has been small time, for Breslin's suppliers have been unreliable in terms of the quality of their product. The word in New Orleans is that Tommy Breslin is looking to significantly increase his share of the trade.

The word in New Orleans is that Tommy Breslin thinks he can move ten million dollars a week, maybe more.

'You boys are full of piss,' says Breslin, echoing his wife's sentiments. 'This deal should have gone down weeks ago but all I've heard is frigging excuses. Can't

---

do business like that. I've got to be able to count on you or I'm gonna have to count you out. Maybe I should take a little trip down to Beirut and find myself a player who ain't got his finger stuck up his ass. You get my drift, Aleksei?'

Rykov smiles, though only with his mouth. 'Save yourself the plane fare. We need to be satisfied about the people we do business with and it takes time to be satisfied. You understand, I'm sure.' He shrugs to indicate his complete indifference.

'So?' says Breslin.

'We're ready to do business now.' From his inside jacket pocket Rykov produces a slim wad of crisp one-hundred dollar bills and places them on the table. 'These are samples,' he says. 'The rest are immediately available. You know the terms.'

The tension is electric. Even on the videotape it is palpable.

Tommy Breslin nurses his drink, slouched down in the folds of the sofa, never taking his eyes from Rykov's face. He lets the moment stretch. Finally he says, 'Rick, fetch the bag.'

Watching the tape, you don't really notice the bystanders until now for they have played no part in the drama. Rick in particular is almost invisible because he stands motionless, his back against the wall, his arms folded across his chest. If you look carefully you can see that his right hand is inside his modish linen jacket, resting on the shoulder holster that he is no longer attempting to conceal.

_____

At Cutter's command, he pushes off from the wall. His limbs are heavily muscled but he walks towards the camera with an easy grace. The camera cannot follow him for it is stationary, its fibre-optic lens embedded in the wall. He goes out of frame. The soundtrack picks up the noise of a door opening, then closing, then opening again, then closing once more, and Rick returns into view.

He has his back to the camera now and we can see that in his left hand he is carrying one of those cases that, despite the claims of its manufacturer, will not quite fit under an aircraft seat. The case is obviously heavy, even for Rick. We cannot see his right arm because it remains folded across his chest.

He walks to where Cutter is sitting and places the case on the coffee table where Cutter has propped his feet. For a few moments he blocks our view of Cutter while he works the combination locks and we hear the distinctive click of their mechanisms. Then he steps aside and resumes his position against the wall, to the left of the frame. His right arm remains across his chest as though it is strapped there, the fingers inside the jacket. He leaves the other arm hanging by his side where it will not get in the way; it is the right arm that will do the work, if needs be. Nobody else moves and nobody speaks.

Cutter takes his time. In the transcript of the video the stenographer has noted a pause of twenty-eight seconds and Harry Cohen has timed it and she is right. But, watching it, the pause seems almost eternal, a moment frozen in time. Cutter still holds his glass in both hands, the bottom of it resting on his chest. The angle of the camera is quite low which makes it look as though he is peering at Rykov over the top of the ridiculous parasol. The level of the liquid in the glass has not fallen by more than a couple of centimetres.

Rykov is in profile, to Cutter's left, our right. He is an extraordinarily handsome man with a proud forehead and jet black hair so finely coiffed it might have been spray painted on his skull. There is something old-fashioned about his appearance, more than a passing resemblance to Rudolph Valentino.

When Cohen showed the videotape to A.J. Devereaux, the deputy director of MI5 said in that superior way of his, 'He looks as though he might run a dance band.'

But there is an air of menace about Rykov. Like Cutter, he looks predatory; they have the manner of two jackals, sizing each other up for dinner.

Flint is there, next to Rykov, but she is leaning back into the sofa and there is the illusion that she has shrunk. Her face is very white, which may be nothing more than a trick of the light.

When the twenty-eight seconds have passed, Cutter takes his feet from the table. He does it slowly, as though they are heavy to lift. He leans forward and places his drink on the table, then opens the case. From the viewpoint of the camera, we cannot yet see what is inside, but Cutter tells us.

'Hundred-dollar bills. Real ones. Five hundred to a

bundle, fifty-six bundles, makes two point eight million. Count it.'

We can see now that he is holding in his hand a two-inch thick stack of bank notes. He tosses it onto the table in the direction of Rykov and there is a loud thud on the soundtrack, for it was inside one of the hollow legs of the coffee table, the one closest to where Rykov is sitting, that the tech boys concealed their primary microphone.

Rykov still does not appear to move, nor does Flint. The nod of his head is imperceptible until we slow the video down to one frame a second.

The tall man, the one who'd been missing the top of his head in our picture, now comes forward and we can see that he has not, as it seemed, been scalped. There is another revelation: he is truly, hideously ugly. In the shadows where he'd been standing, behind and to the left of Rykov and directly opposite Rick, we could not see his face in any detail. Now that we can, what dominates our senses is the sight of the purple weal than runs from ear to ear across both cheeks and underneath his nose, as if his face has been sliced in half and then rejoined by some incompetent welder. The scar has the effect of elongating his mouth into a gash of fantastic dimensions. The weal gives him the permanent greedy leer of a shark. Flint cannot take her eyes off him.

Devereaux was appalled by the sight of him. Cohen heard the sharp intake of his breath as Devereaux realized that the disfigurement was real and not some blemish on

_____

the tape. 'Oh, my dear boy,' he said, 'what monstrous creation is this?'

'His first name was Vladimir – or at least, that's what Rykov called him,' Cohen said. 'They never established his real identity.'

'And who, or what, did that to his face?'

Cohen shrugged, not knowing the answer.

Devereaux's outfit also has its tech boys and they had provided equipment that allowed him to freeze a frame and enlarge and enhance any portion of it. On the screen, Devereaux pulled up Vladimir's face until it was six feet wide.

'Behold the noble savage,' he said. 'I fear for our heroine, Harry.'

'With good reason,' Cohen replied.

As the video continues we are not spared Vladimir's fearsome countenance. Cutter has moved and is now standing by the bar, looking bored. Vladimir has taken his place on the sofa, directly facing the camera, and is methodically emptying the case of its contents.

He takes each stack of bills and manipulates it with his long bony fingers until he is satisfied with its symmetry, then places the stacks side by side in neat rows until they cover most of the surface of the coffee table. We can see that it is uniformity he seeks; he is making sure that each of the stacks is of precisely the same thickness. He runs his hand over the paper plane he has created like a carpenter measuring the smoothness of a piece of wood.

Apparently satisfied, he selects one of the stacks at random. He neatly slits the wrapper with his thumbnail and, holding the bills with one hand, he flicks through them with the other. He does it several times, like a card dealer looking for the Joker. Then he spreads the bills into the shape of a fan and we can see that he is reading the serial numbers. We assume that he does not find two that are the same for eventually he closes the fan and manipulates the stack between his fingers until once again it is perfectly aligned.

Now he counts the bills one by one. He does it very quickly but at irregular intervals he pauses and submits a particular note to minute scrutiny, examining the texture of the paper and the regularity of the print. For a moment we think he has finished but we are wrong. He takes another stack of bills from the coffee table and slits the wrapper, and the process begins all over again.

'Fussy bugger, isn't he?' said Devereaux. 'What do you think the chances were of short-changing young Vladimir?'

'Slight,' said Cohen.

Finally Vladimir is satisfied, though he does not say so. He gets up from the sofa and returns to his position in the shadows where we can no longer see his hideous face. It is Rykov who says, 'Very well.'

'So what now?' says Cutter who has remained leaning on the bar, careful not to obstruct our view of Rykov – or Rick's.

'Now it's your turn to be satisfied. Naturally the merchandise is not here.'

'Naturally,' says Cutter sarcastically.

'It is not far away, Mr Breslin, and it is secure. Your men can go and examine it now. Slavitch will take them.' Rykov nods in the direction of the small man with skin like alabaster who is lounging insolently against the door of the private elevator on the periphery of our vision. 'It is not something that you and I need concern ourselves with.'

'Fine. So what are our concerns?'

'You are a perceptive man, Mr Breslin. You are right, we do have concerns because this is the first time we have done business together and though your reputation is excellent we cannot yet be certain how things will turn out. It is like making love to a beautiful woman for the first time.' He glances at Flint. 'You hope her passion will equal her beauty but it may not be so. In life, as in love, Mr Breslin, we must prepare ourselves for disappointments.'

'Rykov, get to the frigging point. How do you want to do the exchange?'

'With great care.' It is evident that Rykov is enjoying himself. 'Your men will go with Slavitch. You and I will go downstairs to the coffee shop – with the money, of course. I'm told the food is excellent. There are a lot of people there. Nothing bad will happen to either of us in the coffee shop, I think. And then we wait. When your men have satisfied themselves about the merchandise, they may take it. It is in a truck which you may keep with our compliments. They go to wherever they wish and then they call you and tell you everything is as it should be, and I leave with the money. Our business is complete and the next time we meet I shall apologise to you for my foolishness.'

'And him?' Breslin nods towards Vladimir.

'As I said, you are very perceptive. Vladimir is my insurance. He will remain here with your wife. When everything is completed satisfactorily, I will call him on his pager and he will leave. If something goes wrong and Vladimir does not receive a call from me . . .' Rykov leaves the sentence unfinished.

No, no, no, no, no.

Grace Flint is screaming but the sound is only audible inside her head.

One floor below the Alhambra Suite, in a nearly identical living room, though this one cluttered with electronic paraphernalia, Kevin Hechter, the team leader of Operation Harvest, felt as though his lungs had been punctured.

He closed his eyes for a moment while his brain began to calculate how much of his team's time, and the government's money, had just been rendered wasted. Then he said to himself, 'To hell with it.' There would be, he knew, no shortage of other people ready to make that computation.

'Okay, folks, this thing's unravelling,' he said into the microphone attached to the headset that he wore. 'Cutter's going to have to abort and we don't know how Rykov will react. I want everybody in position. Now.'

The effect of his words was extraordinary. Throughout the hotel and in its immediate vicinity men and women abruptly stopped whatever they were doing and moved with great purpose to the posts they had been pre-assigned.

The maintenance man fixing the air conditioning in the Granada Suite walked out the door saying, 'Need to get a wrench,' though he was already holding one in his hand. A chambermaid replenishing mini-bars on the third floor abandoned the liquor cart in the middle of the corridor. Waiters and bellhops and parking valets deserted their duties and the hotel's clients with no more explanation than a hurried 'Sorry.'

And in the atrium lobby four young men who looked as though they had just come from the tennis courts punched in the code that allowed them access to the Alhambra Suite's private elevator. Once inside, and once the doors were closed, they unzipped the bags they were carrying and prepared themselves for combat.

At least they had something to do. Hechter could only watch the grainy images being relayed to his television monitors from the room above, and listen to the silence, and wonder how Cutter was going to play it.

Soft or hard? 'That's not the way I do business,' and try and reason with Rykov? Or, 'Fuck you, Rykov,' and throw them out? Either way, Cutter would have to do it well, otherwise a lot of people were about to get hurt.

Finally Cutter spoke, and for an instant Hechter did not believe what he had heard. Then Hechter said, 'Oh, you fucking bastard, Cutter. Cutter, you cannot fucking do this.' But he had.

* * *

'What do you say, honey? You wanna stay here with Vladimir while we take care of the business? That okay with you, sweetheart?'

Thomas Breslin's voice has taken on a wheedling tone, as if he is cajoling a petulant child. He is still standing by the bar, with his back to the camera, so we cannot see his face but that is not what frustrates us. It is Flint's face we want to see. If ever there was a moment for a close-up, this is it.

She has remained in her prone position on the sofa. She still looks shrunken and her face still looks very white. We no longer believe this is a trick of the light.

'Shouldn't be more than a couple of hours,' says Breslin. 'Right, Rykov?'

Rykov nods. He is watching Flint as carefully as we are. But he is much closer to her. He can see her eyes.

She smiles at him. It is not the false smile of a badly frightened woman. Enhanced and magnified on Devereaux's screen, it is generous, playful even. It is a lovely smile, a credit to the skills and dedication of the reconstructive surgeons.

She turns her head to glance at where Vladimir is standing and then she looks at Cutter. She is still smiling when she says, 'That's fine, honey. You boys go and finish up your business and me and Vladimir, we'll keep each other company. I feel like a swim.'

'She cannot leave this room,' says Rykov, still refusing to speak directly to her.

'Oh, quit worrying.'

She reaches out and touches Rykov's knee and then

gets up from the sofa and goes behind it to where the drapes form the backdrop to the scene. She fiddles with some mechanism and the drapes slide back to reveal glass doors that fill the wall and, beyond them, an enclosed terrace containing a swimming pool. She strikes a theatrical pose with her hands in the air and says, 'Ta-da!' as though she is a conjurer producing an illusion.

Now she walks towards Cutter – and therefore the camera – and we marvel at her performance. There is nothing in the swing of her hips, or the stride of her long legs, or the set of that beautiful face that says she is in the least bit intimidated by the prospect of spending the next two hours in the company of a man who will kill her if things go wrong.

Yet Grace Flint must know that Aleksei Rykov will not be allowed to walk away from the coffee shop with $2.8 million of the US government's money. She must know that at some point in the next two hours he will find himself lying face down on the floor, with his arms pinned behind his back and a gun to his head, and that Vladimir will never receive the message that all is well, that he is not required to take the life of Tommy Breslin's wife. Then what?

'Vladimir and me, we'll be fine,' she says to Breslin and brushes his lips with her own. 'Now you hurry back, because we've got things to do.'

Rick's silent partner, whose name we never learn, repacks the bag while Rick maintains his vigil. Slavitch presses the button that summons the elevator. (And, though we cannot hear this, Hechter in his lair below

radios the order for the four young men to quit the
car before it can ascend. There is no time for them to
remove their flak jackets before they tumble into the
lobby.)

When the elevator arrives it is Rick who carries the
bag inside. He enters the car backwards, never taking his
gaze from Slavitch, while his silent partner follows him,
watching Vladimir. Slavitch seems amused at their
circumspection. He enters the elevator with the fingers
of one hand pointed like a gun and we see him mouth
the words, 'Bang, bang.'

Rykov and Breslin enter the elevator together, but
before they do so Rykov goes over to where Vladimir is
standing and says something to him, softly and urgently.

Cutter could not have heard the words, nor would he
have understood them if he had, for Rykov spoke in
Russian. But the microphones picked them up and among
the agents now crowded into Hechter's room was one
for whom Russian was the mother tongue.

'What did Rykov say?' asked Hechter.

'She is to make and take no calls. She is not to leave
the suite. If anybody tries to enter the suite before
Vladimir gets the call, he is to kill her. What he actually
said was *"zamochit"*. Literally, it means "waste her".'

Only Vladimir and Flint remain in the room. He has
not moved from his place by the wall, among the
shadows. She sits on the sofa with her back to him,
fixing her nails. The only sound we can hear is the
insistent rasp of her file.

* * *

'Did Cutter have a plan or was he just playing for time, hoping for the best?' said Devereaux.

They had broken for lunch at his club in Pall Mall, saving the rest of the tape until the afternoon. They could have sped through it, fast-forwarding through the fallow intervals when little or nothing happened, but Devereaux would not hear of it. He would not be denied a single frame.

'He never said,' replied Cohen. 'What would you have done? In his place, I mean.'

Devereaux fixed Cohen with that mocking stare of his with which he had, Cohen knew, chilled many of his subordinates at Thames House.

'I cannot conceive of circumstances . . . There *are* no circumstances under which I would ever find myself in the place of Cutter,' he said. 'Cutter's brand of courage, if that's what it is, appalls me. Generals belong high up on the hill where they can survey the progress of the battle, not down there in the muck with the infantry. Or in the coffee shop of the Buccaneer Hotel, for that matter. I assume that's where he went?'

'Yes,' Cohen confirmed. 'Neither Breslin nor Rykov was prepared to let the other out of his sight. Because of the money, of course.'

'So who led the cavalry?'

'An FBI agent called Taylor who's an expert in hostage situations. As soon as Hechter realised what was happening he hit the panic button. Taylor had an FBI SWAT team there in less than forty minutes. They put a perimeter around the hotel and got the sharpshooters in place and then sat back to see if Flint could save herself.'

'Asking a great deal,' asserted Devereaux.

'Too much,' said Cohen.

'Where are you going?'

'The bedroom. I'm going to change and have a swim.'

'No.'

Vladimir does not raise his voice. There is nothing threatening about his tone or his posture. There is simply an air of absolute finality in his declaration. 'No.' It is a statement of fact. Flint will not go into the bedroom. She will not leave his sight.

She is standing near the camera, her body facing us but her head turned away as she looks back over her shoulder to where Vladimir remains standing in the shadows.

'I want to swim,' she says.

'Go ahead.'

Now she turns her body towards him, and away from us. Her hands are clasped behind her back. We can see, though Vladimir cannot, that her fingers are furiously busy. She folds them into her palms and then unfurls them in a sequence that she keeps repeating. She shows the camera eight fingers, then seven; eight then seven, again and again. Eight-seven is one of the codes employed by agents of the Federal Crimes Joint Task Force to communicate their wishes, and sometimes their fears, during undercover operations. Eight-seven is a cry for help. It means: *I do not have this situation under control.*

She stands staring at Vladimir, waiting for him to say something more but he does not. Eventually she turns away from him and begins undoing the buttons of her pant suit. She does so slowly but there is nothing remotely erotic about the way she sheds her clothes. She is merely getting undressed. Vladimir and the camera do not exist.

She allows the pant suit to fall to the floor and steps out of it. Naked now except for a pair of white underpants, she walks across the room to the glass doors that lead to the terrace and the swimming pool.

I do not have this situation under control.

But this is a consummate actress giving the performance of her life. If we did not know better we, like Vladimir, would be thoroughly deceived.

In the living room of Hechter's suite, a dozen anxious men watched the screens on which nothing moved and listened to speakers which broadcast no sound, acutely aware of their own impotence and increasingly irritated by it. Occasionally one or other of them spoke urgently into a telephone or a walkie-talkie radio but nothing they said or heard could save Grace Flint.

Only Taylor of the FBI seemed unaffected by the mood of pent-up frustration, perhaps because having played no previous part in Operation Harvest he felt no share of the blame.

'The problem with the elevator?' he asked. 'Run that by me again.'

'We can't use it because he'd hear it coming,' said Hechter. 'By my reckoning it takes eleven seconds to reach the suite from the lobby, which is about three times as long as he would need.'

'And the fire escape?'

'Leads off from the bedroom. She tried to make it in there but Vladimir's too cute for that.'

'Push bar, outward opening?'

'Check.'

'We could blow it with a shaped charge.'

'Great, but then it's twenty-five feet to the bedroom door. He hears the bang, he's going to be splattering her brains all over the terracotta. You might as well call him, tell him you're coming.'

'What's he carrying?'

'Looks like a MAC–10, but we haven't gotten a proper look at it.'

Taylor went closer to one of the television monitors to better examine the picture of Vladimir who now sat in an armless chair a few feet back from the glass doors, watching Flint. He had his back to the camera so there was nothing to be learned about the type of weapon he cradled in his lap. Taylor continued staring at the screen.

'I've got five men on the roof,' he said. 'Perhaps we'll get a shot at him.'

'Trouble is, he hasn't put his nose outside the room,' said Hechter. 'What about tossing a stun grenade in there, or some smoke?'

Taylor continued staring at the monitor. 'It's about twelve feet from the roof to the top of the doorway and they can't lean out far enough to get a decent trajectory.

We might have to risk it, but I'd rather wait and see if anything else develops. How long have we got?'

'They've been gone ninety minutes, so another hour maximum is my guess. If he hasn't heard from Rykov by then, Vladimir's going to start thinking something's wrong.'

Taylor weighed the options, still watching the screen. He found no inspiration there and turned away.

'Okay, we'll give it fifty minutes, see if he makes a mistake. How's the girl doing, by the way?'

Hechter smiled. 'Flint's doing great. Looks like she doesn't have a care in the world. She's sunbathing.' He did not mention her silent screams for help. There seemed to be no point.

Flint lies flat on her stomach by the side of the pool, her arms crossed in front of her, providing a pillow for her head. Her face is turned to where she can watch Vladimir, watching her, through half-closed eyes. She can see very clearly that the weapon he holds in his lap is indeed a MAC–10, a submachine gun capable of firing thirty rounds per second at sufficient velocity to slice her body in half.

There are people on the roof above her, she is sure of it. Though they had crept to the edge of the asphalt on tiptoe, scarcely daring to breathe, she had heard – or perhaps it was sensed – their soft noises. She knows that at any moment they will come for Vladimir, exploding into action with terrible violence. She wills her muscles to relax so that Vladimir will receive no warning from her of what is about to happen.

Come on! What are you waiting for?

She knows precisely what she will do. She has chosen where to lie down with great care. One complete turn of her body, one sudden twist, will take her into the pool. However quickly Vladimir reacts, he will not be able to get off even one short burst before she disappears from his sight. Then her powerful legs will take her down to the bottom of the pool where Vladimir's bullets will not, cannot, reach her – not through eight feet of energy-absorbing water. And, anyway, by then Vladimir will have other things to think about, like an instant decision between life and death; his own death, not hers. If he makes the wrong choice, as she hopes he will, 'Freeze' will be the last word he hears.

Come on! Do it now!

With a lazy grace that will not provoke alarm, she rolls over onto her back to double-check her calculations. Her left elbow now rests on the edge of the pool and her fingers play with the water. One more half-turn and she will be in the pool and then under the surface, safe in its milky warm embrace.

She shades her eyes with her right hand and squints up into the sun. From her perspective the roof looks like the summit of a black cliff towering above her. Any second now, she prays, the stark rectilinear plane will be briefly broken by the shapes of men tumbling over the edge before they plummet down towards her. The shapes will be black, too – appropriately.

She raises her right knee until the leg is bent at a

forty-five degree angle, ready to provide the thrust that will send her spinning into the pool.

Now!

'Come here,' Vladimir says.

She turns her head towards him.

'What?'

He does not speak again. He sits in the chair, his left hand in his lap, his right hand, his gun hand, extended towards her, holding the MAC-10, pointing the ugly mouth of its barrel at her head.

She knows what he said, knows that he meant it. As slowly as she dares, she gets to her feet.

You have to come now because if I go back into that room it will be too late. This is your last chance. Hell, this is my last chance. You have to come. NOW.

Twenty feet away from her, barely hidden from her sight, the agents who were selected and trained at the FBI academy in Quantico for just such emergencies as this, crouch on the rooftop, waiting for the command that does not come. They are attached to nylon straps, with quick-release buckles, that will allow them to moderate their descent to the terrace. They are also equipped with Glock automatic pistols with which they routinely achieve the maximum possible score on the firing range and – a much more difficult trick – on the assault course. They are supremely confident that they will not miss the target when, but also if, they are given the order to move.

But they do not come because the men in Hechter's living room – in the command post of this ruined operation – will not give Flint the benefit of the doubt. They have not guessed that she has a plan; that she is able and ready to remove herself from harm's way. So, for her sake, as they see it, they will not give the order.

Vladimir watches her walk towards him.

He is, essentially, a man immune to human emotion but there is something about Grace Flint that has reached and aroused him. Perhaps it is her aloofness, her apparent indifference to the effect on him of her near-nakedness.

That, at least, was Harry Cohen's theory – for how else to explain Vladimir's momentary lapse into carelessness?

As Flint answers his summons and walks into the room, and as she goes to pass him by, he moves the gun from his right hand to his left and reaches out for her. His right hand hooks inside the top of her thighs and what should have been his trigger finger begins probing the fabric of her underpants.

She does not resist. She opens her thighs to make his exploration easier. His shark's mouth seeks and finds her breasts. She puts her hands behind his head and pulls him closer to her.

From its fixed position the camera offers only glimpses of the spectacle but what it clearly shows, and what Hechter immediately sees, is that the MAC-10 is in Vladimir's left hand, pointing at the floor.

'He's right-handed,' says Hechter, the significance of what he's seeing washing over him like a wave. 'The stupid bastard's right-handed.'

Taylor presses the transmit button of his walkie-talkie radio and says, 'Bravo One, GO!'

Long after it is necessary, long after they've stopped listening to him, Taylor continues to repeat the command: 'Go! Go! Go! Go!'

IV

The coffee shop at the Buccaneer Hotel was called Le Café, which accurately reflected its pretentiousness. It served more *kir royales* than coffee, and dishes such as *agneau de pré salé*, and wild strawberries the size of peanuts, flown in 'fresh' from France, and yours for just $26 a helping, plus service and tax. The room was predominantly white, the furniture dark green, the table linens pink. Everywhere there were potted plants not indigenous to southern Florida, of the kind that do well in the shade. The French doors opened out onto a patio and through them the privileged patrons of Le Café could only rarely hear the distant sounds of the ruder world outside.

'What was that?' said Rykov.

'Sounded like firecrackers,' said Cutter, alias Tommy Breslin.

Other people at other tables had also heard the ragged volley of sharp cracks and briefly paused their conversations before deciding that whatever the cause or the consequences of the disturbance it was no concern of theirs.

But Rykov was unsettled by it. For all of his conceit
the waiting was beginning to tell on him. He had
reviewed the plan that had seemed so perfect, and felt
the first doubts creeping in. He had drunk more coffee
than was good for his nerves. He badly needed to go to
the men's room but he could not, would not, leave Breslin
alone. He, too, was held hostage, he realised – by $2.8
million packed in a suitcase that sat under their table,
steadfastly guarded by Breslin's plump legs.

'You better not be fucking with me because Vladimir
will do exactly what I say. If you fuck up, or your friends
fuck up, you don't have a wife, you understand me?
You're going to be a widower. You get to go to your
wife's funeral.'

'Hey, Rykov, get cancer,' said Breslin, suddenly
emerging from the languid stupor that seemed to have
overcome him. 'Jesus! What's the matter with you? Just
relax, will you? Nobody's going to fuck up, unless it's
you. Have some more coffee.'

'Why is it taking so long?'

'Hell, I don't know. Maybe the traffic's snarled up.
Maybe the car broke down. Maybe your frigging Slavitch
got lost. Anyway, they've not been gone a couple of
hours. You worry like this all the time? You're gonna
give yourself a heart attack.'

But Rykov continued to fret. He called the waiter and
told him for the third time that they were expecting an
important call. He smoked one cigarette after the other.
He drank more unwanted coffee and felt the pressure
build in his bladder. He could not sit still.

Finally: 'I have to take a piss. You come too.'

'Hey, Rykov, I'd love to go to the bathroom with you but that way we're gonna miss the call. You go ahead. I'll tie a knot in mine.'

'No,' he said, but he wasn't sure how much longer he would be able to tolerate the pain.

It was the telephone that saved him, brought to the table by their waiter who plugged it into an adjacent jack saying, 'Call for you, Mr Breslin.'

'See, Rykov, you gotta have a little faith.' He picked up the telephone and said, 'Yeah?'

All of those agents who could see Cutter's face – and there were by now five of them within twenty feet of his table, and three more posing as waiters – agreed afterwards that his performance was nearly flawless. As he listened in silence to whatever was being said to him he allowed only the merest trace of a smile to dance across his mouth. He returned Rykov's intense stare with one of his own, his faded-blue eyes unblinking, giving absolutely nothing away. Then suddenly he winked at Rykov and gave him the biggest, boldest version of his hallmark smile. 'Sounds good to me, Rick,' he said into the telephone. 'Let's do it.' Then he hung up.

'Well?' Rykov said.

'Everything's just as it should be. Everything's fine.'

'Then I think the bag is mine.'

'Sure is,' said Breslin, and he used his legs to push the suitcase under the table until Rykov could feel it against his own. He visibly slumped as the tension left his body. At least for a few moments, he forgot the pain in his

---

bladder. He grinned back at Breslin, who was still grinning at him and, as an afterthought, he stuck out his right hand. 'Pleasure doing business,' he said.

Breslin took his hand and shook it, saying nothing, still grinning. Anybody watching the two of them, anybody who didn't know, must have thought them delighted by each other's company.

Then Rykov became earnest and leaned forward to emphasise what he was about to say. 'I will leave now. You must stay here for twenty minutes. You must not go to your room until then, until Vladimir has left.'

'Fine,' said Breslin.

Rykov stood up. 'And you must give my apologies to your wife for . . .' He hesitated. 'For the inconvenience.'

Breslin shrugged as if to say it didn't matter, that no apology was necessary, that for one man to hold another man's wife hostage was nothing more than a tiresome business formality, like requiring credit references. Breslin was so genial, so quiescent, that Rykov should perhaps have smelled the rat.

The suitcase was much heavier than he had anticipated, and he was having difficulty getting it out from under the table, so he did not see Grace Flint's approach, did not know she was there until he heard her speak.

'Hi there, sweetie,' she said to Cutter, and kissed him on the top of his balding head. 'How's the food? I'm famished.'

Rykov had lost all interest in the suitcase. He stared at Flint in disbelief as she took her place at the table and pretended to study the menu. She was wearing a man's shirt – one of Hechter's – that was two or three sizes too big for her, tied at the waist with a belt. She looked pink and scrubbed, as if she had just stepped out of a hot shower. It was an accurate impression. It had taken a lot of hot water to get rid of the blood.

She looked up at Rykov and smiled. 'You want to be careful lifting heavy bags, Aleksei, you'll give yourself a hernia.'

'That's what I keep telling him,' said Cutter. 'He's gotta take better care of himself.'

'Perhaps we can help,' she said. 'Aleksei, sit down.'

He was too confused not to obey her. He slowly lowered himself onto his chair as if it might explode and said, 'Where's Vladimir?'

'Vladimir won't be joining us, Aleksei,' she said. 'Vladimir is indisposed. Vladimir has a hole in his head the size of a grapefruit. It's called an 'exit wound' but in his case I think 'wound' is something of an understatement. Vladimir is dead, Aleksei.'

While she let this sink in she took her purse and placed it on her lap under the table, and opened it, and took out a semi-automatic Hechter had given her, and worked the slide all the while smiling at him as though he were her lover.

Cutter leaned across the table towards them. 'Hey, guess what, Aleksei?' he said. 'We're federal agents and you, you sonofabitch, are under arrest.'

Rykov looked at their faces as though they were vaguely familiar, as though he was trying to remember where he had seen them before.

'There are a couple of ways we can do this,' said Cutter. 'We can put you up against the wall, and cuff your hands behind your back, and drag you out of here like the piece of garbage you are, but that's going to upset all these nice folks, not to mention the hotel management. So, what I suggest we do, Aleksei, is this: The three of us are going to get up and we're going to stroll out of here like we don't have a thing to worry about, and then we're going out through the lobby and into the car that's waiting for us.'

With the hand that was not holding the gun, Flint picked up Rykov's cup and sipped the cold coffee. Her hand was rock steady. Her eyes never left his face.

'Before we go I have to tell you something,' Cutter went on. 'You have rights. Even dirtbags like you have rights. You have the right to an attorney, Aleksei, which is just as well because you're going to need one. If you cannot afford an attorney then one will be provided for you but, to be honest with you, this isn't the moment to be a cheapskate. Get the very best you can, Aleksei. He won't be good enough but then at least you'll know you tried.' He paused.

'Finally, you have the right to remain silent. This is an important right and if I were you, Aleksei, I would keep silent because if you say anything smart to us, anything at all, it is possible, even probable, that Mrs Breslin here will blow your balls off. You have no idea how much I would like her to do that, Aleksei. No idea.'

The pain was now too much to endure. Aleksei Rykov finally lost control of his bladder.

two

A.J. Devereaux's interim review of what he had codenamed Operation Hades was not yet complete and he pressed Harry Cohen for a working lunch. 'In the country,' he said, conceding it was a Saturday. 'Somewhere special. My treat.' They headed south in Devereaux's Daimler, grinding through London's drearier suburbs clogged with traffic, saying little of consequence until they crested the long hill of Purley Way and Devereaux began, 'When I asked you to find Flint . . .'

'Asked?' said Cohen sharply. He had been reflecting on the troubled history of their relationship and his resentment had been building.

Devereaux glanced away from the road to look at Cohen with mock surprise. 'What would you prefer, Harry? When I *persuaded* you? When I *begged*?'

'Cajoled, I think. Perhaps manipulated is nearer the mark.'

'Dear boy, what on earth are you talking about?' said Devereaux as though he had no recollection of coming unannounced to Cohen's office on a thick, humid evening in late summer, bullying his way past the secretary with his imperious charm. He had slipped into Cohen's room, catching him unawares, and shaken his unwilling hand and said 'Hello, Harry,' as though they were on the best of terms. 'Before you say anything,' he had instructed, laying a thin blue file on Cohen's desk, 'there's something I want you to read.'

'What if I'd thrown you out?' Cohen asked, shifting in the passenger seat, fixing his stare on Devereaux's profile.

'Ah, but you didn't, did you?' Devereaux smiled, relishing the memory. 'You read young Gracie's file.'

A pedantic file hastily assembled by Scotland Yard for Cohen's benefit – or rather not for his benefit since it was prepared according to A.J.'s sly instructions and Cohen had sworn that he would never again be a part or a dupe of Devereaux's intrigues, which was why they had not spoken for the previous two years.

In Harry Cohen's office Devereaux had seated himself in the best armchair as though he was a valued guest and Cohen could not find the energy to resist him. He went to his desk and opened the file warily, not yet sitting down, scanning the first page. He saw that it described in strict chronology the police career of one Grace Elise Flint, and he saw that it was written in the dead hand that marks all law enforcement reports. But the facts were there, linear and stark, and despite himself – despite the animosity he felt towards the bearer of these tidings – Cohen's imagination was soon fleshing out a narrative. Now leaning on his desk, now lowering himself into his chair, he had felt the tug of unwonted emotions. He was aghast at the recklessness of Grace Flint's courage. He was enthralled by the demons that drove her.

They reached a stretch of dual carriageway and the Daimler surged forward, quickly overtaking the line of cars they seemed to have been following for an eternity. 'Laggards,' said Devereaux, savouring the Daimler's power. 'If anyone cajoled you, Harry, it was young Flint, no?'

Young Flint, Constable Flint, barely out of training college, still a probationer, working at the Yard as a glorified filing clerk, plucked from the ranks of the obscure for her first undercover operation. The file said she was chosen 'because of her appearance' and Cohen had found himself flicking through the pages, looking for a picture of her. There was none – one of Devereaux's teasing touches, no doubt – only the briefest of physical descriptions. She was 5ft 10ins, 130lbs, Cohen had learned. Black hair, hazel eyes.

Tallish then, and slim, with eyes the colour of amber, and Cohen could see her in a tight pencil skirt with her warrant card hidden in the top of her sneakers, walking alone in the moonlight, bait for a monster.

For that's what he was, Flint's first target: a hooded giant of a man who ravaged women on Hampstead Heath, looming out of the darkness, beating them into submission with his fists, sending four of them into intensive care.

Cohen had imagined Flint on that first night setting out to cross the Heath, chattering with fear, holding onto the solemn promise of the back-up teams that they would never be more than a few hundred yards away, feeling in the top pocket of her denim jacket the comforting bulk of the police radio on which she was to call if so much as a shadow moved. But nothing untoward had happened on that first night, nor on the five subsequent nights that she crossed the Heath. Her fright would have waned, Cohen knew, together with the vigilance of her guardians.

On the seventh night they did not recognise the small gasp she gave when he appeared before her, stepping into her path from the bushes, close enough for her to smell him. She would have been prepared for the black leather balaclava that reached down to his shoulders – narrow slits for his greedy eyes – for all of the previous victims had spoken of it. What she could not have expected was the embellishment he had made to his costume: brass studs embedded across the width of his forehead spelling out his intention. RAPIST.

She must have felt the studs in her face as he butted her, sending her sprawling to the ground. And she must have felt her helplessness as he lifted her up by the waist of her skirt, shaking and pounding her, driving the breath from her body, spilling the radio from her pocket – and only then did the back-up teams start running. They arrived in time to prevent the rape of Flint, but not the severe bruising to her groin nor the bites to her neck and breasts.

It was six weeks before she was able to return to work and a week after that, Cohen had read, shaking his head in astonishment, she was walking another heath in search of another sick miscreant; rape bait for the second time.

Then a third time and a fourth and a fifth and a sixth, and Cohen had begun to skip the details, his irritation growing with his disbelief.

'This is madness,' he said. 'Why would she keeping putting herself at risk? Why would her superiors allow it?'

'Read on,' Deveraux replied. 'You don't know the half of it.'

But Cohen had pushed aside the file like an unfinished meal.

'Alan,' he said, refusing to indulge Devereaux's whim to be called A.J. 'What is it you want?'

'I want you to find her. We have great interest in Grace Flint but, careless buggers that we are, we've lost her. We'd very much like you to get her back.'

'We?'

'The Service.'

'No, Alan.'

'But, Harry, you must.'

'I *must*?' Cohen, incredulous, had risen up from his desk, his voice also rising. 'Have you forgotten what happened?'

'*Au contraire*,' Devereaux said wearily. 'You were right, Harry. Spot on. You were right and I was wrong and now I need your help. I need you to muck out the stables, clean up the mess. There's no one else I can trust. You do see that, don't you?'

In the reassuring comfort of the Daimler they rode

south in silence as Cohen considered Devereaux's latest question: was it Flint or Devereaux who had enticed him onto this uncertain path?

'No, it was you,' he finally announced. 'Your line, your hook.'

'Conceded,' said Devereaux laughing at the metaphor, 'but Gracie was the lure.'

Two years before, when Harry Cohen had resolved to quit the British Security Service, better known by its acronym MI5; when his despair at the inexorable escalation of his wife's illness had become all-consuming, it was on A.J. Devereaux's polished desk that he had laid his two-line letter of resignation. Devereaux had listened to Cohen's scant supplementary explanation and said 'Oh, my dear chap' and insisted that they leave Thames House immediately – 'Not another word' – and led them at a furious pace to a wine vault in Pimlico. Within its gloomy subterranean chambers – safe from eaves-droppers, Cohen supposed – they had drunk an indiffer-ent Chardonnay while Devereaux probed and parried, seeking the real reason for Harry's desertion. No fool, A.J., however much he tried to foster that impression.

'This business with Annie is awful, quite awful,' he said, his voice weighted with concern. 'You must take indefinite leave, of course. However long it takes, however long she needs.' He paused and then he added, 'Until she's better.'

'She's not going to get better, Alan.'

'Then, however long *you* need, Harry.' He reached

out and gripped Cohen's wrist. 'We'll manage without you, somehow. And if there's anything we can do, anything at all . . .' He left the promise hanging. 'We take care of our own, of course we do. Enough said, I think.'

'I don't.'

And then and there Cohen had sensed the chill as Devereaux's suspicions found their first footing on solid ground.

He withdrew his hand and studied Cohen's face with hooded eyes. 'So, this is not really about Annie,' he said eventually, matter of fact.

'Yes and no.'

'A riddle, Harry?'

'Yes, because Annie needs me, however much she believes to the contrary. No, because I would have resigned anyway, sooner or later.'

'Because?'

'Because I'm not allowed to do my job.'

Devereaux gave a hollow laugh as though Cohen had told a poor joke. 'Nonsense! You're our conscience, Harry, our *consigliere*. "Run it by Harry, make sure it's legal" – that's the DG's mantra, as you know perfectly well. You keep us honest. Nothing of any consequence happens without your nod.'

'Nothing is supposed to happen,' said Cohen quietly.

With one finger Devereaux traced idle circles around the lip of his wineglass.

'I'm sidelined, Alan, out of the loop. It's been going on for months. Ever since I vetoed Ice Trap.'

'You did not veto Operation Ice Trap, Harry Cohen,' said Devereaux, mounting his high horse. 'I did.'

'On my advice.'

'Precisely. I asked you if their perfidious little scheme was legal and you said no and that was the end of it. "Back to the drawing board," I told them. "No hacking into Abdul's bank account. You want to know where his dinars are coming from, you find another way – and you damn well run it by Harry before you raise so much as a finger." '

'Which they did not do.'

'So? We lost interest in Abdul, didn't we? He went off the boil, as I recall. We can check the file.'

'I already did.'

'And?'

'There is no file, Alan. The index says it was "Closed, No Action" so it should be in the morgue, but it's not.'

'Then some shoddy wretch has misplaced it,' said Devereaux impatiently, dismissing the revelation. 'One of Shilling's lads no doubt, or one of his lasses. I'll have them flayed.'

'It's not the only file that's gone.'

'Really?'

'There are seventeen files missing from the morgue – or seventeen that I know of. All of them the same; all operations that I challenged for legal reasons. All of them signed off as "No Action." Your signature, or Shilling's. All of them gone.'

Devereaux did not blink as he absorbed the implications. He watched Cohen watching him with an expression so impassive it was impossible to guess what he was thinking. Give him his due, Cohen thought and not for the first time: he's never more dangerous than when he's under fire. Only the tenor of his voice gave him away.

'I see,' he said icily. 'You think that Shilling's louts have been working off the books and you didn't see fit to bring the matter to my attention. Is that right?'

'I told the DG.'

'Did you, indeed. And why was that, Harry? Forgive me if I'm missing something but in my vanity I supposed that you reported to me?'

Cohen did not reply.

His voice now loaded with sarcasm, Devereaux continued: 'So our *consigliere* thinks that our hallowed Service is running black operations and he does not tell his master? A master, I might add, who brought Harry Cohen into the inner circle and kept him safe from his numerous enemies. For how long have I done that, Harry? Eight years? And now you turn on me? Why? Could you have possibly believed that I was part of it? That I'd gone rogue? Is that what you thought, you ingrate?'

'Yes,' said Cohen.

Devereaux raised himself up from the table as limp as a tired flag.

'We've got some straight talking to do, Harry Cohen, you'll allow me that at least.' He looked around as though he was unsure of his surroundings. 'I'll find the phone, call my girl, tell her we've gone AWOL. Why don't you get us something more palatable to drink?' He turned to leave and Cohen barely heard his muttered addendum: 'Something to take away the taste.'

He never did come back.

Harry Cohen at their table watching tears of condensation sliding down the ice bucket, the acid truth dawning, the new wine untouched.

A.J. in a taxi racing back to Thames House.

Cohen in his wake, following on foot. Knowing what awaited him, he saw no point in making haste.

'Sorry, Mr Cohen, sir.' One of the grim gatekeepers barring his way. 'I'll have to ask you to wait here. If you'll just take a seat . . .'

Cooling his heels in that ghastly lobby, waiting for Payne of Personnel.

'Sorry, Harry.' Payne contrite, retrieving Cohen's smart card and his picture ID. 'A clean break . . . Best, in the circumstances.'

Payne handing over a Jiffy bag containing the few personal possessions they had plundered from Cohen's desk: the pipe he no longer smoked; a pair of gold cufflinks he had bought at Aspreys and now thought vulgar; a photograph of Annie taken in the days when she glowed.

'Just a formality . . .' Payne obtaining Cohen's signature on the document reminding him of his eternal obligations under the draconian sanctions of the Official Secrets Act.

Not a word, Harry Cohen.

A.J. Devereaux in his lair on the sixth floor of Thames House, watching the proceedings on a CCTV monitor.

Not one damn word will you speak of these secret things you think you know.

No longer chief legal adviser to the Security Service, Cohen went home to his wife who no longer glowed. The eyes that watched him slip softly into her room were dull black puddles growing exponentially in her shrinking face.

In Harry Cohen's student days – halcyon days, viewed from the crumbling parapet of his middle age – he established a friendship with Quentin Klein that would outlast all others. They clerked together and trained together and qualified on the same day, and Klein never wavered in his determination to lure Cohen into the plush world of private practice. 'Forget the cloak and dagger stuff,' Klein would say from time to time, whenever he saw his friend disillusioned. 'Come and make some decent money.'

In the event, after his breach with the Service, that is what Cohen did, joining the commercial litigation department of Klein & Partners, which Quentin's father had founded. Cloistered in its comfortable offices in Bloomsbury Square, engaged in complex disputes that involved vast sums but not – usually – any risk to human lives, he saw himself as content as he was likely to be. He would not have believed that anything could persuade him to re-engage the treacherous milieu of counter-espionage.

Until Devereaux came calling, slipping into Cohen's office like a burglar, coming to steal his resolve.

Late into that evening Devereaux had made his pitch. He glided rather than pounced, setting out his stall with practised care. Flint's allure was what he had to sell; that and the flattery of the insinuendo that only Cohen might save her. He proffered them like rosy apples, a barrow-boy's cocky bargain, 'Five for a pound, guv' – but Cohen still wasn't buying.

His blandishments running dry, Devereaux suddenly got up from the armchair and paced the room, working it like a stage. Hands on hips, he glowered at Cohen, then turned his back, then pirouetted to face him once more. Slumped behind his desk, exhausted by Devereaux's performance, Cohen awaited the finale.

'You know, Harry, you amaze me. I'll admit that I'm a hypocrite but now I see I'm not even in your league. For years you bored me to distraction with your pious lectures on the "moral obligations of the state", and God knows how many operations I allowed you to nitpick to death with your petty objections, your legal niceties. Then you speak to me of "black operations" and "rogue agents" and I send you packing with your tail between your legs because I thought you'd gone too far. That's what I told the DG: "Harry's lost it," I said. "He sees conspiracies in his sleep." And now I come to you repentant and I say, "Damn it, Harry, have I got a conspiracy for you! Never mind a few off-the-book operations, how about a whole parallel agenda? Never mind a few files missing from the morgue, what about files that never existed? Operations that never happened – except that they did." I tell you of evidence that implicates not only my deputy but also reflects badly on the DG himself. I tell you that I need your help, and what does Harry Cohen say?'

Cohen said nothing, refusing his lines.

'I go to the Home Secretary to warn him the Barbarians are inside the gate. "Minister," I say, "they stalk the halls of Thames House!" I tell him the evidence is compelling but the details are meagre. I tell him that I do not know their number or their names, that I cannot tell friend from foe, that I need help to seek them out. I need an outsider, I say – someone outside the Service but with an insider's knowledge, someone I can trust. I tell him there is only one candidate: *you*, Harry Cohen; you with your sharp mind and your fine principles. "Then enlist him," says the minister. "Implore him. Tell him he has whatever resources he needs and the unwavering support of Her Majesty's government." And what does Harry Cohen say?'

Another silence that Devereaux was obliged to fill. 'Harry Cohen says, "Leave me out of it."'

Devereaux shook his head as though he could not believe Cohen's intransigence.

'I had only one card left to play. If I could not appeal to Harry Cohen's patriotism then, surely, I could reach his sense of chivalry? A damsel in distress! – that was my line, and Lord knows I was not exaggerating. I tell him of Grace Flint stumbling into this pit of vipers. I describe as best I can her plucky endeavours and the fate I fear

for her: Missing In Action, presumed lost – but perhaps
not! Maybe she's still alive! I ask Harry Cohen – I *beg*
Harry Cohen – to read her file; to apply his terrier's
instincts to the clues she's left us. "Follow her scent,
Harry, see where it leads" – that's all I asked.'

Devereaux walked slowly towards the door, preparing
his exit.

'But Harry Cohen doesn't care about Grace Flint, any
more than he cares about his country.'

He opened the door and stepped into the corridor.

'Goodnight, Harry. And damn you, damn you to hell.'

Cohen went after him, too late. 'You've forgotten
your file,' he called into the darkness of Bloomsbury
Square. 'Like hell he's forgotten it,' Cohen said to
himself. He returned to his office determined not to read
one more word of it – determined as any alcoholic
swearing off the booze.

II

Too late to prevent it, Cohen realised where they were headed. Approaching the town of East Grinstead in Sussex, the Daimler turned onto a meandering minor road that led eventually to a restaurant housed in an eighteenth century manor. It was where Cohen had proposed marriage to Annie. Four of their subsequent wedding anniversaries were celebrated here and, perversely, it was here that he came after she died. He liked its aura of permanence and soothing tranquillity. Its gardens were designed by Capability Brown, and Cohen had strolled in them for hours in search of inner truths and Annie's ghost.

He felt the impulse to demand how Devereaux knew: 'The Service spies on its own does it, Alan?' But of course it did, and Cohen would not give him the satisfaction of denying it.

'You'll like this place,' Devereaux said roguishly.

'I'm sure I will,' said Cohen, ready now to play the game.

They sat in the garden, awaiting lunch, overlooking a paddock where a girl exercised a lively colt that she was evidently determined to tame. She rode well but the horse was not yet willing to concede her authority. Cohen was content to sit and watch their contest and allow Devereaux to make the running. He saw parallels between the two events that had to do with giving rein.

'So, how was Miami? Not much to recommend it, I expect.'

'You can get Hatuey.'

'I'm not with you, old boy.'

'Cuban beer, like they used to drink in Old Havana. It's brewed in Florida but it's still very good.'

Devereaux cleared his throat. 'And Cutter was cooperative?'

Cohen replied, 'Impeccably so.'

'Hold anything back?'

'Why would he? He's as keen as we are to find Flint. And to pin the blame for Hechter, of course.'

'Quite so,' said Devereaux, pursing his lips. 'And he gave you the goods on Rykov,' he went on, rehearsing what he already knew, 'who sang like the proverbial bird. Looking at twenty years in the federal pen, all his dirty little secrets came tumbling out.'

'More like life.'

'Whose life?'

'Cutter saw to it that Rykov was charged with counterfeiting, conspiracy to murder and, for good measure, racketeering under the RICO statute. Given his record, he was facing a minimum of forty years with no possibility of parole. In practical terms, life.'

Devereaux smiled. 'Instead of which he drew death.'

'Prison is a dangerous place. Especially for those who betray their friends.'

'Indeed.' Devereaux twirled the stem of a glass of *blanc de blancs*. 'Well, we'll shed no tears for Comrade Rykov, shall we? Not much doubt that he got what he deserved. Which is more than can be said for Cutter.'

Cohen lifted his eyebrows, feigning surprise.

'Come on, Harry! Cutter exposed Flint to enormous danger. He did that knowing what she had been through. His actions were, at the very best, foolhardy. The fact that she survived does not mitigate his neglect of her safety. Am I missing something?'

'I don't know,' Cohen said.

Down below, the girl had been thrown. The colt was free to run but it stood watching her, the reins just out of her reach. She picked herself up and walked away across the paddock. Puzzled or intrigued, the colt followed.

'Oh, for heaven's sake,' Devereaux complained. 'Flint emerges from the escapade with friend Vladimir – barely, as you said – knowing that Cutter would have seen her sacrificed for the sake of his operation as readily as he might swat a fly. And yet this episode marks not the end of their relationship but the beginning of it! From this point on they are inseparable. Cutter and Flint, a team!'

'And Hechter.'

'Never mind Hechter. It was Cutter who press-ganged her into his ridiculous operation, and Cutter who abandoned her to the tender mercies of Vladimir. When Rykov pulled his stunt, he should have aborted the operation – with uncertain consequences, I admit, but at least he would have been there to share them. Instead, he swans off to the coffee shop and leaves her to her own resources.'

'I'm not sure he had any realistic choice.'

'Twaddle. He threw her to the wolves, Harry. All he cared about was nailing Rykov. That, and not losing the money. She was damned lucky to get out of there alive.'

'More than luck, I think. She put her knee in Vladimir's groin.'

'Yes, but that didn't stop him, did it? When they shot him, he was trying to position young Gracie as his shield. Almost pulled it off as well. It's on your video. The bullets could only have missed her by a hair's breadth.'

Over Devereaux's shoulder, Cohen watched the maître d' approaching their table. 'All undercover operations carry an element of risk,' he said quietly.

'But that's exactly my point.' Devereaux fidgeted in his chair, showing his impatience.

The maître d' coughed discreetly to announce his presence. 'Luncheon is ready, gentlemen.'

Devereaux waved him away.

'Cutter should never have involved her in an under-cover operation, not after what Buller did to her in that stairwell. She was sent to Miami as a liaison officer, for God's sake. A desk wallah. Cutter should not have permitted her within a mile of Rykov and his hoods. But, here's the thing, Harry. When it's all over, does she have a word to say against Cutter? No, she does not. When the brave boys back at the Yard raise their eyebrows and sharpen their quills, when they suggest that Special Agent

Cutter might have been a tad reckless, she says, "Nonsense, that was the plan." She defends Cutter. She *glorifies* him! Explain that to me, if you will.'

'You think I'm holding something back,' Cohen said.

Devereaux slapped his knee. 'She fell for him, didn't she, Harry? Went to bed with him. Our young Gracie and Agent Cutter? Is that it? Am I right?'

Cohen drank the last of his wine and carefully placed the glass on the table. 'Last May – no, this May, six months after Annie died . . .' he began, and then he paused as though he'd lost the thread.

'A year or so ago,' he began again, 'I went to New York on business with one of the associates in the firm, a young woman, about the same age as Flint, I suppose. She was ferociously clever and extremely knowledgeable of the case we were pursuing but my motives in taking her to the States were not entirely honourable. To be blunt, I thought, I hoped, I might seduce her, and one weekend in the middle of the trip I proposed that we drive out to Connecticut for lunch. We went to a hotel where, if things went well, I intended we should spend the night. Together.'

Devereaux wore an expression of increasing puzzlement.

'After lunch we sat in a garden not unlike this one while she told me about her life. I poured out wine and she poured out the secrets of her soul. Oh, certainly we spent the night there but only because I was in no condition to drive back to New York. We took *two* rooms. At some point I realised that to her I was from a different millennium. She liked me, I think. God knows, she liked talking to me. But the possibility of us sleeping together never even crossed her mind.'

'So?' said Devereaux.

'So, after we returned to London the fact that we had spent the night in Connecticut became public knowledge within the firm; from the expense chits, I suppose. The fact that we had spent nine other nights at the same hotel in New York was not considered relevant. New York was work, Connecticut something else. And by that token we – or, rather, she – was condemned. It was taken for granted that she and I were lovers. When I proposed that she be made junior partner in the firm – a promotion she richly deserved, by the way – they thought I was recompensing my mistress for her services. That she was a brilliant lawyer was not disputed, it was simply ignored. The senior partners thought I was behaving like a fool and I was too much of a coward to fight them. We let her go with a glowing reference.'

'Harry, you talk to me in riddles! I ask you about Cutter and Flint and you tell me your sad tale of unrequited love. The point is, were *they* lovers? Is that the glue that held them together?'

'The point is, I don't know. Oh, there is no shortage of people who will tell you that Cutter and Flint slept together but, so far as I'm aware, nobody really knows. We see in others what we want to see, not necessarily what is there.'

'Spare me your homilies,' said Devereaux gloomily. 'Did you ask Cutter?'

'No. Nor will I, unless it becomes blindingly relevant.'

They sat in broody silence, watching the girl, who had remounted the colt and was driving him hard.

'Shall we go inside?' Cohen suggested.

Devereaux followed him sulkily into the manor. They did not speak again until their first courses had arrived.

'In any event,' Devereaux said eventually, changing tack, 'Cutter gave her Rykov, and carte blanche?'

'She and Hechter.'

'Grilled him for days, squeezed every last drop out of him?'

'Apparently.'

'*Apparently*! Don't cavil, Harry. Rykov told her where to go, no? Gave her Robertstown and Maitland? Gave her the New World Bank and Trust? The key to the kingdom, no?'

'Yes.'

'And Rykov gave her Frank?'

'Indirectly, yes.'

Devereaux heaped *foie gras* onto a triangle of warm toast. 'Tell me, Harry. Tell me about Rykov's legacy.' He popped the toast into his mouth. 'Gracie's inheritance.'

'Or her death warrant,' said Cohen.

III

From her vantage point on the veranda of Josephine's Tea Shop, Grace Flint memorised the bankers' shingles she could see. Next door, sandwiched between where she sat and Hetty's Hardware Store, were the offices of Citibank, and Chemical, and Barclays International, and the Royal Bank of Canada. On the other side of the street, NatWest, Société Générale and the Banco de Bilbao shared the prime site above Honest John's Liquor Store, while in the Prince Albert Arcade nineteen other leading financial institutions from seven countries occupied three wooden A-frames, together with the Robertstown Visitors' Center.

Josephine's fruit punch was the colour of vermilion, spiked with ruby rum, and in the afternoon heat Flint felt soporific and hugely content. Kevin Hechter had been right. Here where she sat, less than two hours' flying time from Puerto Rico, on an island too small to make much impression on any map of the Caribbean, there were probably more banks per capita and per square mile than any other place on earth. But, for now, only one of them mattered to Flint.

The New World Bank & Trust Company sat apart from the rest. It occupied what had been a Baptist chapel set on Independence Corner, where the Tarmacadam of Queen Victoria Street gave way to the rust-red dirt of Sidcup Hill, and where a procession of ramshackle trucks risked losing their exhausts in deep ruts that ran like tram lines. The dust kicked up by the traffic hung in the air and coated the walls of the chapel so that they were no longer a brilliant white; more a warm *blanc cassé*. At exactly five o'clock the double doors closed for the last time, and Flint watched as Maitland locked them, fussing with the handle until he was satisfied the premises were secure.

'Skinny, sharp features, slicked-back hair, looks like a polecat,' had been Hechter's succinct description of Maitland, and it was close enough to make him unmistakable. Flint watched her quarry strap his briefcase to the pannier of a sit-up-and-beg bicycle, and tuck the cuffs of his trousers into the top of multicoloured socks. Swinging one bony leg over the crossbar, he mounted the saddle and pushed off, navigating an unsteady course between the ruts until he reached the summit of Sidcup Hill and headed down towards the harbour; down to where, Flint knew, Mrs Maitland would be waiting.

Her name, Flint also knew, was Lisa and in her long cotton dress, buttoned at the neck, pinched at her slender waist, she looked like a refugee from another place and time. Unless the pattern changed, she would be sitting under a parasol alone and aloof from the other expatriate wives, who also awaited their banker husbands on the broad terrace of the Royal Yacht Club. On the two previous afternoons, while Flint had watched, Lisa had spoken to no one until her husband had arrived to peck at her cheek, and no one had troubled her.

Waving goodbye to Josephine, Flint climbed over the rail and dropped down from the veranda into the saddle of her bicycle, a much newer model than Maitland's; aluminium frame, ten gears, top-of-the-range and $10 a day from Harvey's Bike Rentals. She waited for a truck to pass and then set off along Queen Victoria Street in leisurely pursuit of the bony banker. No need to hurry. She free-wheeled down Sidcup Hill, dodging the ruts, feeling the warm breeze tugging at her hat. She supposed that when it rained the roads turned into a quagmire, but Hechter said it never rained much in Robertstown. Not rain rain, he said. In Robertstown it mostly rained money.

He was waiting for her, looking ridiculous, sprawled in a lounger on the lawn of the Harbour View Guest House. He had removed his black lace-up shoes and his navy-blue socks, and rolled the trousers of his wash-and-wear suit to the top of his brawny calves. The sleeves of his white shirt were also rolled up, above the elbows, but his maroon tie was in place, and tightly knotted. With his short-cropped hair and his wary eyes, he looked like an off-duty copper obliged to take a furlough in some exotic clime, and not at all at ease with the concept of leisure. From where he lay, Flint noted, he had given himself an uninterrupted view of the Yacht Club's terrace on which the Maitlands now sat in the shade of Lisa's parasol.

'Boo!' said Flint creeping up on him, crouching low, keeping the sun behind her, like they taught at Quantico. 'Bang! You're dead!'

Hechter shaded his eyes with one hand as he squinted up at her. 'You can't shoot me now because I got it.'

'You did?'

He patted the pocket of his shirt.

'Mr Maitland?' Hechter towered over them. 'Andrew Peter Maitland?'

Maitland's sharp face froze into a mask of hostility. Only his small eyes moved, darting from Hechter to Flint and back again. He did not look at his wife but her hand scuttled across the tabletop like a spider crab and their fingers entwined.

'I'm Special Agent Hechter of the United States Treasury Department and this is Detective Inspector Flint from New Scotland Yard. We need to talk to you.'

'Hello, Lisa,' Flint said, sitting down beside her. Mrs Maitland stared at her husband in disbelief, as though she had just received news of a death in the family.

'This is a private club,' said Maitland. 'Are you members?'

Hechter lowered his bulk into a spare chair and drew it close to Maitland until their knees touched.

'Because if not,' Maitland continued defiantly, 'I'm afraid I'll have to ask you to leave.'

His voice was haughty but just below the polished

surface the broad vowels of his native Essex were easily detectable, at least to Flint.

'Listen to me,' said Hechter. 'Two days ago, Inspector Flint was sworn in as a special constable of the Lawrence Islands. That means she has full police powers and she has deputised me to assist her with her investigation. This morning, acting on information in our possession, I went before a judge in chambers and swore out a complaint against you – you personally, that is – and your employers. This afternoon, we were granted a search warrant.'

From his shirt pocket, Hechter withdrew a white envelope emblazoned with the crest of the High Court of the Lawrence Islands.

'This warrant. Read it.'

The envelope now sat on the table in front of Maitland, but nothing, it seemed, could have persuaded him to touch it. He watched it warily, as though it was a letter bomb.

'Okay, I'll tell you what it says. This warrant' – Hechter picked up the envelope – 'entitles us to search your home and the premises of the New World Bank & Trust Company. It entitles us to examine any document and any record – written, computerised or otherwise – and it further entitles us, if we see fit, to seize them. We will see fit, Maitland. Count on it. You're in so much trouble I don't know where to begin.'

'I want to talk to my lawyer,' said Maitland, his voice now diminished, the polish stripped away by the sandpaper of Hechter's relentless certainty.

He stood up but Hechter took hold of his arm. 'Later,' he said. 'When I say so. You can call from the bank, if you behave.'

IV

Give them their due, Harry Cohen said. The Lawrence Islands may be the nirvana of every doper, mobster, swindler, tax evader and despot with money to hide; it may allow any bank or financial institution of 'good (but undefined) standing' to hang up its shingle; it may impose banking secrecy laws that make those of Panama, Liechtenstein, the Bahamas, the Channel Islands, Switzerland and even Antigua look positively feeble; it may, in short, be the haven of more hot money than an abacus could count. But, continued Cohen, light a fire under them and you surely got results.

'And what kindling did Hechter provide?' asked Devereaux. 'I assume it was Hechter?'

Cohen nodded and took a sip of wine. 'Petroleum,' he said.

High-octane petroleum. Moses Saunders, the prime minister of the Lawrence Islands, the man whose epitaph will doubtless say he 'led his people to freedom', might have devised the banking laws that brought Robertstown its veneer of prosperity, but when it came to guarding his own prosperity, Cohen said, Saunders had precious little faith in them.

'You know that in financial circles he is known as Sir One Percent?' Cohen said, and Devereaux smiled to allow that he did.

'His arrogance is extraordinary.'

'We have only ourselves to blame,' said Devereaux. 'It was quite the fashion at the time. Entice our black brothers over from the colonies to train them as lawyers, give them a solid grounding in the infallibility of the law – *our* law, naturally – and then send them home to keep the natives in order. Of course, it was entirely wrong-headed. Once they got back they invariably became rabble-rousers. And that, more or less, was the end of the British West Indies.'

'Now it's *Sir* Moses Saunders.'

'Indeed.'

'Knight commander of the Grand Order of the Empire, member of the Privy Council.'

'Quite.' Devereaux frowned and pushed his plate away, his meal half-eaten, unwanted. Then he brightened: 'So, tell me, Harry, what did Hechter have on him?'

'Three bank accounts, all of them in the United States, containing a little short of eighteen-million dollars.'

Devereaux gave a low whistle.

'While half the world, it seems, was sending its money to Robertstown, Saunders was getting his out – most of it funnelled through New World, by the way. Given that he is the son of a sugar-cane cutter, given that he's never practised law, and given that his official salary is thirty-thousand dollars a year, Hechter believed the provenance of the eighteen-million dollars was highly suspect. He thought he might seize it.'

'Did he, by heaven! Could he have done that?'

Cohen shrugged and pushed his own plate away. 'Plausibly. Under their seizure law the onus would have been on Saunders to show he had obtained the monies legitimately. But that was hardly the point.'

'Of course not.'

'The point was to let Saunders know that while the Secret Service was powerless to act against New World in the Lawrence Islands, it was far from powerless to act against *his* interests in the United States.'

'Blackmail, Harry?' Devereaux beamed.

'Hechter called it a trade.'

The waiter came to clear away the debris of their meal.

'So, they got their warrant and marched young Maitland off to the bank?'

'Hechter did,' said Cohen. 'Flint elected to stay with Lisa. She had the feeling that for all her apparent timidity, Lisa was the strong one in the relationship. With the men out of the way, Flint thought she might persuade her to see sense and cooperate. She's good at that.'

'Weaving her spells?'

'If you like.'

Devereaux became distracted, staring at the table, his fingers searching the cloth for imaginary crumbs. Then he looked up and fixed Cohen with his baleful glower. 'We've all done that, haven't we Harry? We've all fallen under Gracie's spell.'

V

'Lisa, how old are you? Twenty-eight?'

Mrs Maitland twitched her head up and down to answer yes.

'And how old is Andrew? By the way, what do you call him? Andy?'

She nodded again. She had not spoken a word to Flint for almost half an hour.

'And Andy's what? Thirty?'

A long silence then, at last, 'Thirty-two. Last Tuesday.'

'Do you love him, Lisa?'

Hands in her lap, twisting at a handkerchief, Mrs Maitland quietly cried. They had gone inside the Yacht Club to escape the evening's mosquitoes, and they had the place to themselves. Somewhere out of sight, the barman waited desultorily for them to leave.

'Lisa, do you love him?' Flint asked again.

She wasn't yet capable of answering.

'Lisa, you can help Andy. You can make this nightmare go away.' Flint let the prospect float for a moment. 'But you have to be strong.'

Though the temperature was in the low eighties, Mrs

Maitland's thin body trembled with the cold she felt inside.

'It's not Andy I want,' Flint continued. 'He's done some wrong things – some bad things – but he can make them right, if you help him. You're the only one who can help him, Lisa. Do you know that?'

Lisa did not reply.

Maitland and Hechter had been gone for two hours, and Flint had warned her they would probably not be back until morning – perhaps late morning. Hechter's search of the bank would certainly take all night.

'Andy listens to you, doesn't he, Lisa? On important things? When you have big decisions to make? Well, this is a *really* big decision. I'll bet it's the biggest one you've ever had to make, so you can't let him down, not now.'

She remained frozen in her chair, strands of thin blonde hair stuck to cheeks that were so pale they seemed almost translucent.

'Lisa, are you hearing anything I'm saying to you?'

Mrs Maitland wiped her eyes. 'Are you married?' she said suddenly.

For a moment, Flint was thrown by the question and there was a pregnant pause before she replied. 'Not really. Not any more.'

'Did he die?'

Another pause.

'No. We're separated.'

'Do you miss him?'

If only you knew, Flint thought. What she said was, 'Sometimes.'

'I couldn't live without Andy. I mean, if he went to prison, or . . .' Her voice trailed off as she stared into that empty void.

'Yes you could, Lisa. You could if you had to. But you don't have to. Andy doesn't have to go to prison.'

'Why did you split up?'

'Because I couldn't give him what he wanted,' Flint lied. 'I wasn't strong enough to help him, and so I lost him. I wasn't as lucky as you are.'

'What's his name?'

'James. But I called him Jamie.'

'Do you still love him?'

'I don't know.'

She had stopped crying now, and her body no longer trembled. She blew her nose into the handkerchief.

'Promise?'

'Promise what?'

'That I won't lose Andy?'

'Not if you help us. Not if you persuade him to tell the truth. Will you do that, Lisa?' Stepping back from the void, Mrs Maitland nodded.

'Come on, I'll take you home,' said Flint – *and stay with you, and never let you out of my sight*, but she left that part unsaid.

VI

'So, Flint was right about Lisa.'

'Absolutely. Once she had made up her mind to cooperate Maitland didn't stand a chance. Hechter and Flint could hear them arguing in the bedroom, and, judging by Flint's notes, Lisa had a fish-wife's grasp of expletives.'

'Breeding will out,' says Devereaux provocatively, but he doesn't get the rise he is looking for.

Cohen is comfortably slumped in the rear seat of Devereaux's Daimler, parked outside Cohen's rambling house in Holland Park. Devereaux is in the front passenger seat, placing the last tape into the cassette player embedded in the walnut fascia. For some two hours, since leaving Sussex, the tape-recorded interrogation of Andy Maitland has absorbed him, and Devereaux insists on hearing what he calls the Final Act. There is a hiss as the tape begins, a tap of the microphone, and then Flint's flat monotone reciting the time, date and place, asking Maitland to once more identify himself 'for the record'. Maitland is used to this by now, enjoying it even. As he resumes his wholesale betrayal of his employer's secrets his voice takes on a supercilious edge. Only occasionally does he falter, when Flint's remorseless questioning leads him into thickets of self-incrimination, and then, more often than not, it is Mrs Maitland's voice we hear, firing warning shots across his bow.

Flint resumes her interrogation. 'Andrew, the bank has a non-executive director, is that correct?'

'Andrew', never 'Andy', as though Flint has drawn a line in the sand that she will not cross.

'Yes.'

'Will you please identify him.'

'Roberto Suárez.' Maitland places all of the stress on the first syllable so that it comes out as *Swars*.

'And what nationality is he?'

'Venezuelan.'

'And prior to his becoming a non-executive director of New World Bank & Trust Company, what was his occupation, if you know?'

'He was the Venezuelan ambassador to the Soviet Union. You'd call it Russia now, but this was before it all went pear-shaped.'

'And what does Mr Suárez do for the bank?'

'Not much. Introduces new clients from time to time.'

'How does he do that?'

'Fax. Sometimes I get a phone call from him, but it's usually a fax. "Mister So and So is on his way to see you, please extend him every courtesy." That sort of thing.'

'And these clients he sends you, do they have anything in common?'

'A lot of them are Russians.'

'From Moscow?'

'Not any more. Nice, in the south of France. That's where Suárez is based as well.'

'Why Nice? If you know.'

'Because it's become their bolt-hole. The place is full of them. According to Suárez, you go into just about any restaurant now and you can have the menu in Russian; Cyrillic script.'

'So, these Russians living in Nice that Mr Suárez recommends to you come to Robertstown to see you and open accounts. Is that correct?'

'Lately he's sent a few Serbs as well. You know, from the former Yugoslavia. Yes, they open accounts.'

'In their own names?'

Maitland chortles, as if Flint has told a joke. 'Not often,' he says, still chuckling.

'What's so funny, Andrew?'

'Look, I don't even know their names, not their real ones. Suárez, when he faxes, just makes up any old name: Yeltsin, Krushchev, I've even had a Lenin and a Trotsky. It doesn't matter. All he's doing is tipping me off that the next Russian who walks in my door and says he's Leonid Brezhnev, or whatever name was in the fax, is kosher.'

'Meaning?'

There is a pause on the tape, until Lisa says sharply: 'Andy!'

'Meaning not law enforcement, or the Revenue.'

Hechter is merely an observer to these proceedings, but he has developed a nagging cough. We hear it now, and that tells us he is there.

'Do you take any measures to establish the real identity of these new clients? For example, do you ask to see their passports?'

'No.'

'Do you, or the New World Bank, have any interest in their real identities, or the source of their funds?'

'No.'

'In fact, is it the deliberate policy of the bank to help its clients disguise their identity?'

'Yes.'

'And the source of their funds?'

'Yes.'

'Why?'

Five seconds elapse. We can sense that Lisa is about to interject when Maitland says, 'You know why.'

Flint's tone is steely. 'I can't answer for you, Andrew.'

'Because they're crooks, most of them. Gangsters, hot money men, old KGB thugs. You only have to look at them to know.'

'Very well. Now the names that Mr Suárez chooses to introduce these new clients to you, are these the names you use when you open their accounts?'

'No. We fix them up with an off-the-shelf trust company with a couple of nominee directors, and then the company opens the account.'

'Who are the nominee directors?'

'Miss Pringle.'

'Who's she?'

'Peggy Pringle, my chief clerk. Or any of the girls who work at the bank. Whoever's around at the time.'

'All right. Now, for the record, I am showing you a ledger that was found on your premises last night, in a safe in what I believe to be your office.'

A copy of the ledger now sits on Devereaux's lap, open at the first page.

'Do you recognise this ledger?'

'Yes.'

'Did you maintain it in the normal course of business?'

'Yes.'

'And is the handwriting yours?'

Maitland yawns as he once more answers, 'Yes.' He is beginning to sound bored. Flint presses on regardless.

'Now on each page there are six columns, and each line has a similar entry. Is that correct?'

'Yes.'

'The first column contains what appear to be dates. What do these dates represent?'

'The date on which each account was opened.'

'All right. I'm going to take the first entry on the first page and ask you what each column represents. Twelve, six, ninety-two. Is that 12 June 1992?'

'Yes.'

'The next column has the word "Tindale". What is Tindale?'

'The trust company I set up for this particular client.'

'The third column contains the figures eight-hundred and fifty-thousand. What is that?'

'The amount of the initial deposit.'

'In what currency?'

'US dollars. All our transactions are in dollars.'

'And how did you receive these funds? A cheque? A wire transfer?'

Maitland snorts. 'Hardly,' he says. 'Cash.'

'Okay, let's pause here for a moment. Are you saying that all transactions through the bank are in cash?'

'All incoming transfers, yes. Outgoing transfers could be a wire but more usually a draft.'

'A draft drawn on your bank?'

'No. I withdraw the funds in cash from the client's account and then buy a draft from one of the main banks here. There are plenty to choose from.'

'So I've noticed,' says Flint. 'But you're saying that all deposits are made in cash?'

'Yes.'

'Which the clients bring personally to Robertstown?'

'Or they send a pigeon. You know, someone who carries it for them. That's usually what happens.'

'What do you mean by "usually"?'

There is a brief pause before Maitland answers, 'Sometimes I go and collect it, if that's what the client wants.'

'Go where?'

'Wherever the client directs. Paris, London sometimes, Zurich, Amsterdam. Hamburg a couple of times. Cyprus.' Another pause. 'New York.' Maitland's voice has grown quieter. 'Miami. Los Angeles.'

Hechter coughs sharply and Flint picks up the signal.

'How many times have you collected cash from the United States? Approximately?'

'I can't say off-hand.'

'A dozen times? Less? More?'

'More.'

'Twenty times? More?'

'I'm not sure.'

'Oh, for God's sake, Andy.' This is Lisa, sounding furious.

'Six or seven times a year,' says Maitland quickly. 'For the last six years.'

'So, since 1993, on at least thirty-six occasions, you have exported cash from the United States. Did you do that legally?'

'Pardon?'

'Don't play games, Andrew. You know that if you carried more than ten-thousand dollars out of the country you were required to report it. Did the amounts exceed ten-thousand dollars?'

'Sometimes.'

'What does that mean?'

'Usually.'

'And did you report that? You are shaking your head. Does that mean no?'

'There wouldn't have been any point to the exercise, would there?'

'Cheeky bugger, isn't he?' says Devereaux.

Flint is remorseless. 'I'll ask you again. On any or all of the occasions that you carried more than ten-thousand dollars out of the United States in cash, did you file a declaration?'

'No.'

'Thank you,' Flint says sarcastically. 'All right. Let's return to the ledger.'

'Please do,' says Devereaux. He turns in his seat to look at Cohen. 'On the home stretch, are we?'

'Coming up.'

'Now, Andrew, the fourth column contains a seven digit number. What does that represent?'

'It's the number I give the client to identify him as the owner of the trust company. He uses that number in all transactions and that allows me to make sure that the right account gets credited or debited with the funds. It's like a Swiss numbered account. If a client wants a draft, or funds transferred, or he sends a pigeon to pick up cash, he encloses this number with his request and that's my authorisation.'

'And this ledger is your record of which account is which?'

'Well, I can't keep them in my head, can I? There are rather a lot of them.'

'You can say that again,' says Devereaux. When Cohen first gave him a copy of the ledger, he had counted the number of lines on the first page, and multiplied that by the approximate number of pages filled with Maitland's scrawl, and by his rough calculation some sixteen hundred numbered accounts were recorded.

'But other than the number of each account, you have no record of the account holder?'

'None. As I've told you, I don't know their real names.'

'Any moment now,' says Cohen, and Devereaux leans forward to increase the volume.

'Except this one,' says Maitland.

Judging by the tone of her voice, Flint was not expecting this admission.

'Tindale? You know the real identity of the owner of the Tindale account?'

'Yes.'

'How do you know?'

'Because he was my first client. Actually, setting up New World was his idea, the reason I came out here. In fact, he's rather more than a client. I suppose you could say he's my partner.'

'What's his name, Andrew?'

'He's got more than one but his real name is Harling. Frank Harling.'

We may have imagined the sudden intake of breath we think we hear, but not the paroxysm of coughing that erupts and continues until the tape is turned off. It is Flint's cough, not Hechter's. She sounds as though she is choking.

three

Andrew Maitland said to Flint: 'It was 1987, the year of the crash, and I was a half-commission man, if you know what that is. I was working for a broker but only freelance, so I had to split the commission on all the trades I brought in. Anyway, what people don't understand is that it doesn't matter if the market's going up or down, the dealer still makes money, and I made a killing. Working night and day, mind you, but I was twenty-one and hauling it in. *Loadsa* money, as we used to say.'

He smiled at the memory and reached for a cigarette. 'I'm supposed to have given up but in the circumstances . . . Do you mind?'

Flint shook her head. He could smoke opium for all she cared, so long as he kept talking.

'Anyway, I said to Lisa – we weren't long married – I said, "Let's take some time off." Once the market hit bottom it stayed there, so there weren't many trades to be had. And, to be honest with you, I was getting tired of dealing. It seemed like a good idea to take a break. We didn't have kids or a mortgage. So – end of '88, beginning of '89 – I said to Lisa, "Let's go somewhere. Let's have some fun." She was game, so that's what we did.'

'Where did you go?'

'Australia first, then Bali, Malaysia, Singapore. We spent some time in Thailand and then we ended up in Hong Kong. We both really liked HK so we decided to stay for a while. I got a job with one of the banking outfits and that's how I met him. Frank, I mean.'

Though the tape was running, Flint took notes. It helped her to concentrate on what Maitland was saying; helped her block out the question that was screaming to be asked.

'Take it slowly,' Cutter had warned her on the telephone from Miami. 'Let him go at his own pace.'

When she had not responded Cutter said: 'Look, Grace, I know how badly you want Harling, but Maitland mustn't know that. You push him on this and he's going to think that Harling's the crown jewels, so far as you're concerned. He'll want to trade you for him and I don't want any more trades with this asshole. I want everything he's got with no exceptions, so just let him tell his story in his own sweet time. There's a lot more riding on this than Harling or your revenge.'

'This has nothing to do with revenge.'

'The hell it hasn't! You're obsessed with Harling, and I don't blame you. But we've got other fish to catch. You understand? Now, either do as I say or back off and leave Maitland to Hechter.'

She couldn't help herself. 'You're forgetting something,

Mr Cutter. This is not Hechter's jurisdiction, or yours. Hechter's here only on my say-so.'

There was a silence on the line that made her stomach churn.

'Flint,' said Cutter softly.

'Yes?'

'You want me to call London? You want me to call Commander Glenning and tell him that I think you're unfit for duty? You want me to tell him that your obsession with Harling has clouded your judgment; that you're about to jeopardise the most important joint operation we've ever conducted? You want me to do that?'

'No, sir.' She tried not to gag.

'Because I will, Flint, count on it. Unless you give me your word that you'll conduct Maitland's debriefing in a professional manner, I'll have you kicked off that island so Goddamned fast you won't have time to take a plane. Are we clear on that?'

'I'm sorry.'

'I don't care if you're sorry, Flint. I asked you if we're clear on that. You do this my way or not all.'

'Got it.'

'And Hechter sits in. You don't say a word to Maitland unless Hechter's there.'

'I understand.'

'Do you give me your word?'

'Yes, sir.'

'Then let's do it,' said Cutter.

* * *

Grace Flint said to Maitland: 'What was the date, approximately? If you remember.'

'When I met Frank? Late March or early April, 1992. It'll be in my diary.'

In the shadows of the Maitlands' sparse veranda, out of Maitland's line of sight, Hechter stirred.

'What diary is that?' Flint asked casually.

'I've always kept a diary. Who I meet, where and when, telephone numbers, that kind of thing.'

Flint had read Hechter's scrupulous inventory of the documents they'd seized from the bank and the Maitlands' house. There was no mention of any diary.

'Well, I *used* to keep a diary,' Maitland corrected himself, seeming to read her mind. 'Once we got here, it didn't seem like such a good idea.' He glanced at Lisa who sat on a child's swing in the garden, plaiting bracelets of mimosa for her thin wrists. 'If you know what I mean.'

'The diaries you used to keep, where are they now?'

Maitland stayed mute, watching threads of smoke curling from the tip of his cigarette.

'Andrew?'

'I was coming to that,' he said.

Lisa got up from the swing, placing her bracelets on the seat with a care that belied her obvious tension. She came towards them, lifting her long skirt as she climbed the steps to the veranda. To her husband she said, 'I'll get them,' and pushed open the screen door. Hechter got up from his chair as though minded to follow her inside the house but instead he positioned himself by the open window, his arms folded, leaning his back against the frame. From there, above the drone of the flies, he could hear her cross the living room and the squeak of a drawer being opened; a drawer of the bureau he had already searched, if he was not mistaken. Then he heard her coming back, and the soft clink of metal.

'The records you've seen,' said Maitland, 'that's only some of them.'

Neither Flint nor Hechter seemed to have heard him.

'There's more. Quite a lot more, actually.'

Lisa came out onto the veranda, her right hand balled into a fist that was concealing something; something she would give them but not yet, evidently. Her husband had more to say.

'There's a warehouse . . . Well, it's more of a shed really, but it's pretty big. Not here, not Robertstown. It's at Ellis, on the other side of the island, if you know where I mean. There's an old sugar plantation that we bought for a song because Frank had it in mind to do up the house for himself. You know, somewhere he might come and hang out for a while if ever things got too hot for him. Well, they did get too hot for him in England but he already had another bolt-hole they didn't know about and when that proved secure he changed his mind. About Ellis, I mean. About coming here. Decided he preferred Italy.'

At his own pace, Grace. In his own sweet time.

Flint didn't trust herself to speak.

'Anyway, in the meantime, I'd had some work done on the shed, new roof and so on, and I thought I may as

_____

well make use of it. So, that's where I put the archive, all
the records we didn't need on a regular basis. And I put
some of my stuff there, including my diaries. And some
of Frank's stuff as well.'

Hechter said, 'You jerk.'

Lisa glared at him.

Maitland said. 'There's no need for that.'

Hechter looked ready to hit him. 'Why didn't you tell
us this two days ago? Why have you been holding out?'

Lisa screamed. 'That's not bloody fair!'

Without warning she drew back her fist and threw
what she was hiding at Hechter, hitting him squarely in
the chest before he had time to flinch. A pair of keys for
mortise locks clattered onto the deck at Hechter's feet.

'Jesus, Lisa!' Maitland said sharply as she flounced
down the steps to the garden, but Hechter seemed
unconcerned. He bent down to pick up the keys, curious
to know why they had not registered on him during his
search. There was tag attached that read 'London flat',
and now he remembered why he had thought them
unimportant.

'Holding out in more ways than one,' he said.

Lisa sat down heavily on the swing, crushing the
mimosa, angry red blotches mottling her face. Flint
thought she looked as though she might burst into tears,
and suddenly the prospect seemed unbearable. Suddenly
she wanted to be finished with these people, tired of
their tantrums and petty deceptions. Suddenly she didn't
care what Cutter thought or did.

'Andrew,' she said. 'You said that things got "too

hot" for him in England. Do you know what that was about?'

'Some. A policeman got killed. It wasn't Frank's fault but he was there when it happened. It was some kind of trap, a sting operation, and it all went wrong. Frank was with a client who pulled a gun. Frank said it was totally out of order. He had no idea this idiot was armed or he wouldn't have been within a mile of him. Anyway, the gun went off accidentally and Frank got the hell out of there.'

Accidentally!

Flint saw that Hechter was studying her face, waiting for her reaction. She willed herself to show none.

'This accident,' she said neutrally, 'you hadn't heard about it before – read about it in the newspapers, perhaps?'

'No. I'd been out of the country for five or six years when it happened. Never saw the papers much.'

'And after the policeman was killed, what happened then?'

'I told you, Frank got out of there as fast as he could. It happened somewhere near Victoria station and he just ran for it and jumped on a train.'

'Where did he go?'

'I don't know. All I know is that Frank got off at the first stop, found a phone and called some people he knew, and they sent a car for him.'

Abruptly, Maitland stood up. 'Do you fancy something to drink? A coffee or something?'

'What people?'

'Friends. "My funny friends", Frank used to call them. Look, I have to go to the toilet.'

'Who were these friends, Andrew?'

'I don't know.'

'Yes, you do.'

Maitland was backing towards the door, Hechter moving silently to block him.

'I don't want to know.'

He turned his back on Flint and found himself face to face with Hechter, only inches between them with nowhere to go. His body tensed and for a moment it seemed he was prepared to fight, then his courage left him and his shoulders sagged.

'Please,' he said.

'Leave him alone! Fucking leave him alone.' This was Lisa shouting as she came out of the swing, running recklessly towards them, tripping on her skirt, falling headlong on the skimpy lawn.

Maitland said: 'Oh, Jesus, I'm so bloody scared.'

II

Pre-dawn over Biscayne Bay, an acid-yellow light staining the horizon.

Fifteen nautical miles due south of Miami, the motor yacht *Invincible* rides the sullen swells in the lee of Elliott's Key. On the flying bridge an alarm warbles a soft warning. Jackson Kurlack puts down the night-vision glasses through which he has been studying his surroundings and rises stiffly from the helmsman's chair. His right knee is shot, the cartilage gone, and the pain he feels is never-ending. Sparing the leg as much as he can, he uses the strength of his arms to lower himself to the deck.

In the chart room aft of the main cabin he limps to the radar screen, watching the sweep of the oscilloscope as it confirms there are no other craft within five miles of *Invincible*. His face a ghostly green in the light of the screen, he listens to the radio crackling with static but there are no transmissions to be heard. Kurlack is satisfied he is alone, far beyond the range of any parabolic microphone.

He checks the digital clock above the chart table that measures time in one-second intervals. There is a little more than two minutes to go.

Rhapsody in Blue is playing in the cabin, the Alicia Zizzo piano version that restores the four minutes of spiralling cadenzas missing from all other recordings. Kurlack will not tolerate what he contemptuously calls the Reader's Digest adaptations of Gershwin's original score. The lost cadenzas are supposedly too difficult to play but Kurlack has mastered them. Waiting for the call, he plays them in his head.

The clock tells Kurlack that Taggart is late. It is twenty-two seconds past the hour when the telephone rings. It is a satellite phone connected to a STEALTH scrambler that constantly reorders the sequence of the signals it transmits, rendering them indecipherable.

He hears a high-pitched tone as the scrambler interrogates its twin on the other side of the Altantic. Then it goes silent.

'Are we secure?'

A clipped English voice coming over the speakers in Dolby sound.

Kurlack says nothing until he sees the STEALTH's red light change to green.

'Go ahead.'

'We have a problem. Our young friend on the island is MIA.'

'Since when?'

'Two days ago. And his premises are closed.'

'Bogeys?'

'We think so. We're still making inquiries but it looks that way.'

'Mine or yours?'

'One of each, apparently. The same pair, I wouldn't be surprised. We should have that confirmed in a day or so.'

'But that could be too late.'

'Exactly.'

Reviewing their dilemma, Kurlack rubs his nagging knee. When he was deputy director of the Defense Intelligence Agency he was renowned for his decisiveness.

'I'll take care of it.'

'If you think that's best. I can send someone from here if you'd prefer.'

'Quicker from this end. I can have my people down there in a few hours.'

'Well, I'll leave it in your capable hands.'

'One more thing. Eagle should be warned.'

'Of course. I'll pass the word.'

'I'll signal when we need to talk.'

'Roger.'

Kurlack cuts the line. In the dark recesses of the world these two men occupy, small courtesies are not expected.

He hauls himself up to the bridge and starts the engines. The dawn that has arrived is unpromising, blankets of dirty grey haze obscuring the rising sun. The sea is grey, too, and growing restless. Kurlack pushes forward the throttles as far as they will go and sets a course for Fisher Island. Surging through the spume, *Invincible* will take him there within the hour.

I'll pass the word and at the Villa Donati, high in the hills above Lucca, a telephone rang, the scramblers secured the line and a disembodied voice told the eagle to fly.

The call was not expected but neither did it come as any great surprise. Frank Harling had long accepted that his sojourn in Italy was temporary; that however long it lasted, and however pleasant it became, it was merely an interval. A cadenza, if you like, bridging yet two more passages of his eternal flight.

The eagle must fly but not precipitously. Panic, Harling knew, makes a poor travelling companion.

In his patient restoration of the Villa Donati, Harling had insisted on the finest materials: natural pigments for paint, the best wood, the most authentic tile and stone. And when it was completed, he had insisted on premium fittings. He went to his kitchen and opened the fridge, a Whirlpool imported from America at exorbitant cost. From the back of the freezer compartment he took a Ziploc bag containing another American import: a Ruger P97 automatic pistol, down-sized and easily concealed.

As an afterthought he also removed from the fridge a bag of offal and marrow bones – food for his dogs – and the juxtaposition of the two events led him to consider if he should shoot them. Or was it better to leave money and a note for the grasping crone who cleaned his house in the faint hope that she would look after them? He postponed his decision and went out onto the terrace to feed them.

Lingering there in the soft evening light, he smoked a cigarette, surveying the long driveway that would soon be crowded with the dark blue Fiats of the *carabiniere*.

Harling did not speculate on what had brought about this turn of events. He knew there were too many possibilities, too many points of his own vulnerability. He flicked away the cigarette and watched it spiral onto the gravel. He allowed himself the briefest moment of self-pity – 'That's your life, Frank Harling, a fucking fag end' – and then he snapped out of it. Time to move. Time to prepare.

In his Italian period (as he would come to think of it) he had taught himself to cook; nothing fancy, mind, but solid peasant food: rich, meaty stews of wood pigeon and wild boar; pork braised in wine, flavored with a generous shaving of the black truffles found beneath the ancient oaks on his land. Returning to the kitchen, he set a pot of *ribolita* on the stove to warm and he opened a bottle of Vino Nobile di Montepulciano.

The condemned man ate a hearty meal, he thought. *And then he bloody scarpered.*

Leaving the wine to breathe, he fetched a cold chisel and mallet from the tool cupboard and began chipping away at the grout surrounding one of those authentic tiles covering the kitchen floor. Beneath it lay a leather pouch containing his escape kit: a passport and driver's licence in the same assumed name; a thick wad of Swiss banknotes in large denominations.

The eagle will fly first class, thought Harling, and the prospect cheered him.

His cache retrieved, his supper eaten, he disassembled the Ruger into its five component parts to clean them. Running his finger along the Ruger's fibreglass-filled polymer frame, Harling was confident it would not be readily detected by the tame security precautions that most airports employ.

III

Freedom Field; not much of an airport. Set between Twin Peaks, the highest points around Robertstown, the single runway calls for a precipitous approach and there are no lights, no nav aids worth talking about. A single Portakabin serves as the passenger terminal and Immigration Control. When scheduled flights are due, Harvey Nichols is sometimes there to examine the passports of arriving passengers, or, if he is detained by his customers at the No Name Bar, he sends his wife, if she's amenable. Sometimes – often – Immigration Control is a neglected formality on the Lawrence Islands.

Neither of the Nichols was present when the De Havilland Twin Otter arrived from Puerto Rico bringing nineteen passengers and a small amount of freight. Peggy Pringle, waiting in the rutted parking lot beside her small Rover car, felt a flutter of relief though she could not say why. The visitors she expected were perfectly respectable, she was sure, since they represented Mr Maitland's overseas associates. No reason at all why they would not pass muster at Harvey Nichols' podium, had he been there to man it. Still, she could not deny her own nervousness; the prickles of anxiety that had kept her on edge and sleepless ever since she'd made the call to the emergency number Mr Maitland had provided.

She spotted them coming down the Otter's steps, or thought she did: three men set apart from the other passengers by their white skins and their sharp suits. As they headed towards the terminal, Peggy adjusted her Sunday-best hat and raised one arm in a tentative wave. The tallest of them peeled away, stilling his companions with the slightest gesture of his hand, coming towards her with an athlete's gait. His hair, she thought, was a little too long and he wore trainers with his suit; the jacket unbuttoned, flapping in the slipstream of his own momentum.

When he reached her, towering above her, looking down at her pensive face, she swallowed hard and bravely said, 'I'm Goldfinch' – the codename Mr Maitland had told her to use.

'Snipe,' he replied and then he grinned, showing her the whitest teeth she'd ever seen. 'Ridiculous, isn't it, all these damn birds?' He came to her side, put a long arm around her shoulder and lightly kissed her cheek like a son might kiss his mother. 'You're Peggy and I'm Brad and it's a pleasure to meet you.' His breath smelt of spearmint; wholesome, she thought.

In the Rover, Brad beside her, his silent companions squeezed into the back with their banker's cases between their knees, they chugged up Sidcup Hill, the engine whining in second gear.

'I was right to call, wasn't I?' she asked, not taking her eyes from the road.

'Absolutely right,' Brad assured her, touching her arm. 'Right as right can be.'

Settled on the veranda of Josephine's Tea Shop, just down the street from Independence Corner and the New World Bank, Peggy Pringle told her story; timidly at first but, buoyed by Brad's smiles and his patient understanding, her confidence grew together with her sense of righteous indignation.

Imagine! she said. Standing there as if she owned the place! *Mr Maitland is not available.* The cheek of the woman!

Let's go back to the beginning, said Brad. Let's not miss anything out. Let's just take it easy, Peggy, one step at a time.

Very well, said Peggy, starting over, not displeased by their polite attentiveness.

Thursday morning, five minutes to eight, arriving at the bank to open up, same as always. 'Good morning, Miss Pringle,' said the waiting girls, same as always, knowing that she valued civility as much as good timekeeping. She had taken the key from her purse and slipped it into the lock and tried to turn it, and it would not turn. She had tried again. Same result. Imagine, she said, standing there for all the world to see, fiddling with the lock, trying not to notice the giggles that her staff could not quite suppress. Mind you, she was no fool. It did not take long for her to realise that the lock had been changed. Why would Mr Maitland do that? She had imagined some emergency in the night; an attempted break-in perhaps, triggering the alarms. But, surely, in that event, Mr Maitland would have called her immediately? She was, after all, his most trusted employee, his deputy in all but name.

You're indispensable, his right hand, said Brad. We've always known that.

She had sent the girls home, she said, giving them the morning off. No point in their hanging around, engaging in their tittle-tattle. And no point – *more* to the point – in attracting attention to themselves, and local speculation.

Quite right, said Brad, nodding his approval. And then?

And then she had taken herself off to Cornhill Rise, to Mr Maitland's house, last one on the right as you come around the corner. Not as fancy as you might expect, given Mr Maitland's standing. It was also rather small, but then there was just the two of them, sad to say. Such a shame, them not having children when Mrs Maitland wanted a baby so badly.

And then?

Well, then she'd parked in their driveway and tooted her horn, not having called in advance to tell them she was coming. And that's when *that* woman appeared, Miss High and Mighty, coming around from the back of the house, demanding to know one's business.

Let's take this bit carefully, said Brad. Step by step. Let's not neglect a single detail.

Did she tell you her name?

No she did not!

Say who she was?

Certainly not!

What did she look like? Tall? Short? Fat? Thin?

Peggy rolled her eyes as if to say, 'Who notices? Who cares?'

She was wearing shorts, Peggy said, as if that told him everything.

Brad persisted. Was she fairly tall, say about five-ten, about 130 pounds? Good legs, short black hair that had a tendency to flop over her forehead? Was she early to mid-thirties but with a face that seemed sort of ageless? Did you notice her eyes? Were they like a doe's eyes large and sad and more yellow than brown?

Peggy Pringle looked at him in wonder.

From the breast pocket of his shirt Brad produced a photograph of a woman's face taken with a long lens.

That her?

Peggy Pringle nodded.

IV

As the crow flies it is only eleven miles from Robertstown to Ellis but the clay road takes an ambling route with any number of digressions.

The open Jeep that Hechter had hurriedly hired was a rattletrap and most of its basic accessories no longer worked. But it did have four-wheel drive, which was just as well, Flint thought. Climbing the vertiginous rise of Sawyer's Mount, the road twisted and strayed ever-nearer the edge of a gorge until there was nothing between her and plunging eternity. She hung to the grab-handle so fiercely her knuckles were white. She tried not to look at the drop or at Hechter, who clung to the wheel with equal determination. Each time the clay turned to powder and the wheels lost traction, she heard him say 'Sweet Jesus' and she would hold her breath until he gained control.

Cumulonimbus clouds were building above them like huge cathedrals.

'Looks like thunder,' Andy Maitland said cheerfully from the back seat. 'Sometimes when it rains the road gets washed away.'

FUCKING SHUT UP!

She'd had it with Maitland. She didn't know if it was the whine of his voice or the weakness of his face or, more likely, his association with Frank Harling. Whatever it was, she was growing to detest him.

Wrong, Flint. Stupid, Flint.

She imagined Cutter dressing her down, disapproving of her lack of professionalism.

You don't hate informants, Flint. They're ciphers, nonentities, a means to your end. You don't feel anything about them. You don't let them get to you. Ever.

From the summit of Sawyer's Mount she looked down on the road that plummeted towards Ellis and the sea; a twisting red snake of a road on which they would surely die. She closed her eyes and willed herself to think of anything but the terrifying imminence of their descent.

'Hold on,' Hechter commanded. 'Here we go.'

In her mind she focused on Maitland's ferret face and rehearsed the copper's universal lexicon of terms of contempt: *Asshole, creep, scumbag, dirtbag, slime . . .*

A long-abandoned plantation house with its boarded-up windows and sagging porches; a cane field choked with rampant vegetation; a rusted truck with no doors or wheels, its bonnet gaping open, the engine gone. Finally, incongruous in this setting of decay, a shed about the size of a double garage with freshly painted walls and a new corrugated roof. The door was also new, and Flint took close-ups of its two sturdy locks with the evidence camera.

'Chubbs,' said Maitland brightly. 'Triple mechanisms, top of the line.'

Hechter shooed him back to the Jeep where his sullen wife waited.

Inside the shed, vibrantly lit by three banks of fluorescent tubes, steel shelving lined the walls, stacked from floor to ceiling with bankers boxes. Each one was neatly labelled with the name of an account and dates 'from' and 'to'. Each one was sealed with tape on which Maitland had written his bold signature. The first tape that Hechter slit with a penknife secured a box that was different from the others in that it bore only the initials 'F.H.'

Flint photographed Hechter as he removed the lid. She wanted a shot of the box's interior before the contents were disturbed and she asked him to wait while she found the right angle. The next shot had his hand reaching inside, his fingers lifting one corner of a large manila envelope on which was written this sanction: 'Only to be opened in the event of my death.'

Sorry, Frank, no can do. What about: In the event that creep Maitland becomes your Judas?

Flint's camera faithfully documented the opening of the envelope, the removal of its contents: a thick document, bound with a scarlet ribbon. Then Hechter held the first page towards the camera and Flint flipped the camera to micro mode to make the opening words entirely legible.

I, FRANK ARTHUR HARLING, of the Villa Donati, Vorno, Italy, MAKE OATH and say as follow:

1. I am the principal owner of the New World Bank & Trust Company, located and registered in Robertstown, which is the capital of the Lawrence Islands. The bank holds funds and provides financial services for clients who, for various reasons, do not wish their identities to be known. These clients include certain intelligence agencies who have used the bank to receive and distribute funds in support of covert operations. I am concerned that these operations may have involved illegal activities, and that my knowledge of them may have placed me in danger. I am therefore making this affidavit as a form of protection, or, in the event that anything untoward should happen to me, to place on record what I know. Except where otherwise stated, all matters deposed to herein are within my own direct knowledge.

Holy, holy, holy shit!

Hechter handed Flint the affidavit and said: 'Let me check on what they're doing.'

She squatted down onto her haunches and laid the camera on the floor. She was vaguely aware of Hechter scolding the Maitlands from the doorway, but she couldn't take in what he was saying. Her mind racing, she scanned the pages of Frank Harling's sworn statement, trying to absorb the meaning of his terrible admissions.

V

It was after midnight and in Harry Cohen's cluttered basement study the lighting was subdued, matching his mood. The day had seemed endless and A.J.'s appetite for information insatiable. Lying on the sofa, his waistcoat undone, Cohen watched Devereaux through half-closed eyes; watching his plodding progress along the white board that ran the height and length of one wall on which were mounted one hundred or so photographs, settled in five discrete groups.

There were crime-scene photographs of a stairwell in Belgravia, of a man's body lying in a lake of chocolate-brown blood; alongside them, ghastly Polaroids of Flint's ruined face.

The next group portrayed the interior of Flint's small flat where Cohen had gone to get a sense of her, picking at her things, feeling all the time like a thief. There were shots of her clothes hanging in the wardrobe, her underwear neatly folded in a drawer; a meagre collection of cosmetics in the white-tiled bathroom, and Extra-Strength Tylenol imported in bulk from the States; letters on her bedside table from a doting father who called her

'Amazing Grace' and signed himself 'John'; face-down in a drawer, a framed photograph of a smiling man who had married Grace Flint but not loved her enough.

Cohen had examined her books one by one, discovering her taste for the novels of Elmore Leonard and Lorrie Moore, and then her collection of compact discs. Finding Pachelbel's Canon, he had put it on to play while he pondered the small mystery of why she also collected albums when there was no turntable included in her compact stereo system. It was in the album sleeves that he found Flint's notes, written in her spidery hand, one page per sleeve, snuggled up with the vinyl; notes that A.J. Devereaux did not yet know existed

The third group of photographs on Cohen's wall documented with commendable thoroughness every nook and cranny of the Villa Donati, raided by the *carabiniere* at Scotland Yard's urgent request but too late to capture Frank Harling. As policemen tend to, they had timed their raid for dawn and by then Harling was long gone, slipping into the night, the barking of his dogs the only signal of his departure.

The fourth group, before which Devereaux now stood, showed Ellis: the ruined house, the cane field, the rusted truck. Mostly, it showed the shed and its contents, each print embossed with the date and the precise time it was taken. Flint had used up a lot of film capturing extracts from the affidavit.

2. In approximately the third week of August of 1994 I was detained for questioning by detectives

attached to the Serious Fraud Office (SFO) in connection with a transfer of 7.5 million US dollars that had been made on behalf of one of our clients, from New World Bank & Trust Company to the National Westminster Bank in Bishopsgate, London. I had been instructed by the client to collect these monies on his behalf. The SFO alleged those funds were part proceeds of a large fraud perpetrated by the client and I was initially informed that I would be charged with dishonestly handling stolen money. The fact that I was not charged was due to the intervention of a certain 'Mr Brown' whom I know to be a senior British intelligence officer. I will now describe the precise sequence of events.

Deveraux could have read the whole affidavit, for the original sat on Cohen's desk. But there was something compelling about reading the extracts Flint had selected as important; reading it through her eyes, as it were. Reading it through Cohen's eyes, too, for three of the prints had been enlarged to 10×8 size at his request, and he had emphasised what he thought the most explosive passages with a yellow marker pen. Devereaux adjusted his glasses and leaned forward to read them.

42. I next saw 'Mr Brown' sometime in early May. As usual, we met outside the gates of Kensington Palace and this time he led me to the Royal Garden Hotel where we sat in the lounge. After some small

---

talk, he told me that he knew of my association with Clayton Buller, a Los Angeles attorney who had been a client of my bank for some two years. From time to time Mr Buller would fly to London and hand me large amounts of cash belonging to his clients that I would then deposit to his account. 'Mr Brown' now told me these monies were the proceeds of drug trafficking – an allegation that I found extremely alarming. I said that I would immediately end my relationship with Mr Buller and close his account, but 'Mr Brown' was insistent that I do no such thing. He said that I should continue to accept monies from Mr Buller but that henceforth . . .

Devereaux turned to look at Cohen and said: 'Monies? Henceforth? This is lawyer's language, Harry. This is not our Frank unburdening his soul.'

'Very expensive lawyers. Harling had his affidavit prepared by one of the top three firms in the city.'

'Did he, indeed? And they listened to all of this and wrote it down and did nothing else about it? Told no one?'

'Client confidentiality covers many sins.'

'Balls,' said Devereaux. 'They're not priests! Since when did your precious *confidentiality* permit the concealment of treason?'

Cohen waved a hand as if to say he was too tired to argue. 'Finish reading, would you?'

. . . that henceforth 'Mr Brown' and his associates
would expect a 'levy' of fifteen percent on every
transaction. In other words, I was to deduct that
amount from every deposit that Mr Buller made,
and pay it into 'Mr Brown's' account at my bank. I
was told to inform Mr Buller that he was also
required to make an 'ex gratia' payment of one-
million US dollars to cover past transactions. In
return, 'Mr Brown' said he would 'watch Buller's
back', meaning he would be warned if he was ever
in danger of being arrested. He told me to describe
this to Mr Buller as 'an insurance policy'. After the
meeting, I conveyed this information to Mr Buller
in Los Angeles by telephone.

43. Mr Buller was extremely disturbed by this
development. He agreed to pay the 'levy', and he
instructed me to transfer one million dollars to 'Mr
Brown's' account. But he was now very nervous of
personally conducting any further transactions,
fearing that he was under surveillance by the
authorities. In a second telephone conversation the
day after my meeting with 'Mr Brown', Buller told
me he was going to find a 'cutout' to transfer future
deposits directly to my bank.

44. Some six weeks later I received a message
from Mr Buller asking me to meet him in a National
Car Park adjacent to Victoria Station. He said he
would be bringing with him an investment banker
from Zurich who wanted to discuss with me the
practicalities of the transfers. I assumed this woman

to be the 'cutout'. I knew she was female because Buller referred to her as 'a hot chick'.

The next three passages were coloured entirely yellow. For good measure, Cohen had used a red felt pen to draw an angry exclamation mark in the margin.

45. On the day of the meeting I received a call on my mobile telephone from 'Mr Brown', who seemed very agitated. He instructed me to go to a public telephone and call him on an 'emergency' number be had previously provided. (To the best of my recollection, the number began with the digits 0171 304. I do not recall the last four digits but I know they included 4 and 0.) I did as I was told, calling from a public phone in Victoria railway station. 'Mr Brown' then informed me I was walking into a trap. He said that, unbeknownst to Mr Buller, the woman he believed to be a banker was in fact an undercover police officer. He told me her name was Grace Flint and that she was a detective attached to the Major Crimes squad. He instructed me to go to the meeting, inform Mr Buller of the true situation, and assist his escape.

46. Naturally, I demurred. I pointed out to 'Mr Brown' that Miss Flint, the police officer, was unlikely to be alone. He admitted that there might be a 'back-up team' of other officers hiding in the vicinity, but he said they would be unable to reach the stairwell where I had arranged to meet Mr

Buller. He did not explain how that had been achieved. He just said, 'that's been taken care of', or words to that effect.

47. I then asked 'Mr Brown' what I was supposed to do about Officer Flint if she attempted to arrest us. I remember 'Mr Brown's' reply very clearly. He said: 'Do whatever's necessary. Just get Buller out of there.' He pointed out to me that if Mr Buller was arrested he would likely tell the police about his 'insurance policy'. He said: 'That will bring them after you, Frank, and that would make us very nervous. We can't have you telling tales to the police.' I perceived this as a threat. Because I was frightened of 'Mr Brown' and what he might do to me, I agreed to follow his instructions. He then repeated that I must do 'whatever's necessary'.

Around the final two words of Harling's mitigation, Cohen had drawn a red circle and then a slashing line with an arrow point that directed Devereaux's attention to an enlargement of a few words from the Report of the Inquiry into the Murder of Detective Inspector Peter Pendle. They described what Harling had said in the stairwell as Clayton Buller worked the slide of his Browning in his fervent attempt to also kill Grace Flint; what Frank Harling, on the instruction of his masters, had found it 'necessary' to do.

Finish it, Buller. For fuck's sake, get it done.

Devereaux removed his glasses and rubbed the bridge of his nose.

'We've got to find her, Harry,' he said. 'Save her, bring her home. We owe her that, don't we?'

Cohen was thinking of a videotape of television news coverage he had found in Flint's flat, a kaleidoscope of strident sounds and haunting images. Of throbbing blue lights and keening sirens, of police cars abandoned at crazy angles; of lurid yellow tape sealing off the scene and the yellow jackets of stone-faced cops, some of them armed; of Pete Pendle's body on a stretcher covered with a sheet, carried away in an ambulance with pointless haste; of Flint on a stretcher, shielded from the cameras by men who did not want her face exposed to the public gaze; of Frank Harling's face filling the screen, wanted for questioning, dangerous, believed armed.

Cohen said, 'Reading that, learning the truth, I wonder what she thought?'

'Listen to this bit, Kevin. This'll make you laugh.'

Flint sat on the floor in a corner of the Maitlands' living room, her back against the wall, her legs splayed, Harling's affidavit cradled on her lap. She was un-naturally calm and her eyes were brilliant, her voice pitched a little too high for Hechter's liking.

'Frank's an eagle! I'd have thought vulture was nearer the mark but, no, Frank's a soaring, sodding, eagle. That's his codename! That's what they call him! They've got a whole aviary of birds. Starling, Bullfinch, Snipe . . .'

'Grace, don't do this.'

'Do what?'

'Torture yourself.'

'Oh, I'm fine. Why wouldn't I be? You'll like this one, Kevin.'

'Grace!'

'They put him in a safe house until the fuss died down and they brought in a makeup artist to change his appearance. They called her Thrush. Frank says she was pissed off because they wouldn't give her time to do a proper job on his face. Well, Thrush was right to complain wasn't she, Kevin? It takes a while to make a mask.'

Hechter said, 'We'll have him, Grace. In just a few more hours. Then we'll get them all, every last asshole.'

'Oh, don't count on it, Kevin. I wouldn't be at all surprised if Frank isn't on a plane right now with a new face and a new name and—'

Abruptly she pushed the affidavit from her lap and stood up.

'Well, they've done it before, haven't they?' she said, glaring at Hechter, daring him to challenge her.

She went to the Maitlands' coffee table where her evidence bags were neatly stacked and began rummaging among them.

'They've certainly done that,' she said.

Flint found what she was looking for and marched up to Hechter to show him the items one by one: items supplied by Mr Brown to create Frank Harling's new identity; items Harling was supposed to have destroyed after his escape but which he'd kept, and hidden in his box, as compounding proof of his allegations.

'Exhibit A,' she said, holding up the first bag. 'One

driver's licence issued in the name of Peter Michael Kordas.'

She dropped the bag at Hechter's feet.

'Exhibit B,' she continued, showing him the next one. 'One Visa credit card issued by Barclays Bank to one P.M. Kordas. Exhibit C: An American Express credit card in the name of Mr P.M. Kordas. Exhibit D – a nice touch, this one – a leather wallet with gold initials, PMK.'

'I know, Grace, I know.'

She pressed on, the pace of her narrative growing breathless. 'Business cards stating that Peter Kordas is the Regional Sales Manager for Midas Computing. A diary listing his appointments – oh, and his expenses. Supporting receipts in date order. And this one, this one I really like: One photograph of a woman and two children. They didn't just give Frank a new life and a new job, Kevin, they gave him a whole bloody family.'

There was one more evidence bag left in her hand, containing the British passport of Peter Kordas, immaculately forged. She removed it from the bag and opened it to the last page to show Hechter the picture: Straight-back-and-sides Frank Harling in his thick-rimmed glasses, his complexion olive – thanks to Thrush – hinting of Mediterranean origins.

'Do you see he's smiling, Kevin? Do you see that? Well, you can't really blame him, can you?'

With all of her strength, she hurled the passport across the room.

Then her body convulsed and before Hechter could reach out to help her she doubled over as though her spine had snapped. He lifted her limp shoulders and held her in his arms and stroked her hair. He felt the fluttering of her breath on his neck, and the gentle warmth of her tears.

Since giving up their harvest of secrets at Ellis, the Maitlands had done little else but sleep. 'The sleep of the innocents,' Flint had called it with a copper's heavy irony. Now she too was sleeping, lying on the Maitlands' rattan sofa in the living room, Hechter watching over her.

Evening had approached with tropical suddenness and he turned on a table lamp, adjusting the shade so that the light did not reach her face. Nor did it reach the spot by the window where, from time to time, he would stand and examine the garden and the road beyond, looking for who-knew-what. He had no reason to think they faced any threat but Cornhill Rise was a cul-de-sac and therefore a trap, and it was not in Hechter's nature to take anything for granted. He wanted them out of there just as soon as Cutter could come up with the means. Prowling the room, pacing between Flint's improvised bed and the window, Hechter willed his mobile phone to ring.

'Listen up,' said Cutter when he finally called. 'I've got you wings.'

Hechter asked him to hold on while he stepped out onto the terrace.

'Flint's asleep,' he explained.

'How's she doing?'

'Okay. She was a little shook up at first.'

'I'll bet.'

'She's over it now.' Wild horses could not have dragged from Hechter the truth about her breakdown. 'She's fine,' he added loyally.

'Good. When she wakes up you can tell her she's going home. First flight out. The reservations are all set.'

'She's not going to like that.'

'I don't care what she likes, Kevin. She's not the only one who's shook up. Glenning wants her back in London for a de-brief, and he wants her there yesterday. She's got a problem with that, you have her call me. Now, I've got you Hal Greene and his Lear. He should be with you in a couple of hours.'

'A Lear's not going to do it, sir. Maitland's papers, there must be . . .' He broke off and stepped back into the shadows. Cupping his hand around the mouthpiece he said, 'Wait one.'

The lights of an approaching vehicle edged towards the house around the bend of Cornhill Rise.

'Visitors. Maybe.'

'Stay on the line,' Cutter ordered. 'Something's going on, I want to know about it.'

Hechter slipped the phone into his shirt pocket and bent down to draw a small revolver from the concealed holster that was strapped to his ankle. The protocol covering visits to the Lawrence Islands of foreign law enforcement agents do not permit them to go armed, and it was the only weapon Cutter had allowed him to bring.

He took off his shoes and made a crouching run down

the steps of the terrace and across the lawn to the cover
of the privet hedge. Through a gap in the foliage he
watched as a small car reached the apex of the bend and
the lights were extinguished. Slowly – much too slowly
for Hechter's liking – it approached his position.

'One car, no lights,' he said to his pocket, hoping
Cutter could hear. 'Looks like one occupant but it's too
dark to make them out.'

Squatting at his side Flint said softly, 'One old lady
with an attitude problem,' and the fright almost poleaxed
Hechter.

'Christ almighty! You could have given me a heart
attack.'

'Or a bullet in the back of your head. You're getting
old, Kev. And you've started talking to yourself.'

He feigned a punch at her grinning face.

'She was here before, looking for Maitland,' she said.
'Works at the bank and doesn't take no for an answer. I
had to send her away with a flea in her ear.'

'Well, she didn't get the message.'

Peggy Pringle's Rover stopped in front of the house,
just yards from where they were hidden, and they could
see her face at the driver's window.

'Maybe I should give her a heart attack,' Flint
murmured. 'Who's she talking to, Kevin?'

'What!'

'Watch her lips. She's either talking to herself or there's
somebody hiding in the back. You think we should take
them down?'

Before Hechter could respond the car pulled away,

making a tight U-turn and accelerating down the road, the lights coming on just before it reached the bend.

Hechter stood up and took the phone from his pocket. 'Hello?'

Cutter said, 'You two pilgrims through playing games?'

Hechter was right: Flint didn't like it.

She cussed Cutter to hell with a proficiency that Hechter hadn't heard since leaving the Marine Corps. He tried to calm her down, make her see sense, reason with her, but nothing worked. Finally he lost patience and said, 'Call Cutter' – and so she did.

'You know, Grace, you're getting to be a pain. I'll say this once. I've got a Lear and a C-130 coming down. The Lear's for Hechter and the Maitlands. The big bird's for the documents, and it's got a whole crew to load them. You, you're out of there on the six a.m. bucket to San Juan. Your connection to New York is at noon, and then you're on the overnight BA flight to London. You get in at six forty-five a.m. and the Yard's sending a car to meet you. Now, is that clear?'

Flint surrendered, knowing that nothing she could say would change Cutter's stubborn mind.

Taking her to the airport in the pre-dawn, Hechter said, 'Just tell yourself the boss is almost always right – that's why he's the boss.' Refusing to be mollified, she replied, 'You believe that?'

'Usually.'

'Christ, Kevin, I once had a puppy dog called Hector.

Different spelling but I see the connection.'

  Later – all to soon – she would have given the world
to take that back.

VI

In repose Lisa Maitland's face had lost its anger and vixen sharpness. She had always guarded it from the sun and there were no lines or blemishes spoiling the skin. In their coded traffic to Cutter, Flint and Hechter had called her 'angel face', which, looking at her now, her head cradled in her husband's lap, was not much of a disguise.

The Learjet banked ten degrees and the motion caused them both to stir, but only briefly.

Hal Greene lived for flying and there were many who predicted he would die for it. Working for the Drug Enforcement Administration, flying covert missions over Colombia and Bolivia, he had been shot at more times than most combat pilots with no discernible diminution of his enthusiasm. He maintained his airplanes better than he did his marriage. He certainly spent more time on them.

Greene and Hechter sat side by side silhouetted in the soft glow from the lights of the Learjet's instrument panel. They were talking quietly, Greene answering Hechter's unceasing questions about the nature and purpose of each of the controls and gauges set before them. It was Flint's claim that Hechter had emerged from the womb asking questions, and surely would not stop until the lid of his coffin was closed. 'Self-taught' was Hechter's modest description of himself but that was unfair to the countless souls who had endured the merciless interrogations that had made him an expert in, among other things, the slicker arts of accountancy. Now Hechter was learning how to fly a jet the only way he knew how to learn, by osmosis.

'Want to take it? I need to use the can.'

'Sure,' said Hechter. 'No problem, if you don't mind dying.'

'I'm kidding. The autopilot's on.'

He gave Hechter the reassurance of his lopsided grin and squeezed down the aisle, crouching like a hunchback for he was much too tall to stand up straight in the Lear's tiny fuselage. Hechter gently held the yoke, feeling its precise responses to the commands of the autopilot, watching the gauges report the small movements. Then he leaned forward to get a better view of the night sky, which is why he missed the worst effects of the explosion.

The cloud of charcoal-grey particles collected from every crack and crevice in the cockpit hit Hechter full in the face, temporarily blinding him. He felt as if the skin on his head was being stretched by clamps. The rudder pedals under his feet sped in opposite directions, jamming his right knee against his chest.

Anything that was loose in the cabin left it. The

debris flew towards the rear of the plane in waist-high procession and vanished through the gaping hole in the fuselage next to where the toilet had been; next to where Hal had been, and the Maitlands. There was a damp, white rolling fog that enveloped everything.

Unseen and unaided, the throttle cables for the Lear's two engines snapped back to the near-idle position and, robbed of its power, the plane decelerated as though it had hit a wall. Hechter was hurled backwards and stunned by the impact of his head hitting the seat. His ears were filled with an angry roar.

Hechter was shouting: 'Hal! Where the fuck are you?'

He pulled on the yoke with both hands, the muscles of his thick neck bulging with the effort. Even so, he could feel that the nose of the plane was falling.

The explosive decompression of an aircraft at 32,000 feet is like the explosion of a small bomb, and it has a similar effect on those who experience it at close range. And when it *is* a bomb that causes the decompression, in this case a few ounces of Semtex detonated by a timer; when the blast punches a hole in the fuselage allowing the pressurised air in the cabin to escape like gas from a balloon, the effects on those present are dramatically compounded. It is like being hit twice in the solar plexus by some monstrous fist. The first blow sucks the air from the body. The second begins the process of rapid suffocation; although the lungs gasp for relief the air at 32,000 feet is simply too thin to breathe.

Hechter mumbled 'Oxygen' and reached for a mask positioned by his right shoulder and pressed it to his face. He gasped for breath, to no avail.

His body was feeling lighter now, the first consequences of oxygen deprivation. Events progressed in slow
motion and he found himself observing them with
detachment. He knew that he was dying, knew that only
oxygen could save him. He knew that is was available
but he did not know how to get it. He was beginning not
to care.

Some sixth sense told him he had to manually open
the valve connecting the mask to the emergency oxygen
supply. He felt a sudden sweet coldness on his face. He
resisted, keeping his mouth closed, for his brain was too
sluggish to grasp the connection, but his lungs screamed
for relief and finally they got it.

The roar was softer now, perhaps because he was
getting used to it.

Hechter began talking to himself, as if by rehearsing
his thoughts out loud he might better comprehend them.
He said: 'The throttles are at idle, that's why we've lost
power. I need to push the throttles forward, but how far?
And, Jesus, the speed is building up because we're diving.
Put on power and then pull up, or pull up and then put
on power? Lift versus weight, thrust versus drag. I need
to get the nose up, I need to get the speed down. I need
to get her stable and then I need to get her down to
where we can breathe. Come on you jerk, concentrate!
What did Hal say? Remember the pitch-power rule: pitch
to control airspeed, power to control the rate of descent.
Or the other way round? Come on, Hechter, *fucking
concentrate.*'

He was still rehearsing the basic tenets of aerodynamic law when they became academic. When a Gates Learjet exceeds a speed through the air of Mach .82, or 445 knots, supersonic shock waves travel over the wings and destroy their ability to maintain lift. There are remedies available but not readily to novice pilots flying solo on their first lesson.

The Learjet rolled over onto its back and headed down towards a dark, uncaring sea.

In Cohen's study Devereaux stood before the fifth group of photographs mounted on the wallboard: chilling, potent images of the flotsam that attended the violent destruction of the Lear. The plane had come down less than a mile from the Puerto Rican port of Mayagüez, narrowly missing a small flotilla of fishing boats. The rescuers who were quickly on hand had found nothing to do.

'Who knew?' asked Devereaux.

'Knew what?'

'About Ellis? About what they'd found? About the evacuation plan?'

Cohen yawned and said, 'You did.'

'Of course I did, but who else? Let's examine the sequence of events.'

'If we must.'

Devereaux ignored the rebuke and perched himself on the corner of Cohen's desk.

'As I recall, Flint and Hechter took themselves off to Ellis as soon as young Maitland spilt the beans.'

'Within the hour, as soon as Hechter found a vehicle to rent.'

'Taking Maitland with them, and the unfortunate Lisa, of course. But no locals, correct? They told no one? Not the Attorney General or the judge?'

'No one.'

'And when they got back from Ellis the only calls they made were from cellular phones, digital not analog, and not so easy to intercept?'

'As you say.'

Devereaux picked up the original copy of Harling's affidavit. 'So, who did they call first?' he asked briskly.

'Cutter.'

'Flint or Hechter?'

'Both of them. Flint called to tell him what they'd found, then Hechter asked for transportation. He wanted to get the documents off the island as soon as possible, and they needed something large.'

'A Hercules, no less.'

'Hechter also wanted to get the Maitlands off the island – even more quickly, if he could.'

'Hence the Learjet.'

'Unfortunately,' said Cohen, and Devereaux nodded his acknowledgement.

'And who did Cutter tell?'

'No one at his end, or so he says.'

'And you believe him, Harry? Our Mr Cutter somehow persuades the United States Air Force to drop whatever it's doing and provide him with a cargo plane without telling a living soul the reason why? You buy that, do you, Harry? You don't find it a trifle far-fetched?'

'It would be entirely in character. Cutter's very good at getting what he wants. He's also renowned for keeping his secrets.'

Devereaux grunted, far from convinced. He had rolled the affidavit into a tube which he tapped against his lips.

'Glenning,' said Devereaux, changing tack. 'Cutter does call Glenning, and who does Glenning talk to?'

'You.'

'No, not immediately. He calls the Home Office and whispers in the ear of the minister's permanent secretary. Now, why did he do that, Harry? Why not talk to his superiors?'

'The commissioner was away.'

'So?' He pointed the affidavit at Cohen. 'Don't dance with me, Harry. What about the deputy commissioner, the assistant commissioner, the deputy assistant commissioners? God knows there are enough of them. They can't all have been away.'

'He didn't trust them.'

'Didn't he, by George!' Devereaux seemed startled by the revelation. 'Said that, did he?'

'Not in so many words but that was his implication.'

'Well, well, well.' Devereaux slowly shook his head. 'Cutter's not the only one who keeps his secrets, is he? You're a dark horse, Harry.'

'Coffee,' Cohen said rising up from the sofa, feeling in his muscles the length of the day. 'And then, if you'll forgive me, bed.'

On a handsome white oak table that Annie had bought

in the first year of their marriage – one of her many impulsive purchases – sat a gleaming chrome espresso machine bristling with pipes and gauges that she had also bought, for his fortieth birthday. She had watched his delight as he'd unwrapped the present and told him he was the only man she'd ever known for whom coffee acted as a sedative. Six weeks later they had told her that she was dying.

'Not for me, old chap,' said Devereaux. 'I would be bouncing off the walls all night, or what's left of it.' He pulled out his pocket watch and feigned surprise. 'Good Lord, look at the time. Let's just finish up and then I'll be on my way.'

While Cohen fussed with his machine, measuring precise amounts of coffee and water, Devereaux paced the study, punctuating his monologue with his stride.

'Glenning talks to the permanent secretary. He talks to the minister, who runs a mile; doesn't want to know. Then the PS talks to me – and nobody else at the Service, thank God. Tells me to sort it out. I call Glenning and we meet in a filthy wine bar in Victoria Street, as I recall. And that's it. So, it was a very tight circle. "We'll keep this to ourselves until we know the strength of it." That was the order of the day, Harry. "Get Flint home and see what she's got. Until then, don't tell a living soul." And we didn't, Harry, I'm sure of it.'

'No word to your secretary, no note to the file?'

'Not then. Later, of course, after Flint got back.'

'Glenning says the same.'

'So there you are, a club of four. Nobody else had an

inkling, including the director-general – whom, I might add, never forgave me. I sometimes wonder if that's what brought on his stroke.'

Cohen had finished his preparations and was watching thick brown liquid trickle into a cup.

'Someone knew,' he said.

'And there's our conundrum, Harry. And that brings us back to Cutter. Don't you see? He has to be the weak link. Either Cutter was not as discreet as you believe, or . . .'

Devereaux had stopped his pacing, coming to rest at Cohen's side. He was pulling on his overcoat, suddenly impatient to leave.

'Or?' he demanded again.

'Or he's part of it?'

Devereaux gave a sad smile, as though he wished to temper the gravity of his suspicions. 'Give it some thought, Harry, that's all I ask.'

Then he was gone, striding up the stairs two at a time, his coat flapping behind him. 'See you on Monday,' he called as he reached the summit. Cohen heard the front door slam shut. As Annie had slammed it in the mounting moments of her despair.

four

Flint in her flat, her synapses tingling with fatigue, dialled her husband's number and listened to it ring. She could imagine his house with its steep flights of stairs and polished wooden floors; its large kitchen in the basement, gleaming with appliances and artificial light; a second-floor window overlooking the street where late one night, passing by on police business, she had glimpsed Jamie standing, holding in his arms his bastard son.

'Hello.' Caroline's voice, bright and brittle. In the background, as she kept her silence, Flint could hear the chatter of other voices and riffs of laughter. '*Hello?*'

'Can I speak to Jamie?'

'Who's calling?'

'His wife.'

It was the literal truth for they had not yet divorced, but why did she say it? Flint supposed it was for the pleasure of picking at the scab of Caroline's insecurity, of hearing the shudder of her breath. She had vowed not to do it again – indeed, promised not to do it again – but now she had and there was no way to take it back.

She imagined Caroline masking the mouthpiece with her hand and her angry whisper that must have silenced the chatter: 'It's *her*! Your *wife*!' She imagined the stab of surprise on Jamie's face and his instant recovery; imagined him calming her, taking the phone.

'Grace?'

'Is this a bad time?'

'Not the best. We're about to have supper. What's up?'

'I want to see you.'

He barely hesitated. 'Look, I'm on the cordless. Let me go somewhere I can hear you properly.'

She imagined him escaping from Caroline's hearing, heading for the French windows that led to their prim patch of garden, mouthing some apology to their guests.

'Grace,' he said, keeping his voice down, his soft mouth close to the phone, 'you promised.'

'Promised what?'

'Not to call me at home. You know it drives her insane.'

'I have to see you.'

'Well, great. When? Tomorrow? Shall I come to you?'

No. Not that. Not this time. She named a restaurant in Covent Garden they both knew, and said she would be there at one, and then she rang off before her will could wither in the face of his persuasion.

Wrapping her bathrobe more tightly around her, Flint imagined Jamie returning to Caroline, telling her whatever lie about the call he had quickly invented, and – not for the first time – she pondered a conundrum: If your husband cheats on the mother of his bastard son; if, whenever you allow it, he comes cautiously to your flat for lunch and afterwards – on your needy days, on the days when your want surpasses your hurt – you take him into your bed and allow him to fuck you, does that mean you are having an affair?

Orso was brimming with its usual lunchtime crowd but he had secured the table by the back wall that allowed a measure of privacy. He stood up for her, watching her come towards him, merry with pleasure that she had dressed for him: that at the last moment – God help her – she had discarded the severe suit she'd intended to wear in favour of a Thirties dress of faded print that she knew he liked. He wore his habitual City uniform of pinstripe and stiff-collared shirt but that was only to be expected; if he had dressed for her, chosen the clothes she liked to see him wear, how could he have explained that to Caroline?

He took her hands in his and leaned down to kiss her. She turned her face so that his lips brushed only her cheek.

'You look ravishing,' he said.

'Well, I don't feel it.'

He put the tip of one finger under her chin and raised her face so that he was looking into her eyes. 'Then I will feed you with all of your favourite things, and ply you with delicious wine, and make you laugh until we've chased the gloomies away. How does that sound?'

She retrieved her hands, sat down, and asked him for
water. 'Jamie,' she said firmly, 'this isn't one of those
days.'

He was too practised a seducer to let his disappointment show. 'Then tell me what's wrong and what I can
do to make it better. Anything. Anything at all.'

And so she told him, or started to, and as she talked
she watched the mask of sincerity skidding from his
face, banished by a succession of real emotions. With a
welcome detachment she had not anticipated, she noted
that the dark liquid eyes he used to bewitch her with
now betrayed him. As she told him what she wanted him
to do, she saw his confusion blossom into stark alarm.

He broke in: 'Good God, Grace, I can't do that!'

'Why not?'

'Because what you're asking for is absolutely, irrevocably confidential. I can't get it for you. Under any
circumstances.'

'Jamie, just let me finish.'

'No. I'm sorry, Grace. I don't want to hear another
word. You know how I hate your copper's talk.'

'Jamie—'

'No! I will not let you spoil this.'

He waved his hand, summoning a waiter, and began
reading the menu with studied determination.

'Now, let's see if we can find something that will put
you in a better mood.'

She let him do it; let him decide what they would eat
and what wine they would drink. And, as the meal
proceeded, she let him perform for her, telling his

scurrilous stories of life in the City, of tycoons and high finance and aspects of the market that were rarely reported in the *Financial Times*. He had the gift of mimicry, seasoning his anecdotes with a melody of perfectly captured accents and mannerisms. Close your eyes and you might easily believe you were overhearing an indiscretion of the Chancellor of the Exchequer, or receiving blunt advice from Rupert Murdoch. Yet he was never boastful, always casting himself in a minor part in his adventures. By his account, he was no mover and shaker; merely a witty and irreverent observer of Threadneedle Street around whom interesting things happened.

She smiled for him in most of the appropriate places and he grew radiant. But her sense of detachment remained. Part of her existed away from the table – off-stage, as it were – watching a well-rehearsed charade: Jamie Stapleton, in the role of charmer, attempting to win his apparently gullible wife for one more afternoon. Vaguely she wondered why she had not taken his name when they married, what instinct had warned her. And what, she wondered, had changed? Why was she now impervious to Jamie's technique?

When the meal was done and the bill had arrived, Jamie said: 'Are you free this afternoon? I've cancelled my meetings, you see. I thought we might go to a movie, or go for a walk, or . . . ' He left the third possibility unspoken.

She thought that he might leave, that he might just get up and go, so she leaned across the table and took hold

of his wrists with her hands. Misunderstanding, he did
the same, using his long fingers to stroke the down on
her forearms.

'Listen to me, Jamie. Five days ago, a friend of mine,
somebody very special, was murdered. So were three
other people, but it was his body that I had to identify –
or what was left of it. He was in a plane that was
bombed. When it hit the water, he was shattered into a
hundred pieces. They showed me his hand. That was all,
just a hand. It looked like it had been severed with a
butcher's knife. I knew it was his because of the wedding
ring.'

From the look on Jamie's face she might as well have
slapped him.

'I want the people responsible for that and in the
bank's files you have information about a man who can
lead me to them. I don't care if it's confidential. I don't
care what rules you have to break. I don't even care if it
costs you your job. Get it for me, Jamie. Please.'

He was too strong for her. He pulled away his wrists,
knocking over the water bottle, trembling with rage.

'Are you threatening me?'

'Oh, Jamie, just do it, will you.'

'Or you'll do what, Grace?' He made her name sound
like an obscenity.

She sighed as though she was reluctant to impart the
bad news.

'Or what? Say it.'

'Or I'll go to Caroline and tell her the last thing she
wants to know. I'll tell her that every chance you get you

sleep with me. I'll tell her that you've begged me to take you back but that I won't because I know you're incapable of being faithful. I'll tell her what she dreads, Jamie.'

What she saw in his eyes now was hate.

'You bitch!'

It came out in a hoarse whisper, the venom of it turning heads. A waiter on his way to the table changed his mind and found some other task to divert him.

Ice-cold, Flint said: 'I've been called that before by a bigger bastard than you, Jamie. He was stamping on my face at the time. You just trample on people's emotions.'

He stood up, kicking back his chair, flinging his napkin onto the table. Then without another word he was heading for the stairs, pushing his way through the tables, oblivious to the commotion he was causing.

She let him get halfway across the restaurant before she called out: 'This afternoon, Jamie. You've got until five.'

He beat her deadline barely. She was making tea when she heard the clatter of the letterbox. Looking out of her kitchen window, she glimpsed him hurrying away through her garden. The gate slammed shut, frightening the starlings. She heard the engine of his BMW and the grating of the gears.

An unmarked brown envelope lay on the doormat. She felt its weight and guessed there were no more than half a dozen pages inside. She went to her living room and placed it unopened on the mantelpiece above the fireplace. Through the open windows, she heard the raucous voices of children playing in the street and wondered if Jamie's son would ever enjoy such freedom. Given Caroline's insecurity, she doubted it.

She took her tea into the bedroom where the air was cool and lay down on the bed. She felt bathed in calm and blessed with a clarity that seemed unnatural in the circumstances. Hechter's murder had shaken her more profoundly than any of the other catastrophes that had recently come crowding into her life: more than Pete Pendle's death that she had so clearly witnessed; more than her own near-death and the beating she had endured; more, much more, than Jamie's casual treachery. She supposed that was because Hechter had become the only man she believed she could rely on; right there, right then. In the tumbrel of recent events – the resurrection of Frank Harling and the dark allegations of his affidavit – she had clung to her faith in Hechter as all desperate people will cling to whatever they can reach, which is to say unquestioningly.

And then he was gone, and – intercepted at the airport and taken to the mortuary in San Juan where they had shown her his severed hand; on the plane home, cast into a mental fog where she was unable to fix on any bearing; in Commander Glenning's office at Scotland Yard, receiving his avuncular condolences and his concern for her welfare – she had felt like an automaton. She did what she was told to do for she had no will of her own.

Not any more.

After her de-briefing Glenning had said: 'I want you

to take some paid leave, Flint. A few weeks, more if you need it. I'm very concerned about your health. You've been through a great deal. You can rest easy that we'll get to the bottom of all this.'

And Cutter, calling her at home from Miami, saying much the same. 'We'll get them, Grace. Count on it. Now, you take it easy, you hear?'

She had not lied to them. There was no need. Confident in their authority, believing she had been broken, they simply assumed they could sweep her aside.

She let herself drift off to sleep, thinking of the envelope that awaited her attention.

Woken by the Pied Piper call of an ice-cream vendor's chimes, Flint rose from her bed and stripped off her clothes. She took a shower and put on shorts and a sleeveless chambray shirt. From her fridge she took a bowl of cold watercress soup and half a bottle of white wine. From her collection of CDs she chose an Annie Lennox and put it on to play. From her bureau she took a fresh pad of paper and two felt-tip pens. From her collection of long-playing records – records she could not play, for she had no turntable – she took a Jimi Hendrix album and, from within its sleeve, the spidery notes she had made from Frank Harling's affidavit.

Ready at last, she settled at the pine table under the window of her living room, bathed in a summer evening's light, and opened Jamie's envelope.

There were seven pages, if you counted the Post-it note on which Jamie had scrawled his farewell: 'If you

have any feeling left for me, you will destroy these papers.
I never want to see you again.'

'Count on it,' she said, mimicking Cutter's drawl.

She drank the soup and read her notes. *Approx 3rd
week August 94*, she had written, abbreviating one of
Frank's first allegations. *$7.5 million, New World to
NatWest. Proceeds of fraud. FH arrested by SFO. Enter
'Mr Brown'*. And underneath, in letters much larger than
her normal style, she had written *WHO CLIENT???*,
for Harling had neglected to identify him.

Seeking the answer to her question, she peeled away
Jamie's Post-it and there it was, framed in the heading of
a letter sent by National Westminster's lawyers to the
regulatory department of the Bank of England:

STRICTLY CONFIDENTIAL
In the matter of MARIO ANTONIA SILVA

Sipping the wine, she absorbed the letter slowly, taking
in its dreary account of Silva's perfidy and reading
between the lines. He was, it transpired, a stockbroker
with a City firm of some standing who had abused his
clients' trust, taking reckless gambles with their invest-
ments, pocketing the profits when he won, concealing
the losses by means of false accounting when he didn't.
Unwittingly the National Westminster bank had become
caught up in his scheme when Silva had attempted to
transfer a portion of his gains from the Lawrence Islands
to the Bishopsgate branch. Fortunately, alerted by the
Serious Fraud Office – and with the bank's fullest

cooperation, of course – Silva had been thwarted and arrested, together with his suspected accomplice, one Frank Arthur Harling. But now there was blood on the floor, for the bank still held the $7.5 million. Faced with a plethora of competing claims, embroiled in controversies not of its making, the bank had placed the funds in escrow pending resolution by the courts, and would the Bank of England please consider itself so advised.

Flint turned the page.

Here were photocopies of the transfer instructions, the routing slip, the clearing bank's confirmation and the receipt: the receipt Frank had signed just moments before the SFO felt his collar.

The third page carried copies of short press reports recording the arrest of Silva, and of the profound shock caused to his employers. The *Financial Times* gave his address as Montague Square, and Flint made a note of it on her pad. She pictured herself going from door to door, searching for his name on the rows of bell-pushes, hoping to find some trace of him; a wife perhaps. She suddenly recalled an incident when, as a rookie copper, she had spent days trying in vain to locate some minor villain only to have the sergeant bark at her, 'Tried looking in the phone book, have we?' She had not, and her quarry was listed. Smiling at the memory, she reached for the London directory and found a column of Silvas, including some Marios, but none that was resident in Montague Square.

The press reports also recorded that, in due course, Silva had appeared at the Old Bailey where he pled guilty to numerous charges of theft and false accounting. The amounts involved were spectacular: at least £30 million, by Flint's calculations. She moved on to the report of his sentencing, and could not believe what she read: CITY SWINDLER GETS 2 YEARS.

Two years! She thought it must be a typographical error, one of those *Guardian*-esque solecisms that turns fact into nonsense. Twelve years, surely? The body of the report told her she was wrong.

> Passing sentence, Mr Justice Barth told Silva: 'Those who deal dishonestly on the scale you have admitted must expect to receive severe punishment. However, in this case, the court has taken into account your guilty plea, the fact that you have cooperated in the repatriation of much of what you stole, and other matters that were brought to the court's notice. In the circumstances, a more lenient sentence is appropriate. You should count yourself a lucky man.'

What those 'other matters' were, the report did not say.

The telephone rang and Flint waited for her answering machine to pick up the call. She heard herself say brusquely what she had recorded on a bad day and never got around to changing: 'I'm not available. Leave a message after the tone.'

Her father said: 'Gracie, darling, this is John. I was just wondering if you're back and how you are.

Call me when you can. Lots of love.'

She imagined him in his kitchen, his bony frame stooped over the long dining table that also served as his desk. He would be half-perched on a stool, the phone wedged between shoulder and ear, flicking distractedly through the day's post and neglecting his supper. In all probability, there would be galley proofs of his next novel on the counter awaiting his correction. For as long as she could remember, he had chronicled the career of a small market town coroner whose abiding interest in pharmacology allowed him to detect and solve ingenious murders with the minimum of violence. Falling asleep to the sound of her father's typewriter was one of the few certainties of her childhood.

She imagined calling him back to tell him she was fine. Then she imagined him asking what had happened in the Caribbean, and since she could neither lie to him, nor tell the truth, she did not make the call.

The last three pages of Jamie's file consisted of an internal Bank of England memorandum placing on record, in considerable detail, how the financial repercussions of the 'Silva matter' had been resolved.

Quietly, very quietly, Flint learned.

In the event, there had been no need to trouble the courts. She read of rival bids made, compromises reached, deals done, lawyers paid. And then she read the last section of the memorandum that seemed to have been added almost as an after-thought, and the sheer complicity of it chilled her, as though the evening had suddenly turned cold.

SILVA'S CONVICTION AND AFTERMATH

Mr Silva was sentenced by the Central Criminal Court to two years' imprisonment, of which he served eight months, most of it in Ford Open Prison.

On a confidential basis, we were informed by the SFO that, prior to the sentencing, Judge Barth held a hearing in chambers during which he received 'amicus' evidence from a senior representative of the Security Services. This person stated that although Mr Silva was not formally connected to the Security Services he had, on a number of past occasions, performed tasks on their behalf and provided information that was deemed to be in the 'national interest'. Indeed, it was emphasised that Mr Silva's contribution to the 'national interest' had been of 'great importance'.

This may in part explain the leniency of the sentence Mr Silva received.

After his release from prison, Mr Silva left the United Kingdom and is now resident in Paris. It is understood that he now deals in works of art.

As the light faded, Flint burned the file in her grate. When the ashes had cooled, she swept them into a pan and, with her fingers, ground them into feathery dust. Then she flushed the ash down the kitchen sink, letting the tap run until the last speck was gone.

II

A summer squall had come racing in from the Atlantic, catching London unawares. Marooned part-way along Marylebone High Street, Cohen sheltered from the drenching rain in a chemist's doorway, already late for his appointment, waving vainly at the taxis that hurried by. He was about to give up and return to his office when he heard his name being called.

'Harry. Harry Cohen. Over here.'

On the other side of the street, Sarah Spenny's bronzed face beamed at him from the driver's window of a blood-red Mercedes SLK that was causing gridlock, and Cohen felt a flutter of dismay. It was Devereaux's cruel claim that Sarah ate men for breakfast; 'Like the black widow spider, dear boy, she devours her mates'.

'Come on, hop in,' she called. 'I'll give you a lift.'

Other drivers leaning on their horns in protest ended Cohen's hesitation and sent him scurrying across the road. Squeezing into the passenger seat, his briefcase on his lap, he was still fumbling with his seat belt when she accelerated away.

'So, Harry Cohen, why are you avoiding me?'

One hand on the steering wheel, flicking through the gears with practised ease.

'Am I?'

She threw back her handsome head and laughed, taking the corner into Wigmore Street much too fast for Cohen's peace of mind.

'I've called you three times this month.'

'Yes, well, I'm sorry. I've been meaning to phone you.' He flinched as she veered to avoid a cyclist. 'I've been rather busy.'

'Too busy to eat?'

'It sometimes seems that way.'

She fell silent as she took a short cut through a mews, squeezing past a convoy of furniture vans, only inches to spare. The wet cobblestones made the car skittish but she did not slow down. Cohen held his breath.

Devereaux had said, 'Mark my words, Harry, she's determined to have you,' and though Cohen had scoffed at the warning he felt like her prey.

As they sped down Orchard Street she said, 'Harry, you can't lock yourself away forever.'

'I'm not,' he protested. 'I swear to you I'm not.'

'Annie wouldn't want you to do that.'

'I know.'

'So, when?'

'When what?'

'When are you coming to supper?'

He closed his eyes as she darted through an amber light and made an illegal right turn into Oxford Street, sending pedestrians scrambling for the pavement.

'Soon,' he said faintly.

'Friday.'

'This Friday? I'm not sure I'll be here.'

'Bollocks.'

Emerging into Marble Arch, where the discipline of one lane became a free-for-all, she gunned the engine and raced for a gap in the traffic. Then they were speeding down Park Lane, her auburn hair swinging about her face as she looked from left to right, darting from one lane to the next. To Cohen it seemed as though every collision they avoided was by the narrowest of margins.

'Sarah, where are we going?'

'I don't know.' She grinned. 'You haven't told me.'

'God!' he said as they hit the curve of Hyde Park Corner at sixty miles an hour. 'Pall Mall. St James's. Anywhere around there will do.'

'Hold on!'

She swerved to the left and he felt the car slipping as the rear wheels fought for traction.

'Don't be silly, darling, you'll get soaked. Where are you having lunch?'

He gripped the dashboard with both hands as she nursed the skid, allowing its momentum to take them into Constitution Hill.

'The Reform.'

She gave a hoot of jubilation. 'Ah, so you do have time to eat. But the Reform? Don't tell me. You're meeting that old fraud Devereaux.'

He saw her looking at him, demanding an answer, and he nodded his head vigorously, silently imploring her to watch the road.

'Well, give him my love.'

'I will.'

'No, on second thoughts, don't. He's another one who's been avoiding me.'

'You're imagining things, Sarah.'

Another hoot of laughter as she changed down to second gear and swept by Buckingham Palace.

'Harry, do I frighten you?'

Hurtling down the Mall, bracing himself for impact, Cohen opted for a half-truth: 'Only when you drive.'

After she had dropped Cohen outside the club, given him her cheek to kiss and told him to be at her house on Friday evening 'eight o'clock sharp', Sarah Spenny drove her car to the warren of streets off St James's and, finding no better alternative, parked on the pavement alongside a public telephone.

A couple of steps took her from the car to its meagre shelter. She dialled a number she knew by heart, heard the phone ring once before it was answered.

'Starling.'

'Thrush. He's at the Reform Club in Pall Mall. Meeting Devereaux.'

'Did he see you?'

'Of course he bloody saw me. I took him there.'

The line went dead.

* * *

A porter led Cohen across the Reform's great hall and
through the restaurant to a door marked Fire Exit,
claiming that beyond it Mr Devereaux would be found.
Not strictly true. Cohen discovered himself at the top of
a flight of stairs facing a second door with no handle, no
means of opening it. He knocked and listened to the
silence. He had the feeling of being observed.

He knocked again and the door opened a crack. A
tiny woman with faded blonde hair peered up at him,
regarding him stonily with watery blue eyes. From within
the room a voice bellowed, 'Alice, let the poor chap in
before he takes root,' and reluctantly she opened the
door sufficiently for Cohen to squeeze through, closing
it firmly the moment he was inside.

'Don't mind Alice,' said Devereaux, coming towards
him. 'She's just guarding her domain. Very choosy as to
who crosses this sacred portal aren't we, Alice?' She
gave Cohen one last suspicious look and hurried away
towards the far end of the room where a second door led
to her pantry. On her thin legs, dressed entirely in black,
she looked like a mourner on her way to a funeral.

'Alice's other attribute,' Devereaux continued, not
lowering his voice, 'is that she is almost stone deaf.' He
beamed, pleased with himself. 'Well, how the hell are
you, Harry Cohen? We'd given you up for dead.'

Cohen mumbled about his difficulty in finding a taxi
but Devereaux had no interest in his explanation. 'Now,
you know everyone, I think. Tom Glenning, Peter
Nicolson and, of course, our exalted new DG.'

They faced him from the far side of a large polished

table, nodding their hellos, reaching across to shake his hand: Commander Glenning, ginger-haired and freckled-faced, out of uniform for once and strangely unfamiliar in his dark blue blazer; Peter Nicolson from the Home Office, tall and angular, hair slicked back, sharply dressed; the director-general, po-faced, evidently displeased with Devereaux for using her acronym.

'It's not that I mind the fact she is a woman,' Devereaux had said when he'd called Cohen with news of Barbara Dixon's appointment. 'Nor do I mind that she is unburdened by any knowledge of the Service, nor even that she is intent on turning us into an impoverished facsimile of the FBI. No, it's her insistence on familiarity that galls me. She tells me to call her Barbara! Soon, no doubt, it will be Babs!'

'Cut out the DG nonsense will you, A.J.,' she said briskly. 'Welcome, Harry. Get yourself some coffee and let's proceed, shall we?'

Alice handed him an empty cup, pointed to an urn and retired to her pantry.

Dixon cleared her throat. 'So, where are we? How many suspects?'

'Nine in the frame so far,' said Devereaux. 'Six are ours, two SIS, and one from the SFO.'

Nicolson said sharply, 'SIS? I thought it was your people Harling implicated?'

'Not exclusively,' Cohen said, bringing his coffee cup to the table, finding his place opposite the DG. 'Harling always refers to "British intelligence" or "intelligence officers" but he is never precise as to what that means.

Either he didn't know the difference between the Security Service and the Intelligence Service or his handlers never made it clear who they were. We think they come from both services. That is certainly what Flint came to believe.'

Nicolson drooped in his chair. 'Terrific! A plague on both your houses. The minister will go ballistic.'

'Peter, we're only talking possibilities.'

No one seemed reassured by Devereaux's palliative.

The DG took a handkerchief from her pocket and began polishing the large oval lenses of a pair of spectacles with tortoiseshell frames that gave her the appearance of a curious owl. 'Harry, why don't you begin? No notes, gentlemen, nothing that leaves this room.'

From the notes Flint had compiled, from her index and her chronology of events, Cohen had assembled three lists: one of people, one of dates and times, one of transfers of monies facilitated by Frank Harling. He had typed them himself on his computer and when it was done he had erased the files. There was only one printed copy of each list.

Cohen slid the pages across the table until they sat before the DG and then began: 'First page, first column is the list of people Harling says he met together with a potted version of his physical descriptions, taken from the appendix to his affidavit. Eleven in all. The first four were all connected to the Serious Fraud Office, and, as I understand it, we are confident we know their identities.'

'We are,' said Glenning, tamping tobacco into the bowl of his pipe. 'Two Met officers seconded to the SFO, one from the City fraud squad, and one – name of Scaby – who's an SFO lawyer.'

'I don't understand,' Nicolson protested. 'You said there was only one suspect from the SFO.'

'One in the frame *so far*, Peter,' Devereaux repeated.

'You see,' Cohen continued, 'three officers and Scaby, the lawyer, were present when Harling was arrested and taken to Elm House. Scaby served him with a Section 20 notice that obliged him to answer their questions or go to prison in any event, and he was interrogated on and off over several hours. Harling insisted that he had simply gone to the bank on behalf of his client, one Mario Silva, about whom, he said, he knew absolutely nothing. Then he was left alone in the interview room until early evening when one of the officers, an inspector . . .'

Cohen looked at his notes, searching for the name.

'McNally,' said Glenning, helping out. 'One of mine.'

'Yes, McNally. Inspector McNally told Harling he was taking him to Holborn police station where he would be charged with handling stolen money and held overnight, pending his appearance at Bow Street magistrates court.'

'Only he wasn't. My man McNally puts him into the back of a car that was waiting outside Elm House, and that's the last we see or hear of Frank Arthur Harling.'

'According to Harling, there was a man waiting in the back of the car who introduced himself as "Brown of Intelligence".' Cohen paused, to signal they were getting to the nub of it. 'Instead of a holding cell he spent the night at a hotel near Heathrow airport, though presumably still at the taxpayers' expense. The next morning "Mr Brown" explained how Harling might overcome his difficulties with the SFO. By serving his country.'

Barbara Dixon said, 'Shall we stop this "Mr Brown" business? In the confines of this room, let's call him who he is.'

'Patrick Shilling,' Devereaux said quietly. 'My deputy, may he rot in hell.'

'Any doubts about that, Harry?'

'None,' said Cohen.

'He's your deputy no longer, I trust,' said Nicolson.

Devereaux slapped the table with his hand. 'Of course he is!'

'He hasn't been sidelined?'

'No!'

'Why on earth not?'

'Good Lord, Peter, because we cannot frighten the horses. You do see that, don't you?'

There was silence in the room, except for the chimes coming from the pantry; the incongruous sounds of Alice setting out the tea tray.

Dixon pricked the tension with her common sense. 'Let's go back a minute. Tom, what does the file have to say about Harling's arrest? I assume you've got access to SFO files?'

Glenning finished lighting his pipe. 'With thirty of my lads working inside Elm House, you bet I've got access.' He paused to expel a plume of smoke with an aroma of cherries. 'But there is no file at the SFO, Barbara. Not on Harling. Nothing in Criminal Records either, nor in Criminal Intelligence. As far as the record shows, Harling was as clean as the driven snow, until the business with Pendle and Flint.'

Nicolson looked at his watch. He saw there was just over three hours to go before he was due to meet with the minister, bring him up to speed on the scale of this disaster. It was a prospect he was beginning to dread.

'But there should be a record, notes of the interview and so forth,' he said.

'Tapes,' Glenning said. 'Notes and tapes.'

'Which should have been preserved,' Nicolson insisted.

'Indeed. If nothing else, as part of Silva's file.'

'And even though Harling was never charged, your Criminal Intelligence people should have logged him?'

'Indeed.'

'Put him into the computer?'

'Exactly right.'

'So that record was never entered?'

'Or removed.'

'By somebody in Criminal Intelligence?' Nicolson's tone had taken on an edge of incredulity.

'Or somebody with access to the database.'

'You mean records can be removed without proper authority, without leaving any trace?'

'Apparently so,' said Glenning glumly.

Nicolson swung his head to look at Devereaux. 'Does the Service have access to these records?'

'Not directly. Informally. If we ask nicely.'

Back to Glenning. 'What about SIS?'

'If they ask *very* nicely.'

'But they couldn't remove them? Destroy them?'

'Not without inside help.'

Nicolson turned to Cohen. Spittle had collected at the corners of his mouth. 'Well?' he demanded. 'What do you say?'

'That's also my assumption, Peter.'

'My God! How deep does this thing go?'

Harry Cohen excused himself to go to the men's room, and the others took advantage of the break to stretch their legs. Nicolson went to draw back the thick curtains that shrouded one wall of the room, to crack open a window, clear the fug from Glenning's pipe. He was reaching for the cord when Devereaux stopped him with a curt, 'No.'

'What?'

'We're making waves, Peter; sound waves. They vibrate on glass. If we don't keep the curtains closed, any bugger with the right equipment can pick up every word we say. Don't want that, do we?'

Nicolson stared at him, uncomprehending.

'Imagine, Peter, somewhere out there, for all we know, two of Shilling's louts in the back of a window cleaner's van, earphones on their head' – Devereaux cupped his hands to his ears in a mime – 'fiddling with the dials of an Emerson receiver.'

'But I thought the whole point of meeting here was to get away from your wretched spies.'

'Quite so,' said Devereaux, enjoying himself. 'But what if one or more of us was followed here? Easily done. Tom, what about you? Have someone watching your back, did you?'

'I took precautions,' said Glenning confidently.

'Were you followed, Peter?'

Nicolson remained standing by the curtains, uncertain what to do. 'How would I know?'

'Precisely my point,' Devereaux said. 'Any half-decent team of my watchers could follow you for a year and you wouldn't have a clue. Not your fault, of course. Same holds true for ninety-nine percent of the population. It's what we count on. Do you see?'

'Are you serious?'

'Absolutely.'

Nicolson walked slowly back to the table. 'Then I have a question for you,' he said. 'About Cohen. I know you think a lot of him, but I have to ask if he really is the right man to conduct this investigation.'

'He's the *only* one, Peter, because he's the only one we can trust.'

Nicolson stayed silent, obliging Devereaux to spell it out.

'We don't yet know who is in cahoots with Shilling, or how many rotten apples there are, but we *do* know Harry Cohen isn't one of them. He blew the whistle, you see. Two years ago he more or less told the DG that Shilling had gone bad, that he was running operations off the books. Only the DG didn't listen – your predecessor, of course, Barbara.' He touched her arm in absolution.

'So, that puts Harry outside the ring of suspicion,' Devereaux continued. 'He's in the clear, the only insider who is. And he *is* an insider, for all practical purposes. I can't remember an ops meeting that Harry didn't attend, or a de-briefing, or an interrogation.'

Devereaux paused and smiled: 'You might say that he knows our little ways.'

'But does he have the training and the skills to take on people . . .' Nicolson broke off and gestured towards the curtained window and the watchers he imagined beyond it. 'People like that.'

'Does he have the tradecraft, you mean? Is he practised in the arts of deception?'

'He's got me watching his back,' said Glenning but Nicolson ignored him.

'Can Cohen do the job?' he insisted.

'He's what we've got, Peter. He's *all* we've got.'

More than two hours later, his meeting with the minister now imminent, Nicolson was impatient to be done with it.

He felt flattened by the flow of revelations that had been heaped upon him. He could report – would report – that Cohen's investigation to date had been thorough, but there was little comfort to be had from that. The gaps in Cohen's knowledge were all too plain: vast canyons of doubt and uncertainty and alarming speculation; canyons into which a whole government might fall.

'To sum up what we know and what we *don't* know,' he said.

Cohen smiled his apology. 'The second category is by far the larger, I'm afraid.'

'Well, we know at least this much,' Nicolson continued, looking hard for any plus points. 'We know there was collusion between elements of the Service and the SFO that allowed Harling to escape prosecution for fraud. We know that, in return, he was recruited – by the Service, he thought – to provide certain, unspecified favours and then nothing further happened – for what? Nine months?'

'Approximately,' said Cohen.

'Isn't that odd?'

'SOP, Peter: Standard Operating Procedure.' Devereaux held a finger to his lips as if to say he was about to impart some great secret. 'We gather our flock when and where we may. We put them on ice; we save them for a rainy day.'

Nicolson frowned. 'Brown – or rather, Shilling – kept in touch with him, friendly chats from time to time, but Harling was not asked to do anything until the Buller business. Correct?'

'The meetings were not entirely social,' Cohen said. 'Shilling always pressed him for information about one or other of his clients.'

'Names Shilling got from the Service files? Targets of the Service?'

'Targets or known associates,' said Cohen.

'And you believe these targets may have been approached directly by Shilling for the purposes of extortion?'

'It's possible. What we know for certain is the pattern. Shilling would throw a name at Harling, a name from the files. If Harling confirmed him as a client of the New World Bank, Shilling would propose an aggressive operation, without bothering to record the information Harling had provided. Invariably, I objected to these operations. Invariably, the files were marked "no action" and closed. Invariably, they disappeared.'

'That still puzzles me,' said Nicolson. 'What was the point?'

Devereaux gave a theatrical sigh. 'The point was, Peter, that the targets then ceased to exist. They were *erased* from our collective memory, *spared* the consequences of their actions and our dreadful spleen.'

'It was a setup,' Cohen admitted. 'I now realise I was meant to object to the operations, so that these particular files could be closed. By failing to document Harling as the informant, which Shilling should have done, he deliberately failed to show proper cause for whatever action his people proposed, which was usually the basis of my objection: "no proper cause". It wasn't very subtle but I fell for it, I'm afraid.'

'How were you to know?' Devereaux protested. 'And, Harry, you were the clever one in the end, weren't you? You checked the archive, you discovered that the files were missing.'

For all the good that did me, Alan.

Dixon said, 'Let's move on.'

'Buller is the first certainty,' Cohen obliged. 'The first one we know of who certainly paid Shilling for protection. One million dollars. We also know that he got what he paid for.'

'As Flint could testify,' Nicolson said. 'If, that is, you could find her.'

'Quite.'

'Explain something, if you would. How could Shilling have known about the Buller operation?'

'McNally?' suggested Cohen and Glenning nodded his agreement.

'Buller was basically an SFO case. We only got involved because we had the undercover know-how. More to the point, we had Flint. She'd been running this cover as a dodgy banker for almost a year, on and off. So, when Buller went looking for his cutout, and the SFO got wind of it, Flint was exactly what they needed to bait the trap. In fact, they asked for her specifically. McNally sat in on the briefing.'

MCNALLY!? Written in Flint's angry capitals, top of the list that Cohen had found hidden in her flat; the list of those she thought might have betrayed her. It was a long list and Glenning's name was also on it.

'In any event,' said Nicolson, 'we know that, after Buller, Shilling instructed Harling to extort money from a succession of the bank's other clients in return for "protection" from arrest?'

'Eleven in all,' Cohen said.

'All of whom paid up?'

'Some forty-seven million dollars between them.'

'And then it stopped.'

'Yes.'

'And that's all we know?'

'Not quite,' Devereaux interjected. 'We know, or can surmise, there was American involvement, because nine of the victims – if that's the proper word – were the exclusive targets of American investigations; DEA, or FBI, or, in some cases, both. Nothing to do with the Service, or Intelligence or the SFO. Somebody across the pond was feeding Shilling names.'

'But you don't know who,' said Nicolson, adding to the mounting litany of Cohen's failures. 'Not who, nor why, nor what Shilling and his friends did with the money.'

'Flint knows,' said Glenning.

'Does she? How can you be sure?'

'Because when she went to France she was already covering her tracks. We're pretty sure she flew to Paris under a false name, probably using a passport left over from one of her ops. She shouldn't have kept it, of course – it should have been handed in when the op was over and destroyed – but she's not the first undercover to have held on to a bit of fake ID. It's their security blanket, you see. Anyway, the point is I know Flint better than I know my own daughter and I know she wouldn't have done that unless she had a lead to follow; something that took her to France. And the fact she then vanished tells me that the lead was solid. She's following it wherever it goes.'

'Then why hasn't she reported in?'

'Who's she going to report to, Peter? Think about it. Who's she going to trust?'

'Well,' said Nicolson, pushing back his chair, standing up, buttoning his jacket, 'thank you all for your time and your... How shall I put it? Your frankness.' He leaned across the table offering his hand to Cohen. 'And I'll tell the minister you'll find Flint, shall I, Harry? Reassure him on that?'

'You can tell him that I'll do my best.'

'Good, good. Your very best is what we need.'

He said his hurried goodbyes to the others and headed for the door.

'By the by,' he said as an afterthought, 'if Flint travelled under an assumed name, how do you even know she went to Paris?'

'She was spotted at Heathrow,' said Glenning.

Crossing the park, heading for his office and his meeting with the minister, Nicolson took some comfort in that. At least somebody was on the ball.

III

There was a security alert at Heathrow. Nothing too heavy, judging by the lack of armour, but sufficient to back up the traffic halfway to the M4. In the back of a black cab, Flint fidgeted with impatience. The stench of exhaust fumes trapped by the humidity and the rattle of the cab was giving her a headache, and an edge to her concerns. For six days she had been calling Jamie at home, just to tell him he was free and clear; just to reassure him that no forensic scientist could ever pore over the photocopies he had purloined, trying to match the blemishes from the drum, the tiny scratches from the glass. No matter what time she called, there had been no reply.

Crawling towards the tunnel, she could see a police Land Rover parked on the traffic island alongside the pint-sized mock-up of Concorde. Four young coppers inside, stiff in their flak jackets and their peaked caps, glaring at the cars. As it came their turn to edge by, her cabbie gave them a friendly nod as if to say he appreciated their vigilance. They examined Flint with sullen eyes and dismissed her. She was not who they were looking for.

The meter clicked once more, telling her that she now owed £42. For want of anything better to do, she calculated that at this rate of progress it would cost another £2 to get through the tunnel and wind their way to Terminal Two. Add the tip and call it £50. Another £160 for her ticket, £30 at the duty free, say 250 francs for the taxi fare into Paris, then dinner tonight for Dominique and Gilles, though he would fight about that. Still, she would prevail, and she would take them out to eat at least once more. Add a hire car, if the target was mobile. Say three days, until she could establish his pattern, say 500 francs a day. Café bills, lunches, tips, *métro* fares, incidentals. Call it another 250 francs a day. If she was there a week, call it 2000 francs. All in all, she reckoned – still only halfway through the tunnel – she was looking at the best part of £1000, or twice her monthly mortgage, one tenth of her savings. She had withdrawn half of that precious reserve in £50 notes that now formed a hefty lump in the pocket of her linen jacket. She wondered if she should keep receipts; if the expense of breaking her implicit word to Commander Glenning might be tax deductible.

At least there would be no hotel bill. Dominique had been adamant about that.

'My best friend is coming to Paris for the first time in *years* and she thinks she is going to stay in an *hotel*?' Dominique had said with feigned indignation, referring to Flint in the third person. 'Has she gone mad?'

'Dominique, it's not been years, and it's not fair on the children.'

'What's not fair?' she had demanded, and Flint had imagined her mentally shooing the boys out of their bedroom, driving them into their sister's room, dismissing her mild complaints. 'Besides, how can Gilles help you if you stay in an hotel?'

There was no logic to that but also no point to further argument. Flint, surrendering, said: 'All right, but let me sleep on the sofa.'

'What sofa?'

'The big white sofa, Dominique. The one in your living room.'

'We have no sofa. That is a chair. How can you work if you sleep in a chair?'

They broke into daylight at the end of the tunnel and the cabbie asked, 'Which airline, love?' She told him Air France and felt the cab accelerate as the traffic cleared. Ostentatiously armed cops, Glock automatics on their hips, MP5s braced across their chests, patrolled in pairs outside the terminal. Two of them were posted at the entrance where the cab set her down, and she instantly recognised their type. Cocky warriors, made potent by their firepower, they selected their marks to suit their prejudices: blacks, Arabs and, for the sport of it, any half-pretty woman.

'Excuse me, miss, where are you travelling to?'

Cropped, ginger stubble running up the sides of his head, insolent eyes, a trace of freckles on his face; more a boy than a man but large and fit. Flint could imagine grappling with him on the mat at Hendon in the hand-to-hand, smelling his sweat, feeling him grope her if he got half the chance.

'Paris,' she said.

'Won't keep you a minute.' He looked her up and down with brazen interest. 'I'll need to see your ticket and your passport. Nice blouse.'

She knew from his tone that he meant 'nice tits', and she knew that he meant her to know.

'I'm collecting my ticket at the desk,' she said. *A ticket that's not in my real name, but I won't trouble you with that little detail, officer.*

'Your passport, then.'

She hesitated – barely, but it seemed like an age – while she considered which one to show him: her real passport in her jacket pocket that did not match the name on the ticket, or the fake one in her bag that did. Some instinct made her reach into her pocket.

'So, what takes us to Paris, then, Ms Flint?' He had opened the passport to the last page and was calculating her age from the simple code. 'Business? Pleasure? Husband? Boyfriend?'

'Why?'

'Why what?'

'Why do you want to know?'

'Because I do.'

'It's none of your business.'

He stiffened, puffing up his chest. 'Step to one side, miss,' he said, moving his body towards her, obliging her to move away from the door until her back was pressing against the wall. 'I'll ask you again. Why are you going to Paris?'

Now from her jacket she took out her warrant card, and held it up close to his face so that he could see her photograph and her rank.

Stepping back, he said, 'Sorry, inspector. We've got a security alert.'

'Who are you looking for?'

'Couple of Algerian tearaways.'

'Male?'

He nodded.

'Not white, middle-aged women?'

He grinned and shook his head, a recalcitrant boy caught in the act.

'Then do your job, constable, and get the hell out of my way.'

He shrugged and moved aside, watching her go. She could feel his eyes on her back, searching the linen for the line of her bra strap, thinking of the things he'd like to do.

five

This was Grace Flint's worst nightmare, the one that jerked her into consciousness, damp with clammy sweat.

Her father is standing in the driveway of their house in Mid Compton, talking to the postman whose name is Tom Price. 'Looks like bad news,' says Tom, handing over an envelope that bears the imprimatur of a distinguished optometrist in London's Harley Street. Price's gloomy analysis of the letters he delivers is part and parcel of his service.

Dr John Flint, veterinary surgeon, grins. Out of the corner of one eye he sees his daughter begin her suicidal run down the steep grass bank on which the house stands.

'Why's that, Tom?'

He catches his hurtling daughter effortlessly and swings her up in a wide arc onto his shoulders. Grace Flint, aged four, shrieks with delight.

'Nothing good ever came out of London,' says Price. 'Mark my words. How are you today, young Grace?'

'Lunch,' Grace announces gravely. Her father gives her the envelope to hold.

'Can I have a quick word with you about Bess?' says Price.

'Of course. What's up?'

'Getting old, I suppose, like me. The thing is, past few days she's been all listless and I think she must be going deaf. Doesn't come when I calls her, not like she used to.'

John Flint, who keeps his patients' records in his head, says, 'Well, she is eleven, which is getting on for a Lab. You'd better bring her in.'

'This evening suit?'

'This evening's fine.'

'About seven?'

'Seven it is. See you then, Tom.'

'Right you are, doctor. Take care, young Grace.'

Price climbs into his postman's van and executes a tight circle in the driveway. With a farewell wave, he takes the curve into Allen's Lane.

'Lunch,' repeats Grace, leaning over her father's shoulder to study his face through the thick lenses of spectacles designed to correct the deficiency in her vision. 'Mummy said now.'

'Then now it is, muppet. Let's go.'

'Gee-gee,' says Grace.

'Okay, saddle up.'

Perched on his shoulders, Grace tucks her feet beneath her father's arms for stirrups, takes hold of his neck for reins.

'Giddy-up,' she says.

The grass incline is steepest near the summit and Dr Flint almost stumbles as he mounts it.

'Giddy-up, giddy-up, giddy-up,' hollers Grace, urging her father on towards the house, using as her switch the envelope from London.

But now the house is much further away, a dark silhouette set up on the hill, and it is late October, after the clocks have gone back and the dusk comes creeping ever-earlier. Nervous in the twilight, Grace is hurrying along Allen's Lane, her young Lab – much younger than Bess – bounding ahead with a puppy's enthusiasm. She rounds a bend and sees Tom Price coming towards her through the gloom. He is waving his arms, yelling words that Grace cannot understand. Now she's on his shoulders and he is running, Grace hanging on for dear life, bruising her buttocks on his bones.

They are in the driveway heading for the barn. They pass his van skewed carelessly where he has left it with the headlights blazing. They enter the barn which is dark except in the far distance where her father stands over his operating table bathed in a pool of light. Grace calls to him but he does not hear. As they get closer she can see that his surgeon's gown is stained with splashes that are ruby red, the colour of cherries. There is something in his hand.

Then he steps out of the pool of light and she can no longer see him. She urges Tom on – 'Giddy-up, giddy-up' – and he responds and they are flying through the darkness towards the light and then he stops so suddenly that Grace loses her grip around his neck and tumbles over his shoulders, and she is falling head first until he grabs her, and she hangs suspended at his midriff, staring upside down to where her mother lies on the operating table. Lifeless. Teeth bared. Hammer holes in her skull.

She is lying on her back, her legs bent, her dress pulled up around her waist, her pants ripped open from the waistband to the crotch, specks of blood on her thighs. There is much more blood on her head and face, a sticky brown stain that mats her hair and runs down the right side of her forehead into the lobe of her ear.

The image is indelible but it is the sound that brings Flint's nightmare to its unbearable climax: from somewhere deep within her, the dinning echo of her father's spectral howl.

II

Standing on the steps of the Reform Club that were still sleek from the rain, Devereaux sniffed the freshened evening air and asked: 'What say you, Harry? Shall we take Shilling's lads for a canter? See if they're up to scratch?'

'You watch my back and I watch yours?'

'That sort of thing.'

Cohen sighed. 'After spending so long in Peter's gloomy company, I think I'd rather have a drink, if it's all the same to you.'

'Splendid idea. Tell you what, why don't I take you home and you can say hello to Belinda?'

Lady Belinda, in fact, but you called her that at your peril. Though she was heir to one of those grand estates that still own the freehold to a substantial portion of London, and distantly related to the Queen, Bel was a rebel; a sort of conscientious objector to her class who campaigned noisily for any number of unlikely causes – against fox hunting and selective education, for example; for gay rights and the abolition of the House of Lords. Angular, whippet-thin, model tall, her long blonde hair

pushed carelessly behind her ears, she always stood out
in a crowd and after she had been photographed at yet
another public demonstration, some bright spark at
Thames House – unaware, presumably, that she and
Devereaux were lovers – had submitted her name for the
Service's 'watch' list of potential subversives. Cohen
vetoed the submission, on the grounds that the State had
little to fear from a woman whose picture also regularly
appeared in advertisements in *Country Life*, modelling
elegant rainwear for Burberrys. And, no, he did not think
it relevant that she donated her modelling fees to
Amnesty International.

Cohen adored her. She and Devereaux lived in Eaton
Square, sharing an apartment that rambled over two
floors, and, after his abrupt departure from the Service,
Cohen most regretted that he and Annie no longer went
there for her impromptu, pot-luck suppers and boisterous
conversation. When Annie died, Bel's scrawled note of
condolence was the only one that did not jar on him as
boilerplate, or pious or cloyed with sentiment: *I'm so
angry for you, Harry! SO FUCKING ANGRY!*

In Cohen's view, there was not an ounce of nonsense
in her – and she would not pretend now that his return
to Eaton Square was a spontaneous event. She intercepted
them in the hallway, glowing with pleasure, hugging him
hard. 'Drinks upstairs in the study so you can have your
natter, and then you're mine, Harry Cohen, for the rest
of the evening.'

Devereaux poured two generous measures of malt
(from a Highland distillery owned by Bel's family) and

tacitly admitted his deception. 'I thought we might have a private chat, just the two of us. Exchange ideas. Do you mind?'

'No,' said Cohen. 'I'm only alarmed that you think I have any ideas beyond the obvious one.'

'Find Flint.'

'Exactly. The question is how? If you want the truth, I don't have the slightest notion.'

Devereaux nodded as though Cohen had said something wise.

'Paris is the key, of course. But there's nothing in Harling's affidavit nor in her notes to even hint at why she went there. If she'd gone to Nice then I could have assumed she was following up Maitland's assertion that many of the bank's Russian clients were based on the Riviera, but why Paris? I have a very strong instinct that something happened in those few days after she got back from the Caribbean and before she disappeared. She learned something, some fact or clue that sent her scurrying undercover. But what?'

'Talk to anybody, did she? Any phone calls?'

'Two,' said Cohen. 'One to her estranged husband to arrange lunch, and one to the restaurant to book the table. Nothing significant about that, apparently. He says they remained on friendly terms and met from time to time. He also says their lunch was uneventful. As per usual, she didn't talk about her work, and she made no mention of going to Paris.'

'Friends?'

'She has none that I can discover. Of course, that's not

surprising, given her line of work. She couldn't very well risk bumping into some chum any time she was posing as a Swiss banker, or whatever.'

'No,' said Devereaux.

'*Grace!*' said Cohen, adopting a high falsetto voice, '*fancy seeing you here!*'

'Quite so.'

'*Grrrace!*' said Cohen in a pseudo-Russian accent. '*I thought your name was Hildegard!*'

Devereaux chuckled. 'Wouldn't do at all. What about family?'

'She has no siblings and her mother's dead. Her father's still alive and he called her; left a message on her answering machine asking if she was back from her trip. According to her phone records, she never returned his call, but I mean to ask him about that.'

'Going to see him, are you?'

'I thought so.'

'Good. When one gets lost, I say, go back to the beginning.'

From the floor below came the peel of Bel's raucous laughter.

'What makes her tick, Harry? Our Gracie? What drives her?'

'Anger,' said Cohen quietly. 'Rage.'

III

Cohen took his time getting to Mid Compton, dawdling up from London in his venerable Alfa Romeo. He wanted time to think. He also wanted to delay the moment when he must raise the ghosts he had found in a pine trunk that Grace Flint kept at the foot of her bed. Sitting at her table, searching her adolescent journals for clues as to what had shaped her, he had found himself enlightened and appalled.

Avoiding all motorways, he headed west out of London, following the flow of the Thames to Swinford where he turned north, still loitering on minor roads. He had been as vague to Dr Flint about the time of his arrival as he was about the purpose of his visit, claiming to be 'with the Home Office', saying 'I have some questions about your daughter.' The doctor had not pressed him. He said that if Cohen made it to Mid Compton in time for lunch they should meet at the Horse and Hound. 'Only pub grub, I'm afraid, but better than you would get out of my kitchen.'

In the newspaper photograph of him, pasted into one of his daughter's journals, Flint had the look of Lord

Byron. It was, evidently, a photograph from the file and
its use in the circumstances seemed highly inappropriate
to Cohen, sitting as it did beneath a bold headline that
declared 'Concern Grows For Vet's Wife'. With his head
set at an angle that emphasised his broad forehead and
long nose, a half-smile on his sensuous mouth, he looked
anything but concerned. Rather, he reminded Cohen of a
line from Byron's *Don Juan:* 'Cool, and quite English,
imperturbable.'

Twenty-eight years on, the solitary occupant of the
snug bar at the Horse and Hound, he looked wrecked
and neglected. The collar of his shirt was frayed, a button
missing from his jacket. On the underside of his chin
Cohen could see a small thicket of grey stubble that he
had missed while shaving. Though he was not yet sixty
years old he seemed fragile and defeated. Only the
strength of his grip and his convictions belied Cohen's
first impression.

'Grace is alive,' he said firmly as they exchanged the
usual pleasantries. He did not release Cohen's hand. 'If
she was dead I would know, you see. Nothing bad has
ever happened to Grace without me being aware of it.
It's like physical pain. Do you understand?'

Cohen said carefully, 'I have no reason to believe that
Grace is dead.'

'Good!' Flint smiled, his mouth suddenly as generous
as it ever was, bringing his whole face alive. 'Then we'll
get along fine. Now, what can I get you?'

He brushed aside Cohen's insistence that he should
pay for lunch and busied himself behind the bar as though

he owned the place, pouring their drinks, handing Cohen a copy of the modest menu.

'Since I'm not much of a cook, I practically live here,' he said by way of explanation.

Cohen sipped the glass of lemonade he'd requested and looked for an opening.

'You never thought of remarrying?' he said, stepping into the minefield, wondering as he asked the question if it was much too abrupt.

Flint shook his head. 'You'll want to know about that, I expect. About Grace's mother, I mean.' He smiled again but now it was impoverished, as if his mouth had shrunk. 'Grace's mother,' he repeated. 'Strange, isn't it? After all this time, I still can hardly bear to say her name.'

Marie-Madeleine Flint, née Gilbert, was her name, 'Mad' to her husband and her numerous friends. American by birth, French by descent, she was an unlikely spouse for an English country vet and John Flint remained certain that nothing less than destiny had brought them together. She had been in her sophomore year at Barnard College when her parents' Volvo – en route from Bethesda to New York for Barnard's Family Weekend, Mad's younger brother restless in the back – tail-ended a gasoline truck on Interstate 95, nine miles short of Newark. All three Gilberts perished in the conflagration.

'Perished,' Flint repeated, seemingly distracted by the word. 'Odd way to say it, I used to think: they *perished*. But then, it derives from the Old French – *periss* – and that was one of her passions. Her great-grandfather came from La Rochelle and French was her major at Barnard. She got her degree, by the way, which I thought pretty remarkable in the circumstances. But then, she never was one to quit. Not . . .'

Flint let the thought die and stumbled back to his narrative.

It was only after she graduated *cum laude* from Barnard that Mad took the time to come to terms with her loss. The insurance settlement and her parents' legacy gave her the means to do pretty much what she liked and she headed for France for a sabbatical of unspecified duration. For six months or maybe more (Flint wasn't sure), she explored the land of her forefathers, following her whims and the vagaries of the weather. Provence in early August proved too hot for her taste and she was returning to Paris somewhat earlier than she had expected when she met John Flint in the buffet car of the express train. They talked for three hours and when they arrived at the Gare de Lyon he insisted on buying her lunch at the Train Bleu; an extravagance he could ill afford since he was still a student at the Royal Veterinary College. They lingered over lunch for much of the afternoon. By the end of it he was thoroughly smitten, certain he had met his future wife. She was more ambivalent, or so she said. She thought him too impetuous, too crazy – whatever that meant – and, while we're at it, much too tall.

But how could he not be impetuous when he was looking at the loveliest thing he'd ever seen? Who would not be driven crazy by her heartlessness? If his height bothered her, he said, he would cut himself off at the knees.

Refusing to leave Paris, he wooed her relentlessly and at the end of that magical August, in a small hotel on the Avenue Mozart, they became lovers. When he was obliged to return to London at the start of the new term she accompanied him. With no ties left to bind her, she never went back to Maryland.

'We were married one week after I qualified,' Flint said in a monotone. He had forgotten to order the food. He stood behind the bar, his hands on the counter, staring into the void.

Nothing about life with Mad Flint disillusioned him. She was filled with New World optimism and energy that were infectious, reducing reckless propositions into mere challenges. She believed – and made her husband believe – there was no earthly reason why, fresh out of school, he should not set up his own veterinary practice. With her money they bought the old farmhouse on Allen's Lane, and converted the barn into his surgery, and spent lavishly on equipment, and then they hung out his shingle. And while the business slowly built, and in the fallow periods when he would amuse her with the forensic detective stories he invented, she came to believe – and made him believe – there was no earthly reason why they should not be published for profit. And then, to their mutual delight, Mad became pregnant. In the late evenings, after the inpatients had been settled down for the night, while Flint fashioned the draft of his first manuscript, she would lie on the old leather sofa in his study and propose improbable names for his characters. The manuscript was bought by the first publisher who saw it for the amazing sum of £500. Three days later Grace was born, and for the second time in his life Flint knew the meaning of unquestioning love.

'This must all sound like sentimental drivel,' Flint said, snapping out of his reverie.

'No,' said Cohen. 'Not to me.'

'No? You're married? You have children?'

'We had hoped to, but . . .' He felt the swell in his throat. 'My wife also died.'

'I'm sorry. Do you mind me asking how?'

'Cancer. She had a false negative on a cervical smear. By the time they realised the mistake, it had spread from her cervix to her lymph glands. Then it metastasised to both breasts. Then it spread to her lungs. She was thirty-four years old when she died.'

Flint flinched. 'Christ! You poor sod. I sometimes forget I'm not the only man who's lost his wife.'

'But what's worse?' asked Cohen. 'Watching someone you love die, or never knowing how and why?'

Flint's face was the colour of putty. His sentences were punctuated by long pauses, as though he had difficulty in recalling the events. Cohen had lost all sense of time. He listened mostly in silence because there was little useful he could say.

'It was a Saturday . . . In October . . . I'd taken Gracie on my rounds. We got back about five and there was no sign of her mother or the dog. I guessed they'd gone for a walk but it was very unlike . . .'

Flint broke off and Cohen waited for the outcome of his inner struggle.

'Mad . . . It was very unlike Mad not to be there when Gracie got home wanting her tea. Anyway, I put Gracie in front of the television and went looking for them. I was away for about an hour . . . No sign of them. Then I got worried about Gracie being on her own. Or, I thought, maybe her mother's arrived home wondering where the hell I am. So, I was heading back to the house when I saw Tom Price in his van coming along Midford Gap . . . He's the postman, or was . . . I waved him down, told him, told him about Mad, and he said he would do a circuit of Allen's Lane, see if there was any sign of her . . . I went back, got Gracie, and took the path across the fields. She was too tired to walk, so I put her on my shoulders. We got to the lane and it was beginning to get dark, and I felt this awful foreboding . . . I started to run . . . God knows where I thought I was going but as I came around a bend I saw Price's van. The driver's door was open and the headlights were on and it was parked at this crazy angle . . . It turned out that Tom had spotted something in the ditch. He'd stopped the van and gone to take a look and it was Hector, our dog . . . Gracie's dog, really . . . A young Lab . . . He was lying on his side looking as though someone had given him a terrible beating. There was a lot of blood coming from his mouth. He wouldn't let Tom anywhere near him . . . Snarling like a wolf . . . Then Tom saw us, and he came running,

trying to warn me . . . I didn't listen. I didn't hear a word
he said . . . I just ran to the ditch, and Gracie fell, and I
grabbed her and there she was, hanging upside down, a
couple of feet from her dog. All I could think of was . . .
her mother. I knew something terrible must have happened to her . . . I couldn't move . . . You know what I
did? I just stood there . . . I had my daughter suspended
over that snarling little puppy and I just stood there
howling like a bloody banshee.'

He lifted his head and softly howled, mocking himself
with the memory.

'Anyway, I pulled myself together . . . Eventually . . . I
got Tom to take Gracie back to the house and I told him
to call the police while I started looking for . . . my wife.
It was getting pretty dark and I didn't have a torch . . .
Well, it was hopeless . . . I couldn't see a thing. I decided
to stay with Hector and try to calm him down, but I
could tell he was going into shock, so I ran up to the
barn to get my bag . . . Just as I got back to the lane,
Frank Dawson turned up. He's the local bobby, or was
then . . . We don't have one anymore . . . Anything
happens now, we have to call Banbury, which is a fat lot
of use . . . Mind you, Frank wasn't much use either. Not
really. Not for something like that . . . Anyway . . .'

Flint shook his head to clear the fog.

'I gave Hector a shot to sedate him. Poor little bugger
tried to bite me but he couldn't because his jaw was
broken . . . I knocked him out with pentobarbital, and
we put him in the back of Frank's car, and took him up
to the barn. I gave him a quick examination and decided

there was nothing broken, except for the jaw, but his back and flanks were badly bruised and I was worried about internal damage . . . Odd when you think about it . . . There was my wife, lying out there somewhere, dying or dead, or I thought she was, and there was me fussing over a dog . . . Don't you think that's peculiar? I mean, I know it's what I'm trained to do, but, even so, what was I thinking of?'

The conundrum stalled him so Cohen said, 'There was nothing you could do. Not in the dark. You said it was hopeless.'

'Even so . . .'

'What did Dawson do?'

'Oh, he'd called Banbury from the house and they said they'd send over some men, and we were to wait for them and not go searching on our own . . . I don't know why they said that.'

'Routine, I expect,' said Cohen. 'They didn't want you trampling on the evidence, if there was any. I'm sure you did the right thing taking care of the dog. And you had Grace to take care of as well.'

'Actually, I didn't. She kept trying to come to the barn. She was hysterical . . . I didn't want her to see Hector again, not in that state. There was a lot of blood. I asked Tom to take her home with him. Get his wife to look after her.'

'And then?'

'The police arrived, the ones from Banbury. It seemed like hours but it probably wasn't. Uniformed chaps, four or five of them . . . I don't remember. One of them stayed

with me while Frank took the others down to the lane to
show them where I'd found Hector. Then a couple of
detectives turned up. They wanted to look around the
house for signs of forced entry... I told them, "We
never bother to lock the door" ... Not then we didn't.
Then they wanted to know if anything of hers was
missing. Her bag, any clothes, her cosmetics ... Bloody
silly, I thought. We've just found the dog half-beaten to
death, and they're asking me if she might have had a
reason to leave. Any rows? Was she depressed? Was
there somebody she might have gone away with, or gone
to see? They thought the dog might have tried to follow
her and got hit by a car, you see. I told them: "That dog
wasn't run over. That dog was beaten with an iron bar."
I'm afraid I lost my temper with them.'

'They didn't search for her that night?'

'Not much, or so Frank told me. But, to be fair, it was
very dark ... There was no moon and it started to rain
and it turned into a filthy night. They put a tarpaulin
over the spot where we'd found Hector and they sealed
off the lane. They left a couple of chaps in a patrol car
on guard and the rest pushed off until first light ...
Wasn't much more they could do, I suppose.'

'But then they did a proper search?'

'Oh, I'll say. They started on the Sunday, searched all
day, and on the Monday they began bringing in reinforce-
ments from all over the county. There must have been
two hundred of them at one point ... Dogs, helicopters ... Then they brought in the Territorial Army ...
No, I've no complaints about that. They did everything

they could: house-to-house inquiries, checkpoints on the major roads, plastered her picture everywhere.'

A picture of a laughing woman who was fetching rather than beautiful, Cohen had thought when he'd removed it from the inside cover of Grace's journal; her mouth a little too generous, her nose slightly crooked from some childhood accident.

'And they found nothing, nothing at all?' he asked although he already knew the answer.

'Nothing. It was as though she never existed.'

Like mother like daughter, Cohen thought.

Flint had trouble fitting himself into the Alfa. His legs were too long and he sat untidily in the passenger seat with his knees up around his chest. Cohen drove carefully, following Flint's directions, taking the long way round so that they approached Glebe Farm from the west, avoiding the spot where, in all likelihood, Mad Flint was abducted. 'Silly, really,' said her husband apologising. 'Because I can see it perfectly well from the house.'

It had been a long time since Glebe Farm had lived up to its name. Most of the land had been sold off until only a half-acre garden remained, sloping down to the lane. A driveway bisected it, leading to a quadrangle where Cohen parked the Alfa alongside Flint's muddy Land Rover in the lee of a Dutch barn; Flint's surgery, evidently, for Cohen could hear the baying of animals coming from inside. A flight of stone steps led up from the quadrangle to the top of a bank where the house stood. It was sturdy red brick but Cohen saw that the decorative mouldings

above the ground-floor windows were crumbling, paint
flaking from the louvred shutters – small blemishes that
gave the house the same air of slight neglect he had
noted in its owner.

Flint led the way, pushing open the front door, setting
off down a bare corridor with his long lope, Cohen in his
wake observing the details. The seagrass on the floor
had seen better days and there were no pictures or
fripperies to break the monotony of the faded white
walls. Four closed doors, two on either side, led to rooms
that Cohen suspected were rarely used. A broad staircase
headed up into darkness. Beside it, at the end of the
corridor, was an open door through which Flint had
already disappeared. A man's house, Cohen thought,
from which the two women in Flint's life had been
removed against their will.

He wanted me out of the way!!! Grace Flint, aged
fifteen, had written in her journal. *Why???* The ink she
had used was vivid green, the colour of paranoia.

'The longer it went on, the worse it got,' Flint had
explained to Cohen, hurrying through this part of his
story, anxious to be rid of it. 'For the first few weeks and
months we were living on tenterhooks, waiting for them
to find the body – or I was. I don't really know what
Gracie was thinking. She was so quiet, so withdrawn, I
couldn't reach her. As the months and then the years
passed, I thought it would get better but it didn't. In the
end I couldn't cope. I don't mean in a practical sense. I
hired a live-in housekeeper, so taking care of her was
fine. It was Gracie's sense of loss that became unbearable.

In five years, almost six, I don't ever remember seeing her laugh. She'd come home from school and go to her room and stay there until it was time for supper and then she'd sit at the table and not say a word unless I asked her a direct question. I'd go babbling on about my day, about the patients, about what we might do at the weekend, and she'd just sit there watching me. She had no friends, she never played. Can you imagine how strange that is? A little girl who behaves like an old woman; an old woman who's had a stroke? After supper she'd go straight to her room and go to bed and when I went to say goodnight she'd pretend to be asleep. Or, perhaps she wasn't pretending; perhaps that was her escape. I tried to get help for her but grief counselling wasn't up to much in those days. They just kept saying that she would grow out of it.'

'And, of course, there was no closure.'

'What a bloody awful term – but no, you're right. No closure.'

'Were there any suspects?'

'Not really. The police decided she must have been abducted and they thought it was somebody local and they questioned every man and boy for miles around but there was no physical evidence to go on. He might have got some of her blood on him, mud on his clothes, but that doesn't stand out in the country. I mean, you would expect people who work on the land and with animals to get muddy and occasionally bloody, wouldn't you? Oh, they developed the odd suspect, and tested clothing for her blood, but it never amounted to anything.'

'Nobody was ever arrested?'

Flint did not hesitate. 'Well, eventually, me.'

'The police thought you'd killed your wife?'

'Gracie did.'

Cohen had come prepared for that.

HE KILLED MUMMY!!! Angry, green capitals, written in a child's hand.

In John Flint's kitchen, seated at a long rectory table made of oak, Cohen watched the tea being made; two bags of Earl Grey, two mugs of water heated in the microwave. He said: 'And you had no idea what she'd been harbouring for all those years? Despite your affinity?'

'None. Not a clue. Milk?'

Cohen declined. He would have asked for lemon but he didn't want to break the spell.

'I woke up one morning . . . I suppose it must have been August 4 or 5 of 1982, something like that . . . Almost eleven years after she disappeared . . . It was about six o'clock in the morning, and I heard this racket in the drive. I looked out of my bedroom window and I saw three or four cars and a bunch of men coming up the steps. The only one I recognised was Frank Dawson. When I answered the door, he wouldn't look me in the eye so I knew something was very wrong.'

Flint sat down wearily opposite Cohen, pushing one of the mugs across the table.

'At first I thought something had happened to Gracie. She'd been at Tudor Hall for about four years, and there had been some problems. Nothing too serious, but she'd taken to absconding for the afternoon. They would find her in the fields with some of the lads from the local boys' school, and more than once the headmistress threatened to expel her. She was smoking cigarettes, that sort of thing. Anyway, I thought . . . Well, you can imagine what I thought . . . After what happened to her mother . . .'

Cohen thought, *How could you ever let her out of your sight?*

'She had this chum, another girl at the same school. Her name was Olivia and they became the terrible twins; leading each other on, always getting into trouble together. I could have cared less, frankly. I was so pleased that she had finally found a pal. I didn't even mind that, come the holidays, she would always ask if she could go and stay with Olivia's folks. They lived near London and I just assumed that was a much more enticing prospect for a teenage girl than Mid Compton . . . And then there were the memories, of course. I understood – I *thought* I understood – why she didn't want to come here.'

'She never came home?'

'Oh, occasionally. Tudor Hall's less than an hour away and she would come home for the short breaks, the odd weekend. To be honest with you, the whole business had become so wearing, I thought it was better if she didn't come home. I didn't know what to do, you see? How to help her. I thought she needed space. I didn't understand.'

'Until the police came.'

'Exactly. I was numbed. There was this detective

inspector from Banbury, a man called Shawcross, sitting where you are now, and he said something like, "Dr Flint, we have reason to believe you may have been responsible for your wife's disappearance" . . . I couldn't take it in. I said something banal – "What reason?" Huffily, I expect. Standing on my dignity. It seemed so absurd. He said, "Your daughter believes that you raped and killed her mother". Imagine. I *raped* her? *Mad*?'

Flint stood up from the table and stretched his back, pushing at the hollows with his palms. 'I need to check on my patients. Do you want to come?'

Cohen said, 'Of course,' and they left the house by the kitchen door to cross a broad terrace where ragged weeds grew in the cracks between the slabs. At its edge Flint paused and, standing side by side, they looked down onto an undulating meadow that fell away in green waves before rising again to meet the copse that crowned the opposite hill. In the valley, perhaps half-a-mile away, Cohen could see a twisting brown ribbon that marked the easterly progress of Allen's Lane.

'Of course, it was a terrible mistake,' Flint said, breaking their silence.

'Yes,' replied Cohen, having no idea what he meant.

'I should have kept her here – or, better still, we should have moved away. Gone to a town, maybe. Somewhere different. A fresh start, and all that. Money wasn't a problem because I'd inherited Mad's estate and that was more than . . . Well, it was a good amount, far more than we needed.'

'London, perhaps,' Cohen suggested.

'Or gone abroad. I thought about that. Africa – bring some adventure into her life. I thought of Serengeti and working with the lions. I even made some inquiries and found out there was an international school near the park where Gracie could have gone when she was a little older.'

'But you couldn't leave here.'

'No.'

'Because it would have been too final.'

'Exactly.'

Cohen said: 'I still live in the same house with the same furniture. I still sleep in our bed.'

'Yes.'

'I have friends who think it morbid.'

'Yes.'

Cohen let silence do some work and then abruptly, as though the question had only just occurred to him, he asked, 'What happened to Hector?'

'I put him down. I don't mean then, not immediately. It would have been four or five years after Mad disappeared. He never really got over the beating he was given, or that's my theory. His jaw healed well enough but he was part-lame in the hind quarters and then he developed osteoarthritis. I did what I could: cortisone treatment and, eventually, arthrodesis. Didn't work, I'm afraid. In the end, I put him out of his misery.'

'And Grace never forgave you.'

'No.'

'Nor for packing her off to boarding school.'

'That was a couple of years later. When she was twelve.'

'Young. Too young, perhaps.'

'It seemed best. At the time.' Flint ran the fingers of one hand through hair that was thick and untidy and prematurely white, and then he pointed towards the valley. 'You see down there, where the lane swings round to the right, just beyond the telephone pole? Do you see the tree?'

A solitary white ash, spindly from this distance, leaned over the hedgerow marking the spot where something appalling had happened to Mad Flint.

'Grace planted that,' Flint said. 'I gave her the sapling for her tenth birthday because that's what she asked for. I knew what she'd do with it, I thought that it might help her, but after it was in the ground she never went near it again. About a year later, maybe a little more, I came down early one morning and found her sitting here on the terrace, perfectly still, just staring at the tree. I asked her what she was doing. She said she was willing it to die.'

Cohen coughed to clear his throat. 'Did she say why?'

'No. She wouldn't say. Just, "Everything dies".' Flint ran the knuckle of one thumb across his eyes, as though he was trying to dislodge a speck of dust. 'She was eleven years old.'

'So, you thought it best . . .' Cohen began.

'I thought it best if she went away from here. Tudor Hall had a reputation for dealing with girls with problems, so I went and saw the headmistress and talked the whole thing through with her, and she seemed very sympathetic. Then I took Gracie to meet her. I thought that if she got a look at the school, met some of the staff and other girls, then . . .' Flint ran out of words.

'How did she react?'

'She didn't,' he said, shaking his head. 'She barely said a word, either on the journey, or when we got there, or when we got home. I tried to discuss it with her, make it her decision whether she went there or not. Nothing. She just watched me with those melancholy eyes . . .' He broke off and suddenly changed tack. 'You never met Gracie, did you?'

'No.'

'But you've seen photographs of her?'

'Oh, yes.'

'So you know what I mean about her eyes?'

Cohen wondered if he should lie, or at least hedge the truth. He decided on a neutral course. 'They didn't seem melancholy to me. Not exactly.'

'No?' said Flint, turning to look down at him. 'How would you describe them?'

'Beautiful, certainly.'

Flint continued to stare, demanding more.

'Somebody, an American policeman, told me she had the most enticing eyes he'd ever seen. On the one hand they made her look lost and vulnerable and, on the other' – he thought furiously how to paraphrase Cutter's crude description – 'extraordinarily fetching.'

'You mean bedroom eyes?'

'Well . . .' Cohen felt a flush of embarrassment.

'Oh, I know men found them sexy,' Flint said, turning away, ready to leave the terrace. 'She knew, too. "Fuck-me eyes" she used to call them. Now, in view of what happened to her mother, in view of what she thought I'd done, isn't that the saddest thing you've ever heard?'

They were edging down the grass bank heading for the barn, Cohen in the lead trying to keep his balance, when Flint said: 'I'll tell you what her eyes reminded me of the day I told her she was going to Tudor Hall. I once had a foal, a patient I couldn't save – though God knows I tried. On the night I came down here to put her down, she watched me come into the stall. She was lying on her side. She couldn't stand up. She knew what I was going to do, knew she couldn't stop me. She just lay there watching me, waiting for me to get my courage up. I thought of Coleridge. Do you read him? "Poor little Foal of an oppressed race! I love the languid patience of thy face." That's what's in Grace's eyes, Mr Cohen. It's not sex. It's resignation.'

IV

In marked contrast to the house, Flint's barn was pin-bright and cared for, smelling of carbolic, all gleaming glass and polished wood and honey-coloured tiles.

'They dug them up,' Flint said. 'Every single one of them. And the concrete beneath.' An orphaned kitten no more than a few days old, still sightless, searched his shirt for its mother's nipple. 'Then they brought in a JCB and dug down five feet.'

Not just idle suspicion then, Cohen thought; not if they went to that much trouble. The barn was eighty feet long by his calculations, stretching from the surgery to the waiting area. It must have taken the police two weeks to establish that wherever the bones of Mad Flint lay it was not here.

'She was so convincing, you see.' Flint shook his head as though he did not quite trust his recollection. 'So sure she'd seen it.'

'You burying the body?' Cohen suggested.

'Me standing over her mother, blood all over me, a hammer in my hand. Me digging the hole, dumping her body into it.'

While he spoke of mayhem, Flint fed the kitten milk from the tip of a small pipette.

'She'd repressed it for years – or that was their theory. Then she started having these recurring dreams – nightmares, really – where everything about the night her mother disappeared became mixed up. She dreamt she was on Tom Price's shoulders when she slipped, not mine. And it was here, not in the lane. And it wasn't Hector lying there all bloodied, it was Mad.'

He placed the kitten back in its cage on a bed of straw and took out one of its siblings. There were three more orphans waiting their turn to be fed.

'I didn't know most of this, of course. I got a telephone call from the headmistress saying that Gracie had developed a range of worrying symptoms – recurrent nightmares, intense headaches, panic attacks – and the school doctor could find no physical cause and that he'd recommended urgent psychiatric therapy. I went rushing over there. By the time I arrived she was catatonic. She was admitted to a psychiatric clinic in Oxford that same afternoon.'

Cohen now knew where this was heading; knew what they had done. 'How long was she there?'

'Two months? Perhaps a little more.'

'And they wouldn't let you see her?'

'They said it was best if I didn't. They said she had developed feelings of profound hostility towards me.'

Cohen felt his anger building. 'And what was her treatment? Transactional Analysis?'

'To begin with,' said Flint, surprise in his voice, not

expecting that, then catching on. 'You've been there, haven't you?'

Oh, you bet I have, thought Cohen. Annie in a clinic, undergoing what they called 'counselling' – refusing to see him, blaming him for her cancer, learning to hate. 'Towards the end my wife was in a kind of therapy,' was all that he said.

Flint studied his face.

'Then what?' said Cohen brusquely. 'Hypnosis? Regression therapy? Guided imagery?'

'All of that. Plus what they called "drug-mediated interviews".'

'Sodium amytal?'

'Yes. She was sixteen years old!'

'Holy Christ!'

Bound by common experience and mutual rage, they stood in silence while the kittens mewed.

Flint, perched on the operating table, the scene of his imagined crime, said: 'Of course, she was absolutely mortified. Those charlatans had convinced her that what they'd induced was her "recovered memory", as real as it could be, and they persuaded her to go to the police. When the police found nothing . . . Well, you can imagine how she felt.'

Cohen, slumped in a chair, thought of Annie never learning that she had no reason to hate him.

'She couldn't face me, couldn't face the school, couldn't face anybody . . . least of all herself.'

'What saved her?'

For the second time since Cohen had known him, Flint's face was transformed by the glow of his fullest smile. 'The most wonderful – and I mean this . . . The most wonderful man in the world: one Doctor Richard Holt.' He paused, as though expecting Cohen to guess the rest and then continued: 'A psychiatrist, believe it or not . . .'.

He caught the flash of distaste on Cohen's face.

'Oh, I know. I felt the same. I wanted to murder the lot of them. I told Shawcross. I said, "You can leave the hole, inspector, because now I really am going to fill it with bodies". Then, when I'd calmed down a bit, I wanted to sue, but . . .' He lifted up his hands in a gesture of hopelessness. 'Instead, I went up to London and demanded to see the head of the Royal College of Psychiatrists, and told him *exactly* what I thought of his bloody profession and, to his great credit, he listened. He agreed that what they'd done to Grace in Oxford was monstrous, and then he set about persuading me that the only way to undo the harm of bad therapy was good therapy. It wasn't an easy sale for him, I can tell you. I was with him all afternoon and most of the night. We went out to dinner, and then back to his house – where I drank far more whisky than was good for me . . . Speaking of which, would you like a drink?'

Cohen looked at his watch and, thinking of the long drive that faced him, said without much enthusiasm, 'I should be getting back.'

'Oh, stay the night won't you? I'll find us something to eat and you can sleep in Gracie's room. After dredging all this up, I'd rather like some company, if you don't mind.'

'Of course.'

'Good man! Where was I? Oh, yes, let me finish this part and then we'll go up to the house . . . To cut a long story short, I was eventually persuaded that Gracie should re-enter therapy, but under very different circumstances. Enter the good doctor Holt. The college strongly recommended him. Of course, I didn't just take their word for it. I went to see him and grilled him like a sardine, poor chap . . .'

Flint smiled again and hurried on; over the worst part of the story now, freed of the burden, running downhill.

'I've never known anyone like him. To say he's the most compassionate person I've ever met doesn't come close to doing him justice. I knew that putting Grace in his hands would be like putting her in balm. He warned me the treatment would take a long time, he warned me it might not work, he warned me that I mustn't contact her unless and until she was ready – but I never doubted the outcome. And then . . .'

Flint jumped from his perch on the table, and swung around so that his back was to Cohen.

'Some fifteen months later, on what was Gracie's eighteenth birthday, I was right here, finishing up an operation' – with great exaggeration, he mimed the stitching of a wound – 'when I heard a noise behind me . . .' He turned to face Cohen. 'And there she was, Mr Cohen, my lovely, smiling daughter. And do you know what she did? She put her arms around me and she gave me the longest hug in the world.'

Flint stood wrapped only in his own arms, rocking on his heels, tears sliding down his face, tears of unbearable pain.

'Where in God's name is she, Mr Cohen?'

They were back in the kitchen, sitting at Flint's counter, a bottle of whisky between them, a third of it already drunk. The embarrassment of Flint's breakdown also sat between them like a deadweight, dulling them into long and uncomfortable silences.

Cohen forced himself to look for a way forward. There had been no mention in Flint's personnel file that she had ever received psychiatric therapy.

'This psychiatrist,' he began hesitantly, fearing he might be tearing at the wound. 'Did you say his name was Richard Holt?'

'Ri*shard*,' said Flint, softening the consonants, stressing the last syllable. 'He's French.'

Cohen felt a flutter in his chest. 'French? But he practises here?'

'No, no. Paris – or he did then. That was one of the reasons he was recommended. To totally change Gracie's surroundings. And then there was the fact that her mother was French by ancestry. Richard thought that might help. She lived in Paris all the time she was in therapy.'

Cohen heard the words all right but tiredness – or was it alcohol? – was sapping his brain's ability to absorb them. He stared at Flint as though he was mad.

'What's the matter?'

'Grace was in Paris for fifteen months?'

'I just told you that.'

'And did she ever go back? Did she stay in touch with Dr Holt?'

'Yes. But, more so his daughter, Dominique. She's Gracie's very best friend. Why?'

'So, whenever she was in Paris, she would see or call her friend?'

'Always.'

'Why didn't you say so before?' Cohen was incredulous.

'What are you talking about?'

'*Paris!*'

'What about Paris?'

'It's where she disappeared, for God's sake.'

'Gracie disappeared in *Paris*?'

They were both on their feet now, two bewildered men, shouting to be heard in a gale of confusion.

'They didn't tell you that?' said Cohen, growing evermore agitated, trying to remember what else was in a brief police report in the Grace Flint file that concluded:

'*Dr Flint says he has no knowledge of his daughter's whereabouts.*'

'Who?'

'The police!'

'They didn't tell me anything! They asked me when I last heard from her, and I said it was just before she left for the Caribbean. From Miami.'

'So you thought . . .'

'I thought she'd disappeared in the Caribbean.'

'She disappeared in Paris. The last thing we know is that she took a flight from London and . . .'

There was no point in continuing for Flint could not hear. He was already through the door, crossing the terrace, heading for the barn and the drawer of the desk where he kept his book of telephone numbers.

V

La Palette had been almost deserted when Grace Flint arrived two hours early. She sat at one of the tables on the pavement, shaded by a canopy, where her view of the Rue de Seine was unrestricted. Prim in a loose, calf-length cotton dress, her hair pulled back, she took out her book, ordered a *citron pressé* from the bored waiter, and gave every impression of settling in for the duration.

Thirty feet away, directly in her sight-line, the Galerie Pythéas slumbered in the July sun. In the window, apparently suspended in space, illuminated by hidden spotlights and set against a backdrop of crimson satin, hung an exquisite silver dish perhaps two feet in diameter, decorated in niello and bearing a Latin inscription. A small plaque set on a plinth identified it as 'Imperial Roman, 4th Century AD'. There was nothing else to be seen from the street. Apparently short-sighted, Flint had leaned against the tempered glass and satisfied herself it was thick enough to be bomb-proof. She had also established that the door was locked from inside. A discreet notice invited visitors to ring the bell if they wished to enter.

No one took up that invitation while Flint watched, seemingly engrossed in Proust's *Swann's Way*, lingering over her drink. At about six o'clock, as customers began arriving, greeting each other like regulars, she ordered a small carafe of white wine to renew her claim to the table. To give the impression she was waiting for someone, she consulted her watch at regular intervals and, mercifully, Gilles arrived a good fifteen minutes earlier than he had promised. She spotted him coming down the street, hurrying towards her with a lop-sided grin on his face, hair dishevelled, tieless, pulling on a rumpled cotton jacket, thin as a boy.

He hugged her, kissed her on both cheeks. 'You have long legs, you will travel far,' he said solemnly, slipping into their routine.

'You have large eyes, you see much,' she replied, trying not to laugh.

He hugged her again, almost lifting her off her feet. Then he stood back to examine her face, searching for signs of fatigue. 'In the circumstances, you look pretty good.'

'I'm okay.'

'Dominique said you looked exhausted.'

'And too thin?'

'Oh, much too thin,' he said, and they both smiled. 'Have you seen him?'

'Not yet.'

'Let me get a beer and then I'll tell you what I know.'

It wasn't much. Mario Antonia Silva, aged forty, proprietor of the Galerie Pythéas, dealer in antiquities.

Born in Lisbon, Portugal, once living in Montague Square, London, now legally resident in Paris. Divorced, no dependants. Gallery premises rented on a five-year lease. Apartment at number 30 Rue Jacob also rented. No vehicle registered in his name. No warrants in existence, no lawsuits on file, no complaints. No convictions.

At that last assertion Flint cocked a questioning eyebrow.

'Yes,' said Inspector Bourdonnec of the Brigade Criminelle, 'when he applied for his *carte de séjour* he forgot to mention his little difficulty in London.'

'And could that be a problem for him?'

Gilles shrugged. 'Perhaps. As an EU citizen he's entitled to live here anyway, so nobody's going to get very excited. Mind you, if I decided to take a close interest in the provenance of that plate in his window, then the fact that he lied about his fraud conviction could be relevant.'

'What do you suppose it's worth?'

'Six million francs, or at least that's what he's asking for it,' Gilles said. From his jacket pocket he produced a small leaflet finely printed on expensive paper that briefly described the unearthing of the plate by a farmer's plough in the Lebanon, as well as its almost priceless qualities. It was the addendum, printed in italics, that caused Flint to laugh: *This magnificent work of art is accompanied by an export certificate from the appropriate authority in Beirut. The signatures on this permit have been verified by the Lebanese Embassy in Paris.*

'What do you suppose he means by the "appropriate authority"?' she asked.

'Whoever took the bribe.'

'But there is no doubt it came from the Lebanon,' she said with mock gravity, and Bourdonnec gave her a look that said 'pull the other one'.

So then she knew that Mario Silva remained reckless – what Commander Glenning would call 'a born chancer' – and that had got her adrenaline pumping, for her strategy was entirely based on the assumption that Silva was in some way vulnerable: that by coming to Paris she might find his weakness and exploit it. Silva was her only link to Frank Harling and to the faceless men who had protected him; the men she believed responsible for the murders of Hechter and the Maitlands. Silva knew who they were. One way or another, he would tell her.

At precisely seven o'clock the satin drape parted and two men stepped into the window – one, young and willowy with foppish hair that fell across his forehead, the other matching the description of Silva that Gilles had given her when she'd called him from the airport: 'About one metre seventy, thick-set, fancy dresser even in this heat; darkish complexion, black hair swept back over the ears, curling at the back, receding at the front.' Silva held the plate across his chest while the boy detached the nylon lines from which it was suspended. They withdrew together, carrying the plate between them.

'He's got a walk-in vault at the back of the shop,'

Gilles told her. 'Time locks, by the look of it, and some pretty tricky alarms.'

'I can imagine. If I had a million dollars-worth of looted silver on the premises I'd never leave.'

'Ah, but watch.'

They did not have long to wait. Within a few minutes the steady flow of traffic along the Rue de Seine was brought to a standstill by a blue Peugeot van with no markings that pulled up outside the gallery. Two men, identically dressed in dark shirts and matching trousers that were gathered into polished boots, emerged from the rear doors with no great haste, ignoring the protests of the drivers whose progress they had impeded.

'Cops?' Flint guessed.

Gilles pulled a face. 'Goons,' he said. 'The riot squad. CRS.'

They unloaded grips from the back of the van and then one of them closed the doors, slapping the roof with the palm of his free hand to tell their driver he could pull away.

'Is this official?'

'No, they're moonlighting. There's a bunch of them running a private security racket. Arrogant bastards, aren't they?'

Grips in hand, they stood in the middle of the road surveying the bottleneck, rulers of the Rue de Seine, fuck-you expressions etched on their faces. Only when Silva opened the door of the gallery did they move quickly to the pavement and disappear inside.

'Do they stay all night?' Flint asked.

'Until midnight, then a couple more just like them take the graveyard shift until Silva or his boy turns up in the morning at around eight. At least, that's the way it's been all week.'

'Expensive.'

'It's not just the plate. He's got several other pieces on display inside. The whole lot's insured for twenty-two million francs. He's got it on consignment, supposedly from a private collector in Zurich.' He hesitated and then he teased. 'Guess what? According to Customs, he's got another collection coming in next week. That will be the fourteenth this year.'

Flint stirred. 'Always from Zurich?'

'Or Geneva, or Basle. But always from Switzerland.'

Now it was Flint's turn to pause while she examined his clues. 'Does he have to pay import duty?'

'Nope. Not until they're sold, and not even then if the goods are re-exported outside the EU – which they always are. Know why?'

'It's a laundry,' said Flint, fast as a rat.

'Not bad. But how does it work?'

'Vapour sales. The collections are on loan or they're fake. It doesn't matter because the buyers don't exist. He puts the stuff in his window for a couple of weeks, "sells" it' – she brought up two fingers of each hand to put quotation marks around her words – 'to some offshore "buyer" ' – up came the fingers again – 'who wires the money to Silva's bank here in Paris. How am I doing?'

'Go on.'

'Silva takes his commission and wires the rest of the
money to the collector in Switzerland – except he doesn't,
of course. It just goes into a numbered account. Then he
ships the stuff back to Switzerland, supposedly on "the
buyer's" instructions, passes everything through the
books, and there's several million dollars – or whatever
– nicely washed every couple of weeks. All it costs them
is a cut for the collector, the rent on the gallery, the
freight and insurance, and the price of a few guards.
What have I missed?'

'Not much,' said Gilles laughing. 'I always said you
were quick.'

'Oh, I'm way ahead of you,' said Flint getting up
from her chair, feeling a familiar prickle of excitement as
she watched her quarry emerging from his lair; watched
him scanning the street with a fugitive's care. 'This isn't
a one-man show. It can't be. He has to have a partner
working the other end of the racket, and I'll bet you the
price of that plate I know who it is.'

Mario Silva, strolling up the Rue de Seine in the evening
sun, no longer watchful, not a care in the world, smiling
at all the pretty girls, on his way home by way of ritual
diversion. Just beyond the junction with Rue Jacob, in a
daily market that sells vegetables and cheese, charcuterie
and pastries that are arguably the best in Paris, Mario
goes shopping for his supper. Grace Flint is right behind
him, next in line.

VI

Pretty woman in a fuck-me dress sits comfortably in a brown leather club chair sipping champagne, watching the world over the rim of her glass, watching Mario Silva watching her with undisguised carnal interest. He is sizing her up, considering his strategy: how best to get close and get what he wants.

He is ten feet away from her, leaning against an ornate wooden mantelpiece that bears a bust of the first Emperor Napoleon. The lighting is subdued and he is not yet sure what he sees in those eyes that return his stare unwaveringly. Her lips are parted but her expression is entirely neutral. An invitation – or get lost? He cannot decide and his vacillation makes him edgy.

One of the girls provides a welcome diversion, swinging her hips as she approaches to refill his glass. Silva cannot remember her name but it scarcely matters. She is one of a dozen, all of them luscious in revealing gowns. There is nothing neutral about her expression, or her explicit invitation. As she pours champagne, she stands much closer to him than is strictly necessary, pressing his arm with her breasts, reminding him of their past encounters.

But it's not her he wants, not tonight.

He looks over the girl's bare shoulder to the chair where the woman sits, still watching, still neutral. Riding his luck, nothing to lose, he raises his glass to her in a silent toast.

The Club Elégance occupied the first two floors of a suitably refined eighteenth-century house near l'Abbé de l'Epée, overlooking the southern aspect of the Luxembourg Gardens. The discreet plaque confirming its existence said it was a private club for members only, but these were misleading truths, for anyone who rang the bell and passed muster on the CCTV camera could join on the spot. Inspector Gilles Bourdonnec paid 2,000 francs for three-months' membership, and a 500 franc 'guest fee' for Flint. The receptionist, who looked as though she might have been plucked from the front desk of the Crillon, told him to write whatever names he chose for himself and his guest in the members' register. Flint studied the brochure that invited applications for corporate accounts.

'He's gone to a brothel,' Gilles had said, tapping on the door of the boys' room, urging her to wake up. What he actually said was *une maison de tolérance* and she had lain in Gaspard's small bed struggling with the euphemism, trying to recall where she was. She had turned on the light, seen the Dune posters on the wall and the fearsome artillery of a helicopter gun-ship that was suspended in mid-air above her head, and *then* she remembered. Hastening from the bed, she pulled on a T-shirt that was long enough to make her decent and opened the door.

Gilles was in that crook of the Bourdonnec's apartment that served as the kitchen, already half-dressed, spooning Nescafé into two cups.

'What time is it?' Flint asked.

'A little after midnight. My guys just called. They were about to give up because he hadn't moved all evening and when they saw the lights go out they figured he'd gone to bed. Then a taxi pulls up, and there's Mario looking like Don Juan, all spruced up for a night on the town. You'd better get dressed.'

'We're going to a *brothel*?'

'Well, it's more of a club. Swingers, singles, anyone looking for some action – but, yes, there are prostitutes. Mario can get himself laid, if that's what he wants. Let's go and see – and quickly. My guys should have been off duty an hour ago, and they want to go home.'

Flint said, 'Yikes,' and ran her fingers through her hair. She hurried into the bedroom and then she hurried back.

'What do I wear?'

'Whatever swingers wear,' said Gilles, pouring water into the cups. 'Something sexy but not tarty. Something elegant.'

'Thanks,' she said, wrinkling her nose. 'That's my wardrobe exhausted. Is Dominique awake?'

'She most certainly is, and she's furious. She wants to come and I've told her she can't.'

Flint had found Dominique lying in her bed, watching a rerun of a movie on an oversized TV set that dominated the room. She tried to be grumpy but she couldn't keep it up. Pulling dresses from her wardrobe, holding them up, building untidy piles of 'possibles' and 'rejects' on the bed, she became part of Flint's operation vicariously and that, it seemed, was enough.

They settled on a simple black dress of liquid silk that hung from two slender shoulder straps. Beautifully cut, it revealed very little of Flint's body, merely hinting at what lay beneath.

From her jewellery collection, Dominique produced for Flint's neck a silver band, for her ears, two white-diamond studs and, for her wrists, fifty threads of silver gossamer. Despite Flint's stout objection, she rescued from its hiding place her most treasured possession, a gift from her father, a silver Patek Philippe watch.

'Dominique, I can't!'

'You must. It's perfect!'

'If you go on like this,' said Gilles, watching from the doorway, 'you'll be valuable enough to hang in Silva's window.'

They had all laughed at that, but as Flint sat before the dressing-table mirror, watching Dominique applying a gel to her hair so it lay sleek against her head, she felt the bubbles of her excitement evaporate. She must have been through this – or something like it – a hundred times and this was when the buzz came, or should have done; when, preparing for deception, adopting her disguise, she would feel the delicious tingle of anticipation, like a parachutist checking the harness, waiting for the green light. But gazing back at her own reflection, observing quite objectively that her face was truly beautiful, she could not escape from the memory of the circumstances which had led to its creation, and of the last two occasions when, following the metaphor, her chute had failed to open.

It was irrational, she knew. Nothing was going to happen. This was merely a recce, a must-take chance to get a close look at the target when his guard was down.

Yet even as Gilles urged Dominique to hurry up and finish, all she could think of was the warmth of Pete Pendle's blood when it reached her. Of a jackhammer boot crushing her face. Of Vladimir's trigger-finger probing her vagina.

She stood up and smiled at them, and gave a mock curtsey to acknowledge their applause. She said, 'Let's go,' and led the way, and damned the nagging voice inside her head.

GRACE! DON'T DO THIS!

Beyond reception, the ground floor of Club Elégance was divided into five sitting rooms, one leading to another, with an ambience that reminded Flint of an Edwardian gentleman's club – or rather, never having been in one, what she imagined the ambience to be: club chairs with button-backs, the leather appropriately faded; mahogany tables, probably reproduction; a tall gilt-framed mirror above the fireplace; table lamps with crimson shades that matched the hue of the carpet and the heavy swagged curtains. From where she stood in the first sitting room, Flint could see only two striking incongruities: the vases of freshly cut flowers that adorned every table; and, just inside the entrance to the bar, the stiletto-heeled shoes and splayed legs of a woman, naked to the waist.

She thought they were disembodied – some kind of erotic decoration – until, taking her arm, Gilles led her into the room, and the tallest woman Flint had ever seen stood up from the sofa where she had been sprawled.

'Welcome,' she said, beaming down at them, not troubling to close her gown. 'Whatever you desire is here.'

Gilles stared at her as though he was transfixed and Flint felt the urge to giggle, and a flutter of relief. The panic had left her. She would be all right.

'Well, a drink to begin with,' she said brightly, tugging at his arm, pulling him towards the bar.

They sat on red leather swivel stools and sipped champagne and surveyed their surroundings. By Flint's count, there were thirty people in the room, not including themselves or the barman or the half-dozen near-naked hostesses, as she assumed they were called. It was surreal. Eight men, who appeared to be Japanese, sat together engaged in animated conversation, paying no heed to the women they had presumably come to buy. Four others, American by the sound of them, argued about a baseball game. Nine couples in three groups chatted and laughed as they might in any bar or restaurant.

No sign of Silva.

'If this is sex I think I'll give it up,' she said, feeling a little light-headed. 'Where's Mario, I wonder?'

'Maybe upstairs in one of the bedrooms,' Gilles suggested, nodding towards a staircase on the opposite side of the room that was guarded by a scarlet rope.

Flint was about to say that she thought the rope meant the staircase was off limits when three of the couples rose in unison and headed towards it. A hostess unfastened the rope and let them pass. She waited until they were part-way up the stairs when she called something after them, and they stopped and turned and laughed and beckoned her to follow.

'I think I'll take a look around,' said Flint. 'See if I can spot him.'

'Don't get too close,' Gilles warned.

'Just a friendly chat, if that's what he's up for.'

'I'll watch your back.'

She nodded, and slipped off the stool, and took her glass, and wandered from the bar into the next room, ignoring the American who said 'Hey, babe' as she passed by.

This was the largest of the rooms she had seen so far and she counted forty heads, not including the hired help, none of them Silva's. She drifted among them as though she was lost, receiving their glances and their smiles, their implied invitations. Feeling a hand stroking her arm, she looked at the fingers and saw nails that were painted a brilliant red. 'Mmm, aren't you pretty?' said a woman's voice, and Flint felt the nails digging into her skin.

It was in the fourth room that she found Silva – or
rather, he found her. She had thought at first it was
empty. She sat down for a moment and closed her eyes,
trying to clear the fuzziness in her head. When she opened
her eyes he was there, just a few feet away, directly in
her sight-line, staring at her, she staring back, too startled
to look away.

So here we go, she thought, opening her lips to breathe
through her mouth and increase the oxygen supply; keep
the panic at bay.

Above the fireplace where Silva stands there is a mirror,
reaching almost to the ceiling, tilted at an angle that
allows Grace Flint to observe that the girl refilling his
glass is rubbing her breasts against him. Flint is not
happy about this level of competition. The girl is too
young, too alluring, and Flint will not be surprised if any
second now Mario succumbs, heading for the scarlet
rope and the staircase beyond. All she can do is continue
to stare at him, declaring an interest, hoping that Mario
is not entirely driven by his most basic instinct. Given
their surroundings, that seems unlikely.

But then – surprise, surprise – behind the girl's back
he raises his glass to her, and though Flint has been
trained to let the target make all of the initial running,
she raises hers in response. Not by much, and not
immediately; she delays a few moments, and then only
by an inch or two.

It is enough, apparently. Now the girl is leaving and
Mario Silva is coming towards her. He stands in front of

her chair and says, 'Good evening' and 'Do you mind if I sit down?' Out of the corner of her eye, she sees Gilles come slowly into the room. The hostess is with him – the one with the endless legs.

'My name is Mario. I don't think I've seen you here before.'

Silva remains standing, awaiting her permission to sit down.

'No,' is all that she says.

'I'm certain I would have remembered you.' He smiles and points inquiringly at the club chair alongside hers. She shrugs as if to say, 'It's a free world.'

Sitting down, he asks: 'Did you come here alone?'

'No,' and she points her glass at the wall against which Gilles is leaning.

'Oh, I see.' Silva sounds confused, unsure of his ground.

'He's just a friend. I didn't want to come here alone. Not the first time.'

Silva nods and says: 'May I ask your name?'

His French is correct, much more so than hers, but his accent is curious. He sounds like a man who speaks too many languages.

'Katia,' she says, repeating the harmless lie Gilles has written in the members' register.

'But you are not French, I think?'

'Not altogether.'

He smiles at her evasion and presents one of his own. 'I belong to no country. I regard myself as a citizen of the world.'

She mocks him with her silence.

'The accident of my birth occurred in Portugal,' he confides, and she smiles a little to reward him for his honesty.

'And may I ask what you do?'

At last, thinks Flint, and she baits the hook. 'International finance.'

'Oh, really? That covers many sins.'

She does not reply and Silva seeks another avenue to explore. 'Your friend seems to be enjoying himself.'

Against the wall, the Amazonian – for that is how Flint sees her – is resting her arms on Gilles' shoulders, her hands clasped behind his head. Her robe is still open. Their bodies are separated by no more than the thickness of his clothes.

Flint says, 'That's the point of coming here,' giving him the opening he wants.

'And why did you come here?'

'Curiosity.'

'Curiosity about what?'

'Who I might meet. What might happen.'

'Well, you've met me.'

'Yes.'

'And what do you think might happen?'

'I don't know.'

She is looking at his face and she can read every emotion he is feeling. She knows that any moment now he will move closer towards her in order to touch her: her arm, her knee; if he's bold enough, her thigh. He is also watching her face but he can read nothing. All that he sees is a mask.

He edges forward in his chair, and places one hand on her knee and asks, 'Have you seen upstairs?'

'No.'

'There are bedrooms.'

Now she leans forward, and for a moment he misunderstands and squeezes her knee, and then she rips away his delusions. 'I'm not a hooker. I don't sleep with men in brothels.' She says it quietly but the contempt in her voice is withering. He takes away his hand as though it has been scalded.

'I didn't mean . . .'

'What did you mean?'

'I just . . .'

He's floundering now and she must help him. 'Do you live alone?'

'Yes. Entirely alone.'

'Where?'

'Not far from here. Rue Jacob near St Germain-des-Prés. Perhaps you know it?' Hope in his voice but also puzzlement. He's off-balance now, as he is supposed to be, according to the training manual.

'Then perhaps you will invite me to visit.'

'Of course. When?'

Flint considers, calculating how quickly Gilles can make the necessary arrangements: the hidden cameras, the microphones, the all-important back-up team next door. She looks to him for guidance, as if he can somehow transmit the information to her by osmosis. He is far too engrossed with the Amazonian to notice.

'Tuesday,' she says, a wild guess.

Silva looks crestfallen. 'But I leave for Zurich this morning. I will not be back for several days.'

Thoughts cascade through Flint's mind but the prominent one is that her fish is getting away. He's taken the bait, he's on the hook, but the line is snagged on the obstruction of his schedule.

There is a voice inside her head screaming to be heard but she refuses to heed it. She cannot believe what she hears herself say: 'Then shall we go?'

six

On a stone terrace overlooking the rose garden of
Compton Hall Sir Adrian Taggart said, 'He's
becoming a nuisance.'

The lines on Patrick Shilling's face creased into crevices
of scorn. 'Cohen? He's getting nowhere.'

'That's not what Devereaux thinks.'

'Devereaux's a fool.'

Sir Adrian raised an eyebrow. 'Hardly that,' he said.

Out of hearing, in a distant part of the garden, Sir
Adrian's pretty wife – his second – tended a rose bush,
snipping at the dead wood with pruning shears. Beyond
her, the Solent glittered in the sunlight, its surface like
glass.

'Our friend in Florida is concerned.'

'Because?'

'Because Cohen is hand in glove with Cutter, feeding
him everything he gets. And Cutter is anything but a
fool.'

'Then perhaps our friend should take care of Cutter.'

'He thinks that would be . . . unwise.'

His wife stood back admiring her work.

'Unwise if anything were to happen to Cutter over there,' her husband continued.

'But not unwise if something were to happen to Cohen over here?'

'Not if we thought it appropriate, no.' Sir Adrian toyed with a glass of white port. 'Not if something were to happen in, say, Paris.'

'Paris?'

Sir Adrian nodded.

'Cohen knows about Silva?'

'Apparently.'

Satisfied with her pruning, his wife gathered the severed twigs into a neat pile for future collection.

'Are you sure?'

'Devereaux was not precise but, yes, I think it would be safe to assume that Cohen will be on his way to see Mario before too long.' Sir Adrian smiled, watching his wife walk up the garden towards them, admiring the grace of her body.

'I'll talk to—'

'No names,' said Sir Adrian.

'I'll look into it.'

'Yes, why don't you do that? If it seems appropriate.'

She was within earshot now. 'Well,' she said, drawing near, smiling brightly, 'if you two will stop gossiping about the office we'll have lunch, shall we?'

II

For the novelty of it, Cohen took the train to Paris. He left Waterloo station at nine o'clock in the morning and was walking out of the Gare du Nord in ample time for lunch, having found the passage through the Channel Tunnel mildly disappointing; the eventless nature of the journey, he thought, did not do justice to the scale of the achievement.

His expenses were unlimited – or, at least, not queried by Barbara Dixon's committee – but he shunned Devereaux's advice that he stay at the Crillon, securing instead a room at the Relais Christine in the Latin quarter. It had once been a monastery and therefore appropriate, Cohen thought, to his own enduring sense of solitude. There had been nobody since Annie and sometimes he doubted that there ever would be.

His room was called a duplex, with the bedroom set on a mezzanine above the sitting room where Cohen now sat looking out onto a courtyard largely unchanged for four-hundred years, waiting for the telephone to ring. Inspector Bourdonnec had been adamant and not a little brisk: 'I'll call you. Wait in your room.' Without

Commander Glenning's intervention, without his contacts and his deep knowledge of how to navigate the
bureaucratic channels, Cohen doubted the inspector
would have conceded even that. To judge by his tone on
the phone, Bourdonnec was not in the least inclined to
discuss police business with a total stranger who had no
credentials, no official pretext for his curiosity.

The call came late, after it was dark, startling Cohen
who supposed he must have fallen asleep. Reaching for
the table lamp, scrambling for his thoughts, he grabbed
the phone as if it might not ring a second time.

'Yes?'

'This is Bourdonnec. What is it you want?'

'A meeting, inspector.'

'Why?'

'Because there are things I should tell you, things I
cannot say on an open line.'

Waiting through the pause, Cohen prepared his next
move.

'I can't help you.'

'Inspector, you are the only one who *can* help me.' He
hesitated for two beats. 'The only one who can help
Grace.'

'Who are you? *What* are you?'

'Please,' said Cohen. 'See me.'

In the silence he sensed the weakening of Bourdonnec's
resolve.

'Inspector – Gilles, if I may – I know how close you
are to Grace, you and Dominique, and I know how
much she means to both of you. Her father told me.

Believe me, Grace needs your help very badly. She needs you to see me. Let me tell you what I know, what I can't say now on the phone, and then you can decide if you will help. I think you may be able to save her life.'

'Wait.'

'*Comment?*'

'*Ne quittez pas.*'

Bourdonnec did not put down the receiver or muffle the mouthpiece for Cohen could hear his breathing as, presumably, he listened to the turmoil of arguments inside his head: his copper's innate caution and suspicion versus his curiosity; that, and – Cohen fervently hoped – the strength of his loyalty to Flint that might tip the balance.

Bourdonnec reached his decision. 'You have a pen?'

'Yes.'

'Write this down. On the right bank, across the Pont Saint-Michel from your hotel, there is a Metro station called Chatelet for a little castle that is no longer there.'

'Yes.'

'From Chatelet you take the Rue des Halles to the old market that is also no longer there. Beyond Les Halles there is a large church, Sainte-Eustache, and, to the right of the church, Rue Montorgueil. Follow it until you come to Rue Tiquetonne. At number thirty-eight there is a door, *une porte cochère*. At this time of night you need a code to open it. The code is A2C4. Inside, you will find a passage leading to a courtyard. At the end of the passage, just before you reach the courtyard, the glass door on the right, there are eight bells. One of them has my name on it. Do you understand?'

'Yes. When should I come?'
'*Maintenant.* Now.'

He was not at all as Cohen had imagined him, his looks
far younger than his voice with none of the stiff formality
he implied on the telephone. Climbing (and counting)
the 137 stairs that led to the Bourdonnec's small apartment, Cohen had expected to be met by a parodic French
functionary, all neat and precise and burdened with
rigidity, not this disarming boy of a man with his unruly
hair and rumpled clothes. Standing in the kitchen, using
the sink for an ashtray, Bourdonnec smoked a chain of
Philip Morris cigarettes while Cohen told his story,
keeping his voice low for the sake of the children. The
inspector was a good listener. He did not interrupt Cohen
except to utter an occasional obscenity, punctuating the
more astonishing revelations. If he did not receive the
whole truth, it was certainly a fuller version than Cohen
had intended to give him.

'*Bordel de merde!*' he said when Cohen was done. 'I
had no idea!'

'Grace didn't tell you?'

'About MI5 and your Mr Brown? Not a word. Sure, I
knew about Harling. He was her hang-up, her *idée fixe*.
And she told me about the plane and the bomb when she
called from London to ask for my help.'

Cohen kept his expression neutral.

'But the rest . . .' He raised his hands to show his
exasperation. 'If she had told me, I would never have
agreed.'

'Agreed to what, Gilles? What did Grace ask you to do?'

Cohen saw a flicker of hesitation in Bourdonnec's eyes but then it was gone.

'She asked me to find a man, Harling's partner. Here in Paris. It wasn't difficult.'

'What was his name?'

'His name?' Bourdonnec ran the tap to wash away the ash and then he grinned, lighting up his face. 'Now it's my turn, eh? We'll walk, get some air, and I'll tell you about Grace's other obsession: a man called Mario Silva; dealer in antiquities, *putain*, whore.'

They walked through the night, passing the Louvre, crossing the river by the Pont des Arts, heading up the Rue de Seine, pausing in the shadows opposite Silva's gallery; Bourdonnec telling his story with pedantic thoroughness, Cohen forcing himself to be patient. They pressed on towards the Sénat and the Palais du Luxembourg and then skirted the gardens until they arrived at the Abbé de l'Epée, the vantage point from which they could watch the comings and goings at the Club Elégance. The inspector's timing was immaculate for he had just reached the point in his chronology when Grace Flint had announced to him in an urgent whisper her reckless intent to spend the night with Mario Silva.

'I told her, no way was she going to his apartment. Not then. Not without the precautions in place. I had sent my guys home so there was no back-up team. No wire, no camera, no plan, nothing. I told her, "You think

I'm going to let you go home alone with this animal?"
No fucking way, I said. But . . .'

'She's stubborn,' Cohen said.

'Stubborn! She's impossible! *Entêté!* A mule! She said,
"He's not an animal. I've been there, Gilles. I know how
they smell." And then she kissed me on the cheek and
went off with him like she was his lover. You should
have seen the look on that fat shit's face.'

'There was nothing you could have done to stop
them?'

'I could have broken his legs, but . . .' Bourdonnec
shrugged, acknowledging his failure. 'I followed them
back to his apartment and I rousted my guys from their
beds. We considered busting in, taking him down, but . . .
In the end I decided to trust her instincts. The last thing
I said to her was, "If he starts any trouble, scream your
lungs out. Throw something through the window. *Merde*,
throw *him* through the window." I decided to believe
she could handle it.'

'And did she?'

The door of the club opened and a shaft of light came
towards them. 'I don't know,' Bourdonnec said carefully,
watching the couple that emerged. 'I know she got what
she wanted. I don't know what she had to give him in
return.'

The light retreated as the door closed and they could
hear the clack of the woman's heels on the paving stones
and the tinkle of her laughter.

III

Grace Flint lying on Silva's bed, listening to the sounds he makes as he edges towards her in the darkened room. He has removed her dress so it will not be crushed, and covered her body with a starched linen sheet that tickles her skin. She feels his weight as he sits down on the bed beside her and places his hand on her brow; on what she thinks of, at times like this, as the 'bad side' of her head. Even though his touch is light the pain is unbearable. She flinches. He whispers '*désolé*' and moves his hand to her bare shoulder, stroking it with the tips of his fingers.

Softly he says, 'Is there nothing I can get you, nothing that will help?'

She considers his offer and its implications.

In truth, there is something he can get her; something that will hasten her progress towards the cathartic moment when the nausea will become overwhelming, sending her reeling, retching, to the bathroom. Afterwards, please God, will come the epiphany: her exquisite recognition of the slackening of the band that is presently crushing her skull. The feeling of euphoria, she knows, will be otherworldly, but here's the rub: if she allows Mario to bring her respite from the indescribable pain; when she has heaved up the contents of her stomach all over his bathroom floor; when she is lying once more on his bed limp as a rag, will he still want to fuck her?

Probably, she thinks.

He's not an animal, Gilles. I know how they smell.

But even as she replays this brash assurance in her mind, she feels Mario's fingers under the sheet, straying towards the rise of her breasts.

'Coffee,' she says abruptly. 'Caffeine.'

His fingers halt and withdraw, retreating back to her shoulder.

'Need to vomit.' A kind of aphasia is robbing her of the ability to speak coherently but she must and she forces herself to go on. 'Need to be sick. Coffee works for me, sometimes. Strong coffee. So strong it coats your teeth.'

She can hear herself slurring the words as though she is drunk. He does not move.

'Didn't come here to be a cliché.'

He does not know what she means.

'Don't want this headache. Hurts too much. My head is going to explode. Do you have ice? Could you wrap some ice cubes in a towel for me? Can you do that, please? God, it's so hot in here! Can you open the window? But don't let in the light. I can't bear the light.'

The flow of her words has become torrential.

'There's some maniac drilling a hole through my forehead. He's inside my brain. Oh Christ, Mario! Do you have Tylenol, aspirin, anything? Jesus, Mario! Do something.'

She is exaggerating her hysteria but not by much. Right now the spike of pain driving through the left side of her frontal lobe is so intense she would welcome a lobotomy. She wants to scream but she fears that if she does Gilles will come running from the street, crashing through the door, ruining everything – and there is a part of her brain that stands apart and aloof from the pain, coolly assessing the situation.

Don't blow it now!

Nevertheless, she tells Mario Silva, 'I'm going to scream.'

This gets him moving. He's off the bed, feeling his way through the dark, heading for the door, promising to return with what she needs. She lies on his bed focusing on her cerebral arteries like a Yogi seeking *yama*. She tells herself – and half believes – that if she concentrates hard enough she can shrink those dilated vessels through the sheer power of her will.

Oh, really?

He brings her ice cubes wrapped in a stiff napkin that feels as though it was starched by the same laundry that worked on the sheet. She places it on her temple to freeze the pain. On a surface level it works – for she feels the bad side of her forehead growing numb – but the tip of the spike is now deep inside her cerebellum, far beyond the reach of any local anaesthetic.

Next, from his bathroom, he brings her a potion that he tells her is Sedaspir, and that takes her by surprise.

There is little she doesn't know about painkillers and she rates Sedaspir as one of the big-hitters because it's laced with codeine, derived from morphine, and she once knew an Air France pilot who took it for the high, until the airlines began random drug testing. It also contains a slug of pure caffeine, and she wonders what ailment Mario's got that requires such a potent brew.

As gently as he can, he raises her head from the pillow, offers her a glass of water and says, 'One or two?'

She says, 'Give me the packet,' but she settles for the two tablets he gives her. They won't help the pain much but he doesn't know that. She hears him moving about the room again and then he settles in the overstuffed armchair he keeps by the window, waiting for the drugs to work, biding his time.

She must have fallen asleep, for something in the room has changed. She is now in that phase of the attack where her senses are so acute she believes she can taste the air or hear a butterfly sigh. This is the false dawn, when the pain shrinks and curls up in the back of her skull like a small creature, but she knows it is only resting. She lies in the eye of her very own hurricane, grateful for the respite, sniffing the atmosphere for clues about her present situation.

Mario is no longer in the room, of that she is sure. Her certainty is based not merely on the absence of his breathing. In her heightened state, she would feel his presence even if he was dead.

Carefully, she opens her right eyelid – the one on the

'good side' – and waits for the pupil to adjust. She sees that the light forming the lining around the edges of the curtains is the bland grey of dawn, not the yellow of the street lamps. So, she calculates, at least three hours has passed since she swallowed the Sedaspir. She wonders how Mario has spent the time. Did he turn on the light to watch her, pull back the sheet to look at her body? Did he touch her?

From her prone position her one eye can search only portions of the room. Slowly, gingerly, she opens her left eyelid, ready to snap it closed at the first sear of pain. Now she is able to confirm that Mario is indeed not present, unless he is beneath the angle of her vision.

Come on, do it! You've got to be sure!

She is terrified of doing it but she *does* have to know. She has to know if her plan has worked.

She had come to Silva's apartment with no thought of what she would do, or what she might achieve, or how she might dampen his expectations. She had played for time, accepting a drink, asking him about himself, smiling at his lies. Then she had told a few of her own, inventing a plausible persona in response to his civilised inquiries. She was running out of ideas on how to maintain the verbal foreplay when his face swam out of focus. She felt a rush of irrational panic and then a sudden giddiness that sent her stumbling, spilling the glass from her hand. She heard him say, 'Are you all right?' and felt his hands on her shoulders as he steadied her. And in that moment of the aura, the part of her brain that was not involved in these proceedings, the part not dazzled by the kaleidoscope of hallucinations, conceived her plan: he would have to let her stay and he would have to leave, bound by the commitment of his scheduled departure to Zurich.

With great trepidation, fearing an explosion of pain, she lifts herself from the pillow until she is propped on her elbows, and now she can see the floor. No Mario. No pain either, except for the nagging creature at the back of her skull.

The door leading to the living room and the kitchen beyond is open and they are in darkness. She cannot sense his presence. He is gone, she is sure of it, leaving her a note, perhaps: *Let yourself out when you're feeling better* – that sort of thing. Maybe he will have added a small reproach: *I'm very disappointed at the way things turned out*. Well, he's entitled to that.

She is contemplating her victory when two things happen in quick succession. A bell rings with unbelievable loudness, as though it is inside her head, triggering an intense pulse of agony that travels down her spinal cord like an electric shock. And then she hears a lavatory flush and the bathroom door opens, flooding her with light, and she cannot close her eyes because the lids are frozen, and, still propped on her elbows, she sees Mario coming towards the bed, his trousers undone at the waist, her plan, her cockeyed scheme, in ruins. She opens her mouth to scream but there is no sound.

Mario picks up the telephone on the bedside table – the source, she now realises, of the dinning bell. He listens for a moment and says, '*Merci.*'

To Flint he says, 'My alarm call. I'd forgotten.'

He sees her staring at his midriff and he turns away from her to fasten his trousers. Turning back, icily polite, he asks, 'May I call you a taxi?'

'What?'

'I have to leave for the airport in thirty minutes. I'm going to Zurich. Remember?'

'Of course.'

'Then I'll leave you to get dressed.'

She watches him go to the armoire that serves as his wardrobe and retrieve the dress that he had carefully removed and hung for her, so that it would not be crushed; the fuck-me dress that lied. She can taste her failure. It has the flavour of bitter almonds. Most of her is resigned to it, but not that carping, chivvying part of her brain that is not engaged with the pain.

He's getting away! Do something!

Like what?

Anything!

She lowers herself onto the pillow and says, 'Mario, when can I see you again?'

He comes to the bed, holding the dress over one arm, and looks down on her. He pretends to be smiling but it looks more like a sneer.

'See me?'

'I'd like to see you again.'

'Why? Why would you like to see me again?'

His eyes have grown bright. This is not good. His frustration, his disappointment, are edging dangerously towards anger; appropriate anger from where he stands.

He's gaining the high ground and she needs to find the strength to pull him back. She needs to find a little anger of her own.

'Oh fuck it, Mario, why do you think? You think I came here to be ill? You think I've been putting on an act?'

The vehemence of her questions surprises even her.

Defensively he says, 'Why did you come here?'

'I was bored, Mario. I thought, what I'd really like to do tonight is find some guy and get him to take me home so I can have a bloody migraine in his bedroom. I thought, I'll wind him up and then I'll get ill, and that will really piss him off. It's my idea of fun, you see?'

She sits up, letting the sheet fall from her shoulders, and swings her legs over the edge of the bed. She feels a swooning sensation which she ignores. She engages another gear.

'I don't believe this. I've known you for five minutes and all you care about is that you didn't get to fuck me.'

'That's not true.'

'Really? Then why are you standing there like a little boy who's lost his marbles? Give me the dress.'

He does not do so. He stands there staring at her nakedness, no longer sure of his ground. That's as it's supposed to be, according to the training manual.

'Listen, Mario, I didn't come here to sleep with you.'

She doesn't need the manual to tell her there is no more effective lie than a half-truth.

'I came here because I wanted to know more about you. You were the only person in that club I was interested in. I wanted to spend some time with you, or I thought I did. I wanted to see how you lived, what you liked, what you thought. I wanted to know who your friends are, whether I might like them too. I'm not a one-night stand, Mario. I need to like someone before I go to bed with them. I didn't know if I would spend the night here, or not. Is this making any sense to you?'

'Of course.'

'All right, then I got sick. I'm sorry about that. Sometimes I get these attacks, without much warning. I felt a little light-headed at the club but I put that down to the champagne. I didn't know it was going to happen. I didn't *want* it to happen. What I *wanted* was to know more about you, and I still do. I want to know everything about you. But if you're going to behave like I'm a piece of meat, some cheap hooker whose failed to deliver the goods, then, screw it, Mario. Screw you.'

She pauses – not for effect but because a sudden rush of nausea is filling her stomach.

She says, 'Quick,' and reaches out her arm and, misunderstanding, he tries to hand her the dress.

'I need to get to the bathroom,' she manages to say.

He cottons on and helps her to her feet but she cannot stand without his support. Together, awkwardly, they stumble to the bathroom where he lowers her to her knees before the lavatory bowl. She wants him to leave but she has no time to tell him before the retching begins. Mario is the witness to the seismic scale of her eruptions.

She has no sense of time; no sense of how long she kneels on the cold ceramic tiles, clinging to the bowl.

She does not know if he turns his face in disgust or leaves the room. All she knows is that when the convulsions finally end, when it feels as if every drop of bile has evacuated her body, she slumps to the floor in a foetal position and then she is floating, her arms around his neck. She is weightless, helpless, but alive and counting her blessings.

He carries her to the bedroom and lays her softly on the bed. He covers her with a duvet and fetches a warm, dampened flannel from the bathroom to bathe her face.

She says, 'I'm fine, now. Just give me a few minutes.'

He wipes flecks of debris from the corners of her mouth and tells her to shush.

IV

Inspector Bourdonnec was flagging. In the stark, fluorescent light of an all-night café off the Boulevard Saint-Germain, two blocks from Silva's apartment, his boy's face looked crimped and aged, his skin as brittle as old paper stained by the nicotine of too many cigarettes.

He coughed into his hand and said, 'Where was I?'

'The taxi arrived,' Cohen reminded him.

'Right. One of my guys went over to talk to the driver. He said the reservation had been made the day before: six-thirty sharp, a Monsieur Silva at number thirty; one-way to Roissy, the airport.'

As Cohen knew from their recent discreet observation of the building where Silva lived, the Rue Jacob was narrow and the street parking intense. There had been no convenient spot for the taxi to wait.

'I had one of our cars moved so the driver could park. I wanted time-stamped pictures of Silva coming out of the door, getting into the taxi, just in case, and it was the perfect set-up.'

'Just in case?'

'In case he'd hurt her.'

Cohen nodded. 'You weren't concerned that the driver would tell Silva what was going on?'

'No. We more or less told him that Silva was a suspected contact for an Arab terrorist group we were keeping under observation.' Bourdonnec gave a weary smile. 'We've had too many bombs, you see. You tell that to anyone in Paris, they'll do almost anything for you.'

Cohen, distracted, fidgeted in his chair and Bourdonnec put a hand on his wrist and said, '*Doucement* – he's watching you in the mirror. You know him?'

'No.'

'But you've seen him before, perhaps?'

'Once, maybe twice. Yesterday, when I arrived at the Gare du Nord, he was behind me in the taxi queue. Not looking as he does now but it was certainly him. And this evening – last evening – when I left the hotel to come to you, I saw someone in the street who looked vaguely familiar. I couldn't place him then. Now I'm pretty sure it's him.'

Bourdonnec laughed loudly as though Cohen had told a joke and, removing his hand from Cohen's wrist, he swept his coffee cup onto the floor where it shattered with a satisfactory crash. He jumped up from his chair as though he had been scalded and shouted, '*Merde!*' Other customers took note of the commotion and the *patron*, wiping glasses behind the bar, threw down his cloth in disgust. But the broad-backed man who was making Cohen nervous remained studiously hunched over the counter, nursing a small glass of red wine. Cohen caught his glance in the mirror and the man looked away.

The *patron* arrived with a broom, grumbling at the loss of his cup. Bourdonnec brushed at the imaginary splashes of coffee on his trousers and said quietly, 'Jean-Paul, the guy at your counter, have you seen him before?'

'Never, inspector, and you don't have to smash up my place to find that out. You can just ask.'

'When did he come in?'

'A few minutes after you.'

'I'll pay for the cup.'

'That'll make a change.'

Bourdonnec shooed him back to his counter and sat down at the table. He was grinning mischievously and his face looked refreshed: *faire du cinéma* had clearly chased away his fatigue.

'Tell me about yesterday,' he asked Cohen.

'There's nothing much to tell. At the station, there was a long line waiting for taxis, one of those snaking lines, and he was a few places behind me. At some point, as the line turned, we were standing next to each other, and I said something trivial to him about the delay, and he agreed with me, and that was it. I only noticed him because he was carrying a briefcase rather like mine.'

'And now he's a *loubard* – and you *still* look like a lawyer!'

Cohen gave him a small smile.

'And the second time?'

'He looks like he does now. The singlet – if that's what you call it – the jeans. Oh, and his hair seems much shorter than it was yesterday. I think he's shaved his head.'

'A master of disguise,' Bourdonnec said theatrically. 'But he hasn't changed the shape of his nose or his mouth or his chin, or the space between his eyes.'

'No, he hasn't.'

'You surprise me – for a lawyer. We'll make a detective of you yet!'

'I hope not.'

Bourdonnec leaned forward and abandoned his bantering tone. 'I'm going to make a phone call. I need you to keep our friend interested in you rather than me. Go and pay the bill, please, and argue with Jean-Paul about the price of the cup. Make a big thing of it, he'll play along. Offer him ten francs and settle for fifty. I need a few minutes, that's all, and then I'll see you outside.'

Cohen said, 'Fine,' and – not displeased by the inspector's passing compliment – he did as he was told.

They resumed their journey, recrossing the river to the right bank, heading north, Cohen resisting the temptation to glance behind, Bourdonnec picking up his narrative as though nothing had occurred.

'Silva came out of the building at six-thirty-one a.m. spoke to the driver and went back inside. After a few moments, we saw the lights in his apartment go out and then he reappeared at six-forty, this time carrying a small case and a garment bag. No sign of Flint. My instinct was to seize him but then I thought, What's the point? He wasn't going anywhere except the airport; I sent four of my men and two cars to make sure of that. And long before he got to Roissy, I thought, we would know what had happened, what he'd done.'

'You feared the worst?'

'Not necessarily. I've known Grace a long time, as long as I've known my wife. In fact, the first time I met Dominique the two of them were together – like sisters, only closer. Don't turn around.'

'No.'

'He's there. The blue van that just went by, it's one of mine. You see it's turning left? That's the signal.'

'And what happens now?'

'We will make the same turn. Our friend has a surprise coming.'

So do I, thought Cohen, and he felt a quiver of irrational fear.

'Ever since she became a cop, Grace has been involved in one scrape after another. She never talks to me about her *histoires* but she tells Dominique, which is the same thing. I think she gets scared half to death but she knows how to survive. So, no, I did not necessarily fear the worst. It was only one of the possibilities. *A gauche*.'

The road they turned into was little more than an alley, apparently deserted and excessively dark. The street lights were off and Cohen wondered if Bourdonnec could possibly have arranged for their malfunction. There was no sign of the van which was strange, for Cohen thought they were in a cul-de-sac until he saw a brief reflection of light in one of the distant windows and guessed there must be a dog-leg turn to the right. Bourdonnec paused to light a cigarette – a signal, perhaps? – and Cohen steeled himself for what he imagined was about to happen.

'But then I did begin to worry when she didn't answer the telephone. I kept calling Silva's number from my portable phone. No answer. Relax, my friend. You will spoil the surprise.'

'Sorry.'

'We could not get into the building because we did not have the code for the front door. I rang Silva's bell. I kept it pressed for maybe half a minute. Nothing. Now I did, as you say, fear the worst. *A droite.*'

They reached the dog's-leg and now Cohen could see lights and people in the near distance. He did not understand. The best moment for an ambush had surely passed.

'So, I just rang every bell until somebody answered and opened the door. We created quite a commotion, I can tell you. We were running up the stairs and people were coming out of their apartments in their night-clothes. They were yelling, "What's going on?" and we were yelling, "Police! Police! Get out of the way!" Quite a scene. Then I was banging on Silva's door, calling for Grace, and there was still no answer. We will go up here. Do you know where we are?'

'No,' said Cohen taking in a bewildering array of signs promising 'peep shows' and 'live sex' and 'videos rated XXX!' 'And I'm confused. I was expecting something to happen back there.'

'So was he,' said Bourdonnec. 'Now he thinks we

have come to find some girls, and he is right.'

They strolled up the Rue Saint-Denis like a couple of punters checking out the gaudy come-ons of the sex clubs and video parlours, and the lubricious women who loitered in the doorways with their painted faces and ballooning thighs.

'What did you do when she didn't answer the door?' Cohen asked.

'We broke it down.'

V

The last day of summer term. July is not yet ended and all of August lies ahead – halcyon days to be spent on an island that is pretty much deserted, sun-swept, cooled by breezes that carry the scent of lemon trees and thyme. She emerges from the gates of Tudor Hall, her beauty blossoming, surrounded by her many friends who are reluctant to be parted from her even for a few weeks. Her handsome parents wait in an open car, indulgently patient as she says her goodbyes, smiling at the sight of her.

They are on the island, on a rocky path. It is early evening and somewhere in the distance there is the clamour of bells and a chorus of voices calling them home from the beach. Mad and John Flint, arm in arm, Grace hurrying ahead, laughing, always laughing.

Her mother calls to her, 'Gracie darling, be careful,' for the path is steep and strays close to the edge of a crumbling cliff. But she must hurry for the peal of the bells is incessant and the voices demanding: 'Grace! Grace! Grace!' Her Lab is with her, urging her on.

She turns to tell her mother she is fine, but her mother

is no longer there. Her father stands on the edge of the cliff, staring out to sea. He wears a hospital-green gown that is stained with the juice of cherries. In his hand he holds a hammer.

She calls to him, 'Daddy.' She wants to tell him she has a recollection of pain, though it has faded – like the memory of a past lover whose name she has forgotten. He – her father? her lover? – cannot hear her above the tumult.

Grace! Grace! Grace!

There is the sound of an explosion in which her mother dies.

Gilles is standing at the end of the bed, his boy's face white, quivering with rage.

'What in God's name do you think you are doing?'

She is trying to remember where she is.

'*Answer me!*'

She's never seen him like this and he frightens her. Tentatively she asks, 'Gilles, what's wrong?'

'What's *wrong*! You're naked in his bed and you ask me what's *wrong*!'

It's coming back to her now, flooding back. She pushes herself up the bed, distancing herself from Gilles and his anger, pulling the duvet up to her chin.

'It's not what you think.'

'You fucked that fat shit.'

'No!'

'You let him fuck you.'

'*No!*'

'Jesus, Grace, how could you?'

'Nothing happened.'

'*I can't believe this.*'

'*Nothing happened!*'

She's shouting now, as loudly as he is, and their ruction brings a man to the bedroom door; one of Gilles' men, she supposes.

'Everything all right, chief?'

'No. Go away.'

Gilles turns and slams the bedroom door and then turns back to grab the bottom of the duvet, pulling it from her. She is not, in fact, entirely naked for she is wearing underpants. She hides her breasts with her hands.

'Where are your clothes?'

'I don't know. I don't know where he put them.'

'Jesus!'

'Gilles, listen. I got ill, a migraine attack. I could barely stand. He undressed me and put me to bed. All right? Later on, when I started to be sick, he took me to the bathroom. That's it. Nothing else happened.'

He goes to the bathroom and turns on the light as though he is checking on the evidence. He returns to stare at her for a moment and then he asks, 'What did *you* get? What did you find out about Harling?'

'Nothing.'

'Not a thing? Harling's name never came up?'

'No.'

He shakes his head as if he pities her. 'So, was it worth it, Grace, your night with Mario?'

'Gilles, *please.*'

'Get dressed, Grace.'

He leaves the bedroom with the air of a priest who's been badly let down and part of her feels crushed by his disapproval. But the rebellious voice inside her head has a question to ask, it is demanding to know: *What's it to you who I sleep with, buddy? What's it to you?*

She cannot find her bra or even remember if she was wearing one. She knows she was wearing tights but they are not in the bedroom or the bathroom, so far as she can see. The dress hangs in the armoire but she does not put it on. She can tell from the voices she hears that there are several men in the apartment and she does not want them looking at her in *that* dress, imagining what Mario night have done.

In his chest of drawers she finds a white warm-up suit of the type tennis players wear. The waistband of the pants is far too large for her and she folds it over, secured with one of Mario's expensive neckties. She fastens the jacket all the way to her throat and goes to examine herself in the bathroom mirror. She looks ridiculous, like a child in her father's clothes. For the first time in a long time she laughs.

They are crowded into the kitchen at the front of the apartment, three young men in casual clothes who examine her with open curiosity. They nod their hellos but they do not speak to her. Nor does Gilles, who is examining the front door that will not close. He brushes past her, saying to no one in particular, 'Get a carpenter up here. The lock seems okay but the frame is ruined.'

Half-listening as the arrangements are made, she wanders from the hallway into the living room. She looks for the spot on the carpet where she spilt her drink but there is no trace of it. She tries to remember the subsequent events. Was it here or in the bedroom that Mario undressed her? Casually, she lifts the cushions from the sofa one by one, looking in vain for her tights.

She sits down on the sofa and closes her eyes, trying to evoke the ambience of the room when it was lit by the soft glow of table lamps, and there was music playing on the stereo – Sinatra, she recalls – and she and Mario were exchanging lies, edging towards intimacy. She wonders what would have happened if the migraine had not arrived. Would she, could she, have slept with Mario?

Never.

Not even for Frank Harling's head?

Never in a thousand years!

Oh, really?

To dismiss these troubling thoughts she opens her eyes and fixes on the coffee table where, propped against a figurine of a geisha, she sees an envelope addressed to 'Katia'. It takes a moment before she recognises her pseudonym; the name Gilles chose for her on a whim, the only name by which Mario knows her. She opens the envelope and reads the note it contains: Mario's farewell and, as it turns out, his unwitting testimony.

Ma chère Katia:

Forgive me for leaving you to sleep. I am sure it is best if I do not disturb you just to say goodbye.

And forgive me a hundred times more if I let you think for even one moment that all I wanted was your body. You were right: if we are to become lovers, we must first come to know each other. Whatever happens, I want to see you again. Stay here as long as you wish and use whatever you need; my home is yours. There is a set of keys for you on top of the refrigerator.

If you were still here when I returned, then I would think myself the luckiest man alive. If not, perhaps you will leave your phone number, or you will call me, or . . . who knows? Think of me fondly, as I shall think of you. Bien à toi, Mario.

She takes the note to the kitchen where Gilles sits at the counter, talking into his mobile phone. She squeezes past his posse of three – 'excuse me, amigos, coming through' – and places the note before him. He continues his conversation – with Dominique, apparently – but he reads Mario's words.

To Flint, he mouths a soundless, 'Sorry.' Into the phone he says, 'She's fine. She did great.'

He smiles at her as if to say he forgives her for his doubts. Her nagging voice still asks: *What's it to you?*

The police search of Mario Silva's apartment is hurried and routine. They do not know what they are looking for, since Flint herself does not know and her guesses are random. 'Correspondence, notes, a diary, phone books – anything that might contain Harling's name.'

They check the obvious places: his desk in the living room, the drawers of his chests and cupboards, the speed-dial numbers programmed into his phone. They search for a concealed safe, or a false panel in the wall. They look behind his pictures and under his bed. They probe the toilet cistern and the chimney of the fireplace and the freezer compartment of his fridge. They roll back the carpets, looking for loose floorboards that might conceal a cache, and they take and flick through the pages of each and every book on his shelves.

The search is suspended when the carpenter arrives to fix the doorframe, and it is continually inhibited by Gilles' concerns that what they are doing is both unofficial and illegal. There is no warrant to search Silva's apartment. Gilles veers between his reckless notion to trash the place and make it look as though they arrived too late to prevent a robbery, and his inspector's respect for private property: nothing – *nothing* – he tells his men, is to be damaged.

'Has it occurred to you,' he asks Flint, somewhat tetchily, 'that whatever he has, he carries it with him?'

'Yeah, but I don't buy it. Mario's the kind of guy who keeps careful records. He's not going to risk having his briefcase stolen or getting stopped at Customs.'

'Then perhaps he keeps everything at the gallery?'

'I was thinking about that. Any ideas?'

'Forget it.'

'Oh, come on, Gilles. I got us into here, didn't I? I'll bet you I can get us into the gallery.'

'*Forget it!*'

She laughs. Now that they have stopped imagining her as Mario's whore, she has shed the warm-up suit and borrowed one of his T-shirts and a pair of shorts. They are also much too big for her but the change of costume has lightened her mood.

'Gilles, go home. Let the guys go back to their wives and you go home to Dominique. I'll do better on my own.'

'You can't stay here.'

'But I *can*. He wrote it: "Stay as long as you like, use what you need." His home is my home. He left me a set of keys!'

She holds them in her hand, showing them to Gilles.

'There's something here, I know there is. Let me find it.'

He hesitates. Then he says abruptly to his men, 'Let's wrap it up, let's get out of here.' Gently, forgivingly, she kisses his face.

VI

They had reached that part of the Rue Saint-Denis where the sex business defers to the rag trade but there were still places where a woman or two lingered. Their coquette waited for them at the mouth of a passageway – an *impasse* – daubed with mindless graffiti and Bourdonnec said, 'Just follow my lead.'

She had skin the colour of copper and proud lips that were painted scarlet. She cocked her hips when she saw them coming and laid her head against the wall.

'Hey, boys,' she said in a siren's voice that Cohen thought might raise the dead. 'How about I have the two of you together?'

'You think you can cope with that?'

She ran her insolent eyes over the inspector and said, 'Trust me.'

'My friend's a little shy.'

She looked at Cohen, holding back, and came towards him lazily holding his gaze. When she was very close, she ran her fingers down his chest like a pianist playing a riff. 'You have no idea what I can do for you,' she said. Her teeth were large and very white.

'Have you got a room?' Bourdonnec asked.

'Sure.' She nodded towards the passage and, taking Cohen's arm, drew him to her. 'Come on, honey. This is going to be the best night of your life.'

He doubted it. Allowing the girl to lead him into the dark uncertainty of the passage, he felt like the bait in a trap. Bourdonnec had gone ahead of them, and vanished. Above the echo of her heels on the cobblestones, Cohen strained to hear any sound that might warn him of the imminent attack. She knew it, too. He could feel her tremulous against his arm.

They reached the end of the passageway and stood before a door in a lightless courtyard where the girl released her grip on Cohen's arm and fumbled for her keys. The van, or one that looked very like it, was parked in a corner of the yard. It was empty, so far as Cohen could see, clicking and sighing as the engine cooled.

The girl dropped her purse and cursed. She went down on her knees to gather the contents and Cohen joined her, feeling the ground with his hands, wary about what he might touch. There was an eerie silence and then an explosion of sounds: the onrush of feet, the thud of an impact, a heavy grunt, a muffled cry.

In the darkness Cohen could just make out the shape of figures coming fast and hard, charging towards them. He knew he should move but the frantic messages from his brain weren't getting through. He came up off his knees much too late, feeling a blow to the side of his head that sent him sprawling. He cannoned into the girl and came down on top of her, hearing a startled scream that died in her throat.

And then came the unmistakable report of another even more violent collision: the sickening sound of flesh and bone and cartilage meeting metal at high velocity; yielding, splitting, cracking.

There were three of them, Cohen could now see, and they had run the *loubard* headfirst into the side panel of the van as though he were a battering ram. He lay on the cobblestones like a sack, his head and shoulders still covered by the improvised hood with which they had blinded him.

Bourdonnec said, 'Cuff him, get him into the van.'

Beneath Cohen, the girl moaned and struggled feebly to be rid of him.

'Are you all right? You cut your head.'

They were in the girl's small room, Cohen sitting on the rumpled bed that occupied most of it. She was in what passed for the bathroom, throwing up volubly.

'You want her?' Bourdonnec asked. He was leaning his back against the wall, watching the door, his hands in the pockets of his jacket.

'No!'

'She's paid for.'

Cohen took his handkerchief and dabbed at his forehead, flinching as it stung.

'No, I don't,' he said a little less vehemently. 'Thank you all the same.'

'Okay, but I need you to stay with her for a while.

Talk to her, take her out for a drink. Anything. I don't want her running off her mouth to the next guy who comes along. Can you do that?'

Cohen examined the handkerchief to assess the damage. There were only a few flecks of scarlet staining the linen. 'If you say so,' he said stiffly.

Bourdonnec didn't like his tone, evidently. 'What's the matter? You think we were a little rough out there? You think we should have let him jump you?'

'You don't know what he was going to do.'

'Right.' The inspector's right hand emerged from his jacket holding something that glinted in the light. 'Catch,' he said, tossing it to Cohen.

It was a slim case about five inches long with a fancy metal frame inlaid with ivory, or so it seemed to Cohen. He turned it over in his hands, feeling its weight, looking for the catch to open it.

'Watch yourself,' Bourdonnec said. 'And press the switch.'

Recessed within the frame where his thumb naturally fell was a button that Cohen pushed forward. There was the click of a release mechanism and from within the housing snapped out a steel spike resembling a stiletto.

'That was in his hand when he came for you, when we stopped him. You think he wanted to sell it to you?'

Cohen suddenly felt cold, as though a void had opened inside his chest. Without wishing to, he imagined the spike entering his back just below the shoulder blade, heading inexorably for his heart.

'I'm sorry, I didn't . . .' He saw that his hands were

trembling and willed them to stop. 'You think he meant to kill me?'

'I would say so,' said Bourdonnec, reaching down to take the weapon. 'That is what stilettos are for.' He shrugged. 'It is one of the things I intend to ask him. One of many things. Listen, when you are through with the girl, go back to your hotel and wait. I will call as soon as I have anything.'

'I still don't know what happened to Flint.'

'We'll get to that.' He pressed the button and the spike retracted like a trap. 'For now, I think, this is more important.'

The girl was over it now. From the bathroom came the sounds of running water and her ablutions. When she opened the door she looked like her own much younger sister, her face scrubbed and pale, small without her heels. Her cheap pink dress was unfastened at the back and stained with splashes of water. On her left cheek and reaching to her clavicle Cohen could see the first ripening of a bruise he knew he had inflicted. He saw her as vulnerable and lost and somehow appealing.

Bourdonnec placed a hand on her bare shoulder and she grimaced. 'You did well tonight,' he said. 'Do you know why?'

It was Cohen she watched wide-eyed as she shook her head.

'Because now you have me for a friend. If anyone gives you trouble, comes asking you questions about tonight, you just tell me and I will take care of it. You know nothing, you understand?'

She nodded once but she still did not look at him until, from inside his jacket, he produced a *carte d'identité* that was apparently hers. 'I have a note of your details, Eloise, in case I need to find you. Here, take it. My telephone number is inside. Just remember, you know nothing, you saw nothing. If anyone says differently I want to know.'

His business concluded, he turned to Cohen. '*Bon!* Now I must leave you. Be generous to her, my friend.'

Then he was gone, and the girl was watching Cohen and he smiled to reassure her. 'It will be all right,' he said. 'He really is your friend.'

She also smiled, showing him her teeth, and then she came towards the bed slipping off her dress. Cohen said 'No' but she did not believe him.

She had stood before him naked, pulling his face to her belly, and for moments he had rested there feeling the softness of her skin. He could still smell her scent, sharp and tangy like limes.

He raided the mini-bar and paced his room at the Relais Christine, waiting for the phone to ring, his lawyer's mind straining to bring some order to the chaos of events. He struggled to concentrate on what he had learned about Flint, attempting to push away images of the girl; pushing away, too, the resonant snap of a spring-loaded stiletto emerging from its housing.

Which is not to say that he succeeded.

This was in his hand when he came for you. Five inches of steel honed to a needle point.

Come inside me, make me come. The girl pressing him down, writhing against his face.

Inspector Bourdonnec on the phone, urgent, commanding: 'We have a problem. He is nothing, scum. But the shits who hired him know where you are. They will come for you. Lock the door. Barricade it. Stay away from the windows. I have people on the way.'

In the distance he could hear police sirens and the echo of her heels. He heard her cry out to him and he wished it had been real.

The writing desk jammed against the door, he climbed the spiral staircase to the mezzanine hunched like a target. He lay down on the floor beside the bed and thought of Flint in Mario Silva's apartment; Flint probing the hidden places, searching for the underside.

Searching for what? Finding what?

He heard her cry out to him and wished that it was real.

VII

Flint in Silva's flat, sitting cross-legged on the floor of
the living room. Now she is alone, she has shed his
T-shirt and shorts and is wearing instead one of his
Hermès silk shirts that is soft to her skin and deliciously
cool. The French windows are wide open, letting in the
light of the sun and the passive sounds of a Sunday
afternoon. She is vibrant: on the brink of that heady
moment that every investigator knows when a significant
truth is about to reveal itself; when a fragment of skin
discovered on a trigger, or a human hair found in the
waste trap of a sink, or the stumbling prelude to a
confession, promises a resolution to the conundrum. She
is about to discover what it is that Mario Silva seeks to
hide.

Delaying the moment, extending her anticipation, she
goes to his kitchen to find something to drink. There is a
wide choice set before her on the worktops, for she has
removed and examined every item stored in his cupboards, drawers, refrigerator and freezer.

Similarly, she has emptied every drawer, cupboard
and cabinet in his bathroom, his bedroom and his

living room. Every toiletry, cosmetic, towel, blanket, sheet, pillowcase; every shirt, tie, sock, pair of under-pants, glove, scarf, sweater, jacket, coat; every letter, book, magazine, painting, picture, record, CD, tape, video; every *objet*, appliance, gadget – *everything* that Mario possesses now sits neatly on the floor, adjacent to where it came from. It is as if she has unpacked his life.

In the kitchen she decides to raid his carton of Tropicana orange juice because it reminds her of Florida and another heady moment: *Vladimir won't be joining us, Aleksei. Vladimir is indisposed. Vladimir has a hole in his head the size of a grapefruit . . . Vladimir is dead, Aleksei.*

And, metaphorically, so is Mario – or so she believes.

With all the canny certainty of a woman who hides her own secrets in the sleeves of record albums she cannot play, she knows what Mario has done.

It was the camcorder that gave him away, an expensive-looking Sony High-8 that she found on the top shelf of his armoire, together with a machine for splicing videotapes. So Mario, she had figured, makes and edits amateur movies and she had raced to an assumption about their subject matter; dirty movies, no doubt, starring Mario and women he brought back to his apartment from the Club Elégance. She had half-expected – and steeled herself – to find a tape on which she played a co-starring role: inert, virtually unconscious from the Sedaspir, closely examined by Mario and his camcorder.

But, to her puzzlement, there were no videotapes in the apartment, other than his collection of mainly American commercial movies. And then it had dawned on her – and now she returns to the living room where the tapes are waiting for her, stacked in neat piles on the floor in front of his VCR.

She has arranged them in the same order as he did on the shelves of his bookcase and, one by one, she plays them. To accelerate her review, she makes good use of the fast-forward button on the remote control.

But now she has come to Polanski's *Frantic* and she lets it play at normal speed because, for her, the movie has resonance on several levels. It is set in Paris, filmed in locations very close to where she once lived and to where she now sits. It concerns the abrupt, unexplained disappearance of a woman not unlike her mother. The woman's husband searches for her frantically, rather as John Flint searched frantically for Mad. He, like her father, is not above police suspicion.

She sits on the floor sipping Tropicana, watching Harrison Ford take a shower and his wife take a phone call.

The set-up is worthy of Hitchcock. The camera is with Ford inside the shower, looking over his shoulder, showing us only part of the hotel bedroom beyond the bathroom door. He is singing 'I love Paris in the Springtime' and does not hear the ringing of the telephone, but we do, and we see his wife answer it, and we see that she becomes agitated by what she hears. She calls to him from the bedroom and he says, 'Honey, I can't *hear* you.' She tries again and then in resignation picks up her dress from the floor. The last we see of her, she is dragging a suitcase out of shot.

Cut to a close-up of Ford shaving in the bathroom mirror. Flint knows the movie more or less by heart and she says the next three lines in unison with Ford. 'You're awful quiet in there, babe . . . Haven't gone to sleep on me, have you?' For the pay-off she mimics Cutter's drawl: 'I ain't in here shavin' for drill.'

And then the room bell rings, and rings again, and Ford's next line is, 'Are you gonna get that, babe?' – but he never gets to say it.

There is a jagged cut and several moments of blackness as though the tape has broken. Flint knows better and she waits, and now it is Mario Silva's face looking into the camera. He is sitting in the armchair against which she leans, suave, composed, soberly dressed. He waits for a moment and then he begins to speak in that curious accent of his, the intonation of a man who knows too many languages:

My name is Mario Silva. I am making this tape in order to place on record certain events and activities of which I have become aware. I am doing this for my own protection and to ensure that if anything happens to me those responsible will not escape. I am placing a copy of this tape with my attorney together with instructions that in the event of my disappearance or death from anything but natural circumstances it should be delivered to the authorities.

There is another pause and Flint holds her breath as

though she is afraid the slightest noise might distract him.

He taunts her with his silence for what seems like an eternity, and then:

I am going to tell you a story, a true story, about a man named Frank Arthur Harling and something called The Enterprise . . .

VIII

He had expected the cavalry but, in the event, the evacuation of Harry Cohen from the Relais Christine was achieved with no great fuss.

Bourdonnec calling from the front desk, telling him to pack his things; three of the inspector's men sent to escort him from his room and watch the lobby while he settled his bill; a couple of patrol cars at the hotel's entrance; Bourdonnec waiting for him in the back of an unmarked Peugeot that pulled away as soon as Cohen was inside. No sirens, no flashing blue lights.

'I have to say that you put the fear of God into me,' Cohen said, feeling relieved but also deflated by the anti-climax. Then he sensed the tension in Bourdonnec and saw the ugly profile of a sub-machine pistol cradled on his lap, saw him checking the mirrors and the street up ahead.

The radio crackled and a voice said, 'Clear so far. We're five-hundred metres behind you.'

Bourdonnec took a hand-held set from his pocket and said, 'Close up. René, where are you?'

'Up ahead. Corner of St André and Séguier. I see you in the mirror.'

'Okay. Pull out now. Let's make this a baguette.' He gave Cohen a rueful smile. 'How do you say it? We're the meat in the sandwich?'

Cohen had a dozen questions, and the sense not to ask them.

'Got him,' said their driver, a slab of a man with no visible neck.

Up ahead, Cohen saw a car pulling out of its parking place, accelerating cautiously, allowing them to catch up. The rear window filled with light as the tail car narrowed the gap.

Bourdonnec on the radio again. 'René, keep it steady. Take Saint-Germain to the bridge. Thierry?'

'All clear.'

The tyres screamed as they took the turn onto the boulevard, the three cars now in a compact convoy that muscled its way into the traffic flow. Steady was not the word Cohen would have used to describe their progress.

'Who knew you were coming to Paris?'

The inspector's question had already occurred to Cohen and he had his answer ready. 'Devereaux and Glenning.'

'Nobody else?'

'Devereaux may have told Barbara Dixon, the director-general. He might also have mentioned it to Nicolson at the Home Office, as an indication that we were making progress. I doubt that Glenning would have told anybody.'

Bourdonnec grunted. 'The *salaud* we picked up tonight, he knew you were coming and when you would arrive. He had the time of the train. Who knew that?'

'Certainly not Glenning. When I last spoke to him I was planning to fly.'

'So, Devereaux.'

'I'm not sure.' Cohen searched his memory to recall the details of their parting conversation.

Well, good luck, old chap. You'll keep me informed, of course.

Of course.

I'd stay at the Crillon if I were you.

Perhaps I will.

And so it had continued, a banal conversation that went nowhere.

Do you need a lift to the airport?

No, no, Alan. I'll manage, thank you.

'I am quite sure I didn't tell him I was coming by train,' Cohen said, and he was struck by that oddity. Why had he been so evasive about his plans?

Bourdonnec's eyes never ceased searching the road ahead of them. They were approaching the end of the boulevard where the traffic lights were red. He tapped the driver on the shoulder and said into the radio, 'René, keep it moving.' Unbidden – or so it seemed to Cohen – a strobe on top of the Peugeot's dashboard began pulsing, filling the car with flashes of intense blue light and the hee-haw of a siren. From in front and behind, two more sirens joined the chorus, two more pulsing strobes. In the windows of the shops they passed, the lights reflected like crackles of electricity that seemed to bounce and dance onto the pavements. Then they were thrusting into the junction, bruisers looking for a fight and, to his right, Cohen saw the lights of cars bearing down on them and heard the squealing of brakes, the protests of angry horns. They made it, barely, onto the Pont de Sully, and the strobes were turned off. As suddenly as it had begun, the cacophony died.

'Who made your reservation?' Bourdonnec said, once more picking up the thread as though nothing had happened.

'I did.'

'On the telephone, perhaps?'

'Yes.' The truth dawning on Cohen.

'Boss, we've got company' – Thierry's voice, urgent on the radio. 'Some idiot who also jumped the lights. Maybe he's just an opportunist?'

'And maybe not,' said Bourdonnec, swinging round to look through the rear window. 'René, take the Quai Henri.'

'You want me to take him out?' asked Thierry.

'Not yet. Let's see what he has in mind.'

Their convoy reached the end of the bridge and took a sweeping right turn onto the expressway that follows the right bank of the Seine, racing towards Disneyland, dipping into a curving tunnel at what seemed like suicidal speed. The car rocked as the driver changed lanes, swerving to avoid a motorcyclist. Cohen closed his eyes and pushed away images of a crumpled black Mercedes that famously came to grief against the thirteenth pillar of another Paris tunnel very like this one. He concentrated on the revelation that his telephone was tapped by somebody who knew a man in Paris, a man who carried in his hand five inches of sharpened steel.

The lessening of the roar told Cohen they had survived the tunnel. He opened his eyes to see Bourdonnec half-turned in his seat, his back wedged against the door, the radio in one hand, the gun in the other, its squat barrel pointing at the roof.

'Thierry, where is he?'

'About two hundred metres behind me, holding steady.'

'Okay, start dropping back, see what he does.'

'Do I let him pass me?'

'If he wants to.' To Cohen he said, 'The piece of shit, he's just a punk, *un petit voyou*. He knows nothing. Some guy in a bar paid him five thousand francs to follow you around, mug you when he got the chance, kill you if he wanted to. We need to know who hired him, and why. Maybe these guys know.'

'Kill me? For five thousand francs?'

Bourdonnec smiled. 'You should feel flattered. Believe me, in this city I can have you killed for five hundred.'

'Inspector, here he comes. Black Opel, two-door, Paris plates. Three occupants, male so far as I can tell, two in the front, one in the back.'

'Let him come. René, did you hear that?'

'Got it.'

The car was filling with light as the Opel gained on them.

Bourdonnec said, 'Jacques, you know what to do,' and the driver nodded, one eye on the rear-view mirror, adjusting his grip on the wheel.

'He's going to ram you, boss.'

'The fuck he will.' To Jacques and into the radio Bourdonnec said, 'Let's do it!' To Cohen he said, 'Hold on!'

Before Cohen could respond, the brake lights of the lead car flared crimson. The Peugeot swerved violently to the right, jolting onto the hard shoulder, and the motion sent Cohen sprawling into the seat well on his knees. He heard the persistent blaring of horns. He saw the Opel passing them, startled faces at the windows. Then the lead car veered into the left-hand lane and now the Opel was the meat in the sandwich, boxed in on three sides, the tail car crowding it as though it was attached. Up ahead, in what was now the middle lane, the rear lights of a lumbering articulated truck grew ever-brighter as the Opel hurtled towards it with nowhere else to go.

The driver must have thought he could make it, or maybe he just panicked. In any event, in the two or three seconds he had to make a decision he made the wrong one. If he had braked for an instant he might have given himself room to pull in behind the Peugeot. Instead he tried to get ahead of them, accelerating and going for a gap that wasn't really there. As he wrenched the car onto the hard shoulder, he clipped the corner of the truck and Cohen saw the Opel stagger, then seemingly recover, then spin wildly into the guard rail before flipping over.

It filled the Peugeot's windscreen as it proceeded before them on its side, deluging them with sparks and the scream of metal. With the grace of a toboggan, it drifted into the path of the truck to be tossed aside as though it was a piece of flotsam.

The last Cohen saw of the Opel, it was twisting in mid-air, hurled there by the vortex of its own momentum, passing over the roof of the Peugeot like some doomed plane that had lost its wings. Their driver was still braking when Cohen heard the awful commotion of the impact. There was a momentary silence and then the crump of an explosion.

Still on his knees in the seat well, Cohen turned to see Bourdonnec watching the flames through the rear window. In their intermittent light his face was angular and impassive, shadowed by dark stubble, nothing remotely boy-like about him.

Cohen lay inert in the back seat of the Peugeot, feeling his bruises and an overwhelming torpor. Reeling from the clutter of the night's events, he had learned about the fate of the three men in the Opel as though Bourdonnec was reporting casualties in some distant, who-cares war. They, their deaths, meant nothing to him.

They were incinerated, Bourdonnec said, and Cohen thought, *How terrible*.

The car was stolen. *Oh, really?*

Two handguns found in the ashes. *Interesting*.

In his mind, tired of the news, Cohen switched channels.

Red and white cones guarding the scene reduced the expressway to a single lane, creating a tailback that stretched towards the city as far as Cohen could see. A small army of gendarmes directed traffic with brisk efficiency, scolding the rubbernecks who dallied for a better look at the wreckage. Pompiers worked to remove the remains. There was a stench in the air of burnt rubber and over-fried chicken; acrid but also sweet.

Bourdonnec said, 'It will take us a while to find out who they were.'

Cohen thought, *This has nothing to do with me*, but he knew better. Of course it did.

'I didn't hear from her all day. Then, in the evening, I called Silva's apartment to see how she was doing, and she said "fine". She said she might spend the night there, which I didn't like. I said, "What if he comes back?" but she just said, "Quit worrying, willya?" in that irritating American accent she sometimes uses. I didn't argue with her. Frankly, I was sick of the whole business by then ... You want more coffee?'

Cohen said, 'No. No, thank you.' If he never tasted Nescafé again it would be too soon.

'Then, at about eleven o'clock, perhaps a little earlier ... I know the children were asleep and Dominique had gone to bed. I was in here, washing up the dinner things. I didn't hear her come in. We had given her a key, of course. Suddenly she was standing where you are now with this look on her face. She was so happy – no, much more than happy. I don't know how to say it. *Radieuse?*'

'Radiant.'

'She was radiant. Those eyes of hers, they can be so sad even when she smiles. But not that night. That night they were alive, dancing. You know how she looked? She looked like a woman in love.'

'*Papa?*'

The face of a small boy peered into the kitchen, examining Cohen with frank curiosity. He wore a pair of glasses with bright red frames and corrective lenses.

'*Oui, chéri?*'

'*Qu-est ce que tu fais?*'

'*On parle.* Come and say hello to a very important man from England. This is Gaspard, Monsieur Cohen.'

'*Enchanté.*'

'Come on, in English.'

The little boy held out his hand and gravely said, 'How do you do. It is a pleasure to meet you.' Cohen smiled and shook the hand and Gaspard reached up to kiss his cheek.

'*Tu parles de quoi?*' he asked his father.

'We are talking about Grace.' He picked up the boy and held him easily in one arm; as easily as last night he had held the gun. 'Gaspard is Grace's favourite, aren't you, *chéri?*'

'*Elle arrive?*'

'Soon, we hope, don't we Monsieur Cohen?'

'*Je vais le dire à Maman.*'

'Okay, why don't you do that.' He put down the boy

and watched him run from the kitchen.

'When Gaspard was three my wife became very ill. It was a viral infection in her lungs that would not go away. Hydrocortisone, antibiotics, the doctors tried everything but she just got weaker. In the end we sent her to the sea, to Brest, to where her father now lives, for the air. The sea air, we thought it might help. She was away for almost two months and it was very difficult for me: my job, taking care of the children. Well, the other two, they can take care of themselves but Gaspard was very . . . *nécessiteux*?'

'Needy.'

'Yes, needy. So, Grace came to Paris, to live here, to take care of Gaspard. She took leave from her job, for a month, maybe more. I had never thought of her as a mother but you should have seen her with that child. *Incroyable!* She adored him. She was so loving, so patient, so . . . *sensible*. After she was gone I told Dominique: within a year Grace will have a child of her own. She laughed at me. "*Jamais!* Grace will never give up her work." I told her she was wrong. I said, "No, Dominique, Grace has changed. This is the new Grace who wants a child at her breast, not a gun to her head." And Dominique said, "There are many Graces, Gilles, more than you know, more than you will ever know." She said, "Grace has not changed, she cannot change. What you have seen is one of the ghosts she keeps inside her; the Grace she might have been." She was right, of course.'

Cohen said, 'And which Grace did you see that night

when she came back from Silva's?'

'That was the old Grace. What I saw in her eyes had nothing to do with *l'amour*. It was exhilaration, *joie*. She had picked up the scent, you see, and she was intoxicated.'

'Harling's scent?'

'Yes. "I know where he is, Gilles," she said. "I know where he is." '

'But she didn't tell you?'

Bourdonnec shook his head. 'She didn't tell me anything. I said, "Where did you find it?" and she said I had to guess. Well, how could I guess? Whatever she found, it could have been anywhere. She gave me some riddle about a camera: "A camera never lies but movies can be misleading." ' Bourdonnec shrugged as if to say what was he supposed to make of that? 'I became a little bit annoyed with her. I said, "Well, maybe he is no longer where you think he is," and she said, "Oh yes he is. He's trapped, Gilles, he can't move. He's mine." I said, "Trapped? Where is he trapped? Europe? Africa?" She said, "Close." I asked if he was in a jail, if that was why he could not move? She said, "I'll bet it feels like one." In the end, I gave up. I wasn't in the mood for playing games. I told her I was going to bed and we would talk in the morning. Except we didn't, because in the morning she was gone.'

'She didn't say goodbye?'

'No. She left a note here on the table. "*Mille mercis et mille bisous.*" And that was the last I heard from or about her, until her father called Dominique.'

Cohen had a question he'd been holding back, wary of how it might be received. 'When Grace disappeared, and the police established that she'd flown to Paris, Scotland Yard put out a bulletin, through Interpol, I think, and—'

'And you want to know why I never saw it, why they did not come to me?'

'Yes. It just seemed—'

'My friend, what I did for Grace was not official. There is no file that mentions her name – or Silva's name for that matter. Nobody knew except for my men.'

'I see.'

'Do you? You think you understand? I doubt it. *Allez!*' He threw the dregs of the Nescafé into the sink. 'We need to sleep. We will be busy this evening. You can have the boys' room.'

'Oh, no. Surely there's a hotel . . .'

'No hotels, Harry. Until we find out what is going on I want you with me, please. If you are killed it will be very bad for my reputation.' He grinned. 'Besides, I like you.' He took Cohen's arm and led him towards the bedroom. 'I will like you even more, perhaps, when you leave Paris and somebody else can worry about who is trying to kill you.'

Cohen did not bother to undress. Under a helicopter gun-ship suspended in mid-air, he lay down on a boy's bed – sometimes Flint's bed – and fell asleep almost instantly.

* * *

At one of the pavement tables of the café La Palette on the Rue de Seine, Cohen and Bourdonnec waited for the closing ritual of the Galerie Pythéas to begin. It was nearly seven o'clock, time for the arrival of the haughty night-time guardians of Mario Silva's plundered treasure. Then, if all stayed the same, Mario would commence his evening pilgrimage to the market – except, on this particular evening, he would get no further than the junction with the Rue Jacob. Three of Bourdonnec's men were lurking on the corner, ready to take him down, while another half-dozen detectives and uniformed police were preparing to storm the gallery. They anticipated – even hoped – that they might meet with some resistance.

'The guards are CRS,' Bourdonnec said. 'Riot police. They have a certain reputation.'

Cohen said, 'I know. I've encountered them.'

'Really?'

'It was 1972. I was an exchange student, fifteen years old, in Paris for the first time, and I fell in love with a woman called Katrina. Puppy love, of course. She was much older than I was – at least seventeen – and she smoked cigarettes and drank Pernod for breakfast, and I had never met anybody like her. I would have gladly followed her to the ends of the earth. Unfortunately, I followed her to a student demonstration on a particularly tense evening when the CRS had decided to clear the street. I was trying to get out of the way when they clubbed me to the ground.'

'And your lover?'

'Never my lover, alas. I have a vague memory of lying

on the ground, covered in blood, and her crouching down, shouting, "Kill the pigs!" I never saw her again.'

'So, you were a revolutionary, Harry Cohen.'

'Hardly.'

'I think so. I think you are full of surprises.'

Thirty feet away, two men stepped into the window of the Galerie Pythéas, one young and willowy with foppish hair, the other precisely matching Bourdonnec's description of Mario Silva.

The inspector said, 'It's time. Stay here, please, and enjoy the show.'

'And then?'

'Afterwards, we'll take Silva to his apartment. Join us there. *A tout à l'heure.*'

He took his leave and strolled across the street towards the gallery, hands in pockets, ridiculously thin. He stood with his back to the window, paying no apparent attention to the blue Peugeot van that came to a halt alongside him. From where Cohen sat, he looked like a boy waiting for his girl – no threat at all to the emerging guards with their fuck-you expressions.

There was no immediate sound when the window shattered. It turned white, then lemon then dirty orange, and Cohen sat transfixed, mesmerised by the stark beauty of its lethal disintegration.

seven

Flint leaving France on the first available train, travelling second-class so as not to squander her reserves. She has paid cash for her ticket, making her anonymous, and in this part of Europe that has no borders there are no formalities – no need to show her passport or any form of identity when she crosses the frontier near Mons. She has left no paper-trail in the wake of her departure, no easy way to establish her destination. In view of what she has learned from Mario's video, she believes this to be a sensible precaution.

She is not invisible, of course. If they come looking for her – as she fears they will – there are any number of potential witnesses to her flight: the ticket agent at the Gare du Nord and the woman at the newsstand who sold her a map and a magazine; her travelling companions on the high-speed TGV to Amsterdam, and particularly those who share carriage number eleven; the barman in the buffet car when she goes to buy her breakfast; the fresh-faced young buck in the seat across the aisle, who tries to catch her eye whenever she glances in his direction.

But if and when the witnesses are asked about the passenger in seat thirty-two, the woman they are likely to describe will not bear much resemblance to Grace Flint. In the privacy of the Bourdonnec's bathroom, working with limited resources, she has fashioned a woman who is older, plainer, more obviously used. Her hair is untidy and streaked with flecks of grey. There are blue shadows under her eyes. Her lips are thin and turn down at the corners. Underneath her unflattering dress, she wears a thick T-shirt – pilfered from Baptiste Bourdonnec's closet – that gives her bulk and flattens the outline of her breasts. She wears glasses and hose and sensible shoes. In short, she is a frump and it bothers her that the boy – a student by the look of him, and American, she guesses – maintains an interest in a woman who is surely old enough to be his mother.

The journey to Amsterdam will take a little over four hours and the magazine does not divert her for long. She stands up to retrieve her bag from the overhead rack and has to grab the back of her seat as the train hits a curve. The boy sees his chance and is on his feet saying, 'Here, let me get that for you.' He is a good six inches taller than she is and he lowers the bag with ease.

'*Merci*,' she says primly.

'You're welcome.' With his good teeth and his liquid eyes he reminds her of Jamie, which is not his fault, she supposes. 'Hi, I'm Jack. You going to Amsterdam?'

Where else would she be going on a train that doesn't

stop? She poses the question in curt French: '*Et où veux-tu que j'aille?*'

He shakes his head. 'Sorry, I don't speak the language.'

In that case, my young friend, kindly piss off.

'*Fous-moi la paix!*' is what she says with just a glimmer of a smile, as though she regrets his unfortunate inadequacy. Uncomprehending, he holds up his hands in surrender and resumes his seat. He will not bother her again.

Left to herself, she retrieves from her bag the notebook in which she has written down verbatim Mario Silva's videotaped declaration that is part confession, part accusation. In her scrawled hand it runs to twenty-seven pages, many of them scored with underlines she has drawn to give emphasis to some of what Mario had to say.

On one page there are vertical parallel bars running like railway tracks alongside the entire text to remind her that every word of this passage is important – though, in truth, she does not need reminding. She will go to her grave recalling this part of Mario's testimony.

I knew nothing of what had happened to Maitland until Harling turned up in Paris. I wasn't expecting his visit; he'd given me no warning. He simply arrived and we sat in this room . . .

Here Mario had broken off and looked away from the camera, as if to indicate where the two of them had sat. There was more than a bit of the thespian in Mario, Flint had decided. The camera was static, the focus fixed, but what began as a dry recitation had become enlivened by the pauses and gestures Mario introduced; the glancing asides he could not resist making.

. . . we sat in this room and Harling described how he had received a phone call the previous afternoon from our old friend Mr Brown – except his name wasn't Brown, of course. His real name, Harling told me, was Patrick Shilling and he was – he is – a senior official of the British Security Service, MI5. So, now I understood that our information came from impeccable sources.

Mario had allowed a flicker of a smile.

What did Mr Shilling have to say on this occasion? I will tell you. He warned Harling of Maitland's arrest, he told him to disappear. He said – and these were the precise words – that Harling should 'stay lost' until 'the threat has been eliminated'.

Mario leaned towards the camera.

Eliminated. What did that mean?

'It meant they put a fucking bomb on the plane,' Flint had said quietly to the screen, talking to Mario as though he was there.

We did not know, how could we know? But three days later we knew. Mario straightened in his chair and his voice became sonorous. *I wish to state for the record that after a further call to Patrick Shilling of the British Security Service, Frank Harling told me that The Enterprise had disposed of Mr Maitland, his wife and an American agent named Hechter.* 'Disposed of' – those were Shilling's words, according to Harling. 'Unfortunately' – Shilling's word again – they had failed to dispose of a British police officer named Grace Flint.

Her 'elimination', Shilling said, was only a matter of time.

Flint's body is on a train doing 180mph across the flatlands of northern France. Her mind is doing somersaults in Mario Silva's apartment.

Now, Miss Flint is known to Harling and, indirectly, to me. He would describe her as the nuisance of his life, and so would I. She has pursued him for as many years as I can remember. For reasons I do not understand, Miss Flint is obsessed with Frank Harling.

'You want reasons, Mario? Ever had a boot stamping on your face, Mario? Ever heard Frank telling some asshole to kill you?'

Mario smiles. *Perhaps she is secretly in love.*

'Cute,' Flint had said.

Mario, serious once more: *But Frank Harling and I have never countenanced violence. We are businessmen who bend the rules. We had nothing to do with the murders of Mr and Mrs Maitland and the agent, Mr Hechter, and it is not we who are hunting Grace Flint even as I speak. If anything happens to her it is not our responsibility. The responsibility lies with you, gentlemen – because, through your neglect, you have allowed The Enterprise to flourish.*

That burden lifted from his shoulders, Mario sipped from a glass of what might have been water.

Now, what if you who are watching this tape are even more culpable? What if you – and here Mario had pointed an accusing finger at the camera – *are part of the deception, part of The Enterprise? I am aware this is*

entirely possible, for I do not know how far the tentacles
reach. Perhaps I have put my trust in the wrong people?
Perhaps even now you are considering how you will
destroy this tape, how you will silence my voice from the
grave?

Another pause and then Mario slowly shook his head,
like a father about to shatter a child's illusions.

No, my friends. You will not silence Mario Silva. Be
aware of this: one month from now, if The Enterprise
has not fallen, several distinguished US senators, deputies
of the Assemblée Nationale, members of the Houses of
Parliament and the Bundestag and the Senato in Rome
and Senado in Madrid; representatives of the Eerste
Kamer and the Folketing and the Assembleia da
Republica – each of them will receive a copy of this
recording. So, too, will the editors of the New York
Times, The Times *of London,* Libération, Die Zeit, La
Stampa, El Pais, Handelsblad, Aftenposten, Expresso;
so, too, CNN and the BBC and TF1 and . . . *Well, you*
get the picture, gentlemen. This tape will be posted on
the Internet. It cannot be suppressed.

Another pause, and then: *Now, for your benefit, or*
perhaps the benefit of a wider audience, I will describe
what Frank Harling and I know about The Enterprise.

Silva rises from his chair and there were moments of
confusion as he came towards the camera and adjusted
its position and refocused the lens. Then the screen was
filled with a white poster board propped on the mantelpiece, Mario coming back into shot with a felt pen in his
hand.

'THE ENTERPRISE' he wrote dramatically in large capitals centred at the top of the board – hamming it up for the camera once more. Underneath, to the left, he wrote 'US'; to the right, 'UK'.

On the third line, in the left-hand column, he wrote 'The General' and, in parenthesis, 'Jackson/DIA?' In the right-hand column, under UK, he wrote, 'The Admiral' and, in parenthesis, 'NATO SAC?'

So, this is the primary structure of The Enterprise, the top of the pyramid, you might say, and these are the men who run it.

Mario, looking over his shoulder, speaking to the camera.

In the United States we have The General, whose name, we think, is Jackson. As I will describe, we have reason to believe he is – or was – a high official of the DIA.

Flint had held her breath.

And here, in the United Kingdom – Mario pointing to the right-hand column of his chart – *we have The Admiral. We do not know his name but, for reasons I will describe, we believe that he is – or was – a high official of the NATO Supreme Allied Command.*

Flint had said, 'Holy, holy shit.'

Mario, now full-face to the camera, like a lecturer before his class: *What was the purpose of The Enterprise? I will tell you. It was to extort money – millions of dollars, more than fifty-million dollars – from those of us who bend the rules. How did The General and his friends do that? By providing us with 'protection' against those law enforcement and intelligence agencies that were investigating our activities. What protection? Information, gentlemen; specific, detailed information about the progress of those investigations. Where did that information come from? From corrupt agents, from those very people who pursued us. Which agents, which agencies? I will tell you.*

Mario turned back towards his chart and drew two vertical lines – one in the left column, one in the right – and began writing two lists of acronyms, providing as he went a spoken running commentary.

DIA, Defense Intelligence Agency; CIA, Central Intelligence Agency; DEA, Drug Enforcement Administration; FBI, Federal Bureau of Investigation; EPIC, El Paso Intelligence Center; FinCEN, Financial Crimes Enforcement Network. And here, under the Admiral – Mario moving to the right-hand column – *MI5, Military Intelligence as it used to be, now the Security Service; MI6, also known as SIS, the Secret Intelligence Service; GCHQ, Government Communications Head Quarters; SFO, Serious Fraud Office . . .'*

'I forgive you, Mario,' Flint had said.

In a corner of the crowded buffet car, Flint drinks hot chocolate and nibbles a *sandwich jambon*. The ham tastes of nothing but she forces it down. She has not eaten for almost thirty-six hours and she knows she cannot afford the weight loss; already the watchband on her wrist is loose.

In her purse is the notebook that she guards as though

it is an heirloom. It is all the evidence she has and that fact is making her uneasy. She now thinks she was wrong to leave the tape in Mario's flat; to return *Frantic* to its position on the bookshelf, as she had restored all of Mario's other possessions to their rightful places. At the very least she could – she knows she should – have made an audio copy. She could have called Gilles and asked to borrow a tape recorder. She did not do so because Mario's accusations had persuaded her there was no one she could trust, not even Gilles. A flush of guilt that she could ever think such a thing now adds to her disquiet.

On the other hand.

Turning her back to the corner so she can watch for prying eyes, she takes the notebook from her purse and finds the relevant passage.

Over time it became clear to us that The Enterprise had sources of official information in many countries, especially in Europe. Italy for one, and Germany, and the Netherlands and, most of all, France. For example, in August of 1995, Shilling gave Harling complete details of a surveillance operation that was being conducted in Paris against one of his clients by the Brigade Criminelle. Harling told the client, of course, and the operation came to nothing.

One more of Mario's pauses and then a rhetorical flourish.

So you see, gentlemen, the tentacles of The Enterprise reached far beyond its natural boundaries.

To the Brigade Criminelle, apparently, of which Gilles Bourdonnec is an inspector. Flint pushes the unworthy thought away but there is no antidote to its poison. She is infected by suspicion. There is nobody she can trust – nobody she will trust – until she has found Frank Harling and pinned him to the wall.

She turns to the last page of her notes and takes comfort in what she has written there; Mario's coda, his final gift to her.

Girne.

Frank's present whereabouts, the haven that he thinks is safe.

When she returns to the carriage Jamie's look-alike is asleep, his long limbs akimbo. She retrieves her bag from under the seat where she had pushed it for safe-keeping and puts away her notebook. There is still more than two hours to go before they reach Amsterdam and she resolves to spend the time refining her plans.

She is heading north because Girne – and Frank – lie far in the opposite direction and her aim is to confuse. Since she is the prey as well as the hunter, she knows she must avoid the predictable moves. Logic would have sent her from Paris to Italy or, better still, Greece; in any event, south. But if she was in pursuit of someone hell-bent on reaching Frank's haven, she would know precisely where to look and where to wait. Thus she will avoid them all, all of the obvious places. If The Enterprise finds her it will not be because she was obvious.

In terms of resources, she is not badly off. Paris was much less expensive than she had feared, leaving her with abundant cash that she has changed into dollars:

nearly $1,600 in her purse, $5,000 hidden in her bag. She has enough of a wardrobe to ring the changes and she still has two passports – though therein lies a danger.

If The Enterprise is half as good as Mario claims, then, sooner or later, it will know that she travelled to Paris as Suzanne Williams, the name on the leftover cover passport she had neglected to return. Escape IDs are meant for one-time use, get-the-hell-out-of-here eventualities, and she now regrets wasting it for trivial purposes.

She had feared that if she used her genuine passport to leave London, Commander Glenning would have learned of her trip, and even the purpose of it. So what? she asks herself with the clarity of hindsight. What would he have done? Barked at her? Certainly. Suspended her? Perhaps. Had her killed? Not likely.

But The Enterprise.

It is not we who are hunting Grace Flint even as I speak.

Thank you, Mario.

Her elimination, Shilling said, was only a matter of time.

So, she cannot use her own passport, nor the escape – which is another reason why she is racing north, not south. In Amsterdam she knows of a man named Klaus who, for $1,000, will provide you with a Canadian passport in any name you choose, according to police intelligence.

There is a carping part of her that rebels at this component of the plan, for Klaus conducts his trade no-questions-asked and his usual customers are the scum of the earth, according to her reading of police intelligence. Which makes him worse, or just as bad, in Flint's estimation, and the carping part of her objects to this pact with the devil.

So what would you have me do?

There is no answer from her conscience. She will fatten Klaus's coffers because she has to. To appease herself she vows that one day she will ensure Klaus gets his comeuppance but for now he is a white knight in dirty armour, a dubious means to a rightful end.

In the Yard's canteen, when she was a mere detective sergeant, they used to kid her about the connotations of her name: 'Got a spark, Flint? Give us a light.' They were implying she was hard.

She shrugs away the memory and concentrates on her plan.

She will get a room near the Central Station at one of the gay-run B&Bs where no one will care who she is or what she calls herself. Klaus works nights in a bar on Herengracht and she will see him this evening, if her luck holds. Two days to get the passport, maybe three. She will spend the time touring the travel shops, looking for the best deal on a flight to the Turkish coast and then a ferry to Girne.

An odd name, she thought. On the map of Cyprus she bought at the Gare du Nord, the pretty little port where she and Jamie spent their first holiday together was still called Kyrenia but its official name was Girne – just one of the enforced changes that has turned the northern half of the island into a pariah state. It is not even called Cyprus anymore, but the Turkish Republic of Northern Cyprus; one half of an armed camp with more rampant soldiers poised on the dividing line than anywhere else on earth, except Korea.

That was Frank's joke, on the cryptic postcard she had found hidden in the sleeve of *Frantic*.

Like North Korea but the food's better. So is the climate.

There was a picture of the harbour and she wonders what has become of the Dome Hotel and the corner room with its wide balcony on the top floor which she and Jamie rarely left before evening. Then they would walk down to one of the open-air restaurants on the quayside and feast on meze and Cankaya wine, and Jamie would read to her from the guidebook, proposing itineraries that were never kept. He would say, 'Tomorrow we really should do something,' and she would say, 'We *are* doing something,' and he would laugh and say, 'No, I mean visit a castle, or something,' and she would say, 'Sure.'

She imagines that it will be in one of those restaurants that she will first encounter him.

'Hi, Frank. Remember me?' Something like that.

And then what? the carping voice demands to know but she doesn't yet have an answer.

Jamie is still asleep – except it's not Jamie, of course. It's the boy who looks like Jamie, or how Jamie used to look in the days when trust was a word still in Flint's vocabulary, before she knew better.

They have arrived at Amsterdam Central and the carriage is emptying and her first inclination is to leave him be. But then she thinks better of it and touches his face. She sees his startled eyes and says, 'Unless you want to go back to Paris, this would be a good time to wake up.'

She's moving down the aisle when she hears him call after her, 'Hey, thanks. Thanks a lot.'

De nada. She once fell in love with a boy on a train, but that was a lifetime ago, before she knew better.

Mingling with the crowd, she moves from the platform to the concourse and follows the directions to the *dames-toilet*. She pays five dollars for the use of a spic and span *cabine* that has a wash basin and a shower and two fresh towels. She strips off her clothes and ties the dress and the hose into a bundle that she will abandon in some convenient litter can.

Now she rids herself of the rest of her disguise, standing under the shower, scrubbing away the makeup from her face and the talcum powder from her hair.

Her mask restored to its near-eternal flawlessness, she chooses what to wear to complete her transformation: a pair of jeans that are just a little tight across her buttocks; brown suede ankle boots with heels that add two inches to her height; a linen shirt the colour of saffron with the top three buttons left undone.

For accessories she selects from her collection a man's-sized watch, a diamond engagement ring, a pair of heart-shaped ear studs and a deep blue silk bandanna that she ties around her throat. She puts mousse in her hair and combs it back behind her ears. A pair of sunglasses perched on her head help to keep it in place.

Examining herself in the mirror she is satisfied that – to the casual observer, the potential witnesses – she bears no resemblance at all to the woman who travelled in carriage eleven, seat thirty-two, of that morning's express from Paris, nor to any official photograph of Grace Flint that Patrick Shilling might obtain from the files.

To complete her new persona she considers what name and nationality to give herself. In her countless different guises she has been everything from Tracy to Ulvhild; from an Essex girl with attitude to a Norwegian enchantress who could melt ice with her allure. Names are important to her for they set the inner tone and the outward appearances, changing the way she walks, the set of her head, even the way she feels. Once, in Miami, she was Neysa and – freed of her English inhibitions – she discovered she could dance the *marimba* as though she had been born to it.

Who will she be today?

On the train, in her mind, she was Enid, a spinster's name in her experience. For Mario, she was Katia, more exotic, more daring. Before that, she was sunny Suzanne, a name . . .

Something's wrong!

The certainty hits her like a slap in the face from an unseen hand. The proof evades her for the moment but she knows in her bones she is on the brink of a catastrophe. It is like that instant on a plane when the engine note changes and the wing drops. She holds onto the basin, waiting for the plunge.

Staring at her own reflection in the mirror, she wills herself to replay her thoughts, and now she gets it. Suzanne! Where is Suzanne?

And now she is down on her knees, pulling her things from her bag, searching for the passport she shouldn't have used. It is not there, and neither is the wedge of one-hundred dollar bills that she had hidden in her underwear. Five-thousand dollars that would have taken her to Kyrenia. Gone.

She leaves the *cabine* looking as though a bomb has hit it, taking only her purse, running onto the concourse with murder on her mind.

Jamie, fucking Jamie.

She means his look-alike, of course, but at this moment they are indivisible to her.

Using her elbows, she barges her way through the crowds, not caring who she offends. In her saffron shirt she looks like a Buddhist monk run amok as she races from platform to platform, from the newsstand to the bureau de change to the coffee shop to the taxi queue to the bus stop, her elbows pumping like pistons, her eyes streaming with tears of rage.

She retraces her steps, running even harder, the crowds now parting as she hurtles towards them.

She runs until she can run no more, until there is nowhere else to look. She lurches into a pillar and grabs hold of it, fighting for breath – fighting for life, as it feels.

Little by little she recovers. She gets her bearings and slowly heads back towards the ladies toilet to retrieve her belongings.

How could she be so stupid? Her anger is turning inwards, for all the good that will do her. She feels what she is: alone, hunted, trapped.

Face it, Flint, you've fucked yourself.

II

Marked by a small brass plate that does not tout for business, the law offices of Stern & Kreindler are located on Dreikönigstrasse in a building that also houses one of Zurich's many private banks. Four days after a Semtex bomb exploded at the Galerie Pythéas, Dr Gerhard Kreindler took the stairs to the third floor for the sake of his heart, arriving at precisely nine o'clock, his customary hour. As was also his custom, he exchanged a ritual greeting with his receptionist – 'Guten Morgen, Herr Doktor,' 'Guten Morgen, Frau Endler' – and then with his secretary, who was also Frau Endler. Else and Lise are sisters, indeed twins – though not identical – who constitute the entire staff of Stern & Kreindler. Stern being long dead, the clients are thus assured that the confidentiality of their affairs relies on the discretion of just three people. In his dignified way, the good doctor will, if asked, point out the advantages of such an arrangement.

The client list is small but extremely lucrative, a fact reflected in the quiet opulence of the offices. White oak panels line the walls, complemented by the beige of the carpets and the soft grey of the curtains and furnishings. Except for Dr Kreindler's mahogany desk – which belonged to his father – the furniture and the lighting are contemporary, thanks to the influence of the Endler sisters. Admiring their taste, and having never married, Dr Kreindler also accepts their advice on some of the additions to his wardrobe.

At his desk, served by Lise with a glass of hot water flavoured by a thin slice of lemon, the next part of his ritual is to attend to the morning post that she brings him in a calfskin portfolio, opened and sorted according to its importance.

On this particular morning – three days after Gilles Bourdonnec had emerged from the operating theatre of the St Claude Clinic following seven hours of drastic surgery – Lise stood by his desk, withholding the portfolio, which was not her usual practice.

'Is something wrong, Frau Endler?'

'Unfortunately, Herr Doktor.'

Now she opened the portfolio, placing it before him, and he quickly scanned the top page of the first letter which regretted to inform him of the untimely death of a mutual client.

It had been sent from Paris by an *avocat* known to Dr Kreindler who was as thorough as he was solicitous. Attached to his letter were reports from Paris newspapers describing the carnage on the Rue de Seine, and follow-up reports of the four police officers who still fought for life. There was a copy of Mario Silva's death certificate, and a second certificate attesting to the death of his assistant, both stamped with a *notaire*'s seal. There was a statement from the Ministry of Justice that roundly condemned their assassinations. Finally, there was an envelope, sealed with red wax, on which was written: 'For Dr Gerhard Kreindler. To be opened only by him and only in the event of my death. Signed Mario Silva.'

Dr Kreindler weighed the envelope in his hands.

'And how did this arrive?'

'By special courier, Herr Doktor.'

He snapped the seal with his fingers and tipped the contents onto his desk. There were two small keys attached to a silver ring, a banker's draft for $50,000 and a note, which the doctor read and then handed to Lise.

'You will prepare a label?'

'Of course,' she said. 'When will you travel?'

'Tomorrow, the noon flight. You might take this to the bank,' he said, handing her the draft.

'At once, Herr Doktor. As soon as you return.'

Taking the stairs to the ground floor, the doctor reflected on his long association with Mario Silva, the most civilized of clients. He would miss their long lunches and Silva's occasional gifts of fine wine almost as much as he would miss the fees.

But Dr Kreindler is philosophical about loss, as he is about most things. Entering the bank, descending to the vaults, he pushed such matters from his mind and contemplated the pleasures of Washington DC. Such a civilised city, in parts. Having completed his simple task, he thought he might linger there for a day or two. A visit to the Corcoran, perhaps, and dinner at Le Lion d'Or.

He was well known to the security guard but – this
being Switzerland – there were still the usual formalities
to be completed. Then he was alone in a locked room
lined wall-to-wall with three inch thick steel doors
guarding who-knew-what; what secrets, what plunder.

Silva's box contained only videotapes. Fifty tapes, all
of them identical, according to the note.

For now, Dr Kreindler was required to deliver only
one of them – personally, to the Director of the FBI.
Unlocking the box, he wondered what might be playing
at the Kennedy Center.

III

Even in his good moods Patrick Shilling wore a scowl that could frighten horses, according to his wife.

Horses and children, apparently, for there was a young girl watching him with a look of terror, unable to take her eyes away, seeming as though she might break into tears at any moment. Shilling stared back at her, wishing to imply that if she did start bawling he might – just might – throw her overboard. She was right to be alarmed by him. He did not like children, period, including his own.

Just now, there were a lot of things he didn't like.

There was a chop on the Solent and the bucking of the ferry was making him queasy. The French team he'd hired had turned out to be idiots and, doubtless, he would now receive the blame for their incompetence. He was pissed that Cohen was still alive, pissed that Flint had not been found. Most of all, he was pissed that Taggart had summoned him to the Isle of Wight in his Admiral's tone of voice, as though Shilling was a rating.

He thought about Taggart's wife and whether he should have her. She'd made it very clear that he could.

The child cried and its mother fussed and Shilling
looked away. He took out a packet of Marlboro and the
cretin sitting next to him pointed at the No Smoking
sign. Staring him down, Shilling lit a cigarette.

Christ! it was hot in here.

He pushed his way out of the salon and onto the
forward deck where a few hardy souls watched the
approach of Cowes through the bow spray. The swaying
masts of the yachts clustered in the harbour looked like
reeds in a marsh.

Taggart had a boat. So did Kurlack, come to that. He
called his *Invincible*, which is how he saw himself. Bit of
a joke, really, considering he was almost lame. He liked
to pretend it was a war wound but Shilling knew better.
The closest Jackson Kurlack had been to a war was
sitting in NATO headquarters in Brussels. Same was true
of Taggart, more or less. They were a couple of decrepit
armchair generals who had never got their hands dirty –
or, let's be real about this: one *brigadier*-general, one
vice-admiral. They weren't even pros in the intelligence
game. They had both been *seconded* to military intelligence when they were fit for nothing else.

The baleful bellow of the ship's horn announced the
ferry's imminent arrival.

Christ! He hated the fucking Isle of Wight.

Katherine Taggart showed him her tits, serving them tea
in what her husband called the library; a bit of an over-
statement when all he had was a couple of shelves of
books. Shilling had five times as many books still in

boxes that he'd never unpacked after moving out of the
marital home. He'd once told his wife he was going to
Borders to buy a book and she'd said, 'Why? You've
already got *lots* of books.' Silly cow.

'Thank you, Kate dear,' Taggart said, beaming at her.
'Now, I'm afraid, we've got business to discuss.'

'When don't you have business to discuss?' she said,
softening the reproach with a smile. To Shilling she said,
'You'll stay for supper, of course, Patrick? Spend the
night?'

You'd like that, wouldn't you? Shilling thought. Me
fucking you rigid in the conservatory while the old man
sleeps.

He was old, old enough to be her father and then
some; the proverbial Ancient Mariner compared to her –
and, not for the first time, Shilling wondered at Taggart's
folly. He spoke of his first wife – and the mother of his
children – as though she was dead, but Shilling knew
otherwise. After their daughter died, Shilling had established, she ran off with an itinerant yacht skipper she
met during Cowes week, and now she worked charters
in the Caribbean on any boat – with any man – that
would have her. Shilling had pictures.

And if Taggart thought that fickle Kate was here for
any other reason than the money, he was clearly delu-
sional. Her refined accent and her mannered ways
suggested a privileged upbringing but Shilling knew that
her mother was an alcoholic, her father a fake colonel
who conned an uncertain living out of old ladies in
Tunbridge Wells, selling them dodgy antique furniture

and *objets d'art*. Any time he wanted to, Shilling could make a phone call and Kate's papa, as she called him, would find himself answering difficult questions at the local nick.

Shilling knew that Kate clipped rose bushes in the garden, and served tea in the library, and endured the groping of Taggart's liver-spotted hands because of the millions he had stashed away; new money, money Shilling had acquired for him, incidentally. She was a gold-digger, pure and simple, a whore. As they all were.

Her husband said briskly, 'I'm afraid Shilling has to get back to London. Affairs of state and all that.'

'What a shame,' she said.

Next time, bitch. Sometime soon.

'What the hell do you think you're doing?'

Admiral Taggart, doing his Nelson impression. He'd have Shilling lashed to the mainbrace and flogged, if he could.

Shilling shrugged. 'It was botched.'

'Good God man, I know it was botched! I want to know how.'

'I called—'

'No names!'

'I spoke to ... a contact in French intelligence and asked him to take care of Cohen – as you wanted. He couldn't, or wouldn't, but he put me in touch with ... some people. They were supposed to be proficient.'

'Proficient! They blew up the Rue de Seine!'

'Hardly, and that was later. After they'd missed Cohen. Twice.'

'And, after they had "missed" Cohen, *twice*, as you put it, you still thought they were suitable for this operation? Have you gone mad?'

If you push it, Admiral, mad enough to snap your skinny neck, Shilling thought.

He said, 'There wasn't time to change horses. I knew Cohen was working with the French police, and I was pretty sure they would move against Silva. Couldn't have Mario running off his mouth, could we? And, as it turns out, I was right. They *were* about to take him.'

'But a bomb? In the middle of Paris in the rush hour? You approved this?'

'A miscalculation. They knew the window of Silva's place was bomb-proof and they said it would contain the explosion. The stupid buggers didn't know that applied only if the bomb was on the outside. As I said, they botched it. What else can I tell you?'

'And now there are four policemen at death's door.'

'Three of them will probably make it,' Shilling said nonchalantly, like a surgeon talking to the housemen after his rounds. 'The fourth, the inspector, he's doubtful, I'd say.'

'Doubtful?' Taggart shook his head in disbelief. His face was sagging, showing its age.

'Listen—'

'No! You listen, Shilling. This operation is totally out of control. I will not stand for your incompetence.'

Taggart was quivering with anger. Shilling contained his, for now.

'I want to know precisely what you're going to do to clear up this bloody awful mess you've created. Where's Flint?'

'Gone to ground.'

'And?'

'It's been more than a month now. Sooner or later she has to come up for air: make a phone call, buy a ticket, draw money, use her credit card – something. Sooner or later she'll show her pretty face, and then I'll know, and then I'll take care of it.'

'How much does she know?'

'I'll ask her.'

'If I'd known,' Taggart began and then broke off, getting out of his chair, walking over to the windows that looked onto the rose garden and the restless Solent beyond. His back to Shilling he said, 'And Cohen?'

'He's on his way to Miami. Gone to see Cutter. He got back from Paris last night and left this morning.' A beat, and then Shilling added, 'Perhaps Kurlack should take care of him?'

'*No names!*'

'His hoods did okay in Robertstown. Why not?'

Taggart continued staring at the garden. 'Why has he gone to see Cutter?'

'I don't know. Ask Devereaux.'

Taggart spun around, venom in his eyes – or perhaps it was panic. 'You damned fool!'

Fuck-me Kate put her head around the door and brightly inquired, 'More tea?'

eight

Cohen took a taxi from downtown Miami to Coconut Grove and waited in Monty's Restaurant for almost half an hour until Cutter came and found him and said, 'You ever thought of investing in a cell phone?'

Cutter was wearing baggy shorts and a loud Hawaiian shirt and he was making the hostess nervous.

'Excuse me?' Cohen said.

'You're in the wrong joint. If you had a phone I would have called you.'

'But you said Monty's. Isn't this . . . ?'

'Yeah, well there's new Monty's and there's old Monty's, and you can't see shit from here. Come on down. They've got conch fritter and jugs of beer and the best key lime pie you'll ever eat. And, there's someone I want you to meet.'

Monty's Raw Bar – the old Monty's – was mainly for the young crowd, apparently. Bronzed limbs on hard wooden benches and a lot of Spanish being spoken. Cutter led the way across the terrace to a table by the water's edge, Biscayne Bay spread out before them glittering in the mechanical sunlight.

'You okay? You look wrecked.'

'A bit of jet lag,' Cohen said. He was not going to admit that he hadn't really slept since Paris; that whenever he closed his eyes he was lurched awake by the shattering echo of the explosion. Gilles had looked dead when he'd reached him, his legs and back shredded to bloody meat by shards of glass. Cohen lifted a plastic cup of beer with both hands to minimise the shaking.

'How's your friend doing?' Cutter asked.

'Not well. His legs are in a terrible mess. He's lost his spleen and one of his lungs is shot to pieces. They may have to remove it if and when he can cope with the surgery. He's still on life support, of course.'

'Any word on the perps?'

'Sorry?'

'The perpetrators. The fucking assholes who did it.'

'Oh, I see. No, no word, so far as I know.'

'Okay, well that's something else we'll ask him about.'

Cohen shook his head trying to clear the fog. 'Him? I'm sorry, I don't—'

'Him. That sonofabitch over there.'

Cutter nodded his bull's head towards the end of the dock where a motor cruiser was moored with its stern towards them, no more than fifty feet from where they sat. Cohen hurried to put on a pair of glasses so he could read the name written on the transom: *Invincible*.

'You see him?'

'No.'

'The guy on the flying bridge.'

Now Cohen saw him: a man sitting in the shadow of an awning who was scanning the shoreline through a pair of binoculars.

'You see, Harry, those assholes, his assholes, they bombed the wrong plane. The Lear never made it, but the C-130 sure did. And, I'll say this for Maitland: he was one hell of a bookkeeper. Fastidious isn't the word. Every last cent accounted for.'

Cohen said, 'I don't understand.'

'Nor did I till two days ago. All we had was a lot of interesting numbers and dummy corporations and bank accounts we can't get into. Then I get a call from HQ, and you'd have thought it was the second coming, and I'm on the next plane to Washington, and guess what I'm looking at?'

'I have absolutely no idea.'

'I'm looking at Mario Silva's last testament, Harry – and that asshole's death warrant, if I have my way. Mario gave us chapter and verse, Harry, or as best he could, and suddenly Maitland's numbers make sense – a *lot* of sense – and now Jackson fucking Kurlack has got more bugs on him than a dead groundhog, and we're going to get the sonofabitch, and then we'll ask him about your friend.'

Cohen felt as though he had lost his shaky grasp on reality. 'Will you please slow down. Who is Jackson Kurlack?'

'He is,' said Cutter, nodding towards the boat. 'Brigadier-General Kurlack, Defense Intelligence Agency, retired. Except he's not retired, not to my way of thinking. He's been working his ass off, he and his partner; his British partner, by the way. That Italian guy, Count Cavour, remember what he said? "If we did for ourselves what we do for our country, what rascals we would be." Well, that's what they've been doing, Harry: they've been doing it for themselves. You following any of this?'

'No,' said Cohen. 'Perhaps if you would just begin at the beginning?'

'Exactly what I plan to do. We'll get ourselves some conch and some pie and then I'll take you to the office. I've got a bunch of my pilgrims standing by to give you the story.'

'Thank you.'

'Yeah, well, you might want to wait before you say that, Harry. Your wife, your late wife, what was her maiden name?'

'Taggart. Why?'

'That's what I thought,' said Cutter.

The headquarters of the Federal Crimes Joint Task Force was a bleak four-storey office block set behind a chain-link fence on an industrial estate just east of the North Dade Detention Center, which – with its heavy metal gate barring the entrance, the steel window shutters on the ground floor – it somewhat resembled. The roof bristled with radio aerials and a dirty grey satellite dish, adding to the sense of embattlement. It looked to Cohen as though the Task Force had prepared for a lengthy siege. Cutter led the way through the metal detector in the lobby, setting off a strident alarm.

A Metro-Dade cop, seated in a booth behind a thick acrylic shield, looked up from his book and said into a microphone, 'You carrying, Mr Cutter?'

'Jerry, you *know* I'm carrying.'

'What about your friend?'

Cutter grinned. 'What about it, Harry, you got a gun?'

Cohen shook his head. 'Hardly.'

The guard looked him over as though he didn't much care for what he saw. 'How about you take all of the metal objects out of your pockets and then you walk through the detector one more time?'

'You've got to do it, Harry, or he won't let us in.'

Cohen did as he was told and only then did the guard hit the button that unlocked the inner door.

'Welcome to the war zone,' Cutter said.

In Cutter's spacious office on the fourth floor – a room that had no windows and the ambience of a bunker – four of his pilgrims waited for them: three young men, casually dressed, perhaps because it was a Saturday, and a small woman with an angry face who said, 'Just so you know, I'm objecting to this meeting.'

'Harry Cohen, meet Carrie Evanovich,' Cutter said. 'Best Assistant US Attorney in the southern district when she's not being a pain in the ass. Carrie thinks that because you're a Brit you're certainly a spy and probably gay. I told her, of course you're a goddammed spy, that's why you're here!'

Cutter had taken off his shirt and was stepping out of his shorts.

The woman said, 'That's bullshit, Aldus. I'm objecting because this is in breach of DOJ regulations,' but Cutter ignored her.

'As for your sexual orientation, well, hey, rumour has it that Edgar J. used to wear a dress. Harry, say hello to Jack Stenning, Dieter Branch, Oliver Barry, and take a seat. Pilgrims, let's get started. Jack, you want to get the lights?'

The room went dark for an instant and then it was lit by the glow of a screen above and behind Cutter's desk. An image appeared, black and white and slightly fuzzy until an unseen hand sharpened the focus. It was evidently a surveillance photograph taken with a long lens: a man waiting to cross the street, his face caught in profile. In the half-light Cohen could see the near-naked Cutter taking a fresh shirt out of its wrapping – getting dressed, apparently.

'Gerhard Kreindler, Swiss national, DOB December 10, 1940. Nothing against him in our files, not listed in NADDIS.' A second image, this one full-face, flashed onto the screen and Cutter continued, 'Runs a two-bit law firm out of Zurich, Stern and Kreindler, except there is no Stern; just Gerhard here and a couple of secretaries. Two days ago, he flies into Dulles, Swissair, first class, takes a limousine downtown and walks into headquarters with a package that he wants to deliver personally – *personally*, mind – to the director. After they'd run it through the X-ray, and calmed down, they let him meet with a deputy assistant director, and Gerhard here explains that he represents one Mario Silva . . .'

An unsmiling face appeared on the screen, one of those photos taken in a booth.

'Look familiar, Harry?'

'Not really. I only saw Silva from a distance before he was killed. Afterwards . . . Well, afterwards, there was nothing left to recognise.'

Cutter grunted and said, 'Correction. The late, lamented Mario Silva. Portuguese national, DOB June 9, 1958, resident in Paris, dealer in antiquities – or so Gerhard would have us believe. A little over a month ago, about a week after Hechter and the Maitlands were murdered, Gerhard gets a call from his client. He's worried. He's got information – dangerous information. He thinks his own life might be on the line. So, he's made a tape and put it somewhere safe . . .'

The screen went blank momentarily and then Silva reappeared, sitting in an armchair, relaxed, his legs crossed, the tips of his fingers held together to form a steeple under his chin, waiting to begin.

'And Mario tells his lawyer, "Anything happens to me, Gerhard, I want revenge. They take me out, you get this tape to the proper authorities" – which is me as it turns out, cause for once Washington put two and two together and didn't come up with five. Dieter, you want to tell us what we're looking at?'

Across the room from Cohen, a voice in the dark said, 'It's not the original. First or maybe second generation copy but it's not been tampered with. No cuts, no insertions. It's what he made.'

'You know what happened to the original, Harry? You want to know what I think?'

Cohen was a mile ahead of him. *She gave me some riddle about a camera*, Gilles had said. *A camera never lies but movies can be misleading.* 'Flint's got it,' he said, and Cutter laughed.

'See, pilgrims, I told you he was smart. Roll the tape, Jack. Let's see how smart he really is.'

They had reached that part of Mario's performance where he stood before the mantelpiece writing on a board, and Cohen felt a stabbing tightness inside his chest as though he was being crushed by the weight of his outrage.

'The Admiral,' Mario wrote, and, in parenthesis, 'NATO SAC?' and now Cutter's barbed inquiry made ghastly sense. Taggart was the family name – as in Sir Adrian Taggart, formerly Vice-Admiral Taggart, formerly of Defence Intelligence, formerly attached to NATO's Supreme Allied Command. Annie's father, Harry Cohen's father-in-law.

Taggart. 'That's what I thought,' Cutter had said.

Cohen stared at the screen but what he saw were images of other things: of the ice in Taggart's eyes when Annie had announced their engagement; of the contemptuous note he wrote declining to attend their wedding; of the letters sent to Annie from Belgium that were always addressed to 'Miss A. TAGGART', the name in capitals and underlined – letters that latterly she hid

from her husband; the one letter he'd found that called
him 'your Jew boy'.

She'd gone to the Isle of Wight to die, her capacity to
resist her father's will exhausted by the cancer that
devoured her. Cohen had not understood her decision
and his anger and confusion had only made matters
worse. They had not spoken at all during the last month
of her life.

And now Cohen saw himself on the car deck of the
ferry, hunched against the wind, going to Annie's funeral,
a funeral to which he had not been invited.

Now he was at the cemetery, standing apart from the
other mourners, Taggart tall in their midst, staring his
defiance. Afterwards he'd said, 'She's back for good now,
Cohen. Back where she belongs.'

Taggart, not Cohen, was the name carved on her
headstone.

'Harry?' Cutter's voice bringing him out of his reverie.
'You okay? You want to take a break?'

'No,' said Cohen quietly – the answer to both
questions.

On the screen, Mario was writing acronyms, glancing
over his shoulder to recite their meaning to the camera.
*And here, under the Admiral, MI5, Military Intelli-
gence as it used to be, now the Security Service . . .*

Well, not quite, Mario, Cohen thought; not exactly
under the admiral.

So far as Cohen knew, Vice-Admiral Sir Adrian
Taggart was only an advisor to the British security and
intelligence services. All of them.

II

'They met at SAC, as far as we know. Taggart was stationed there from May of 1990 to October of '93, when he retired. In that time frame we've got Kurlack visiting SAC on six occasions for meetings that were also attended by Taggart. Of course, they may have met before Taggart located to Belgium. We're still checking on that.'

Oliver Barry glanced at Cutter as if to say, 'We haven't had much time to work with this stuff,' and Cutter nodded his forgiveness. During what he called Mario's dog and pony show he'd put on a long-sleeved shirt and tie and a pair of dark blue pants and he now looked something more like the senior agent in charge of the federal government's most potent task force. The force's motif, chosen by Cutter, was set into the centre of the conference table at which they sat; a rampant bald-headed eagle, the scales of Justice in its fearsome talons.

'Any input, Harry? Know who his pals are?'

'No.'

'Never talked to you about his time at NATO?'

'He barely said a civil word to me about anything.'

Cutter was prepared to let it go but Carrie Evanovich said, 'Why?'

'Because he detested me on first sight, and I grew to detest him.' She cocked an eyebrow as if she knew there was more and Cohen added, 'He didn't want his daughter married to a man he thought was a Jew.'

'Piece of work,' said Cutter. 'Ollie, go ahead.'

'Kurlack took early retirement in June '94, as a consequence of downsizing at DIA. Meaning he was kicked out. What you might call two-cents-worth of the peace dividend. He moved down here – initially to Lauderdale – and three weeks after that we have Taggart flying into MIA – Miami International – paying him a visit.'

From the folder before him Barry produced an immigration entry card and passed it to Cohen. The handwriting was unmistakable: the name TAGGART, written in the same sloping capitals that had addressed the poisonous letters to Annie.

'Taggart was here for three weeks, we think – INS is still looking for the departure stub. That means he would have left on or around July 29, '94. Three weeks later, Harling and Silva were arrested in London by the SFO and Harling was sprung by "Mr Brown", or so he says in his affidavit.'

'A.k.a. Patrick Shilling,' Cutter said.

'We then have a series of get-togethers between Harling and Shilling, culminating in the meet at the Royal Garden Hotel in May '95 . . .'

'And, Jack,' said Cutter. 'Tell us why that date's relevant?'

Jack Stenning had open before him a ring binder holding a sheaf of documents perhaps two inches thick. Cohen could see that the top page bore an elaborate seal and some fancy lettering. 'May 31, 1995, Maitland incorporated the Strongbow Trust. The usual bullshit: off-the-shelf shell company with a couple of nominee directors, girls from the bank.'

Stenning turned the page. 'Same date, Strongbow opened an account with New World, which was Maitland's standard procedure. What's not standard, what grabs your attention, is that the opening balance is shown as zero. All the other New World companies we've looked at – some sixteen hundred and seventy-five – kicked off with an initial deposit of at least a few thousand dollars. Strongbow's had zip until June 8, when Maitland made a transfer: one million dollars taken out of the Tindale account and paid into Strongbow.'

'Buller's "ex gratia" payment,' said Cohen.

'No. Tindale is Harling's piggy bank, remember? Remember Maitland said that Tindale was the only account where he knew for sure who the beneficiary was? Buller didn't pay up until the thirteenth of that month. That's when we see another one million going into Strongbow, transferred from what looks like one of Buller's trusts.'

Cohen showed his puzzlement. 'Harling never mentioned that in his affidavit.'

'No, he didn't, did he?' Cutter chuckled. 'Nor did Mario, come to that. So, the question is, why would

Frank pay a million and why are they so coy about it? Any ideas, Harry?'

'Perhaps,' said Cohen, reaching down to find his briefcase. He had occupied his time on the flight from London working on a chronology that sought to make sense of the welter of events. Consulting it now he said, 'On the day before that transfer, Silva was sentenced to two years' imprisonment for fraud when he might have expected ten. Coincidence?'

'You believe in coincidences, Harry?'

'Not often.'

'Neither do I. You think they got to the judge?'

'I don't know,' said Cohen. 'According to the press reports, the judge spoke of "mitigating factors" that had been brought to his attention but he didn't say what they were.'

'You think Shilling went in to bat for Mario? Whispered in the judge's ear about unspecified favours Mario might have done for queen and country?'

'It's happened.' Cohen fidgeted in his chair.

'No shit! You ever do that, Harry, when you were with the Service?'

More often than I would care for you to know, thought Cohen, but he did not reply. In the back of his mind, the embryo of a suspicion was forming; a notion so malign it made him cold inside.

He held Cutter's stare until he smiled his surrender and said, 'Okay, Jack, go ahead,' and Stenning resumed his litany of payments received by the Strongbow Trust: dates, amounts, a host of transfers from a host of other trusts, all faithfully recorded by Maitland. The detail was lost on Cohen. His suspicion was hardening towards certainty and all he could think of was Devereaux.

Devereaux in the wine bar, his voice laced with sarcasm: *Could you have possibly believed that I was part of it? That I'd gone rogue? Is that what you thought, you ingrate?*

Yes, Cohen had said, and now he damned himself for his own stupidity.

'You still with us, Harry?' said Cutter.

'Of course.'

'Glad to hear it. Okay, so, bottom line, Strongbow takes in – what? About fifty million in a little over a year, Jack?'

'Forty-eight million, six hundred thousand, and change. Beginning with the Tindale deposit in June '95. Last deposit was four million on August 24, 1996.'

Four days before I blew the whistle, Cohen thought. Four days before I told him that I knew.

I'll find the phone, call my girl, tell her we've gone AWOL. Why don't you get us something more palatable to drink?

He never did come back.

'Which goes where?' Cutter said.

Now Stenning began a new litany of out-flowing transfers, money that left Strongbow's account almost as soon as it had arrived. Transfers to banks in Liechtenstein, the Isle of Man, the Channel Islands, the Cayman Islands, Bermuda, Antigua and just about every other bolt-hole and haven Cohen had heard of.

'So what about the rest of it, Jack?'

'Cash withdrawals. Made by Maitland always immediately before he made one of his trips, which are all nicely documented in his expense reports.'

'In that fourteen months, how many of those trips were to Miami?'

Stenning consulted a second file and said 'Nine.'

'And how much did he bring?'

Stenning did some quick arithmetic and said, 'In total, before those particular trips, Maitland withdrew eight-point-five million dollars from the Strongbow account.'

'What about the UK? Maitland make any trips over there?'

Stenning confirmed what Cutter already knew: in the same period, eight trips to London, eleven million dollars withdrawn.

Cutter nodded his head. 'You getting the picture, Harry?'

'I'm not sure. You're implying that Maitland was taking cash to Kurlack, Taggart, perhaps Shilling and . . .' Cohen broke off, unsure of his direction. 'Why? They were transferring money to secure accounts all over the world without any difficulties. Why would they risk Maitland carrying cash?'

'They had bills to pay, of course. Come on, Harry! All those slimeballs they had working for them, all those corrupt cops and spooks and fucking agents – excuse my language, Carrie . . . All those assholes who were selling their operations down the river, they weren't going to take a cheque, were they? American Express, that'll do nicely? Forget it. Oh, maybe some of them, the regular snitches, maybe they set up accounts, took transfers. But the average Joe, when he sells out his brothers, he wants Judas money; thirty pieces of silver in his hand, except nowadays it's hundred-dollar bills. Get it?'

'I suppose so, but it's all surmise, isn't it?'

'You can say that again,' said Carrie, and Cutter grinned at her.

Cohen pressed on. 'I mean, I'm not sure you can even prove that Kurlack and Taggart ran The Enterprise, not on the strength of what Harling and Silva said in their statements. Surely, you need more?'

'You bet,' said Cutter. 'Dieter, play the tape.'

'Now, Aldus, just a minute!' Carrie Evanovich had leapt to her feet as though she was on fire. 'You cannot do this.'

'Calm down.' To Cohen he said, 'Carrie's upset with me because—'

'No, Aldus!'

'Because I made her do something she wasn't too keen on.'

'*Aldus!*'

'Yesterday morning she got a warrant for Kurlack's phone on probable cause that was – well, perhaps just a little *improbable*.'

'*Jesus!*'

'Carrie, we're all on the same team. Who's he gonna tell? Who are you planning to tell, Harry?'

'Nobody,' said Cohen. 'I can't. I don't have the faintest idea what you're talking about.'

'You see, Carrie? It's fine. Harry's like one of those monks. You know? They take a vow of silence? Okay? Relax.'

Evanovich sat down, looking capable of murder.

'Given his intelligence background,' Cutter went on as though there had been no interruption, 'we figured he'd have secure communications – or, what he thought was secure. His problem – General Jackson fucking Kurlack's problem – is that he's been out of the game for four years and the NSA's now got stuff he never even dreamed of. So, Carrie here' – Cutter gave a nod to the still-simmering Evanovich – 'got a federal magistrate to sign a warrant that lets us listen to his calls for five days.'

'Subject to daily review,' she said. 'You might remember that.'

'Sure. And when you play him the first product tonight, he's going to feel like he was Solomon when he gave you the warrant. Roll the tape, Dieter.'

Dieter Branch pressed a button on a remote control and the room was filled with the crackle of static. Then came a high-pitched tone, then a clipped English voice coming over the speakers: 'Secure at this end.'

'Go ahead.'

'Well, I've spoken to him.'

Cutter said, 'Dieter, hold it there.' To Cohen he said, 'Is that Taggart?'

'Yes.'

Unmistakably so. Taggart on the phone: *Let me speak to my daughter.*

Evanovich said, 'Would you swear to that in court?'

'Yes.'

'Any doubts?'

'None.'

If she was mollified by his certainty she did not show it. Cutter nodded and Branch restarted the tape.

'And?'

'His excuses are lame and I don't have much confidence in his proposed solutions. Frankly, I think he's becoming something of a liability.'

'Not now. We need him now.'

'Of course not now! In due course. When and if the current problems are resolved.'

'Maybe. Where's the Jew?'

'With you, apparently. He's talking to the fat man.'

'That's me,' said Cutter in case there was any doubt.

'Does he have anything to tell him?'

'I shouldn't think so. Our friend in Paris had his accident before the Jew was able to contact him.'

'Good. What about the girl?'

'Not so good. She may have seen our friend. She was certainly there.'

'When?'

'About four weeks ago. We have a sighting of her that seems to be fairly solid. We think she's looking for the eagle.'

There was a pause that allowed the static to build and Branch fiddled with the remote control to dampen the pitch until Kurlack was ready to resume the conversation.

'Any leads on the girl?'

'None. We are monitoring the appropriate channels. There's nothing more we can do until she surfaces.'

'Bound to, sooner or later.'

'Sooner, I hope. What about the Jewish problem?'

'Maybe you were right. Maybe we should deal with it over here.'

'Can you locate him?'

'Easily. If he's with the fat man, I'll know where he is within twenty-four hours.'

'Well, that might be best. Best if you dealt with it.'

'I'll let you know,' said Kurlack, and one or other of them ended the call.

III

Flint's sanctuary was on Kerkstraat, high up under the gables of a thin, tall house that creaked with age. Her attic room, the cheapest she could find, cost $265 a week, gnawing away at her reserves until they were almost gone. She had a throat infection and she was running a temperature, which might have contributed to her overwhelming sense of lethargy. She felt drained, as though her will and her fortitude had been sucked away.

Tomorrow, she said; she would get out of bed tomorrow – but she had been saying that for five days. Marcel, who ran the rooming house, wanted to call a doctor but she didn't see the point. All a doctor would do was prescribe antibiotics to get her temperature down, and then what?

Anyway, she couldn't afford to pay for antibiotics. On the chipped, painted table that served as her dresser was $35 and a few guilders, all she had left in the world – or, this bit of the world, which was the same thing. That, and a Visa card she dare not use.

For the umpteenth time she reviewed her plan, a plan of sorts. If she could just get back to England without leaving her scent, she believed; if she stayed far away from London, and most of all her flat and Scotland Yard and anywhere else they might be watching; if she could get to her bank – not her own branch, of course, but one with a manager who wasn't a complete idiot – she might be able to withdraw the rest of her savings without too much delay. If she succeeded Shilling would know within minutes, she reckoned, for monitoring a bank account – like credit card transactions – was child's play for MI5. But, if she came at him from the blind side, she might just be able to get her money and disappear before he had time to react.

In her mind that was giddy from fever she reviewed the devious route she had devised that promised a chance of getting her into and out of England without showing her passport, the one that she was certain would be on the watch list of every immigration official. And, with luck, it might also confuse Shilling's hunters, causing them to look for her anywhere but Amsterdam, while she waited for Klaus to produce her passport.

Rehearsed in the abstract, it sounded okay. She would return to France, take a ferry to Ireland, travel to the north – crossing the one border to the United Kingdom that does not entail passport checks – and take a second ferry from Belfast to Liverpool. She would get her money and then – retracing her steps to the Netherlands – she would pause in Dublin long enough to 'lose' her Visa card. Somebody would find it and hand it in – or, better still, try to use it. Either way, Shilling's goons would waste precious time searching for her in Ireland, while she was back in Amsterdam urging Klaus to get a move on.

Fine. But the inward journey she envisaged was in excess of a thousand miles, and what she hadn't yet come up with was any way of accomplishing it with just $35 and a handful of guilders.

Tomorrow, she said; tomorrow she would pawn the watch her father had given her for her twenty-first birthday, the only personal possession she cared about. She would redeem it as soon as she got back to Amsterdam – if she ever got back to Amsterdam, that is.

If the Special Branch watchers – who haunt the ferries from Ireland – didn't take her for a Provo on an active service mission, and ask for some ID. If the MI5 surveillance cameras at the ferry terminals – linked to a database of photographs posted by the likes of Shilling – didn't recognise her face. If . . .

Deciding there were far too many ifs for her to contemplate, Flint took refuge in sleep.

As he had taken to doing, Marcel brought her supper: home-made chicken broth, and thin slices of coarse brown bread, and apple juice out of a bottle.

He stayed to encourage her to eat and, sitting on the end of her bed, he said, 'Listen, it's none of my business, but are you in some kind of trouble?'

She watched him warily, waiting for the first wrong move.

'We figured you must be hiding from somebody – the cops, a boyfriend . . .'

'Who's we?'

'It doesn't matter. We're not going to tell anyone. We're just worried about you. You seem like a nice person and . . . well. Is there someone you can call, somebody you trust?'

'No,' said Flint.

'Your parents, maybe? Your mother?'

'I don't have a mother.'

Marcel nodded, as though that explained everything. He was in his fifties, she guessed, a roly-poly man with a round face who smelled faintly of baby oil. He had a dog named Apricot, a pint-sized long-haired terrier that followed him around and now lay in his lap watching the food on her tray.

'What about your father?'

'There's nobody, nobody I want to call. I'm fine. I'm just tired, I just need to rest. If you're worried about the rent . . .'

He pulled a face as if to say the rent was the last thing on his mind.

'Look, Marcel, I appreciate your concern, and the food. You're very kind.' She smiled and continued, 'You're also right – about the boyfriend, I mean. You see, it didn't work out and I left and he's upset and . . . Well, I know he's looking for me and I just can't stand another scene, not right now. I don't want him to find me, please.'

'Nobody will find you here,' Marcel promised.

'Thank you,' she said, ashamed for once of the slickness of her lies.

* * *

Is there someone you can call, somebody you trust?

It was a question she had asked herself, over and over, clutching briefly at hopeful answers only to see them turn to straw under the weight of her scrutiny.

After they'd gone – Marcel and Apricot – she ran through the options one more time.

Commander Glenning and Aldus Cutter were both out of the question, and not only because of Mario's warning about the reach of The Enterprise. In the troubling matter of who had betrayed her over Ellis, the two of them stood shoulder to shoulder at the top of her list of suspects, for they were the only ones she had told about Maitland's treasure trove of documents, the only ones who knew about Frank Harling's damning affidavit. Okay, she would concede, maybe neither of them had deliberately caused the bombing of the Lear, the murders of Hechter and the Maitlands; that was probably down to Shilling. But, at the very best, one or other of them had been careless; one or other of them had left the secret unguarded, told somebody, maybe even told Shilling – and she'd ended up in a stinking morgue in San Juan looking at Kevin Hechter's severed hand.

Again she asked herself, could she trust either of them now with the secret of Mario's videotape, a secret that could get her killed? The answer, again, was No.

And on that narrow premise, everyone she knew in law enforcement – every cop and every agent she'd ever worked with, every colleague she'd ever liked and even trusted; even Gilles, and that was the worst thing of all –

was also suspect. Running through the names, seeing their faces, she remembered what the instructors at Hendon used to say about the poison of corruption: Forget the metaphor of rotten apples in a barrel, they'd warned; when corruption goes deep enough, it kills the whole bloody apple tree.

Well, from her bitter perspective, an entire orchard lay dead. At one moment in her delirium she had vividly imagined row upon row of blackened trunks and perished limbs. She knew that she must expose the whole rotten mess, and she had come to know exactly how to do that: she would take the story of The Enterprise to the newspapers, every newspaper she could think of – and thank you, Mario, for your timely suggestion. But the newspapers would want proof, and she had none beyond her scribbled notes. Which is why she needed Frank Harling as her living, breathing witness. Somehow, she told herself, she would make him tell his story; persuade him, fool him – put a gun in his mouth if she had to.

She was aware of the irony that she now saw Harling as her only hope rather than her nemesis. *This has nothing to do with revenge*, she had told Cutter when Frank's name had first surfaced and he'd said, *The hell it hasn't! You're obsessed with Harling.*

Well, yes and no, Mr Cutter.

She would now admit to herself that she was truly obsessed with Frank Harling, for what he might help her to achieve.

If she got to him before The Enterprise got to her.

If, and only if, she could find the money to finance her undertaking.

She had imagined calling Jamie. *Listen, sorry about what happened the last time I saw you, but could you drop whatever you're doing and fly over to Amsterdam and bring me a few thousand pounds? Oh, and by the way, don't tell anybody, including the mother of your bastard son.*

Hardly.

She had imagined calling Dominique, but Dominique had no secrets from Gilles.

She had imagined calling her father and – in the middle of yet another restless night – this had seemed a brilliant proposition for there was no one in the world more likely to do her bidding. But, on reflection, as the dawn light came, she had been jolted by the rigid certainty that he was the last person she dare call. In her personnel file at the Yard there was listed the number of the person to call in the event that she fell in the line of duty. It was her father's number, the first phone they would have tapped. She knew it would still be tapped, and ceaselessly monitored.

Fucking, fucking, fucking hell!

She heard Apricot scratching at her door, coveting what was left of her chicken soup, no doubt.

Well, why not? she thought, getting out of bed to open the door. Right now, Apricot was the only breathing thing she could talk to.

And then the solution struck her with blinding clarity, and she was grabbing her address book and running

down the stairs, Apricot yelping at her heels, finding
Marcel in his kitchen, seeing the astonishment on his
face as she came towards him in her nightshirt, her hair
wild, pouring out her news.

'There *is* somebody who can help me. Please, call this
number in France – I don't want to risk anybody hearing
my voice on the phone. Ask for Dr Richard Holt. Tell
him, please, that his daughter's very best friend is coming
to see him. Tell him exactly that. Say he is to tell no one,
not even Dominique. How do I get to Brest? . . . oh,
never mind. Tell him I'll be there tomorrow, or the next
day at the latest.'

'You trust this doctor?'

'He saved my life once before.'

'You want me to drive you there?' Marcel said, picking
up the phone.

She would have hugged him but he was poised to dial
and she told him the number. For what seemed like an
eternity he listened to it ringing, getting no reply.

IV

Cutter had scoffed at Jackson Kurlack's claim that he could find Cohen within twenty-four hours; that, by implication, The Enterprise had sources within the task force.

'No dirty players on my team, Harry. You know why? Because they'd have to be dumber than dirt not to know what I'd do to them – and I don't hire dumb people. You've got no worries on that score.'

Even so, it seemed to Cohen that he was hustled out of Miami as though he had the plague. Another of Cutter's pilgrims – an unsmiling young man wearing a shoulder holster he did not attempt to hide – had hurried him to the hotel to collect his things and Cohen had said with a casualness he did not feel, 'This is getting to be a habit.'

'What is, sir?'

'The other day, a French policeman implied that if I was going to be killed he would rather it didn't happen on his patch.'

'Well, he had a point, didn't he, sir?'

Cutter had been waiting at the airport, menacing the

supervisor at the British Airways desk with a preview of the difficulties he might cause if they really did close the flight before Cohen arrived.

They didn't bother giving him a boarding card or trouble him with the security checks. Less than five minutes after reaching the terminal, he was standing breathlessly at the end of the ramp, shaking Cutter's hand, as though they were sealing a deal. The purser had pulled him inside the plane and was closing the door when he'd heard Cutter's final reminder: 'Remember, Harry, not a living soul.'

'I can't tell you,' Cohen said. 'I'm truly sorry, Tom, but I've given him my word. And everything I have told you – which is little enough, I know – is for your ears only. Nobody else can know until Cutter's people have got what they need.'

He had declined to meet Glenning at the Yard. Calling from Heathrow airport, reaching him at home – still in bed and groggy from sleep, by the sound of him – Cohen had asked for a rendezvous in St James's Park where they now skirted the lake on which royal swans floated motionlessly, their necks folded, their heads sheltered under their wings.

'Does Devereaux know?'

'No. Nor will he. Not yet. Everybody's suspect.'

'Except you and me and Cutter.'

'Including you, Tom.'

Glenning stopped dead in his tracks and Cohen turned back to look at him. 'But not as far as I'm concerned. I

_____

can't do this alone and I have to trust someone, and I do trust you.'

'But not enough,' Glenning said bitterly.

Cohen dropped his shoulders. There was nothing more he could say to justify the gaps in his story, the yawning chasms of details withheld. He had told Glenning about Mario Silva's videotape and the thrust of his allegations, but none of the minutiae about The Enterprise that might allow him to guess at the identity of its principals. Nor had he revealed any part of the elaborate surveillance operation that Cutter had launched, an operation that even now – please God – was ensnaring Kurlack and Taggart and Shilling and who-knew-who-else in a web of self-incrimination.

Glenning took his time lighting his pipe, staring out over the lake, his resentment weighing on him like a yoke.

'Tom . . .' Cohen began.

'Leave it. There's no point, is there? Nothing you can say to make any difference. You must do what you think is right.' He nodded over Cohen's shoulder towards the Home Office in Queen Anne's Gate. 'What about them? Nicolson, the minister?'

'No.'

'Christ! You are out on a limb, aren't you?'

Cohen said, 'What choice do I have? Think about it, Tom. If you were the one who had sworn me to secrecy, if I'd given *you* my word, what would you think of me if I broke it? If I told Cutter, for example?'

They resumed their walk in silence, Glenning setting

the pace and their direction. He led them out of the park and onto Horse Guards Parade where they stood in the empty square.

'At the Reform,' Glenning said finally, 'when you were out the room, Nicolson asked if you were up to it – up to the job, he meant – and Devereaux said you were all we had – Hobson's choice – and I told them, no. I said you had me watching your back, and I meant it. I won't pretend I'm not offended but I still mean it. Tell me what you need.'

Cohen felt a flush of relief. 'Flint,' he said. 'We have to find Flint before they do.'

Glenning shrugged. 'We're doing all we can. There's an Interpol watch for her worldwide.'

'It's not enough, Tom. Understand something. Flint's got a copy of Silva's tape but she's got something more, something that wasn't on the tape. She knows Harling's whereabouts – she told Bourdonnec: "I know where he is." And I believe she's gone after him – or she will – because she knows that Harling's the only living witness to what's gone on. As evidence his affidavit is useful, powerful even, but there are holes in it; things he didn't say, things he didn't tell us. If we're ever going to get to the bottom of this mess we need him in the flesh.'

'So?'

'They . . . the other side . . .'

'The people you won't tell me about,' said Glenning.

'Can't,' Cohen snapped back. 'Can't, not won't. The point is, Tom, they must know how crucial Harling is, and they'll go to any lengths to keep him hidden. That, or kill him, like they killed Silva. We can't find him – or we never have been able to find him. I don't even know where to begin looking. Our only hope is to find Flint.'

'I've told you . . .'

Cohen turned away, his temper rising. Despite his fatigue, he had not slept on the flight and there was precious little left of his reserves. As Cutter had put it, he was running on empty and now here was Glenning draining the last few drops of his patience.

He heard Glenning say, 'What do you want me to do?' and he swung round to face him.

'I want a proactive hunt for Flint. I want her on every watch list there is. I want her bank account monitored, and her credit cards. I want the phone of everyone she knows, anyone she might call, tapped. I want her picture in the newspapers and on television. I want her description circulated to every police force in Europe. I want her arrested on sight.'

Glenning was staring at him as though he thought him insane. 'Arrested for what?'

'Conspiracy to murder,' Cohen said. 'Hechter, the Maitlands, the pilot, Mario Silva – all of them. And the attempted murder of Gilles Bourdonnec and his men – that should get the French interested. And anything else you can think of. Whatever it takes to find her, Tom. Whatever it takes.'

V

Harry Cohen lying down, stark terror in his eyes. Eyes he can neither fully open nor fully close. It is as though the lids have been glued at the mid-point.

Near where he is lying a telephone is ringing but Cohen cannot reach it for he cannot move his arms or his shoulders. He cannot sit up or roll onto his side or lift his legs, or any other part of his body. So far as he can tell, he is paralysed.

He attempts to speak but his larynx does not produce a sound.

He has suffered a stroke, he is sure. It is the only explanation. He tries to remember where he is, what day it is, but he has no recollection of recent events. The last thing he remembers is getting off the plane, arriving at Heathrow in the half-darkness of the predawn.

Then what? Where am I?

There is a soft glow in the room, on the right periphery of his vision, but it is not sufficient to tell him much about his whereabouts. If he could move his head just a few inches towards the source of the light that might be the display of a digital clock he could confirm what he suspects: that he is at home, prostrate on the sofa in his study.

The bloody phone won't stop ringing, mocking him with its taunting false promise of help. Then mercifully it does cease – only to begin again. On and on, again and again.

All right, assume you are at home, he tells himself. *What day is it?*

The answer to the question is crucial for twice each week, each Tuesday morning and Friday afternoon, Mrs Manning comes to clean the house. She has her own key, she will let herself in and eventually, in her own good time, she will reach the cluttered study where – please God – he lies. Will she think him dead, lying there with his eyes half-closed, unable to move, unable to speak? No matter; she is a sensible woman, she will call for help. *So, what day is it?*

He remembers distinctly that it was Sunday night when he left Miami and therefore Monday morning when he arrived at Heathrow and, reaching for straws, he takes comfort in this knowledge for it is now the night once more. Monday night; perhaps it is already Tuesday morning. In just a few hours, he tells himself, he will hear Mrs Manning's key in the lock and her ritual call coming down the stairs: 'Mr Cohen? Are you home?'

But then it dawns on him there is another possibility: that an entire two days have been erased from his memory; that it is already Tuesday night and Mrs Manning will not return for three more days – and, meanwhile, his brain is dying.

Oh, Jesus!

Is it Monday night or Tuesday night? Whether he lives or dies, he decides, depends entirely on the answer.

He forces himself to concentrate, to try and reconstruct the hours – or the days – that are missing from his life.

Heathrow, you were at Heathrow. You had a carry-on bag, nothing checked. You came through passport control, the girl just nodding when you showed her your passport. Then what? You would have got a taxi at that time in the morning, before the rush-hour. So, you must have gone outside to the taxi rank. Was there a queue? Did you have to wait?

No! Wait a minute. You didn't go outside, not straightaway. You did something else first. In the terminal. Concentrate!

Did you need money for the taxi, did you go to a cash machine? Did you change dollars back into pounds? No, you had money, remember? You had five hundred pounds in your wallet that you never changed into dollars. Okay, so it wasn't that. What else? Bloody concentrate!

Finally the phone stops ringing and Cohen is grateful for this meagre blessing.

Hold on. Just a minute. The telephone. That's it! You made a telephone call! You went to the bookstall and you bought a phone card and you made a call. Who to? Who did you call? Who would you have called? Devereaux? No, not Devereaux – least of all, Devereaux. Glenning? Did you call Glenning?

He holds onto that question, probing at it, pushing it,

pinning it to the walls of his befuddled mind.

Glenning. Glenning. Why might you have called Glenning? Why that early in the morning? Did you want a meeting, tell him something important?

Then suddenly a piece of his memory returns so vividly it might have been projected on a wall, replayed to him in stereo sound.

He is picking up a telephone, not to make a call but to receive one. He is not at the airport but in his kitchen. It is not the voice of Tom Glenning he hears but that of Sarah Spenny: 'Harry bloody Cohen. How are you?'

'Harry bloody Cohen,' she'd said. 'How are you?'

'Sarah. I'm fine, thank you,' he'd replied – and it was true. After leaving Glenning he'd come home to Holland Park feeling light-headed, almost intoxicated; as if, by passing the baton to Glenning, he had unburdened himself of a great weight. He'd gone to bed and fallen asleep and slept for nine straight hours untroubled by dreams of shattering explosions. Taking a shower, shaving the stubble from his face, he'd felt reborn, and ravenously hungry. He was preparing scrambled eggs – shaving a black truffle into the mix – when the phone rang. Sarah Spenny, making her pitch.

'I'm absolutely fine. How are you?'

'Not good,' she said. 'Harry, I need to see you.'

He hesitated for just a little too long and she said, 'For Christ's sake, Harry, this is important.'

'Well, Sarah, the thing is . . .'

'I won't take more than half an hour of your precious bloody time.'

'When?'

'Now.'

He floundered, seeking some delay. 'Can you just tell me what this is about?'

'Not on the phone. It's about the Service, Harry, something I've just found out. I have to tell someone and you're the only person I can think of.' She'd paused and then she'd added in a small, scared voice, 'Harry, somebody's trying to kill me.'

She must have been calling from around the corner for less than five minutes after she rang off the doorbell chimed and she was standing there, smiling at him. She didn't look scared. In a short white dress that set off her tan and her auburn hair she looked fresh and inviting. She put her arms around his neck and kissed him on the mouth, tasting of peppermint.

'Thank you,' she said. 'For seeing me.'

And then before he could say a word she was inside the house, walking down the hall, heading for the kitchen. She got there ahead of him and he heard her say, 'You're cooking eggs for us, you marvellous man.'

'Well,' he said, coming into the room as she perched herself on the counter, hitching up her skirt, showing off her legs.

'What I really need first,' she said, 'is a drink.'

Inwardly Cohen surrendered. He knew that Sarah was immune to anything short of outright rudeness and it was not in his nature to be rude. What the hell, he thought. 'Whisky?' he suggested.

'Please. A large one.' She crossed her legs and clasped her hands around her knees. 'God, it's good to see you, Harry.'

He put ice in two glasses and poured them both generous measures of Scotch and they toasted each other and then he said, 'So, Sarah, what's all this about? You said someone is trying to kill you?' He said it lightly, as if it were a joke.

'Devereaux.'

'*Devereaux!*'

She took a large swallow of her drink. 'Bloody, fucking A.J. Devereaux. Your chum.'

'Sarah, that's absurd. Why on earth would Devereaux want to harm you?'

Another swallow, a hard smile and then she said, 'Because of what I know. About him. About the Service.'

Cohen shook his head in disbelief. 'You're not making any sense.'

She softened the smile and cocked her head to one side. 'Harry, be nice to me, please. I really do need you to be nice.' She came down from the counter and stood before him, very close, looking into his eyes. 'I'll fix us another drink and set the table and you cook us supper and we'll have some lovely wine, and we'll be friends like we used to be, talk about old times. Can we do that, please? And then after supper, if you insist, I'll tell you all about Devereaux – if you promise not be angry with me. Don't frighten me, Harry. I'm already scared half to death.'

'I don't mean to frighten you, Sarah. I just don't—'

She silenced him with a kiss, this one lingering, her lips apart, her tongue gently probing his mouth. Devereaux's forewarning skittered through his head: *Mark my words, Harry. She's determined to have you.*

True to her word, Sarah would not talk about Devereaux during supper. She poured them wine and extravagantly praised Cohen's cooking with almost every mouthful while she talked of the old times – or rather, her version of what had occurred.

To his recollection she was no more than a distant and junior colleague at the Service, one of the countless minions, most of them young women, who worked in the basement of a dreary office block in Curzon Street, where – in the days before Thames House – MI5's Registry was housed. Cohen was based in Gower Street with the rest of the senior management and Curzon Street was an outpost he rarely visited – until the end; until files missing from the Registry became his obsession. But for that, it is unlikely he would ever have met Sarah had she not been a friend of Annie's; a friend from school, someone who came to dinner. He'd thought her bright and pretty, and far too indulged by her long-absent father. Otherwise, he'd not thought much about her at all.

But that was not her memory, apparently.

'Harry, why did you go off me?' she asked. 'Was it because of Annie, what I said to her about you?'

Having not the slightest notion of what she was talking about, Cohen looked at her nonplussed.

'I mean, I know you fancied me, or I thought you did. I certainly fancied you. I thought we were heading helter-skelter for an affair and then . . .'

'Sarah! You're talking nonsense. What did you say to Annie?'

'That if she didn't want you, I did.'

Cohen felt as if the room was turning. 'For God's sake! When did you say this to her?'

'It was one of the last times I came to supper – probably the last time. She was beastly to you all evening – being a real cow, I thought . . .'

'She was ill, Sarah. In awful pain.'

'Yeah, but we didn't know that then – not how ill she really was.' She shrugged and went on, 'Anyway, after-wards, here in the kitchen when we were clearing up, I told her I'd take you off her hands, if that's what she wanted. I said I thought you'd come.'

'How could you?' Cohen would have stood up to emphasise his anger, but he was losing all feelings in his legs.

'I thought she'd told you. I thought that was why you went off me.'

'I don't know what . . .' Cohen tried to say but his words were slurred beyond comprehension.

'I mean, one moment you were all over me, coming to the Registry almost every day – you'd never done that before. "Sarah this, Sarah that, thank you, Sarah" – I was always the one you came to. Remember? All those little compliments, those little hints? "I love that dress." "What's that scent you're wearing?" "Are you going somewhere nice this weekend?" And then, after work, you started taking me to that wine bar in Covent Garden – remember? – where they served champagne, and you wanted to know all about the Registry and how it worked ... What was I supposed to think?'

He spluttered. He would have said, 'I was pumping you,' but he was now incapable of speech.

'I mean, there was the Chief Legal Advisor asking little Miss File Clerk about the Registry, as if I'd invented the bloody thing. Is he really interested in cross-referenced indices? Not likely, I thought. I thought – I hoped – that all you were interested in was getting inside my knickers. In fact, I'll tell you a secret. One evening, when we were in that little alcove by the window, and we sat really close, I went to the bathroom and I took off my tights and my knickers and stuffed them in my bag. I thought that, any minute now, you would slide your hand up my thigh and I had my cunt waiting for you, and you never knew.' She paused. 'Harry, are you all right? You don't look too well.'

He couldn't answer so he shook his head.

She got up and came to him. 'I think you'd better lie down. Here, I'll help you.'

She was much stronger than he would have guessed. She drew him to his feet and put his arm around her shoulders and half-carried, half-dragged him to the hallway. She contemplated the stairs leading up to the bedrooms and chose instead to negotiate the flight that led down to his study in the basement.

'Better down than up – for once,' she said, and she giggled.

He always felt in danger of falling but somehow she got him down the stairs. She led him to the sofa and laid him on it and knelt down on the floor beside him.

'Now here's a thing,' she said. 'Harry Cohen horizontal at last.'

He felt her fingers running through his hair, pushing it back from his forehead, brushing his neck, walking down the buttons of his shirt as though they were stepping stones.

'Now, you know, a girl like me could take advantage of a situation like this.' Her fingers reached his waist and continued to his groin. 'Anything alive down here? Shall I fuck you, Harry? Would you like that? Fuck you till your dick falls off?'

She leaned over him, pressing her breasts against his chest and traced the line of his nose with her tongue. She opened her mouth as if to devour him, and then she brought her lips together and spat into his eyes.

Now the images are less distinct and erratic. Lying in the dark on what he now knows is the sofa in his study, he sees an earlier version of himself, equally helpless, watching Sarah at work, ransacking the room.

She is methodically working her way down the wallboard, removing the photographs one by one. A stairwell in Belgravia, Pete Pendle in a lake of blood. Flint with her ruined face. Flint's things in her flat, invaded by Cohen.

Now she is going through the drawers of his desk, now the filing cabinet. She will not find Frank Harling's affidavit or Flint's scribbled notes for they are secure in a safety deposit box at Cohen's bank.

But she does find Mario's tape in the video player – the copy Cutter had given him – and this arrests her. She lets it play, coming to the sofa to sit by Cohen, leaning against his chest while she absorbs the content and the implications. Mario names names while with the fingers of one hand she knots and tugs the thin gold chain she wears around her neck and nibbles on its small stone. With the fingers of the other hand she knots and tugs at Cohen's hair causing him pain that he cannot express. Her spittle has dried on his face like a scab.

She is picking up the phone, dialling a number.

He hears her say 'Thrush' and then she continues: 'He knows about you, Taggart, Kurlack.' There is a pause during which she is admonished, apparently, for then she angrily defends herself. 'You're not hearing me. He *knows*. Silva's talked. What's the fucking point?'

Now reason is being applied, Cohen assumes, for she goes silent. Turning to watch him, she listens to her instructions.

He sees her walk up the stairs, her legs exposed to the crotch from Cohen's angle.

She returns with a glass and comes to kneel at the sofa and lifts his head. 'Drink this,' she says, and he has little choice as the liquid fills his mouth. It tastes of nothing.

He is in darkness. He does not see her leave.

* * *

The doorbell is chiming and Cohen thinks, *She's forgotten her key!* But it is still dark, much too early for Mrs Manning's arrival. Whoever it is, he prays they will persist and his spirits soar when he hears the sound of breaking glass.

But then another thought occurs to him. What if it is Sarah returning to make sure he's dead? – Sarah, or Shilling or one of his crew, for Cohen now has no doubt that she is – always has been – part of The Enterprise. Little Miss File Clerk in the Registry, perfectly placed to do Shilling's dirty work.

He hears the front door open and softly close, and the thud of his racing heartbeat. He waits for the intruder to turn on the lights but they do not do so. What he sees instead is the faint reflection of a torch beam lighting the wall of the stairway, and he hears footsteps in the hall. Then the light fades and his panic subsides. Whoever it is, they are not coming directly to the study. They are going upstairs, searching the house – and Sarah wouldn't need to search the house, would she? Sarah would know exactly where she left him.

He waits. It is not a large house. Annie's room – what used to be Annie's room that remains untouched – occupies the attic; her private space to which she would retreat, and increasingly as her illness progressed. Two guest bedrooms on the second floor, unused since Annie left. Their bedroom suite on the first floor, Annie's clothes – those she left behind – still in the closets of her dressing room.

Not much to search, not long to wait.

The reflection of light returns, dancing along the

stairway wall, growing brighter, as is Cohen's sense of hopefulness. Then it fades once more but he takes this philosophically. The intruder is thorough, methodical, he tells himself. Of course they will search the ground floor before coming to the basement.

Living room, dining room, kitchen, a small scullery in the back. He imagines the intruder's progress and tells himself to be patient. On the basis of no evidence at all – no rational explanation for the intrusion – he has chosen to believe that this is friend, not foe. Whoever they are they will find him, they will call for help.

The reward for his reckless optimism comes soon enough. The light returns and this time it is no mere reflection but the beam itself chasing down the stairs, probing his study like a searchlight.

Once, twice, the beam flicks along the wall above where he lies, and then it is extinguished. In disbelief he hears footsteps retreating along the hallway, heading for the front door, and Cohen is screaming, *Come downstairs! You never came downstairs!*; screaming at the top of his lungs, not making any sound.

He hears the front door open and then close. A wave of despair washes over him bringing in its wake a rush of nausea that makes him gag. Tears are stinging his eyes. Unable to blink, it feels as though the membranes are drowning.

And then – precious God – he hears voices. Through the mask of his tears he can see a glow more constant than torchlight. Someone, he believes, has turned on the lights in the hallway.

Footsteps are coming towards the top of the stairs, the voices growing louder, more distinct.

'There's nobody here, sir. He must have gone out.'

'So, what's this, then?'

The voice is familiar but Cohen can't place it.

'A key, sir.'

'Does it fit the lock? Tried it, have we? – well, try it now . . . You see. Now, why would he go out without his front door key?'

'Well, he's not here. I've looked everywhere.'

Cohen wants to yell, to damn the lie, but since he can't he listens to his name being called.

'Harry? It's Tom Glenning. Are you here?'

Yes, Tom. Yes, Tom. Yes, Tom. Yes.

'Did you go all the way to the top?'

'Right up to the attic, sir.'

'Look in all the bedrooms?'

'Yes.'

'What about in there?'

'Yes. That's the kitchen.'

Glenning shouted, louder than before, 'Harry? Harry Cohen?'

Oh, please God.

'And down there?'

'Yes, that's his study. I shone my torch around.'

'Did you go down?'

'Well, halfway down.'

'Oh, come on, lad, what's the matter with you? Find the lights. Get down there and take a proper look.'

VI

For the third time the locum said, yes, she knew where everything was, and, yes, she knew the treatment regimes by heart, and finally John Flint climbed into his Land Rover and took the curve into Allen's Lane. When he reached the village he turned left onto the A44, driving south, maintaining the fiction he was heading for London. He drove at a steady forty miles per hour, one eye clamped on the rear-view mirror, obeying his daughter's instructions.

Watch for slowcoaches, she'd said. *Anyone who dawdles behind you. And everyone parked in a lay-by. They may try tagging you from static OPs.*

Static what, darling? he'd asked.

Never mind. Just don't turn off until you're sure you are clear. If you see someone parked, just keep going until you are well beyond their visual range and then find a way to double back.

He'd almost reached Eynsham before he was sure, or as sure as he could be. There were no other cars in sight – parked or otherwise – when he turned onto a side lane that took him to the A40. Now he was heading west towards Gloucester, then turning north towards Moreton in Marsh. Having completed his sweeping, deceptive circle, he pulled into the long driveway of Simkins' Farm.

He had the windows open and the breeze was tugging at his shirt, messing up his hair. He felt exhilarated, as if he'd shed ten years, as if every trouble in the world had evaporated like mist in the morning sun.

He caught himself in the mirror and saw that he was grinning and that made him laugh. He banged the steering wheel with one hand and yelled a whoop of delight.

At the top of his voice he crooned the tune to 'Amazing Grace' and he thought of her pulling a face, a young girl flushed with embarrassment, imploring him to stop: 'Please, Daddy, *don't*.'

But she could not deny him, not today, for she *was* amazing. He was amazing. Everything was amazing.

He started over once more, this time singing with gusto his own irreverent version of John Newton's words.

Amazing Grace, how sweet you are, that saved a vet like me,

You once were lost but now you're found, it's you I come to see.

The night before Sally Barton had put her head around the door of the snug bar and said, 'Call for you, Doctor Flint.'

Flint had groaned. He was used to being tracked down in the evening to deal with some emergency or other but he'd not been in the pub for more than ten minutes;

barely had time to order his supper. He'd asked the barmaid, 'Any idea who it is?' and she'd said, 'Someone foreign,' which didn't do much to narrow the field. Anyone born south of Eynsham was foreign to Sally.

The public phone at the Horse and Hound was located in a passageway leading to the toilets, set in an alcove that was low and not quite the width of Flint's shoulders. He'd squeezed himself into the space – picking up the phone, saying 'Hello?' – and five muffled words had turned his world into bedlam.

'This is about your daughter.' A man's voice, speaking with an accent that was certainly foreign.

'What? Who is this?'

'Listen to me. You must go to another telephone. Not in the village. Not at your house. You must go quickly.'

Quickly? Quickly did not nearly describe the velocity with which Flint's temper was rising. He'd been down this road before, in the months after Mad disappeared, taunted by telephone calls from some perverted creep claiming he had Flint's wife; telling Flint in loathsome detail what he was doing to Mad.

'*Listen,*' he had roared.

'No! You listen! She says to use the phone at Loudon's place. Okay?'

'No, not okay! What the hell do you mean?'

'Wait . . . She says to tell you, Claudius is undone.'

What is this madness? Flint would have said, but suddenly he had known what the message meant; known also that only his daughter could have sent it.

Grace is alive!

Somehow he had managed to speak. 'Got it.'

'Okay. I am going to give you a number to call. Write it down.'

'Hold on,' Flint had said, squeezing out of the alcove, searching his pockets for something to write with, something to write on. 'Go ahead.'

'Now, this is not the whole number. You have to add the international dialling code and the first four digits.'

'And how am I supposed to do that?'

'She says to remember your scribblings. Do you understand?'

Scribblings were how Flint described the mystery thrillers he wrote. 'Yes.'

'She says to remember to send your apologies to Alfred.'

It took a second before the penny dropped. Alfred was Hitchcock and Grace had said she reckoned he owed the master an apology for stealing the title of his best-ever movie and then short-changing him. Flint had called his last mystery *The 31 Missteps*.

'Got it.'

'She says to remember your sister's habit.'

It was Sister Anne's unwavering habit to begin each day with 20 Hail Marys. No more, no less. Always 20, as though her eternal life depended on it. The opening words of *Missteps*.

'Got it.'

'Alfred, followed by your sister, followed by this . . .'

And a minute later Flint had been running out of the pub, wrenching open the door of the Land Rover, careering at madcap speed through narrow country lanes until he reached the Falkland Arms at Great Tew, a near-idyllic village dating back to the sixteenth century, created by a man named Loudon. John *Claudius* Loudon.

It was where they would come for Sunday lunch – while they were rebuilding her face; when she came home to escape the wreckage of her marriage – and, to get her smiling, he would do his daft impression of another Claudius, the Roman emperor who was poisoned by his wife. 'I, Claudius,' he would announce imperiously – a napkin on his head for a crown; about to clutch his throat and slump onto the table – 'am undone.'

The Falkland Arms had been brimming with folk, the overflow spilling out into the garden, and rather than push his way through the crowds he'd used the telephone box by the village green; the old-fashioned kind with a door that closed, giving him some privacy – which was just as well.

'Wait a moment,' said the voice that had answered and then Grace was on the line – unmistakably Grace – saying she was fine, saying that she loved him, saying that she needed him, and he could barely say an audible word. He had been rubbing at the rivers on his cheeks, trying not to let her hear that he was bawling like a kid, but not really caring if she knew. He had just about managed to say 'yes' whenever it was required; yes to whatever she had asked for.

He had driven home in a trance, finding himself back at Glebe Farm with no recollection of the journey. Unable to sleep, he had spent the night in his surgery talking to

his patients, telling them his news. In the morning he
had arranged for the locum and then driven to his bank
to withdraw ten thousand pounds; more than she'd asked
for, but what the hell. As the clerk was counting the
notes for the third time, it had occurred to him that
perhaps Grace did not want the money for herself; that
perhaps she was a prisoner and this was the ransom.

Well, so be it. If that was true she was in the hands of
fools, for they could have demanded every penny he had,
and every penny he could beg or borrow. He would steal
if he had to. There was no price John Flint would not
pay to get his daughter back.

'Pardon?' the clerk had said.

'Sorry, my dear?'

'I thought you said something.'

He had given her his biggest smile. 'Talking to myself,
I expect.'

Schiphol airport, Tuesday evening, John Flint following
the directions to the train that will take him swiftly
into the heart of Amsterdam, following precisely his
daughter's instructions.

The flight from Birmingham had taken less than an
hour but even so the KLM attendant had taken one look
at his height and moved him to a bulkhead seat; more
room for his legs, she said. She'd spoiled him as well
with extra coffee and a schnapps, and beamed at him
when they'd said goodbye. He'd supposed his mood was
infectious.

Timed by his watch, the train journey took seventeen

minutes and he counted them down – as he had once counted down the moments on another train, going to meet Mad after some circumstance had forced their separation for all of three days. Ordinarily the parallel would have made him sad but not today. Nothing could make him sad today.

On the main concourse of Central Station he stood under the clock where she had told him to stand, craning his neck to search the crowds, longing for his first look at her – and only now did he feel a suggestion of anxiety. What if she didn't come? What if she was not *allowed* to come?

'Dad.'

Startled, he stared vacantly at the woman standing before him – her wild hair a multitude of colours, a stud in her nose, her mouth livid with lipstick, a tattoo of a serpent running up her neck. And then she laughed at the look on his face, and threw her arms around his neck, and he was hugging her back, waiting for his heart to burst.

VII

'She gave you GHB, Gamma Hydroxy Butyrate, otherwise known as Great Hormones at Bedtime.' Sitting by Cohen's bed in a private room at the Harley Street Clinic, Glenning allowed himself a glimmer of a smile. 'It looks just like water. A capful is supposed to make you randy, though it's actually a sedative-hypnotic originally developed as an alternative anaesthetic. As far as the doctors can tell, she slipped you a whole bottle. By rights, you should be dead.'

'*Would* be dead, except for you,' said Cohen but Glenning shrugged away the accolade. 'My God, I still can't believe it. Where did she get it?'

'From just about any dance club in the country. The kids call it Liquid Ecstasy, although it's not the same as Ecstasy. It's cheaper and it's worse, especially if you mix it with alcohol – which is what she did to you, of course. In the wine, most probably, or the Scotch, or both. We can't be sure because she washed out the bottle and the glasses. Tidied up after herself very nicely.'

Cohen stretched his arms above his head, luxuriating in the miracle of movement. Wiggling his toes, being able to flex his fingers, was still a novelty that gave him a child's pleasure. It had taken them thirty-six hours to get the poison out of his system and he'd been on life-support for most of it. This afternoon he'd been strong enough to walk to the bathroom, though they still had a drip in his arm, feeding him glucose and multi-vitamins.

'No trace of Sarah, I suppose.'

'No, she's done a bunk, I'm sure of it. So has Shilling. I've got a watch out for both of them, of course. All the ports and airports are covered. But my guess is, they were out of the country on Tuesday, long before you were in any shape to talk to us.'

It had been Wednesday – yesterday evening – before he could speak so much as a word. It had been almost midnight before he'd found the strength to describe what had happened and, by the look of him, Glenning had not slept since.

'I've got good new and bad news,' he said. 'You want the bad stuff first?'

No, not really, but Cohen said, 'Always.'

'Whatever it is you know – whatever it is you wouldn't tell me – if it was written down, taped or photographed, she's got it. There's nothing left in your house that has any bearing. She cleaned you out, Harry.'

Cohen was not surprised but even so he felt the deadening weight of his own failure. Thanks to his stupidity, they had Mario's videotape and Cohen's indiscreet notes of what Cutter had told him.

They knew most of what Cutter knew and so now would Glenning, Cohen decided, for what was the point in holding back? He had given his secrets away to the enemy. How could he deny them to the man who had saved his life?

Carefully, not sparing any detail, he recited what he'd learned in Miami. Glenning received the revelations in solemn silence. When Cohen got to the part about Taggart – 'You know, of course, he's my father-in-law' – Glenning shook his head, as if to say he shared Cohen's disbelief.

'He'll know, of course,' Cohen said. 'Shilling will have told him. Kurlack, too. So, that's the end of Cutter's operation.' He faced up to what he must do. 'I should call Cutter, let him know what's happened.'

'Maybe,' said Glenning in a tone that said otherwise. Seeing the question on Cohen's face, he went on: 'Harry, let's not rush this. Let's think about the implications.'

He got up from his chair and paced the room like a general in his tent before the battle, drawing down on his greater experience.

'Think about it. The thing about rats is they only care about themselves. When they leave the proverbial sinking ship, you don't see them helping each other, do you? It's every rat for itself, and bugger the women and children. They're not like us, you see, rats. They don't know about loyalty, they don't have a conscience. Now, look at it from Shilling's point of view, if you can. He's a rat, no doubt about it. Sarah calls him, tells him what you've got. He knows right there and then that the ship's going down, so what does he do? He's got to believe that Taggart and Kurlack are being watched and listened to every which way there is. Does he contact them, tell them "Save yourselves, lads" – and put himself even deeper in the mire? Maybe, but I doubt it. I've been a copper for thirty-two years, Harry, and I've seen it a thousand times. When the ship goes down, it's every rat for itself.'

'I have to tell Cutter,' Cohen protested.

'Do you? Why? You tell him and he'll pull the plug and get nothing. End of story. You don't tell him and he'll keep listening to Taggart and Kurlack and who knows what he'll get. All right, let's suppose that Shilling is not your average selfish rat, let's say he calls them. He tells them, "The Jew knows everything, but we've taken him out" – which is probably what he and Sarah think. Now, Taggart and Kurlack, they're saying to themselves, "What does Cutter know?" They're in a right panic, babbling to each other about what to do. If Cutter gets any of that on tape, that's solid gold, Harry.'

Cohen looked dubious.

'Do you know who agrees with me?'

Glenning was into the swing of it now, shrugging off his tiredness, persuaded by the force of his own conviction.

'Cutter, that's who. I called him last night, while I was waiting to de-brief you. I told him what little I knew. He was beside himself – concerned about you, of course – but he was over the moon at the thought of what his satellites might pick up. Now, are you going to spoil that for him? Why?'

'Because I gave him my word I wouldn't tell a soul

and I've effectively told the whole bloody world.'

Sarcastic now. 'Grow up, Harry,' said Glenning.

A young nurse, a slip of a black girl, came to take Cohen's temperature and check the drip and she said to Glenning, 'Now, don't overtire him.'

'I'll be going soon.'

'Not before you tell me the good news,' said Cohen. 'I need good news.'

Oblivious to great affairs of national importance, she gave them both a stern look. 'I'll tell you what. The trolley's coming, you can have a cup of tea, and then you' – she pointed at Glenning – 'are leaving.'

Glenning held up his hands in a gesture of surrender.

'The reason I sent a bobby round to your house to check up on you,' Glenning began when the nurse had gone, 'was because I'd been calling you half the night to tell you I thought I had a line on Flint. Now I'm sure I have.'

'You've found her?'

'Not exactly. But close.'

Pacing the room again, Glenning told his story with all due modesty, as though what he had done was merely routine.

'Monday night, while you're entertaining Sarah Spenny, Flint – John Flint, that is – gets a telephone call at the Horse and Hound. Male voice. "This is about your daughter" are the first words he hears. Yes, well,' he went on, seeing the astonishment on Cohen's face, 'you'd told me that he practically lived there so when I applied to the minister for the order to tap his home phone I added the pub for good measure. Nicolson didn't like it but I made him see reason.'

'How?' Cohen said.

'Let's just say I twisted his arm.'

'Tom?'

'I told him I wasn't sure about you, that I thought you were holding back – which was true enough. Then I let him think that you and Flint might have something going on, that you were telling him things you weren't telling us, calling him at the pub. So, the order was very specific. We could only listen to calls between you and Flint, or Flint and his daughter, or any calls that were specifically and obviously about her. Anyway . . .'

'You cunning bastard.'

'Anyway . . . They have a bit of a chit-chat and Flint is told he has to go to another phone at "Loudon's place". Flint doesn't get the message so now the caller gives him a code – from his daughter, supposedly: "Claudius is undone." That does it. Then he's given a number to call with the first four digits disguised by some more code, so we don't know what country it's in. Flint's off the phone and out of the pub in less than a minute. There was no time to trace the call and no time to stick a warm body on Flint, but clearly something was up. That's what I was calling to tell you. When it got to two o'clock and you still weren't answering I knew in my gut that something was wrong.'

'Then thank God for your gut.'

'Yes. Well, Mrs Glenning would not share that
sentiment, still . . .'

There was a babble of voices in the corridor and
Glenning waited until it had passed.

'By Tuesday morning I had some of my best lads all
over Flint. There wasn't much for them to do at first
because he spent a couple of hours on the phone telling
all and sundry that something important had come up
and he was off on a trip. London, he said. Which meant
anywhere *but* London, of course.'

'Why?'

'Because his daughter would have warned him we
were listening, wouldn't she? If she was worried about
the phone at the pub – and she was, because she dreamed
up all those codes, just in case we were listening – then
she's got to be certain his home phone is tapped. Bound
to be. So, she tells him to obfuscate; tell us anything but
the truth.'

'But she must know *you* know that – and that you're
not going to fall for it.'

'Yes,' said Glenning, 'now we're in a game, and we
both know it. Question is, who's better at it?' He took
his pipe from his pocket and sucked on the stem. Even
unlit it gave off the scent of cherries.

'Mid-morning Flint takes himself off to Barclays Bank
in Chipping Norton and draws out ten thousand pounds.
He's not short of a bob or two but he's never done that
before; never taken more than a few hundred in one go,
not in cash. So, now I have a pretty good idea what's
going on. She hasn't touched her account in more than a

month, nor used her credit card, so she's got to be running short of cash. He's taking her money, got to be; follow him, find her. Problem is, she knows that, knows how we do it, so she has to have a plan, some way for him to lose us.'

'And did she?'

'Yes. A lad named Simkins. If I opened the window, do you think they'd mind if I smoked?'

'I think that nurse would cut off your balls.'

Glenning grunted. 'You're probably right. Anyway, Simkins . . . My lads put a transmitter on Flint's Land Rover. While he was at the bank. I didn't want a tail on him because Grace would have told him how to spot it. And though she would have warned him about a transmitter, they're not that easy to find, not nowadays, not unless you know what you're doing or you've got a detector. This one was in a radio aerial. Switched it for his – and he'd never have known the difference. Ten mile radius so my lads could follow at their leisure, which they did. And he led them on a merry chase: south, west, north, south again then east. It took them the best part of an hour to figure it out.'

'He switched cars?'

'Yes. As simple as that. And the thing is, we were watching for it. Knew she might try that. But he'd have to set it up, wouldn't he? Call somebody to borrow their car, arrange the rendezvous? And he didn't – or we didn't know that he had.'

'He called from the bank,' Cohen guessed, and

Glenning said no, he didn't. *He got the bloody manager to call for him!*

'Slipped into the manager's office to say hello – or that's what my lad thought, the one who followed him inside. Door was open and he was quite sure Flint didn't use the phone, and rightly so. He got a bollocking for not checking with the manager afterwards but it wasn't really his fault. I mean, this is not Kim Philby he's tailing, he's a country vet. You don't expect a country vet to pull a stunt like that.' Glenning reflected for a moment. 'Unless he's got Grace Flint for a daughter. What do you think's happened to the tea?'

Glenning went to the door and checked the corridor. There was no sign of a trolley.

'So, what Flint does is, he pops his head around the door and tells the manager he's left his wagon on a yellow line – which is true – and would he mind calling Arthur Simkins – who's known to both of them – to say Dr Flint needs a favour, needs to borrow a car, and he'll be popping round that afternoon. And that's what Flint does, with my lads none the wiser. Simkins farms a thousand acres, and Flint takes care of all his animals, so they're pals. "Arthur," he says, "I'm off to London to see the queen but the old girl's playing up and I don't want to risk it on a long trip, so can I swap it for one of yours?" Arthur says, "Of course you can, John" – and then here's the nice touch. Flint says, "I think the differential's out" – or some such nonsense – "Your lad Tommy's good with cars. Can he take the old girl for a spin? See what he thinks?" And that's what Tommy does.

Leads my lads on a merry old chase until they work it out and pull him over.'

Cohen laughed and Glenning gave him a sharp look. 'I'm glad you think it's funny.'

'It was ingenious.'

'Yes, well so am I. As I said, we knew the call to the Horse and Hound was from overseas, so I'm pretty sure he's heading for an airport or a port. Question is, where? Now, she's had him tell me he's going south – that's the cover story. But she knows I'll *know* it's a cover story, so now I'm supposed to think maybe it's not a cover story – he is heading south. Except he's not, of course.'

'You've lost me,' said Cohen.

'She bluffed and then she double-bluffed and then she overdid it, because she had us running round in circles, you see, not knowing which way to look. As I tell my lads, Glenning's first rule: if in doubt go for the obvious. So they did. They looked at a map and asked themselves, what's the closest airport with international flights? – answer, Birmingham – and they headed straight for it – and there's Arthur Simkins' Land Rover nice and snug in the car park. Missed him by a couple of hours.'

'Where did he go?'

'Amsterdam. No reservation, of course. He took a chance there'd be a seat and paid cash for his ticket. My guess is, she had a back-up plan: if there hadn't been a seat on KLM, he'd have flown somewhere else. Anywhere in Europe. Didn't really matter.'

Cohen felt deflated. 'Are the Dutch police looking for him?'

'No, I'm not playing that game. You see, the fact he flew to Amsterdam could mean that's where she's not. Or it could mean that's what I'm supposed to think. Or it could . . .'

'Please don't,' said Cohen. 'The point is, we've lost him. We still don't have a clue where she is.'

'For now.' Glenning smiled. 'He's got a locum standing in for him – but only until tomorrow night. Best he could do at short notice.'

'So?'

'So he's got to come back, hasn't he? Tonight or tomorrow. Can't let his patients die.'

'I take it back,' Cohen said. 'You're not a cunning bastard, you're a crafty old fox.'

Glenning was describing the arrangements he had made when the door flew open and the nurse stood there, hands on hips, silencing them with her glare. 'You,' she said – pointing at Cohen – 'rest. And you' – to Glenning – 'out!'

'We haven't had our tea.'

'*Out!*'

She didn't come up to his armpits but Commander Glenning of Scotland Yard was led meekly from the room.

VIII

'Doctor Flint? Doctor John Flint?'
A thick-set man in a dark blue suit was blocking the passage through passport control, another – who might have been his twin – standing just to one side. They both had small, etched mouths turned down at the corners. The Brothers Grimm, Flint decided.

'Yes, and who might you be?'

'Special Branch.' He reached into his pocket and brought out what might have been a warrant card, flashing it, giving Flint the merest glimpse of his credentials. 'I'll have to ask you to come with us.'

Flint jutted his jaw. Grace had warned him he might face a reception committee when he got back to Birmingham so he was half-prepared for it; ready, at least, to be awkward.

'Come where?'

'This way,' said the speaking Grimm, pulling back his head to indicate a vague direction. The silent Grimm came alongside Flint in a manner that said 'I'll take your arm if I have to' but Flint wasn't yet ready to submit.

'What's this all about?'

'We need to ask you some questions.' Leaning forward in a confidential way Grimm continued, 'You're not under arrest, sir, not yet. But you could be. We can have a scene, right now, if that's what you want.'

'They'll provoke you if they can,' Grace had said. 'Don't rise.'

'No,' said Flint. 'That's not what I want.' Stiffly, like a man holding onto his dignity in difficult circumstances, he allowed them to lead him away. They took him to Customs and to a small room that was depressingly familiar: no windows; a desk with a Formica top and a couple of hard-looking chairs; nothing on the walls except a large No Smoking sign; a carpet that was a vile mustard colour and – the sign notwithstanding – pocked with cigarette burns. He had once spent a lifetime in a similar room, waiting to be interrogated about the supposed murder of his wife.

'They'll lean on you,' she'd said. 'Make it as uncomfortable for you as they can' – and he'd just stopped himself from saying, 'I've been leant on before, darling.'

'I'll take your bag,' said Brother Grimm.

Well, fuck it, Flint thought. Perhaps just a small rise. 'Not without a search warrant,' he said.

'Sit down!' Grimm had a short fuse, apparently. 'I don't need a warrant to take your bag.' Belatedly he added 'sir', making it sound like a slur.

'I do need a warrant to search your bag without your consent but, of course, I can't get a warrant until the morning. And since I can't hold you here overnight that means the nick. Ever been in the nick . . . sir? *I said sit down!*' Flint did as he was told and Grimm leaned on the table with his hands. 'You know, you really don't want to push it too far. You're getting up my nose.'

There was nothing in the bag, nothing that would lead them to Grace.

Give Grimm his petty victory, Flint thought. 'Do what the hell you like.'

Cohen and Glenning in the back of an unmarked police car, rushing headlong up the motorway to Birmingham, not exactly on the best of terms.

Following his pattern, Flint had made no reservation, trusting his luck on getting a seat – pushing his luck, in fact, for it was a Friday evening when businessmen go home and flights are likely to be full. Glenning didn't get word Flint was coming until he'd walked up to the KLM desk at Schiphol and his luck had held.

'I'm coming with you,' Cohen had said.

'I'm not sure you're up for it,' said Glenning, who had brought him home from the hospital that afternoon and remained with him 'just in case'. A police patrol car was parked prominently outside and armed officers had been summoned to spend their foreseeable futures in Cohen's house.

'Whether I am or not, I have to be the one who speaks to him. Alone.'

'Not on your life,' Glenning scoffed, as if the very idea was absurd.

'Why not?'

'Because you're a civilian and Flint is police business.

Do I need to remind you his daughter's a fugitive, wanted for murder?'

'But that's a charade, Tom.'

'It may be a charade to you but it's official. Now, because of you. Your idea. I can't fake this. Officially she's wanted and, for that matter, so is her father. Aiding a fugitive – in case you didn't know – is a criminal offence.'

'Oh, for God's sake,' Cohen had snapped. 'Don't be so bloody ridiculous. We're trying to find Harling, not lock Flint or her father away. That's the point, isn't it? The only point.'

'It's not your call.'

There had been a stubborn set to Glenning's jaw and Cohen – ever the lawyer – had changed tack.

'Tom, you need to understand something. Please. I know John Flint – only for one day and a drunken night, I grant you – but he showed me his soul. I know what makes him tick. Above all else, I know that his loyalty to Grace is absolute. It's not a cliche to say he would gladly die for her, it's a fact.'

'I've got a daughter,' said Glenning.

'I know you have. But her mother didn't disappear as though she had been swallowed by the night. Your daughter didn't spend her childhood coming to believe you had raped and killed her; made hammer holes in her skull, buried her under the floor. Your daughter—'

'I get the point.'

'I don't think you do, I really don't. Flint's love for Grace is unfathomable – deeper than we'll ever know –

because she forgave him. Never mind that he'd done nothing wrong. She thought he had, and he carried that guilt for years, and *she forgave him*.' He stared at Glenning, willing him to understand. 'Let me ask you a question. Would you kill for your daughter?'

'Now you're being ridiculous.'

'John Flint would, Tom. No question. You, me, anybody who might hurt her. He'd poison the water supply if it would save Grace. And there is nothing you can do to him, nothing you can threaten him with, that will make him betray her. We're the enemy now – or rather, you are. Why? Because Harling and Silva have told her that everything in her kingdom is rotten, corrupted. You're corrupt, Cutter's corrupt, anyone she's ever worked with may be corrupt – or so she believes. If only by association, you are all part of The Enterprise and John Flint will not give his daughter to you if you beg him on your knees or flay him alive.'

'I can't let you talk to him alone.'

'Yes you can,' Cohen had said, becoming desperate, grasping at a passing spark of dubious inspiration. 'I'll be his lawyer, represent him. I know he'll agree. Then I can talk to him as much as I want.'

'Really?' Glenning had said. 'You don't think that might raise a slight conflict of interest? Given your present arrangement with Her Majesty's Government?'

And round and round it had gone, an argument that had no resolution. All his persuasions having failed, Cohen fell into a sullen silence that now swathed the back of the speeding car like a shroud. For sixty miles of motorway they did not speak a word.

'Tell you what,' said Glenning as they approached the airport, offering a truce. 'You can do the talking. Most of it.'

Not yet willing to be appeased, Cohen thought, I'll have to – because we'll be bloody lucky if Flint says a word.

They'd turned the key on Flint and left him alone, letting him get used to the idea they owned him, and Cohen said, 'Why not just put him in a cell?' but his irony was wasted on them. And then they unlocked the door and Cohen saw it was a virtual cell, lacking the usual toilet facilities, and he gave Glenning a withering glare.

Flint sat with his back against the wall, his chair tipped back, one arm resting on the table. He looked younger than Cohen had remembered, less worn. He watched the doorway with defiant eyes.

Cohen jostled past the Special Branch minders. 'John,' he said warmly, holding out his hand in greeting, keeping the palm up to show there was nothing there. He got no sign of recognition. 'It's Cohen, Harry Cohen. I came to your house.'

'I remember.' Flint's voice was flat, not a trace of welcome.

'God, look at this place!' Cohen whirled around to face Glenning. 'Isn't there somewhere else we can talk?'

'It doesn't matter,' said Flint, 'because I have nothing to say to you, nothing at all.'

Cohen had a speech in mind but he never got to deliver it.

Glenning said, 'I'm going to find somewhere half-decent and have a drink. You want to come, Doctor Flint? For Grace's sake?'

'And who the hell are you?'

Glenning seemed to think about his answer. 'Next to Harry – next to you, maybe – I'm the only chance your daughter has of staying alive.'

Glenning led them to the pub on the first floor of the terminal, the only place he could smoke his pipe. Without consulting them he brought three large whiskies to the table and said, 'Coppers can't drink on duty so, ipso facto, I'm not – on duty, that is.' He raised his glass. 'To Grace.'

Not touching his drink Flint said, 'I have to go home. I have patients and no one taking care of them.'

'Yes, you do.' Glenning smiled, the bearer of glad tidings. 'I spoke to the locum this morning. She's done some juggling and she'll stay until you get back. You don't believe me? Call her.'

Cohen could see that Flint, for all of his bravado, was coming to the end of his tether.

'Oh, that's terrific!' he said, vitriol in his voice. 'What did you tell her? That I was under arrest? Christ!'

A woman at the next table glanced at Flint in some alarm and edged her chair away from him, whispering urgently to her companions.

'No, because you're not. I told her you had flu. I let

her think I was a friend, maybe a colleague. She's none the wiser. Nobody is. Nobody will be if you keep your voice down.'

But Flint would not be pacified. 'I want to go. If I'm not under arrest I'm leaving.'

Glenning did not hesitate. 'Go ahead,' he said in a tone that implied 'as if I care', and Flint was on his feet and Cohen thought, 'That's it, it's over' – and then Flint's face creased as though he was in pain, and he slumped back into his chair, appealing to Cohen. 'I don't know what to do.'

'If I were you I'd go home,' Glenning said. 'I'd go home but I'd take Harry with me because I wouldn't want to be alone tonight. Let him tell you what he knows, what he thinks you should do, and then you make your decision.' Glenning emptied his glass in a single swallow. 'As for me, since I'm not on duty I'll have another, and then I'll get my driver to take me home, and I'll wait to hear from you. It seems to me you've got one crack at it, one chance to get it right. I hope you do.'

He got up and nodded to them and ambled away towards the bar, as though he were a stranger they'd met who'd grown tired of their company.

IX

Later, when it was all over, Cohen would ask Glenning why he'd changed his mind and Glenning would say, 'Because I saw that you were right; that he would give you Grace' – but it didn't seem that way then.

Well after midnight they sat in silence amid the ragged weeds on Flint's terrace looking down on Allen's Lane, a ghostly silver ribbon in the moonlight, running through the fields. Tomorrow, Flint had said, was his thirty-fourth wedding anniversary – or would have been under different circumstances. Cohen did not share with him the forlorn coincidence that it was also very nearly the first anniversary of Annie's death. It seemed to him there was only so much pain the two of them could endure.

He did not know what ploy to use, how to begin. On the journey to Glebe Farm and since their arrival, Flint had barely acknowledged his presence or spoken more than a few words. It was as if they'd exhausted all there was to say on the subject of his daughter and – Grace being their only mutual interest – they had nothing left to discuss.

But of course they did and Cohen knew he somehow

had to scale the towering cliff of Flint's suspicion. Applying the metaphor, reaching for the first hand-hold he said, 'You told her about me and she thinks I'm one of them, doesn't she?'

Flint turned to look at him. 'One of what?'

'The Enterprise.'

Flint didn't answer, he didn't have to. In the bar at the airport there had been a moment when he'd seemed to question his faith in his daughter's certainties but now it was restored. The coldness that Cohen saw in his eyes was no trick of the moonlight.

'So, how do I convince you that I'm not?'

'You can't.'

'She's wrong, you're both wrong.' Cohen got up from his chair and walked to the edge of the terrace from where he could just make out the spindly ash that stood as Mad Flint's slight memorial and it struck him as unbearable that there might soon be need of another sad reminder of another vanished life.

He said 'Sir Adrian Taggart' and, a moment later, 'my father-in-law' and then before he could stop himself he was blurting out bitter truths he'd had no intention of telling. With his back to Flint he spoke of Taggart's abiding hate for him, the poisoning of Annie's mind, a headstone in a cemetery that would forever deny his existence and his marriage – shaming verities that flowed from him like a confession, as though he had no control over what he was saying. He told what he knew of the partnership between Taggart and Jackson Kurlack and he talked of the monstrous ruthlessness of their henchmen; of Gilles lying in the wreckage of Mario Silva's gallery; of himself lying in the dark, waiting for his brain to die. He felt his rage building and he grew reckless, giving away Cutter's secrets, or far too many of them. He spoke of secure communications that were not secure and of the elaborate operation that was now underway to establish the reach of The Enterprise; to identify and incriminate its component parts. But maybe not in time. *Not in time to save Grace.*

'For God's sake, man . . .'

Out of words, he remained at the edge of the terrace, watching the shadow of an owl describing lazy shadows over the valley. It was hunting for prey, no doubt, as Grace hunted Harling and as they now hunted her.

'I didn't know about Gilles,' Flint said softly. 'I saw something on the news about the explosion but I didn't make the connection.'

Cohen held his breath.

'Grace doesn't know either. Before she called me, she'd tried calling Dominique's father repeatedly but there was no reply. I expect he's in Paris.'

'He is,' said Cohen. 'I met him. He won't leave Dominique's side.'

He heard the scrape of Flint's chair, sensed his approach, saw him waxen-faced, staring at the sky as though he had witnessed some momentous event he could not yet fully comprehend.

'Does she understand what she's up against?' Cohen asked.

Flint slowly shook his head. 'I don't know.' He put

the knuckles of one fist to his mouth.

Cohen said, 'She needs help, John,' and Flint nodded and waited until he could speak.

'She's gone after Harling . . . I took her money and she asked me to buy her a new passport . . . I got it from some villain she knew about, a chap in a bar, somebody called Klaus. You'll want all the details.'

'Please.'

'But you're too late to stop her. She left Amsterdam an hour before I did. Direct flight to Istanbul, then a connection to Antalya, then a ferry to Northern Cyprus . . . Kyrenia, I think. Where Harling is . . . Apparently.'

'Oh, Christ.'

'I know.' Flint gave a sickly smile. 'Pariah state and all that. Not easy for you.'

'No.'

'You'll want the phone, I expect.'

How about a miracle? thought Cohen.

nine

The photograph of Frank Harling was three years out of date and even when it was current it had too many shortcomings to serve as decent ID. It was a low-light surveillance shot snatched in a nightclub in the West End of London and in the original uncropped version there was a woman – one of the hostesses, presumably – sitting close to Frank wearing not very much above the waist. He'd had his arm around her shoulders, pulling her towards him, staring at her breasts with exaggerated wonder, hamming it up for whoever else was at the table. Out of context, with the woman cut out of the picture – his mouth wide open, his eyes popping – he looked ridiculous and not at all as Flint remembered him.

I don't want to talk to your friends. Harling telling Buller but looking at Flint, his mouth tight, his eyes obscured behind tinted glasses. *Know who they are? They're the law.*

Still, it was all they'd had to work with, the one they'd plastered on TV after they'd taken her out of the

stairwell on a stretcher. And it was all she had to work
with now, the only likeness of him she could show to the
good folks of Kyrenia: 'I'm looking for this man.'

She tried to imagine how he might have changed in
the interim.

He'd have likely put on a few more pounds, she
thought. Frank liked his food, indeed, he was something
of a *bon viveur*, according to police intelligence, and he
was not exactly undernourished when she'd met him in
the stairwell – broad-chested, thick arms, a hint of a
paunch, a suggestion of jowliness under the jaw line –
and since then he'd spent most of his time in Italy,
enjoying his sojourn at the Villa Donati. The Italians
said he'd kept himself apart, done most of his own
chores, but that didn't mean he'd been deprived. She
could see him in his kitchen, pasta in the pot, a creamy
sauce in the making, a bottle of red wine on the go – and
damn the calories. No, it wasn't a slimline Frank she
sought, not Frank lite, not likely. Of that much she was
pretty sure.

She thought about the face she would never forget.

In the stairwell – as in the nightclub picture – he'd
worn sideburns and a moustache that turned down just a
little at the corners of his mouth. In the safe house he'd
shaved them off and in the passport photograph she'd
found at Ellis – the one supplied to Frank by MI5 – his
face had seemed diminished. Without hair to mask it,
she'd thought, his upper lip was too weak for the
prominence of his nose and the broad reach of his
forehead, giving him a beaky, predatory look; an

impression that his face was top-heavy, out of balance. Frank needed a moustache to give character to his countenance and he must know that and she wondered if vanity had got the better of his prudence.

And, speaking of vanity, what about his hair? In the passport photograph it was clear that Thrush had done her best to disguise its retreat from his forehead, to lose the widow's peak Flint had seen and fixed on in the stairwell: an identifying characteristic in the jargon; one a perp can't easily change. But it was a lost cause and by now, surely, Frank would have a shiny dome on top of his head – or maybe a toupee. Would Frank wear a rug? Somehow, she doubted it.

She didn't know much about the eyes because she'd never seen them clearly. Even in the passport photograph Frank had worn tinted lenses. And, anyway, eyes were not a good identifier in Flint's opinion. It was too easy to change the shape and even easier to change the colour. She had her own collection of contact lenses that just about covered the spectrum.

Much more reliable as identifiers were his height and his posture. In the stairwell he'd worn boots with significant heels, not unlike the boots that Buller had used to stamp her face into pulp – but she wasn't going to think about that, not now. Without his lifts, if they were standing barefoot and back-to-back, she reckoned she would have two inches on him, maybe three.

So, there we have it, Frank Harling. You're short, fat, balding and ugly – and you can't hide from me.

The monster thus reduced to manageable proportions

in her mind, she slept without dreaming in room 309 of
the Dome Hotel, the windows open to the sea, Frank's
picture on the bedside table to reinforce the notion he
was close to her. Very close. She could feel it.

In Amsterdam, on her father's first night – after she'd
washed the dye from her hair and removed the fake nose
stud and the stick-on tattoo – they had gone to an
Indonesian place for dinner and she'd told him some of
what she knew about The Enterprise, and some of what
had happened to her. She spared him much of the detail
because it had always been her way to describe what she
did in not-to-worry terms, and he would play his part by
affecting to believe her. In these harmless charades the
back-up teams were always in place, the equipment
infallible, her targets benign. Except once, of course, in a
stairwell in Belgravia, for what happened there was
beyond the limits of useful pretence. For both their sakes,
this exceptional anomaly was never mentioned.

She lied to her father mainly through omissions. Thus,
in her laundered version of events, on the Lawrence
Islands there was never any possibility that she might
have been on the Lear when it was bombed out of the
sky; no angry, anguished call to Cutter protesting his
decision to send her home by other means.

Similarly, in her account of Paris, she did indeed wear
a fuck-me dress to the Club Elégance to lure Mario Silva
– and talking of Gilles and his encounter with the
Amazonian she'd made her father hoot with laughter –
but she did not tell him of her night in Mario's flat. From

what he heard – and did not question – John Flint was perfectly entitled to assume that she'd somehow gained entry to Mario's flat, and found the videotape, *after* he had departed for Zurich.

But no amount of dissimulation could have disguised the trouble she was in. She was hunted and alone and he knew it – how could he not? – and the dread he felt had burned in his eyes. She had done her best for him, trying to make him see that if she could just find Harling – and she *would* find Harling – then the nightmare would end.

'But I don't understand, darling,' he'd said. 'If you find him – *when* you find him – what on earth are you going to do?'

Good question. Because in her realistic moments – when the nagging voice in her head forced her to face the cold, hard truth – she knew that Frank Harling would not surrender to her, not in a million years. She could talk to him until the cows came home – trying to turn him, trying to get him to turn himself in – and, in all probability, he would laugh in her face; stamp on her face, if he could. She didn't tell that to her father.

'I'm going to talk him down,' she lied. And then, because he hadn't understood, she'd continued, 'When I was just a little copper, just this big' – and she'd held two fingers an inch apart and cocked her head to peer at the gap, and that had won her a wan smile – 'I chased some young tearaways, I can't remember why... Anyway, one of them – a girl, she would have been about fourteen, I suppose – ended up on the roof of an old warehouse, and so did I, and I was frightened she would jump.

_____

Remember? I'm sure I've told you this story.'

He'd stared at her blankly and she'd thought, *No, probably not: sixty feet from the ground, a pitch-black night, freezing rain on the tiles and a hulking bitch with a knife.*

'Well, I radioed the station for back-up and the sergeant told me to talk her down and I didn't have a clue what I was supposed to do.' She'd fashioned her hand into an imaginary radio and held it to her mouth. 'Crackle, crackle. Crackle, crackle. "How, sarge? What am I supposed to say?" Crackle, crackle' – and she'd put on a gruff voice – ' "You'll think of something, Flint." Crackle, crackle. "You *always* think of something to say." Cheeky sod.' She'd feigned an indignant look when her father had chuckled.

'Natter, natter, natter. I went on and on. I imagined she was Ollie and we were back at school and we'd been sent to bed – in trouble, *again* – and I talked her head off. I wouldn't stop. I said anything that came into my mind. In the end, she practically begged me to let her go down.'

After four hours on a ledge too narrow to sit on, me numb with cold, unable to move. She went down the ladder like a monkey. I was the one they had to peel off the ledge – but that's another story, Daddy dear.

'Gracie, you can hardly think you'll find Harling on a roof.'

'Sort of,' she'd said. 'Or up a gum tree. He's in trouble, Dad – so am I, but he's reached the end of the line. He has nowhere else to go, no one he can turn to. I've got a whole army of people I can go to once I know who's bent and who's not. But, you see, he betrayed his friends when he made that affidavit and he knows it even if they don't – yet. Once they do know they'll kill him. The only chance he has is to turn himself in to me before they find out. But I have to know: who tipped him off about Ellis? Who told him to run?'

'And you think he'll tell you?'

'Yes. I'll talk him down. In the end, he'll beg to tell me.'

Oh, really?

She'd pushed the voice away and held her father's eyes and put her hand to her mouth. 'Crackle, crackle. "You could talk for England you could, Flint." Crackle, crackle.'

'And what if he doesn't listen to you, Grace?'

Then I'll do what I have to do.

And what's that?

Shut up!

'He will, Dad,' she'd lied.

II

There were no decent street maps of Kyrenia to be had – a military precaution, Flint supposed. There were two Turkish frigates riding at anchor beyond the harbour walls and she'd seen Turkish army patrols deploying along the coastal road, setting up chicanes of oil drums. On the Greek side of Cyprus they were promising to install a Russian-built ground-to-air missile system, and the Turks were promising to bomb it if they did.

Isn't that just like Frank, she thought. Here five minutes and he starts a war.

The map the hotel had sold her was hand-drawn and coloured with a wash. There were toy sailboats drawn on a pastel sea and candy-striped umbrellas to designate the beaches. If the scale of the map was to be believed, then the International Hotel and Catering School was the largest construction in Kyrenia.

It would have to do. Over breakfast on the Dome's terrace, she drew a rough circle around the edges of the town and divided it into quadrants that she would canvass one by one, beginning with the segment that embraced most of Kyrenia's tourist attractions – the ones she and Jamie never got around to visiting.

Not that she expected Frank to be posing as a tourist. Wealthy retiree was much more likely to be his cover: just another British lotus-eater lured to Kyrenia by its exquisite tranquillity, the cooling breezes and zero taxes.

She went to her room and dressed for the sun: sneakers, shorts, a loose cotton shirt with sleeves she could roll down if it got too hot, a floppy sunhat with a brim to cover the back of her neck – or obscure much of her face if the need arose. She examined the effect in the mirror and thought she looked harmless, even comic; a typical tourist in a silly hat.

Her valuables stored in the hotel's safe, Frank's picture in the pocket of her shorts, she left the Dome, heading for the harbour.

'You're looking for a man? How about me?' or, 'You've found him' or 'What you need is a real man' – or some such crack – and she was getting pissed off with it. She would show the picture to any likely candidate – any taxi driver who might have driven Frank, any waiter who might have served him – and one time out of three she'd see the leer growing on their faces and know what was coming. In the gloomy interior of a backstreet bar, beneath the obligatory portrait of President Denktash, some jerk had even made a move on her, taking her arm, coming on with his 'You looking for a good time?' and she'd had to bring up her knee to convince him she really did mean No.

It was gone two o'clock and she'd been at it for more than four hours and Harling's picture had not drawn a trace of recognition and it was too damn hot for grunt work. She flopped into a cane armchair at one of the vacant tables set out under canopies along the waterfront. Nearly all of them were vacant – the consequence, she supposed, of rumours of war.

When she'd come here with Jamie – in the evenings, cheerful candles on the tables twinkling like starlight – they'd sometimes had to wait to be seated. She remembered one particular evening when, for almost an hour, they'd sat on the quayside near to where she was now, their bare feet dangling in the water, holding hands, talking nonsense. She'd asked him what he meant by 'love' and – misquoting Saint Augustine, who had been pondering the mystery of time – he'd said, 'I know what it is if no one asks me, but if you ask me I can't say.' Well, that was Jamie for you. She should have known.

A waiter with a sad lopsided smile brought her back, asking what he could fetch her. He didn't seem to be a jerk and she risked showing him the picture, watching his face as he studied Frank's image. He said, 'Maybe . . . I'm not sure . . . Too many people come' and she said 'Not today' and thanked him for trying.

She ordered salad and bottled water and when the waiter had gone she took off her hat and shook her hair loose. An optimistic cat came to join her – grooming itself under the table – and she thought of her father in his surgery waiting for her call.

'Promise,' he'd said at the airport. 'Promise you'll phone.'

'The minute it's over.'

Well, judging by this morning's performance, that could be a while and she knew there wouldn't be a moment when he didn't feel the tug of his anxiety. If only for his sake, she resolved, she would start again as soon as she had eaten. It was like doing a house-to-house: you could knock on a thousand doors and not get the answer you were looking for but you had to keep going, keep knocking, because if you didn't you could bet your pension that the answer had been waiting for you at a house you'd neglected.

'I'm looking for this man' – and sod the Casanovas. She would show Harling's picture to every living soul in Kyrenia if she had to. If that's what it took.

The afternoon shift and she worked the streets methodically: bar to bar, shop to shop, post office to bank. She accosted every taxi driver she came across, every cop, even a group of loitering conscript soldiers.

Nobody recognised Harling, or so they said, and she began to wonder if he had radically changed his appearance. Perhaps Thrush – in the course of her hurried efforts to disguise him – had recommended that he submit himself to cosmetic surgery after his escape? Maybe some Michelangelo with a scalpel had created a mask for Frank, as they had for Flint? If so, even she might not recognise him, even close up as they had been in the stairwell.

It occurred to her that she could walk up to him in the street and hand him the image of his former likeness – 'Excuse me, do you know this man?' – and not have a clue that she was asking Frank Harling to identify himself.

Until he spoke. Then she would know. Unless he'd changed his accent *and* his dialect *and* his speech pattern *and* the resonance, she would know.

Finish it, Buller. For fuck's sake, get it done.

She could hear that voice now, mimic each and every syllable.

In the early evening, just before closing time, she hurried into the one bank she had not yet checked and for a moment she stopped breathing, believing she had found her grail. As the clerk behind the counter studied her picture she thought she saw something in his eyes; something fleeting that triggered her antennae. He said casually – perhaps too casually – 'What's his name?'

Since she didn't know what name Harling was using she could only give the clerk her misused woman's smile. 'He never told me,' she said, dropping her eyes to signal her embarrassment.

He thought about her reply and then he handed back the photograph. 'No, I've never seen him.'

'Are you sure?'

'Certain,' he said – and she was sure he was lying.

After he'd shooed her out of the bank and locked the door and kept watching her through the glass until she'd walked away, she filled her mind with crazy notions of what she might do: follow him, find out where he lived, get his phone records, talk to the neighbors, keep a watch on the bank; twenty-four-hour surveillance until he led her to Frank.

Right! You and which particular army?

Her sudden sense of helplessness depressed her, sapping her will, and she walked slowly back towards the hotel. She felt in need of a shower, a change of clothes, something to drink.

What you need, Flint, is a miracle.

Oh, shut up!

She grew angry with herself. This was only the first day, for God's sake! What did she expect? Harling on a plate? She would have to work for it, push for it, keep on going until she got the break. Because that's the way it was, the way it would be, and feeling sorry for herself was a complete waste of time.

For God's sake!

She made herself walk faster, put some snap in her step, straighten her back. She arrived at the Dome and marched up the steps.

Evening, and she was back on the quayside, checking out the dinner trade for any possible Franks. She had chosen a table near the bottom of the slope that led down from the street, allowing her to get a good look at the other customers as they arrived – not that there were many to observe. Candles burned forlornly on mostly vacant tables. Checking their watches as though they could speed up the night, the waiters idled.

A woman's high voice said, 'Leave me alone!'

Flint looked over to a nearby table where a couple sat, the woman indignant, her companion trying to appease her. Flint had already checked him out. He was a local by the look of him, good looking in a flashy sort of way; unless he'd undergone a total body transplant, he was definitely not Frank Harling. The woman picked up the menu and studied it furiously – rather as Jamie had retreated behind the menu in Orso refusing to listen to any more of her copper's talk. The man reached for her hand and she pulled it away.

Odd, that, Flint thought: until towards the end, she and Jamie had never argued – rarely even had a tiff. She would lose her temper with him sometimes but he would always disarm her with his charm. A bad day at work and she might come home spoiling for a fight over some trivial aggravation, and he'd watch her with those liquid eyes until she got close to boiling point and then he'd say 'I adore you' – or some such – and however much she kept it up, trying to provoke him, he would never fight back. She'd come to the conclusion he had the boiling point of tungsten.

'No,' the woman said. 'I've told you, I keep telling you. No.'

When had he changed? she wondered. It was after Frank Harling had come into her life, that was for sure. When she was in the hospital Jamie had been amazing, taking time off work, refusing to leave her bedside, even though he couldn't touch her – couldn't even hold her hands because the fingers were broken and everything hurt so bloody much. The nurses had tried to make him go home but he wouldn't and for the first couple of nights – until they gave in and brought him a bed – he'd slept on the floor. If he slept, that is. They'd had her sedated to dull the pain and she would drift in and out of sleep and somehow he had always known when she would wake up, or so it seemed. Her abiding memory – even now – was floating into consciousness and hearing his voice very close to her ruined face, whispering all the reassurances she needed to hear.

The woman was talking urgently to a waiter, asking him for something, and the man was grinning at her and Flint began to get the idea that he was not her companion. She spoke with an English haughtiness and Flint decided she was probably a tourist being hit on by a Romeo who wouldn't take no for an answer. He was having his say now, with a lot of gesticulation, and the waiter shrugged and walked away. The woman looked despairing and Flint wondered if she should intervene.

Often she couldn't help herself – it was instinctive. She remembered that the first big row with Jamie came after they'd been out for the evening – for the first time in months, and only to a movie because she couldn't stand people staring at the bruising on her face – and on the way home she'd seen three yobs harassing a young woman. She was black and they were white and they were taunting her – 'jungle bunny' and 'dirty bitch' and worse – and Flint had let go of Jamie's arm and crossed the street and taken the can of Mace out of her bag – the can she was authorised to carry in case Frank Harling came calling – and she'd given one of them a squirt in the face; not a full dose, just enough to make him think his eyes were on fire. The other two had squared up to her and for a moment she'd thought they were going to have a go – and she'd *really* wanted them to try. Perhaps they'd seen that in her scary face because they'd backed off, taking their buddy with them, not even cursing her until they were a safe distance away.

When they'd got home Jamie had been furious, angrier than she had ever seen him.

'Christ! Isn't once enough for you? Are you trying to get yourself killed?'

'I'm a cop, Jamie. It's my job. It's what I'm supposed to do. You know – protect the citizens, keep the peace?'

'You're on sick leave, for God's sake. Can't you ever forget you're a . . . Can't you just leave things alone?'

No, actually. She might have explained to Jamie that she always felt compelled to intervene because she hadn't been there to intervene for her mother, and that's why she became a cop. Or, more truthfully, she might have said she became a cop so she would *have* to intervene, and one day she would push it too far and get really badly hurt – far worse than Buller had done – and then maybe the guilt she felt about her mother would dissipate.

But he would have said, 'Grace, you were six years old, for God's sake!' – or something like it and they would have gone round in circles, she trying to explain something he would never understand.

'Well, you could have done something, Jamie,' she said instead – and that had got him going because he'd thought she was calling him a coward, which in a way she was. Even tungsten has a boiling point.

Another man had come to the woman's table – the restaurant owner, Flint assumed – and he was listening to her complaints. Flint heard snatches of what she said – '... me alone ... pestering me for months ... him to go away' – and then Romeo was getting angry, getting to his feet. The owner started yelling at him and he was yelling back and Flint thought, any minute now they're going to start trading punches.

Then Romeo backed off and turned on his heels and strode in Flint's direction, heading for the ramp. When he was halfway up he turned and shouted something in Turkish that sounded pretty offensive but the woman ignored him. She was studying the menu once more, trembling with anger or anguish.

Pestering me for months, she had said and Flint's mind was racing. As in, *He's been pestering me for months*? Meaning, *I live here*?

When she was sure that Romeo had gone, Flint got out of her chair and walked over to the woman's table taking with her the bottle of wine she'd barely touched.

'Hi,' she said. 'I thought you might need a drink?'

'What?' The woman glared at her. She was in her early forties, Flint guessed, with burnished skin that said she spent too much time in the sun. Her hair was drawn back severely, emphasising her high cheekbones and her long neck. She wore an old shirt and a pair of chinos and tennis shoes and almost no jewellery, as if she couldn't care less what she looked like – but Flint could see why

Romeo found her attractive. She held up the bottle and said, 'I couldn't help noticing. I just thought if he came back I could hold him down and you could break his legs with this – though it would be a pity to waste the wine.'

The woman said, 'I don't think so, but thanks anyway.'

'Sure.'

'I should go home.'

'Okay.'

Flint started to turn away and the woman said, 'I don't mean to be rude.'

'Hey, it's fine. If you don't want company . . .'

A hesitation and then, 'I'm Stella. Stella Montague.'

'Gillian Stone,' said Flint. 'I prefer Gill.'

'I came here for something to eat but that . . .'

'Jerk?' Flint offered. 'Asshole? Creep?'

'All of those things,' said Stella, 'and more.'

Flint could see the tension easing out of her.

'Have you eaten?'

Flint shrugged. 'I'm not sure I care.' She thought about it for a moment and then she said, 'Okay, I will if you will. But, first . . .' She waved the bottle.

'Yes,' said Stella. 'I need a drink.'

Stella Montague was a premature widow, her husband taken from her by a multiple pile-up on a fog-bound stretch of the M4 motorway.

'He always did drive too fast,' she said objectively. 'Practically zero visibility and he was doing eighty – the daft sod.'

Not a sentimentalist then, thought Flint.

Stella said she had left England a year ago primarily for tax reasons and chosen Kyrenia more or less on a whim. It was cheap to live and the climate was stunning but, to be honest, it was a bit of a dump. And it was full of bloody English. There was an English pub, an English shop, an English school, even – would you believe – an English church.

'Really?' said Flint as if she didn't know. 'And do you have much to do with them?'

'As little as possible. Well, I like to play bridge and there's a club that's predominantly English but that's about it. As far as I can, I've gone native.'

Soon after her arrival Stella had started to learn Turkish – which was how she'd met Ahmet, indirectly.

'Ahmet?'

Stella nodded her head towards the slope.

He ran a garage and she'd decided to buy a car because the woman who gave her Turkish lessons three times a week lived bloody miles away, up in the hills, and Stella had got tired of paying for taxis and having them wait for two hours while she struggled with the vagaries of a language that seemed to have more vowels than consonants and lacked any grammatical gender. Anyway, Ahmet had sold her a small Ford in pretty decent condition and she'd taken it back a couple of times to have small things fixed and they'd started chatting and one thing had led to another.

'We had a fling, which was fine, and then I found out he was married. Not that I cared one way or the other, but the silly bugger told his wife, or let his wife find out, and suddenly I had this hysterical woman on the phone calling me every name she could think of.'

Stella raised her eyebrows as if to say you should have heard her.

'I didn't understand half of what she said but the next thing I knew she was banging on my front door, wailing and weeping, showing me pictures of the children. Well, that did it. Ahmet was good but he wasn't *that* good. So, I told him to get lost. Only he won't. That was two, three months ago and he still won't leave me alone.'

'Has he threatened you?'

'Oh, God, no. Quite the reverse. Undying love. He wants to leave his wife and all the little Ahmets. I tell you, I'm at my wits' end.'

'Can't you go the police?'

'You're joking.'

Flint was about to argue but she checked herself. Cutter had once told her, 'You're good, Flint, because you never forget who you're supposed to be.'

'Yeah, you're probably right,' she said. 'You used to let him screw you, so what's the problem? Cops, they're not very good with the subtleties.'

'You sound as if you know.'

'A guy raped me. Problem was, we'd been living together for almost a year – still were living together in a way – so how can that be rape, right?'

Stella lit a cigarette. 'Is that why you're here?'

'Sort of. Let me ask you something.'

There was a wariness now in Stella's eyes, as though

she'd suddenly found reason to be suspicious

'There's an English guy I'm trying to find and I wondered if you knew him.'

'What's his name?'

Flint said, 'When I knew him he was Harling. Frank Harling.'

Stella looked at her blankly. 'Sorry. Means nothing to me but then it probably wouldn't. As I told you, I keep my distance.'

'Yeah, well, he won't be Frank Harling any more. Turns out he changes his name about as often as he changes his underwear.'

'You're pregnant, aren't you?'

'I'm not here to start a fight,' Flint said. 'I just want to talk to him.'

Stella shrugged as if say it was none of her concern.

Flint said, 'I was wondering. These people you play bridge with, you said some of them were English.'

'Most of them.'

'I've got a photograph of Frank. If I showed it at your club maybe somebody would recognise him.'

What you need, Flint, is an army. An army of English ex-pats.

'Perhaps.' Stella seemed doubtful but then she went on, 'We're playing tomorrow night. Come if you like.'

Flint nodded. 'I've got nothing to lose. Where do I go?'

'Where are you staying?'

'At the Dome.'

'I'll pick you up. About six.'

Flint smiled her thanks. 'Let's get out of here. Where's your car?'

'Just up the hill.'

'I'll walk you there.'

They split the bill and they walked up the harbour rise to a narrow, dark street where a small Ford was parked and as Stella fumbled for her keys Flint heard a sound behind her. She swung round dropping into a crouch and saw Ahmet lunging for her. She lashed out with one foot and caught his kneecap and heard him yelp with pain, but he had momentum and he kept coming, sending her sprawling, falling on top of her. She fought like a cat, going for his eyes, and she was on top of him when she felt a prick in her back and a rush of heat running up her spine and an explosion of pain in her head. Then somebody was lifting her, somebody was opening a car door.

'She give you any problems?' A voice she knew she recognised.

'No,' said Stella. 'She couldn't wait to see you.'

'Silly cow,' said Frank Harling.

III

The right wing dropped abruptly as the plane banked on its final approach to Ercan and Cohen felt a rush of irrational fear. He was an uneasy passenger at the best of times and – this being a Turkish Airlines flight – this was definitely not one of those. When he was sixteen Cohen's father had taken him to Paris for the England-France rugby international and if they hadn't got caught up in the post-match euphoria and missed their plane home they would have been – should have been – among the 346 souls on a Turkish DC-10 heading for London that plunged into the forest near Ermenonville, shredding itself into a million pieces. Afterwards, out of morbid curiosity, Cohen had read a gendarme's all too graphic account of what it was like to be in the forest on that Sunday afternoon – like Verdun after the bloodiest battle – and he'd never been able to disassociate Turkish Airlines from searing images of the aftermath of sudden, violent death.

To make matters worse the plane bringing them to Cyprus – or Kibris as the Turkish Cypriots called it – was an ageing Boeing that seemed to groan and shudder

in protest at every demand made upon it. The sound of
the landing gear coming down was excruciating, like
tearing metal, and Cohen gripped the arm rest as though
for dear life.

Alexander Bland said, 'I guess flying's not your thing.'

Bland was Cutter's man – or, at least, Cutter had
made the arrangements. Formally he was a senior
functionary at the US embassy in Ankara. Unless Cohen
was much mistaken he was also – primarily – the CIA's
head of station in Turkey.

'Alex and I go back a-ways,' Cutter had said enig-
matically. 'You can trust him to get things done.'

And that he had. While Cohen had cooled his heels in
Istanbul, Bland had plumbed the diplomatic channels in
Ankara until he'd found a way around the seemingly
insuperable problem of negotiating with a state that did
not exist. Nobody recognised the Turkish Republic of
Northern Cyprus except the Turks – 'and, oh yes,' said
Bland, 'Mozambique' – and nobody recognised its
president, Rauf Denktash. 'Hard to ask a guy for a favour
when you've been calling him an outlaw for twenty-five
years, and you're going to go on calling him an outlaw
no matter what he does for you,' was Bland's blunt
assessment of the problem. 'Even harder when the place
is on the brink of war.'

Still, that's what he'd achieved: not yet the favour but
at least the chance to ask it, face to face. The presidential
limousine was waiting for them on the Tarmac. Cohen
caught sight of it as the plane thudded safely onto the
runway and he could at last unscramble his bowels.

* * *

'So, you are a lawyer, Mr Cohen,' said the president. 'As am I.' On the wall behind his desk there was a formal portrait of a much younger, much slimmer Denktash in black robes, a barrister's wig perched on a head that was now almost entirely bald.

'Merely a solicitor,' said Cohen. 'One of the infantry.'

'Nonetheless, I'm sure you share my perception of the legal complexities of this case; the *daunting* complexities that confront us.'

'It's certainly complicated, sir.'

'Oh, more than complicated, Mr Cohen, surely? Let me see if I have this right.' He perched a pair of glasses on the end of his nose and opened a file that was surprisingly thick. 'Now, the man, Harling, whom you wish us to locate and arrest has committed no crime in this country, so far as I am aware. He entered the TRNC legally under what you tell me is his real name and what he calls himself now is his own affair. As long as there is no intention to deceive, he may call himself what he likes.' He peered at Cohen over the top of his glasses as if to make sure he was following the logic.

'Now, the woman, Flint, on the other hand, did not enter the TRNC legally since her name is not . . .' he paused, looking for the detail in the file – 'Gillian Stone and you tell me that the passport she presented in that name is a forgery; one manufactured in some bar in Amsterdam.'

'Not necessarily manufactured *in* the bar,' said Cohen

pedantically. 'She obtained it from someone who works in a bar.'

Denktash waved a plump hand, brushing away the irrelevancy. 'Wherever it was made it is false, and presenting a false passport in order to gain entry is a crime in my country, Mr Cohen. She will be arrested, you can rest assured.'

'Thank you, sir.'

'No, I don't think you understand. She will be arrested for the crime she committed *here*. She will be prosecuted *here*. If she is found guilty, she will – in all likelihood – be sent to prison *here*. After she has served her sentence she may be deported, but that is a matter for the courts.'

Cohen swallowed and said, 'She's wanted for murder, sir. They both are.'

'So you say, Mr Cohen, but that brings us to the next complexity. Tell me, Mr Bland: if the British came to you with a similar request to arrest two of their nationals and simply hand them over, what would happen?'

At Washington's firm insistence Bland was required to keep out of the discussions, to let Cohen do all of the talking. He was there as the facilitator of the meeting – nothing more. By maintaining this fiction the State Department believed it could plausibly deny that the US had ever negotiated with the unrecognised president of a rogue state. Bland even sat apart, on a sofa as far away from the presidential desk as he could manage.

'I'm not a lawyer, sir,' he said.

'No,' said Denktash dryly, 'you're a diplomat – I'm told. Even so, I'm sure you know there are certain formalities that would be observed. Even among friends, there are formalities: treaties, letters *rogatoire*, extradition proceedings . . .'

Cohen said, 'Mr President, I know that what I'm asking you to do is irregular.'

'Irregular! Mr Cohen, it is unprecedented. You come here with Mr Bland, the representatives of two powerful nations that have done all they can to undermine and isolate my country – a country that is, nevertheless, a democracy with a written constitution and one founded on law – and, in the total absence of any treaty or agreement between us, or any legal grounds, you ask me to break our laws. Is that not the sum of it?'

'Yes,' said Cohen.

'And to add to these complexities we have a conundrum, do we not? Gentlemen, why is the United States government using its vast influence to support this request? This is a British matter, is it not?'

'Not entirely,' said Cohen. 'As I think you know, among other things Harling and Flint are suspected of complicity in the bombing of an aircraft in which four people died. The plane was American and the pilot and one of the passengers were US citizens. In fact, they were both federal agents.'

'Ah, I'm glad you brought that up.' From the file Denktash produced a document that Cohen could see was a faxed copy of the Interpol alert for Flint; the dangerous fiction he had created that had now taken on a life of its own. 'I see from this that Flint is also wanted for a bombing in Paris. Is that correct?'

'Wanted for questioning,' Cohen said.

'But not by the French. A man is killed . . .'

'He was Portuguese, sir.'

'He could have been a Martian, Mr Cohen, but he was killed in Paris and several French police officers were injured in the explosion, and yet there is no word from France in support of your request. Two Americans are killed on an American aircraft that is flying over the territorial waters of Puerto Rico – and Puerto Rico is effectively an American dependency, is it not, Mr Bland? – and though Mr Bland comes here with you he makes no request for these terrorists to be handed over to him; indeed, he says barely a word. It is purely a British matter. Why is that, Mr Cohen?'

Cohen feared that any moment his face would turn red. 'Initially . . .'

'Initially?'

'At this stage,' Cohen began again, 'Flint and Harling are wanted for questioning about conspiracy to murder. It is not suggested that they actually caused the explosions – rather, that they may have been part of a conspiracy that was hatched, at least in part, in the United Kingdom.'

'Oh, I see!' said Denktash as though a dense fog had suddenly lifted. '*Initially* you think Flint and Harling *may* have conspired *at least in part* in the United Kingdom – but what if they didn't? What if it transpires they orchestrated their conspiracy in Paris or New York or even Amsterdam? What then? Will you hand them over to the French or the Americans or the Dutch?'

'Technically . . .'

'*Technically*, Mr Cohen.'

Cohen knew that on the Greek side of Cyprus, where Denktash was detested, they called him 'the donkey'; in Whitehall, for his stubbornness, he was known as 'the mule'. More like a fox, Cohen now thought.

'It is possible, Mr President, that if they were not charged in the United Kingdom for any reason, some other state might apply for their extradition.'

Denktash shook his head. 'So, gentlemen, we are at the nub of it, are we not? In the absence of any treaty between the TRNC and the United Kingdom, in the absence of any formal request from the British government, in the absence of even *prima facie* evidence, you are asking me to ignore a crime Flint has committed in my country and hand her over to you – together with Harling, who has committed no crime in this country – so that you may or may not hand them over to America or France or the Netherlands – perhaps even Portugal? In any event, to a nation that does not recognise this republic, that has no treaty with us, that presents no evidence, that makes no request of us at all. Mr Cohen, you are asking a lot.'

Denktash removed his glasses and closed the file. 'This is not a decision that can be made lightly. I'll have you taken to your hotel. You will be informed in due course.' On his desk he found other urgent matters that required his attention.

Defying his orders Bland said, 'What would it take, sir? For you to say yes?'

'One word, Mr Bland. Not from you. From Washington. From your secretary of state. A telephone call, person-to-person.'

'And, assuming the impossible, what would that word be, sir?'

Denktash did not look up from his desk. 'Please.'

Their hotel overlooked the dividing line between Greek and Turkish Cyprus; the so-called 'green line' that ran through the heart of Nicosia – or Lefkosa to the Turks – that was a forest of blockades and barriers and razor wire. The United Nations maintained the line, had done for a quarter of a century, but from his room Cohen could see trenches that were occupied by Turkish soldiers. Cohen thought it surreal. It was as though the Berlin Wall had not fallen at all, but simply been moved to a warmer location.

Bland was in the room next door working the phone, his line constantly engaged. He had brought with him a complicated-looking box that secured his conversations but there was nothing he could do, he said, about the microphones in the walls, assuming there were any.

'I do assume that there are,' he'd warned Cohen, 'and so should you. And assume they're listening to your calls, as well as mine. In fact, count on it.'

But Cohen wasn't worried what the Turks heard him say. Clearing the clutter from his mind he had re-established the truth: that Denktash was not the enemy.

'It's me,' he said, calling Glenning's direct line at Scotland Yard.

'Twenty minutes,' and Glenning cut the line.

As a safe phone – safe, that is, from a direct tap, but not necessarily from the vacuuming satellites of GCHQ – they had selected the public phone in the lobby of the Crowne Plaza Hotel in Buckingham Gate. Glenning could stroll there from his office in just a few minutes, get something to drink if he wanted to, even smoke his pipe.

'How's it going?' he said, answering on the first ring.

'Too soon to tell. What about your end?'

'A.J. is spitting blood. He's decided you were not entirely frank with him about why you're where you are. Peter's come to the same conclusion and since that's what I told him about you – vis-à-vis the vet – the three of us are now united in our suspicion of you.'

'And?'

'There was talk of A.J. coming out. To "supervise".'

'Supervise what?'

'Whatever nefarious arrangement you may come to. They – we, as far as they know – do not trust you, Harry. There is a strong belief that you've fallen under Cutter's spell – A.J.'s words – and since Cutter won't tell them a thing, you are very definitely in the doghouse.'

'When might A.J. come?'

'For all I know he's there now. On the other side of the line.'

'Understood. I'll call you when there's news.'

'Do that. Listen, Harry, are you sure you know what you're doing?'

'No. But there's nothing else I can do.'

Cohen put down the phone and it rang almost immediately.

Bland said, 'We're back in the ballgame. See you in the lobby in five minutes. And, in case you were thinking about it, don't ask.'

Privately President Denktash may have believed he had achieved for his beleaguered republic the most seismic breakthrough in international relations since Yalta, but he was far too urbane to show it. He welcomed Cohen and Bland back into his office as though they had just stepped outside for five minutes to stretch their legs or get some air. 'Right, gentlemen, we have work to do.'

He had removed his jacket and his tie and all other sense of formality. He sat on one of two sofas set on either side of a low table on which the file was now spread – open to them, its contents ready to be shared, apparently.

'Now, it transpires that Flint arrived in Kyrenia late on Thursday afternoon on the ferry from Antalya.' He handed Cohen the landing card on which she had written the name 'STONE, Gillian' but the president made no mention of that. 'I wonder why she did not fly directly from Istanbul?'

'Airlines keep passenger manifests,' Cohen said. 'Ferry companies don't.'

'Of course. She checked into the Dome Hotel without a reservation. Normally, at this time of the year she might have been lucky to get a room but, sadly, as you know, these are not normal times. Mr Bland, let me ask you a question. Do you think our friends across the line are foolish enough to deploy their missiles?'

'I don't have an opinion, sir.'

'I do,' said Denktash. 'They will back down, they must back down because if they don't they will be bombed.' Bland kept his silence, waiting out the pause. 'Nobody should be in any doubt about that. Nobody.'

Cohen wondered if the secretary of state had raised the question of the looming war in the course of the phone call she would never admit to making. If so, if she was unclear about Turkish intentions, she had her answer now.

'Flint appears to have spent Thursday evening in her room. None of those who have been questioned so far recall—'

'Sir, can I interrupt you?' Cohen couldn't help himself because what Denktash was reporting sounded like the product of a hurried police inquiry into someone who was missing, not someone who was under observation. 'Are you saying that Flint has disappeared?'

'I'm coming to that Mr Cohen. All in good time.'

Oh, Christ!

Cutter had urged him to hurry. 'They're pissing themselves, Harry. They don't know what's happened but they know it's not good. They're into damage control and they badly need Flint to tell them if they're holed below the waterline. Flint is now their number one priority. You need to get there first, buddy.'

'On Friday – yesterday – she was extremely industrious.'

'Please!' Cohen implored. 'Mr President, I really do need to know what's happened.'

Denktash frowned his disapproval but he said, 'She has disappeared and in somewhat curious circumstances.'

'What do you mean?'

'Last evening she had dinner with a woman at one of the restaurants on the harbour. They left together and Flint did not return to the hotel last night, nor has she returned so far today. Her things are still there including her passport – in fact, both of her passports – and a large sum of money; several thousand British pounds. The police think it is curious that she would abandon several thousand pounds – unless, of course, she knows we are on to her. It's possible.'

You're too late! You got here too damned late!

'The woman she was with? Who was she?'

'We don't know. There is a description of her that tells us very little.' Denktash glanced at one of the documents on the table. 'Early forties, perhaps. English, certainly. Rather dowdy by the sound of it. Reddish hair drawn back from her face. She was wearing what appeared to be men's casual clothing and just a little gold jewellery.'

A little gold jewellery.

Cohen said, 'Was she wearing a chain, a chain with a small stone around her neck?'

Denktash checked the page and said, 'Yes, a gold band on her wedding finger and a gold necklace. You know this woman? Another of the conspirators, perhaps?'

'Perhaps.'

Cohen was in turmoil, plunged back into the nightmare of his paralysis, Sarah Spenny leaning on his chest, knotting and tugging at his hair; knotting and tugging at the gold chain she wore around her neck.

Denktash misunderstood his agitation. 'You can be assured there is a full-scale search underway. In addition to the police, the commander of the Turkish Defence Forces has provided men and equipment to assist the search, whatever is necessary, and the area has been sealed off. Since we are dealing with terrorists, he has also provided a special forces unit, men who have experience in such situations.'

Cohen forced himself to speak. 'We need them alive.'

'That will be up to Flint and Harling.'

Denktash stood up and went to his desk and returned with an envelope that was embossed with the presidential seal.

'I should tell you that Harling has also disappeared. The police located the apartment where he was living and it was visited by the special forces this morning.' Denktash paused and smiled. 'I say visited but I doubt if they knocked. In any event, he was not there and nor were his things. A neighbour saw him leaving the apartment complex yesterday afternoon and there is a description of a car.'

Denktash opened the envelope and drew out a sheet of notepaper that he showed to Cohen. Whatever it said was written in Turkish, endorsed with three stamps and three florid signatures that bristled with authority.

'This is a *laissez passer* signed by myself and countersigned by the chief of police and the military commander. It will speed you through the road blocks you will undoubtedly encounter. I have a car and driver waiting for you downstairs.'

'Where am I going?'

'Kyrenia. It is only a matter of time before they are found and – since you can identify Flint and Harling and perhaps the other woman, if she is involved – your presence could be invaluable. Don't you agree?'

'Yes,' said Cohen.

Oh, God, let me get there before it's too late.

'And thank you.' He looked at Bland in a silent appeal: *What the hell do I say now? What the hell do I do?* Bland shrugged and raised a hand in a gesture of farewell.

'Mr Bland and I have other matters to discuss.'

President Denktash took Cohen's right hand in both of his. 'I wish you well, Lawyer Cohen. Good hunting.'

IV

Grace Flint is inside a box, a white box as cramped as a coffin – but coffins aren't white inside, she knows. They're plush red velvet, or plain pitch pine and, besides, you don't have lights inside a coffin – blinding white lights that are sending her optic nerves crazy – nor Annie Lennox singing to you in stereo. *I may be mad, I may be blind, I may be viciously unkind* . . . She is covered with a sheet, or maybe a shroud, that is also white; as white as the skin on her face, as white as her hair. Everything is white and when she stands outside the box she can see that she merges with her surroundings so perfectly she is invisible. She is there but she has vanished and Annie is asking, *Why can't you see this boat is sinking* . . . *sinking, sinking, sinking, sinking.*

She snapped out of the hallucination with a start and for a moment everything was perfectly clear. She was not in a box but in a room, lying on something hard, like a table. There was someone else in the room, someone dressed in white – but that was all of the information she could garner before the clarity skidded away.

She was falling, sinking, back in the box, Annie

leaning over her. *This is the fear, This is the dread, These are the contents of my head* ... Annie dressed all in white, some kind of tunic. Annie pulling at her, Annie hurting her.

'Leave me alone!'

I may be viciously unkind ...

Annie putting something in her arm, Annie slapping her face, Annie screaming at her.

This is the fear, This is the dread ...

'*Leave me alone, bitch!*'

There is something in Flint's mouth, probing under her tongue. She imagines a cattle prod and feels an explosion of pain.

Stella Montague removed a thermometer from Flint's mouth and checked the reading. 'That's fine.' To Flint she said, 'How are you feeling, my dear?'

She was wearing a white tunic buttoned to the neck. Her hair, freed from its constraint, fell about her shoulders. A surgical mask was perched on her head like a bonnet.

Flint resolved to say nothing. Not a word.

'I expect you're thirsty. Well, it won't be long and then you can have some water. Don't try to move, dearie, there really is no point.'

Fair comment. Flint could feel the two straps that bound her to the table.

'I won't be a moment,' Stella said, dipping under a white sheet that was suspended from the ceiling like a curtain, falling onto Flint just below the level of her breasts, obscuring her view of the room beyond that point. She couldn't see beyond the curtain but she could sense that Stella was not alone.

Frank Harling said, 'Let's get it done.'

'Now, dear,' Stella said, 'we need you to raise your hips and just turn your lower body on one side. Just halfway. We need to be able to reach your spine.'

Flint made herself as rigid as a rod.

'Oh, you are being a cunt. Frank, turn her over.'

She felt rough hands on her hips and her thighs and then her buttocks, turning her, twisting her with a power she could not resist, locking her into position.

'Now, you're going to feel a jab. Nothing awful; just a pin prick. But you have to keep still. If you move it will hurt like hell, and then we'll have to do it again. Just relax.'

She felt Harling's fingers digging into her bare flesh like the clamps of a vice and then a prick in the small of her back.

Another man's voice said, 'Just keep her still.'

'You're doing very well,' Stella said cheerfully. 'Just a few more seconds . . . and . . . there, it's done!'

Harling released her. Stella's cheerful face appeared from behind the curtain.

'Now, that wasn't too bad, was it?'

There was a sob working its way up Flint's throat and she fought to keep it down.

'I'll be with you in just a moment.'

Coming from behind the curtain Flint heard the gentle clatter of surgical instruments being laid out. Then she heard the squeal of rubber and Stella reappeared, pushing a trolley that carried what appeared to be a cylinder of oxygen. 'Just in case,' she said. 'We don't want you dying on us, do we?'

'Leave it out,' said Harling. 'Who the fuck cares?'

Ignoring him, Stella parked the trolley alongside Flint's head and fussed with dials attached to the cylinder.

'Everything seems to be in order,' she said. 'Now . . .'

She leaned over Flint and felt her forehead and then pressed her fingers against the pulse in her neck.

'Good, good. You're doing very well.' She sat on the edge of the table and said, 'Now, let me explain what's going to happen.'

Flint wanted a very clear view of Stella and she blinked several times in an attempt to clear the tears that were welling in her eyes.

'We need to know several things. First and foremost, we need to know what Maitland told you, what documents he gave you, exactly what they said, and who else knows what they said. Oh, and where the documents are now, of course. There are a lot of other questions, but that's what we're going to start with. Okay? Now, because you're a cunt you're not going to tell us – not yet, brave little plod that you are.'

'For Christ's sake!' Harling growing impatient behind the curtain.

Stella nudged her on the arm with a closed fist, the gentlest of punches.

'So, here's what we're going to do.' She brought her face very close to Flint's. 'Behind there' – she jabbed her head at the improvised curtain – 'is a surgeon who is going to remove your internal organs. One. By. One.'

This is not real. This is a nightmare. Any second now I'm going to wake up.

'Now, don't worry – he's a very good surgeon. There have been some questions about his ethics and he's not practising at the moment – actually, he's prohibited from practising at the moment – but *technically* he's very sound. So, you're in good hands. Is there something you want to say?'

Fuck off and die.

'All right. Do you feel a nice, warm creeping glow? That's what you're supposed to feel. Look, what I want you to do is see if you can lift your legs. No, come on, sweetheart, you really should try. It's the only way we can tell if the epidural has taken. Believe me, you don't want him cutting you, harvesting you, if it hasn't taken. Come on, try.'

Despite herself, Flint tried to lift her legs. They would not move.

'That's great. Okay, this time it's pretty minor. He's going to take something out and then we're going to let you think about it for a while – and then we'll see how it goes.'

She pushed her hand beyond the curtain and patted Flint's belly.

'Apparently, there's a lot of stuff down here you can do without.'

She ran her hands up to Flint's left breast and fondled the nipple.

'Mind you, if I was you, I wouldn't wait until he got to my heart.'

Stella kissed Flint on the forehead and tousled her hair. 'Now, there's something else I need to tell you. I knew a man who had a hernia operation and they gave him an epidural and it went the wrong way – up as well as down – and he suddenly found he couldn't use his lungs. He managed to tell them just in time to get the oxygen, and then there was this explosion in his head.'

Stella stood up and displayed her hands in a petal. 'Boom. It took them two hours to bring him down off the ceiling. So, if you feel you can't breathe, don't forget to shout.'

Unable to keep her vow of silence Flint said, 'Fuck you.'

Stella said softly, 'No, fuck you,' and disappeared behind the curtain.

'Who'd want to fuck her?' Harling said. 'Look at her, she's all skin and bone.'

'If you'll all just be quiet for a moment, please,' the other man said and Flint, feeling nothing, imagined the cut being made.

She willed herself to breathe and not to cry.

'You know what's really funny?' an invisible Stella said. 'When we were in the restaurant, and you wanted me to believe you were pregnant, I thought, "Who's she kidding?" I mean, next to me, you're the last woman in the world who'd want to be pregnant – and if some fucker's sperm made it up here violating one of your eggs, you'd have it exterminated in a second? Right? I mean, who'd want all of that screaming, all of that shit?'

A five second pause. 'You know, in some ways, Grace, I think we're doing you a favour.'

They were beginning with her ovaries.

ten

On the whitewashed surface of a cinder-block wall in the briefing room of a Turkish army base five miles east of Kyrenia, Grace Flint's mask of a face had been blown up to gigantic proportions.

'The terrorist, Flint,' announced Captain Zulu – freshly arrived from the mainland – and Cohen could not deny that she looked the part. The photograph had been copied from the Gillian Stone passport found in the guest safe of the Dome Hotel and it showed her gaunt and sullen, the mug shot of a woman who had been hiding out for a month and neglecting her nutrition. The enlargement process had also removed the gradations of tone so that she was pure black and white with intense eyes and a dark slash of a downturned mouth. If you didn't know better you might think she was some unyielding leftover from the Seventies, a defiant disciple of, say, the Baader-Meinhoff gang or the Red Brigades.

They didn't know better – *the terrorist, Flint* – and that was Cohen's fault. He had to find a convincing explanation for his lie – if they would listen.

Zulu's men were aware that Cohen had information to contribute, but they were uneasy about his presence. Though he sat among them he caught the looks that said he had no business in this room. Zulu was not the captain's real name, of course, and all of his men also had pseudonyms drawn from the phonetic alphabet, embossed on name tags that were pinned to their chests. They were Bravo, Oscar, Sierra and so forth, while he was '*Mister Cohen*' – a foreigner and all too obviously a civilian.

'So, Mister Cohen, come up and tell us what you know about Flint.' Zulu's English was fluent, tinged by a mid-Atlantic accent.

Slowly Cohen walked to the podium and faced fourteen taciturn commandos dressed all in black who sprawled in plastic chairs. Several of them smoked and the air was pungent with the aroma of strong tobacco.

Zulu said he would provide a translation. 'I don't want any misunderstandings.'

'Good,' Cohen quickly said. 'Thank you, captain. Because I'm afraid there has been some confusion. Let me see if I can provide you with a clearer picture of Flint.' He coughed to clear his throat. 'As you know, she is a serving police officer . . .'

'Is?'

'Was – was a serving police officer.' Cohen nodded to Zulu to acknowledge his correction. 'She has, of course, been suspended for the time being but the point I want to make is that she is not, in any sense, a terrorist. There is no reason to believe she has or ever would use violence.'

He paused, waiting in vain for Zulu's translation. From the floor, the commando designated by his name tag as Whiskey said, 'She blew up a plane.'

'No, no, no,' Cohen said emphatically. 'You see, this is where the confusion has arisen. Other people have certainly done that and Flint is suspected – and I stress *suspected* – of being associated with them . . . in some way . . . that is not really clear.'

'Conspired,' Zulu said. 'The warrant says she conspired with others to cause explosions.'

'Yes it does and, frankly, that is overstating the evidence.' It was hot in the briefing room and the cigarette smoke was making Cohen dizzy. He closed his eyes and searched for words that might edge them towards the truth. 'What is certainly true is that Flint has knowledge – crucial knowledge – about these people and that is why it is imperative that she is found and interviewed. I'm certain that when she understands the situation she will fully cooperate.'

Zulu spoke in Turkish, a mere handful of words. Then he said to Cohen, 'She's trained to use weapons.'

'No, she is not. Only a small proportion of British police officers ever carry firearms and she never has. There is no reason to think she even knows how to fire a gun.'

Zulu said, 'But in America . . .'

'She was merely a liaison officer.'

'But in America,' Zulu insisted, 'she was trained. On

the firing range. And at Quantico.'

'What are you talking about?'

Unzipping the breast pocket of his windbreaker, Zulu withdrew a sheet of paper that he unfolded and read aloud: 'From May 1997 to June 1998, while she was attached to a federal task force in Miami, Flint was trained in the use of handguns. On the firing range she routinely scored in the high nineties . . .'

'But that's utter nonsense,' Cohen protested.

'In June and July of 1997,' Zulu continued, 'Flint attended the FBI National Academy in Quantico, Virginia . . .'

'To become familiar with FBI methods and procedures,' Cohen said.

'And stayed on after the course to observe the training provided by the Critical Incident Response Group.' Zulu broke off from his relentless recitation and said, 'Have you been to Quantico, Mister Cohen? Among other things the CIRG provides excellent tuition in hostage rescue and SWAT team methods. We experienced training on a live range at Quantico. It was very realistic.'

Could it possibly be true? Could Cohen have spent more than a month probing Flint's background and not picked up even a hint of this? He reached for Zulu's sheet of paper. 'Where on earth has this come from?'

Zulu let him take it. It was written entirely in Turkish and indecipherable to Cohen.

'From the military attaché at the Turkish embassy in London,' Zulu said. 'It is based on information received from his contacts in the British security services.'

Cohen felt as though he had been punched in the stomach or – more likely – sandbagged, hit from behind.

'It seems that some of your colleagues don't share your equanimity.'

Zulu took back his dispatch and rapidly spoke to his men and Cohen didn't need to comprehend a word in order to understand the gist of what he said. It was all too clear from the hardening of their faces: Flint was trained and therefore dangerous.

'Now,' announced Zulu. 'The terrorist, Harling . . .'

II

Lying on a camp bed, watching the dwindling light through a small window high in the wall – a window too small for even a child to climb through – Flint knew she was sedated. She had passed out during the operation and when she had come to she was in this room, a catheter in her arm, feeling much as she did now: languid and strangely distant. The outrage at what they had done to her was like an echo, something elusive that she could not yet grasp.

There was a dull ache above her pelvis and she reached down under the sheet with her hand and felt the dressing on the wound. She traced the length of it with her fingertips and felt a tingle that extended just below the bikini line.

So, it would be a hidden scar, she thought dispassionately; nothing too disfiguring. Technically he's very sound, Stella had said.

Jesus! Snap out of it!

She guessed that the sedative was contained in the colourless liquid that dripped relentlessly from a bottle suspended above her head, feeding a tube attached to the catheter. Vaguely she thought of what she might do, what she should do, to stop the drug entering her bloodstream but it was difficult to concentrate, her mind drifting off to subjects of its own choosing.

Had she wanted children? Jamie had. In the early years of their marriage he'd done all he could to persuade her and once, when her period did not arrive like clockwork – and, as the days passed, she grew more certain she was pregnant – she had accepted what seemed inevitable and he had been elated. His dismay when she'd told him it was a false promise – or a false alarm – had been difficult to take.

But however hard he'd pressed her to 'try again' – as if she'd 'tried' the first time – she had found herself ambivalent. She knew she could have a child and return to her career – and there was never any question that she wouldn't – and she was not unattracted by the proposition. What held her back was the knowledge of the risks she took, more often and sometimes much greater than Jamie knew or imagined. She knew that one day she might step too far over the edge and then her child would have no mother, just as she'd had no mother – and she could not bring herself to do that, any more than she could bring herself to come down from the ledge. She was a risk junkie, addicted to adrenaline and – in the end, she'd decided – unsuitable for motherhood.

'Perhaps when I grow up,' she would say to Jamie to placate him, 'maybe next year.' And then Jamie had fathered Caroline's bastard child, and the subject was moot.

Not any more, it wasn't. Now it was irrelevant because they had taken away the option she had left herself.

For God's sake, Flint, concentrate on what you have to do.

She fingered the catheter, willing herself to disconnect the tube. She tried again to grasp the enormity of what they'd done, to find the rage that was her due. The anger was there and it was building. She could hear it moaning, like a wounded animal in some corner of her soul.

Emerging from the kitchen Metin Cadessi asked Frank Harling, 'Shall I feed her?'

'What for?'

Cadessi shrugged as if to say he didn't care either way. 'You want something?'

'Later, maybe.' Harling was lying on a sofa, his eyes half open, watching the terrace where Patrick Shilling and Sarah Spenny sat on a low wall engaged in intense conversation.

'What about them?'

'Metin, this is not a fucking hotel.'

Harling had been in a black mood ever since they had driven up from Kyrenia – he and Cadessi in the Ford with Flint laid out on the back seat like a corpse, Shilling and Spenny following behind in their rented Jeep. Cadessi had been keen to describe his winning performance as Ahmet the persistent Romeo but Harling wasn't interested. As soon as they'd arrived he had told Cadessi to find somewhere in the forest and dig a hole and Shilling had asked him why.

'Why the fuck do you think?'

'No,' Shilling had said.

'What do you mean, no?'

'We need to talk to her. We need to find out what she knows.'

'I know what she knows – she knows too fucking much. You think I'm going to let her walk out of here?'

'When she's talked I'll decide what to do with her.'

'You'll decide?' Harling had said and Shilling hadn't bothered to reply and for a long moment they had stood in the driveway like two tensed cats eyeing each others' throats. Then Spenny had opened her bag and taken out a small black revolver and said quietly, 'Frank, behave yourself,' and Harling had thought about it.

'Later,' he'd finally said. 'We'll talk about it later' – and, having experienced the volcanic quality of Harling's anger, Cadessi had decided that Flint was not the only one who could end up in a hole.

'You want something to drink, maybe.'

'Shit, Metin! Will you cut it out?'

'Okay, okay.' Cadessi kicked the logs smoldering in the fireplace – a fire made necessary, even in summer, by the thickness of the walls. In the day, when the heat outside could be unbearable, the house was deliciously cool. At night, when the mists often came, it grew cold enough to chill the bones. 'What do I care?' he said.

It was Cadessi who had found the house after Harling had found Cadessi. There had been a phone call from a contact in Istanbul mentioning the possibility of lucrative employment, and two days later Harling had turned up at Cadessi's door offering five thousand dollars a month for unspecified services. Five thousand dollars being much more than he usually made selling icons and artifacts looted from the churches and medieval castles that speckle the mountains behind Kyrenia, Cadessi had accepted.

'I need a bolt-hole,' Harling had said, defining the first service he required. Somewhere out of town that he could disappear to if the need arose. Somewhere he could rent or buy through a very private arrangement.

Well, there was Volker's place, Cadessi had said – Volker being his sometime partner in the icon business. Volker had returned to Germany for the duration and Cadessi had the keys and for a price – a steep price since Cadessi saw this as a seller's market – the house was available.

When they had driven up into the mountains to inspect the property – following a narrow, winding track through stunted olive trees and Aleppo pines – Harling had found an ill-restored corner of a ruined monastery: eight draughty rooms on two floors, barely furnished or equipped.

'It needs some work,' Cadessi had conceded, 'but wait until you see this.' On the second floor, at the head of the stone staircase, there was a door that Cadessi unlocked, leading to a large chamber where every inch of the walls was lined with pornographic photographs, some of them life-sized. 'Volker's jerk-off room,' said Cadessi. 'It's included in the price.'

Cadessi was a good five inches taller than Harling, and he kept himself in shape, and in his youth in Istanbul he had tried out for the Turkish junior national wrestling team. He knew, he thought, how to take care of himself. But he had never experienced such a crushing bear-hug as Harling applied, nor been lifted from his feet so easily, nor ever felt so powerless.

Without a word Harling had carried him from the room and thrown him down the stairs. As Cadessi lay at the bottom – trying to decide what was broken and what hurt the most – Harling had arrived and kicked him in the face. He turned away to protect himself and Harling kicked him in the small of the back. He turned again, and was kicked in the head. No matter which way he twisted, nor how much he begged for Harling to stop, he was kicked and stamped until he was senseless. When he had come to, Harling was sitting on the stairs regarding him with cold indifference.

'Don't you ever – *ever* – fuck with me again, Metin. You understand?'

They had renegotiated the rental arrangement on terms very much more favourable to Harling and then he had taken Cadessi to hospital in Nicosia. Two days later when Cadessi was discharged – bruised over most of his body but otherwise intact – Harling had given him twenty-five thousand dollars to furnish and fix the house. Cadessi had obtained receipts for every cent he spent but Harling – having made his point – had never asked to see them.

On the terrace Shilling and Spenny were wrapping up

their discussion, evidently. Spenny stood up and stretched
her bare arms above her head, her skin a burnt orange in
the last light of the sun. She was wearing a skirt that was
very short – for Shilling's pleasure, Harling supposed –
and at this distance she looked girlish, harmless, not the
one to worry about in the coming confrontation. Not the
dangerous bitch that she was.

'Metin, you got a handgun?'

Surprised by the question Cadessi almost lied but he
caught himself in time. 'Sure. Nine-millimetre Beretta.'

'Where is it?'

'In my room.'

'From now on, carry it.'

'You think there's going to be trouble?'

Harling got up from the sofa and shivered. 'Yes,' he
said. 'If you don't get that fire going I'm going to die of
the fucking cold.'

'I'll explain it to you once more,' Shilling said with weary
patience, as though he was talking to a recalcitrant child.
'We need to know what Rykov told her. We need to
know what Maitland told her. We need to know what
documents she found. When we know all that we can
assess the damage: who's vulnerable, who's not; which
accounts have been compromised, which haven't; who's
talked besides Silva; what they can prove as opposed to
what they might suspect. Am I getting through to you,
Frank?' Shilling's voice was rising. 'Is there something
you find particularly difficult to understand?'

'Yes,' said Harling calmly. 'What's the fucking point?

Silva's told them everything they need to know.'

They were sitting at the table picking at the remains of a meal that Cadessi had reluctantly prepared. When Spenny had asked 'What's for supper?' he'd replied, 'This is not a hotel' – mimicking Harling, looking to him for his approval, getting instead a dark look that had sent him off to the kitchen. He'd returned with goulash out of a can and a bowl of fruit and a sour red wine that suited the mood.

'The point is that Silva made a lot of sweeping allegations he's not around to repeat. The point is they don't have a witness – or do they? The point is, Frank, how did they know about Silva in the first place?'

'Maitland?' Harling said, no more than a suggestion.

'Crap. Maitland didn't know that Silva even existed.' Shilling lit a cigarette and allowed the smoke to drift in Harling's direction. 'No, it wasn't Maitland, Frank, and there couldn't have been anything in the bank's records to identify him, could there? I mean, that was the whole point of your bank, wasn't it, Frank? No way to identify the clients? Isn't that right?'

Harling stayed silent.

'Or maybe that isn't right, Frank. Perhaps Flint did find some way to identify Silva from your records – some way you hadn't thought about.' Shilling looked from Harling to Spenny and back to Harling. 'Has that possibility occurred to you, Frank, because it's occurred to us.' Getting no response he continued, 'And, if she was able to identify Silva, maybe the FBI can identify others and, if that's the case, there are any number of people – myself included – who would like to know. That's what Flint is going to tell us. That's the fucking point, Frank.'

Spenny took an orange from the bowl. 'Don't you want to know, Frank? How she got onto Silva?'

'What's that supposed to mean?'

Her thumbnails dug deep into the peel. 'If there was a weakness in your system? That's worth knowing, isn't it?'

Harling shook his head. 'I don't believe you people. What's the matter with you? She tells us and then what? It doesn't matter what she says. Don't you get it? It doesn't matter because Silva's fucked us. He's fucked you, he's fucked me, he's fucked everybody.' He leaned towards Shilling and blew away the smoke. 'That's. The. Fucking. Point.'

'Not necessarily,' said Shilling.

'Jesus!'

Spenny said, 'You're fucked, Frank, I can see that.' She held a segment of the orange to her lips and sucked out the juice. 'You'll have to disappear, find another rock to crawl under, but there's nothing new in that – you've been running for years. And it's not as though you can't afford it. But Mario didn't fuck me because he couldn't. We never met, did we? He'd never even heard of me. And, as for Patrick: well, Mario was an informant and Patrick was his handler, and some of the things he spoke about come close to the truth. It's just that Mario twisted them for his own nefarious purposes.' She shrugged. 'Informants are like that sometimes.'

Harling said, 'Were you two smoking something out there? You think they're going to buy that?'

Spenny smiled and licked her fingers.

'You're out of your minds. Let's just get this done and get the hell out of here.'

'When the bitch has talked,' said Shilling flatly as though he was repeating a mantra.

'Speaking of which,' said Spenny getting up from the table, 'I should check on her.'

As she passed Shilling's chair he reached out and touched her arm. 'Tell her,' he said, 'that tomorrow we take the first of her kidneys.'

Flint heard the key turning in the lock and reconnected the tube to the catheter. Feigning sedation she closed her eyes and kept her breathing shallow.

'Well, my dear,' Nurse Stella said in her most syrupy tone, 'and how are we feeling?'

III

Zulu's commandos stood on either side of a waist-high platform that presented a topographical model of the mountain range behind Kyrenia in which – it was assumed – Flint and Harling were now trapped. The platform was some fifty feet long and about twenty feet wide – one foot for each mile it represented – and it was crisscrossed by a maze of roads and tracks. Tiny villages and hamlets made from papier-mâché dotted the slopes, a hundred or more of them by Cohen's count. With broad sweeps of his hands, Captain Zulu was describing to his men how Turkish ground forces were, even now, conducting a methodical sweep of the area, narrowing the possibilities, tightening the noose.

He said to Cohen, 'It's out of date – twenty-five years out of date, to be exact – but it gives you some idea.'

'It seems like an immense task,' Cohen replied, careful to keep any hint of optimism out of his voice. In the face of the damning dispatch from London and his own culpability, Cohen had abandoned any hope of persuading Zulu that Flint was not a dangerous terrorist. Silently he prayed for time.

'Horseshit,' Cutter had said when Cohen called him from the base to report Flint's supposed firearms expertise. 'The best I know, the only weapon she touched in Miami was the one Hechter let her have to point at Rykov's balls.'

'What about Quantico? Did she receive any training there?'

'It's news to me but I'll check. If it's denied I'll let Bland know, get him talking to the folks in Ankara.'

'He needs to hurry.'

'Damn right.' Cutter had taken a breath and then, 'Harry, who do you think is feeding them this bull? Who's setting her up?'

'If I said A.J. I'd be guessing. A wild guess.'

'Yeah,' said Cutter. 'That's what I thought. Wild.'

Zulu had finished his briefing and his men had divided into two teams. They were checking their equipment, setting up a metallic cacophony as they worked the slides of automatic weapons, tested the firing mechanisms, slapped home clips of hollow-point ammunition. Four of the commandos stood apart, calibrating the night scopes of their sniper's rifles.

Cohen left them to it and went outside to get some air. On a landing pad a pair of assault helicopters waited in the moonlight pointing at him with their ugly snouts and their missile pods, showing him their scorpion's tails.

Flying just above the treetops, climbing and then dipping and then climbing again to follow the topography of the limestone peaks, the Rooivalk hunted its prey. On either side of the cabin observers equipped with night-vision goggles leant out of open doors scouring the gaps in the foliage for any sign of the targets. Squeezed between Alpha and Lima, feeling the hardness of their light body armour, Cohen caught glimpses of the other Rooivalk perhaps a mile away following its own search pattern. Zulu sat on the bench in front of him receiving on his headset possible sightings from the ground, and every now and then he would tap the pilot on the shoulder and the helicopter would veer and climb and chase away to a new location where they would hover, descending slowly towards the blackness of the forest. Suspended above the unknown, Cohen would feel the stillness inside the cabin grow until the observers gave the thumbs-down – negative, nothing there – and Alpha or Lima or one of the others would say something to get a laugh and crack the tension.

They had been doing this for two hours and Zulu said they would keep on doing it for four more – until they found the targets or until they reached the limit of the Rooivalk's endurance. And, in the case of the latter, they would return to base and refuel and start all over again; however long it took, Zulu said, they would find them, deal with them.

Unless Cutter got his denial from Quantico, and unless Bland worked his diplomatic magic in Ankara, and unless Zulu received word from his commanders that there was no need for such extreme measures, then sooner or later the observers would find what they were looking for and the Rooivalks would swoop down and fifteen men hardened on the live range at Quantico would allow Cohen one brief opportunity to negotiate a surrender.

Sooner or later, Zulu said. It was only a matter of time.

Another possible sighting from the ground and Zulu tapped the pilot's shoulder. The Rooivalk plunged onto its side, banking to the right, and dropped steeply towards a ravine. Now they were below treetop height, following the course of a dry river bed, the other Rooivalk on its tail – two birds of prey poised for the kill.

IV

Being the hired hand, Metin Cadessi took the first watch. Spenny had gone to bed, Harling was half-dozing on the sofa by the fire. Cadessi didn't know where Shilling was but wherever he was lurking he would be awake – wide awake – that was for sure. Shilling wouldn't trust Frank any further than he could throw him; wouldn't trust him not to kill the Flint bitch the minute his back was turned.

Cadessi's vantage point was in a copse of carob trees set on a rise about one hundred yards from the monastery. From there he could see the front of the restored wing, the open barn where the Ford and Jeep were parked and the track winding down the hillside, a luminescent white ribbon in the moonlight. He had the Beretta in his waistband and – courtesy of Frank – an M-4 automatic rifle nestled in his hands. It had a firing rate of 700 rounds a minute on full auto and a thirty-round magazine, or so Frank had said. Full of surprises, Frank was. 'Where the fuck did you get that?' Cadessi had asked but Frank had not replied.

Drawing a bead on imaginary targets coming up the

track, Cadessi reckoned he could take out half a platoon with one squeeze of the trigger. On the other hand, he thought, training the gun on the window of the bedroom where Spenny slept, he could cut her in half from a hundred yards, or Shilling – or both of them if he wasted a full magazine.

Lying on his belly, adjusting the sight, he wondered if that was what Frank had in mind.

Flint had drifted off to sleep and she did not hear the key in the lock, the opening and closing of the door. It was his presence that woke her. She opened her eyes and Frank Harling stood at the bottom of her bed looking at her with no particular expression on his face. She would have instantly recognised him in the street or picked him out of a line-up. He had lost some weight, he was tanned and bearded but he was still unmistakably the man in the stairwell.

'It's been a long time.'

'Three years,' she said quietly. 'Three years, one month and . . . Shall I tell you the number of days?'

'Not long enough,' he said. She saw his eyes take in the tube disconnected from the catheter. 'You do that?'

'Yes. I didn't want to be half-drugged when you came to see me.'

He nodded as if she had made a sensible decision. 'Before I kill you,' he said, 'there's something you're going to tell me.'

Before I kill you – said indifferently, like a simple time reference: *Before Christ . . . Before lunch . . . Before*

I leave . . . Her throat was so dry it hurt just to breathe and she struggled to contain her panic.

'Who told you about Silva?'

She watched him coldly, wanting him to feel her hatred.

'Now, you can tell me and it will be painless, or I can hurt you very badly until you tell me – and then I'll kill you. Either way, you will tell me. What Buller did to you, that was nothing. You can't imagine what I will do to you if you make me.'

What terrified her was his apparent apathy, the lack of anger in his voice or in his eyes. *Either way you will tell me* – a fact calmly stated. She could save him the trouble of hurting her but it didn't really matter, he didn't care. *And then I'll kill you.*

'Well?'

She had to say something – anything. That's what the training manual said: Keep talking. Except the manual did not anticipate you being strapped to a bed in a locked room, facing a psychopath who didn't give a shit what you said if it wasn't about Mario Silva.

'Why the hurry, Frank?' She tried to keep her tone as dry as his. 'I thought you wanted to butcher me again?'

'No,' he said. 'That's their thing. I think it's a fucking waste of time. I mean, if you're going to do it that way, forget the anaesthetic. What's the point in sparing you the pain?'

'Oh, there was pain, Frank. Not the sort you mean but there was pain.'

She felt him pull back the sheet and his hands gripped

her feet. 'One more time. Who told you about Silva?'

He was pressing her toes backwards and the pain was beginning and she heard herself blurt out what she was going to tell him anyway: 'You did!'

He didn't release the pressure. 'Go on.'

'In your affidavit.'

'What affidavit?'

She closed her eyes to remember the words as precisely as she could. 'I, Frank Arthur Harling, of the Villa Donati, Vorno, Italy, make oath and say as follows . . .'

Any moment now she would have to scream.

'I am making this affidavit as a form of protection, or, in the event that anything untoward should happen to me, to place on record . . .'

'You fucking bitch!'

'Except where otherwise stated, all matters deposed to herein . . .'

And then he squeezed the phalanges and she felt a pain shooting up her legs that was exquisite. She arched her back and thrust her fist in her mouth and bit down on the knuckles. She was damned if she would scream for him. Not yet.

He let go of her feet and went and fetched the rickety wooden chair on which her clothes were strewn. He threw them on the floor and turned the chair around and sat with his arms folded resting on the back. 'If I have to,' he said, 'I'm going to take this chair apart and I'm going to ram the pieces into places you don't want me to go. Do you understand?'

Oh, she understood all right. There were times even

now – even after all this time – when she would be
haunted by unwanted visions of her mother lying broken
and helpless at the mercy of some animal like Harling.
She would imagine what he said to her, what he told her
he was going to do. And when he was finished with her
she would imagine him digging a hole for her body and
sometimes she was still alive when the clumps of earth
began falling on her. Sometimes . . .

For Christ's sake! Keep talking!

'Take your hand out of your mouth,' Harling said.
'Do you understand what I will do to you?'

'Yes. I understand that you're an animal, Frank.'

'Did Maitland give you the affidavit?'

'Not directly. I found it at Ellis.'

'Ellis?'

'Your bolt-hole, Frank. Your other bolt-hole, I suppose. The one Maitland bought for you. Where he stored
the archives.'

'Who else read it?'

'Hechter.'

Patiently Harling asked, 'Who's he?'

'Was, Frank. He *was* a US Treasury agent until you
blew up his plane.'

'Who else?'

Why does he care?

'I don't know. I don't know if Hechter had it with him
on the plane or if it was kept with the other documents
we seized. If it got to Miami I'd bet that just about
everybody in the task force read it.'

Why does he care? Why does it matter?

'Who did you tell?'

'Aldus Cutter, the head of the task force. My boss in London, Commander Glenning.'

Harling shifted in his chair. 'And what did you tell them – exactly?'

'I don't remember – *exactly*. That you'd taken out an insurance policy: they hurt you, you hurt them. That you'd made a sworn statement that implicated a whole lot of spooks. Something like that. That they'd protected you. Put you in a safe house. Got you out of the country.'

'Who else knows? What did you tell Silva?'

'About you? Nothing.'

'So why did he give you the tape?'

Her heart fluttered like a butterfly in her chest. 'What tape?'

'The fucking videotape he made.'

How does he know about the tape? Nobody knew about the tape – she'd told nobody except her father. *Oh my God!*

'He didn't give me any tape.'

Harling stood up, straddling the chair, twisting the frame in his hands.

'I swear. Ask him.'

'Ask him?' Harling picked up the chair and threw it at her head. 'He's dead, you silly cow.'

'Well? Has she told you?'

Shilling was waiting for him in the living room, sipping a small brandy, standing with his back to the fire.

'Not yet,' said Harling. 'She's a stubborn bitch.'

'Oh, how very perceptive of you, Frank.'

As if he hadn't heard Harling said, 'But she's up to something.'

'Meaning?'

'She's started to talk. She says that Maitland kept records of his own hidden away at a place called Ellis – somewhere on the island, not at the bank. Fuck knows what he thought he was doing. Anyway, he told her where they were. She says she didn't have time for a proper look before they were shipped off to Miami but that Maitland kept some kind of list, evidently, because then she gets a call from Cutter giving her Silva's name.'

Shilling pretended to laugh. 'And you believe her?'

'Of course I don't believe her. Christ!' Harling took a glass and the brandy bottle from the sideboard and poured himself a drink. 'Maitland wouldn't have known Silva if he'd fallen over him, would he?'

'Exactly.'

'So, what's she up to? Who is she trying to protect?'

'Protect? Herself, I imagine.'

'There's more to it than that.' He sniffed the brandy in his glass and grimaced. 'She's lying about Cutter as well. It wasn't him who told her. Know what I think? It was somebody on our side. She's got an informant – probably the same fuck who told her where to find me.'

'Silva told her.'

'No, he didn't. He couldn't have. He didn't know. This stuff smells like petrol,' Harling said, nevertheless taking a deep swallow. He held Shilling's eyes. 'So, who did know, Pat – besides you?'

'Bollocks,' Shilling said angrily. 'You're talking utter bollocks.'

'Am I? You didn't mention it to Taggart or Kurlack by any chance? You didn't tell them, "Our cash machine is now located in the fucking Turkish Republic of Northern Cyprus" – didn't say that, did you? When did you tell her?' He raised his eyes to the ceiling above which Sarah Spenny slept. 'I will find out, you know.'

Shilling bridled and snapped, 'Mind your manners, Frank.'

Harling looked right through him and tossed the rest of his brandy onto the fire. 'Tastes like petrol, too,' he said, watching it flare into an intense blue flame. He pointed his forefinger at Shilling with the thumb cocked. 'I'll catch you later.'

'Where are you going?'

'I'm going to check on Metin, make sure he's still got his eyes open.'

Harling left the house, taking with him the key to Flint's room.

V

During the year when they put Grace Flint's face back together – in between the series of reconstructive operations that seemed eternal – she met a therapist named Adam Ballantine who specialised in the treatment of police officers suffering extreme mental anguish caused by their exposure to sudden violence: violence inflicted on them or, more often, violence inflicted on others that they had observed. Flint would not acknowledge herself as a victim in that sense – for she would not admit to any lasting mental trauma – but she went to see Adam because she knew she had no choice if she wanted reinstatement. When she told him she didn't need counselling he'd said, 'Fine, then we'll just chat' – and 'chat' they did, religiously, three times a week, until she was finally declared fit and ready to return to duty.

They would talk about everything under the sun but always, in every session, they would – sooner or later – return to the stairwell in Belgravia and Adam, in subtle ways, would probe the moment when her terror and her dread had turned to resignation: when she had accepted that she was going to die. Since he asked the question in many different ways, she gave him many different answers but she did not waver from her insistence that she had never accepted it. Feared it, yes, expected it, even – but not for an instant had she acquiesced. Even as Buller had worked the slide of his gun, even as he had brought the heel of his boot slamming down on her face for the umpteenth time, even as Harling goaded him – *Finish it, Buller. For fuck's sake, get it done* – she had clung to the belief that she might survive. Something, she said, something inside would not let her quit – would *never* let her quit – and Adam had called it 'your sprig of hope'.

Well, the sprig was still there and it was growing bigger, nourished by her certainty that, metaphorically speaking, she had Frank Harling by the balls. The chair had hit her squarely in the face and her nose felt as if it might be broken and she could still taste the trickle of her blood – and she didn't care. She didn't care because he cared far too much about what had led her to Mario Silva's door; how she had known.

Who told you about Silva?

You did.

And there it was, staring her in the face – her get-out-of-jail card if she played it right.

You did, you told me – and they don't know that, do they?

Frank had left the room without another word: no more threats to kill her; no menacing promise, 'I'll be back.' He would be back – of that she was sure – and then, icily calm, she would deliver a threat of her own.

'What do you think they're going to do when I tell them about the affidavit, Frank? That you sold them out, betrayed them? You didn't mean to, perhaps, but you're the one who's put them in the hole. You think they're going to let you walk away? I don't think so.'

Fucking cow, cunt, bitch, slag – all the names he would call her, all the names she'd been called before. *I'll kill you.*

'Yeah? How are you going to explain that, Frank?' she would ask. 'They want answers and if I'm not around to give them they'll know you've got something to hide. You know, I wouldn't be surprised if you were the next one on the operating table. You've got no ovaries, Frank, but they can start with your dick.'

He would try to hurt her, of course – smash her face, break her toes this time, take that chair apart and tell her precisely where he was going to ram the pieces.

What Buller did to you, that was nothing. You can't imagine what I will do to you. Oh, yes I can, Frank. I've been there too many times.

And this time she *would* scream. If he so much as touched her she would scream her lungs out until they came and then she would tell them everything – everything they wanted to know.

And then what?

Shut up.

What do you suppose they'll do to you?

SHUT UP!

She needed quiet because she needed to think. No, he

was the one who needed to think.

'Think about it, Frank. They'll kill you, just as surely as they'll kill me. What are we going to do about it, Frank? We've got to get out of here, haven't we? Together.' Then she might give him a wry smile. 'You know, it's ironic, given our history. You and me, Frank. We're the only hope we've got.'

Damn right, Frank.

Clinging to her sprig of hope, she awaited his return.

Hearing the rustle of leaves, the snap of a twig, Metin Cadessi slipped the safety catch on the M-4 and scanned his surroundings through the scope. He was emboldened by the terrible power he held in his hands – and that's what made him careless. Too late he was aware of soft noises behind him. He twisted onto his back and tried to bring up the rifle but his arm was pinned to the ground by Frank Harling's foot.

'Fuck! You could have got yourself killed.'

Harling, looking down on him, said, 'You ever shot anybody, Metin?'

'Sure.'

'And when was that?' Harling removed his foot, allowing Cadessi to scramble into a less undignified position. 'In your wasted youth?' Cadessi had bragged of the days when he ran with a gang that terrorised Kurds in a suburb of Istanbul.

'In the army,' he said, rubbing his arm.

'You were in the army?'

'In Turkey everybody goes into the army.'

'And where did you fight your particular war?'

'Here. When I was stationed here, near Famagusta. One night some Greeks tried to cross the line.' Unarmed Greek Cypriots made reckless by alcohol, as it happened, but Cadessi didn't mention that. 'I shot one of them here' – he pointed to the spot between his eyes – 'from eighty metres.'

Harling nodded as if to say, Not bad. 'And how did you feel about it afterwards?'

'Okay.' Actually, not okay – locked in a stinking guard house for five months until he had ceased to be the focus of an embarrassing international incident. 'Pretty good.'

'Could you do it again?'

Harling's question was casually asked but that didn't fool Cadessi. 'Why?'

'If you had to? If someone had a gun and they came running towards you? Let's say you're here, hidden among the trees, and you saw this fuck coming at you and you didn't know why – all you know is they've got a gun. Let's say they get to about there' – he pointed to the spot about twenty yards away where the driveway leading from the house joined the track – 'what are you going to do?'

'Who's coming, Frank?'

'Some fuck with a gun! What are you going to do?'

'Shoot them, Frank. Right between the eyes.'

Harling considered Cadessi's answer as though it was profound. Eventually, 'That's what I thought. I mean, that's why you're here. Right?'

* * *

She was dozing again when he slipped into the room and the first she knew he was standing over her with a knife, one hand clamped to her mouth.

'Keep quiet,' he said, slicing through one of the webbing straps that held her to the bed. He cut the second strap. 'Get up.'

'Why?'

'Get up and get dressed.'

She stared at him bewildered. This wasn't any part of her plan.

'Come on! Do you want to stay alive?' He fetched her clothes from the floor and threw them on the bed. 'Do it.' He pulled back the sheet and she grabbed the dress to cover herself.

'What's going on, Frank?'

'There's been a change of plan. No more fucking around – they've decided to kill you, and they mean it.'

'*They're* going to kill me? What about you? What you said?'

'That was just bullshit. I know what happens when a cop gets killed – remember? It's been bad enough having you all over me like a rash for all these years. I don't want any part of this. Now, *get dressed*. I'm going to give you a chance to run for it.'

'You're mad.' Either he was or she was. What was he playing at? What was his game? 'I can't run,' she said. 'I've had surgery, remember? You stole my fucking ovaries!'

'No, we didn't,' he said as she felt his fingers probing the dressing on the wound.

'What are you doing?'

He pulled away the gauze and said, 'Look.'

There were no stitches, just a superficial cut across her abdomen.

'We didn't touch you. You only thought we did.'

She stared at where he stood but she could no longer see him. She fell onto her side and curled her body into a ball. She began sobbing, racking violent sobs that made no sound. She cried for reasons she did not know and for reasons that she did.

'For fuck's sake,' he said but he could not reach her. She'd gone to a place he had never been, a place he could never go.

Dressed now, sitting on the floor, her knees pulled up to her chest, feeling a loathing for him that was more visceral than any feeling she could remember, holding in her hand the gun that he had given her, listening to his insane plan.

'You ever fired a weapon in anger, Flint?' – Cutter asking her with his gap-toothed grin after they'd taken Rykov away. 'Could you shoot a guy in the balls?'

Actually, no, sir. Not then. Now she could.

Really?

Oh, believe it.

'You've got to move fast,' Harling said. 'I'm going to say I got careless and you took my gun. Lock the door and take the key. I'll start shouting my head off about thirty seconds after you leave but they'll have to break the door down to find out what's happened and that will give you a bit of time. The front door's to your right and it's open. Okay?'

Actually, no – not okay.

'This is bullshit,' she said. 'Whatever else this is, it's bullshit.'

'*Listen to me!*' She thought he might reach down and shake her. 'When you get outside follow the driveway until you come to a track and keep going. Run as if you're fucking life depends on it, because it does. They're going to come after you – count on it – but you having a gun will slow them down. You know how to use it?'

Actually, yes. It was a Ruger P97 automatic, seven rounds in the clip. She nodded.

'If they get too close, fire off a couple of shots. But remember, they're armed so when you get a decent way up the track find somewhere to hide. You'll have to stay there until it gets light – by which time we'll be long fucking gone, I hope.' He shrugged. 'It's the best I can do for you.'

She didn't move and he came towards her. 'Come on, for fuck's sake. Do it.'

'Okay, Frank,' she said and she brought up his Ruger and shot him.

VI

It had been another false scent and the Rooivalks had lifted out of the ravine and separated, each of them taking a new vector to scour. The monotonous thud of the rotor blades and the constant buffeting of cold air was getting on Cohen's nerves, as was the waiting. He felt the threat of cramp in his legs and longed to stand up and stretch. Not likely: not in this confined cabin; not wedged as he was between the hard hides of Alpha and Lima.

Zulu turned to him and took off his headset and tried to shout above the din.

'What?'

'It's for you. Someone wants to talk to you.'

Cutter, please God, with news.

It was Cutter and he did have news – just about the last thing Cohen wanted to hear. Pressing the earpieces to his head Cohen hunched down to get out of the wind and listened appalled to what Cutter had to say.

'Turns out our unhelpful friend was right. Apparently, while she was in Miami she got pally with a Metro-Dade homicide detective name of Singleton – good guy we call "Blade" who works with us from time to time. Anyway, I found out he used to take her to Metro's range way out somewhere near the Everglades and let her shoot. I just got through talking with him on the phone and – you're not going to like this – he says she was a natural. The Blade knows what he's talking about. He's an . . .'

Cutter's voice was drowned in a squall of interference.

'Say again. Hello, Aldus?'

'. . . in Vietnam.'

'Say again. I missed that.'

'I said Blade's an ex-marine and he knows what he's talking about. He was a sniper in Vietnam.'

Cohen could think of nothing to say.

'Quantico's even worse. First I've heard about it but that girl sure gets around. She tried out with CIRG, did some SWAT exercises, live range work, Hogan's Alley – anything they'd let her try. They rated her, Harry. They said that for a woman she was pretty damn good.' He paused and then he added, 'I'm sorry. I should have known about it. I feel I've let you down.'

'How did he know?'

'Who?'

'Devercaux.'

'Beats me. When the time comes we can ask him but meanwhile, buddy, you've got a big problem.'

Not as big as Flint's, Cohen thought. He thanked Cutter and gave the headset back to Zulu. 'Yes, fine,' he mouthed in response to the captain's questioning up-turned thumb.

But Cohen knew that Cutter's call would have been monitored by the Turks and he could imagine the essence of the warning that Zulu would surely receive on his headset any second now: *She was taught to shoot by a trained sniper*.

He saw the captain stiffen. The pilot must have heard the same transmission for he turned his head expectantly and Zulu gave the order.

The machine bucked as Zulu said to Cohen, 'Reports of gunfire.'

Another veering turn and then they were flying parallel to a ridge that stood above the tree line like icing on a cake. The moon was dropping and it cast a silhouette of a phantom Rooivalk racing ahead of them on the limestone; an arachnid of monstrous proportions leading the way to Flint's likely destruction.

They followed a trail of blinking lights that a foot patrol had laid to guide them in. Nine yellow and the tenth red, then nine more yellows and another red – and so the pattern repeated itself, tracing the twists of a track. One of the observers was counting off the reds.

He held an arm extended above the shoulder. Decisively he brought it down and Zulu spoke into his headset and the helicopter banked and turned away. The pilot cut the engine and there was a sudden silence. Banked on its side, the Rooivalk fluttered towards a clearing like a wounded bird, the blades disengaged to autorotate, providing just enough lift to cushion the landing.

The second Rooivalk was already there, men spilling

out of it, lethally armed. Completing their camouflage, they wore black balaclavas with holes for their eyes. Zulu told Cohen to strip and gave him a black jumpsuit to put on and a hood for his head. Seemingly as an afterthought, he handed him a flak jacket. He held up one finger to his mouth to say, 'Quiet, no talking.'

Almost in a trance, Cohen followed Zulu's shadow into the night.

Stealthy as panthers the four snipers approached the darkened house, working their separate ways through the undergrowth in search of suitable firing positions. Though they no longer wore name tags, they kept their designated call signs for communication purposes and the marksman known as Victor found a hollow some two hundred yards from the front door where he could support the barrel of his Remington on the branch of a scrub pine. Whiskey worked his way to an open barn, taking cover behind a small white Ford, while X-ray and Yankee chose positions in a copse of carob trees set on a rise. One by one they murmured into their headsets, reporting their positions.

'Snipers in place,' Zulu said to Cohen.

Then it was the turn of the two assault teams – designated by their leaders, Alpha and Bravo – five men in each, who were invisible to Cohen until Zulu handed him a pair of night-vision glasses. Now he could glimpse them: flitting spectres bathed in an eerie green light, drawing ever-nearer to their target. The first man had almost reached the house when Zulu said, 'Come on.'

Avoiding the white backdrop of the track, they ran from tree to tree, cover to cover, keeping low, Cohen soon breathing hard in the thin air. They passed the rise and came to a junction where the track joined a concreted driveway.

'Close enough,' Zulu whispered and he motioned with his hands for Cohen to lie down next to him behind the meagre cover of a thorn bush. Propped on his elbows, Cohen peered under the branches to see that the Alpha team was now in place: two men flattened on either side of the front door, the other three crouched under windows, their backs against the wall. The Bravo team had vanished.

Using the glasses, Cohen scanned the face of the house, searching for any signs of life in the darkened windows. On the ground floor he thought he could see the faintest black flickers of a fire reflecting on a wall but otherwise the place was deathly still. It looked to be a monastery only partially restored, the ruins of the greater part looming above and behind the new roof like a skeleton.

Zulu murmured into his headset and held up a hand to show Cohen two fingers: two minutes to go. Two more minutes and then Cohen would perform his miracle – or not. He knew that in this company he was alone in caring about the outcome. On balance, he thought, Zulu and his men would probably prefer that he failed.

Zulu pointed to the roof and Cohen saw five black

shapes posed in the gaping windows of the ruins,
silhouetted like mannequins against a star-studded sky –
the Bravo team taking the high ground without a shot
being fired. Coils of rope hung from their shoulders and
Cohen could see the snouts of their weapons sprouting
from their backs. One by one, they climbed down onto
the roof and edged across the tiles.

One finger from Zulu – one minute to go.

In the Rooivalk, Cohen had endlessly rehearsed his
speech, going over in his mind how he should begin.
'Frank Harling, Grace Flint, my name is Harry Cohen'
or 'Mr Harling, Detective Inspector Flint, I'm from the
Home Office in London' – and any number of other
variations. They all sounded ludicrous. In the end he had
decided he would say whatever came into his head.

Bravo and his men were now perched perilously on
the lip of the roof with their backs to the ground, their
heads half-turned to look down, holding onto ropes that
were secured around the chimney breasts.

'Ready?' Zulu mouthed and Cohen pulled off his
balaclava and nodded. 'Go.'

'Harling, Flint, Spenny – anybody who's in there – listen
to me.'

What the fuck! A naked Metin Cadessi rolled off the
bed onto the floor hugging the M-4 to his chest.

'My name is Cohen. I'm here to tell you it's over. You
are surrounded by armed men. You have no alternative
but to surrender.'

The voice was coming from outside, from the

driveway. Cadessi crawled towards the window.

'Frank Harling, Sarah Spenny, if you cause any harm to Flint you will be killed. You must put down your weapons and show yourselves at a window with your hands in the air. Do it now.'

Cadessi stood up, his back to the wall, and peered through the edge of the glass. There was a man dressed in black standing alone less than twenty metres from the house, his hands cupped to his mouth. Twenty metres was nothing.

'The men surrounding you are Turkish commandos. They are highly trained.'

What commandos? There wasn't another soul out there that Cadessi could see.

'If you don't come out now they will come and get you. You have no chance, no chance whatsoever.'

Fuck you, thought Cadessi. In the manner of the many action-movie stars he much admired, he whirled to face the window and fired from the hip. He pulled the trigger and kept it pulled until the whole magazine was gone.

From his position in the hollow, through his telescopic sight with its ten-power magnification, Victor saw movement in the window he was trained on, saw the glass disintegrate, saw the barrel flashes, saw the outline of the target – and fired. The model of Remington he favoured was designed for accuracy rather than speed: a bolt-action rifle giving him a single shot. It was all he needed. In the sight he saw a human head explode.

*   *   *

Lying on his back, his legs and chest stinging from the chips of concrete that had peppered him like shrapnel, Cohen saw five black shapes coming down the face of the house towards him, rappelling on ropes with the smooth grace of synchronised swimmers. When they reached the windows of the upper floor they hung suspended for a moment until, at some unseen signal, they used their legs to push away from the wall, twisting their bodies to gain momentum, swinging back like pendulums, their legs outstretched, feet first.

And at the instant they crashed through the glass and disappeared from Cohen's view with an almost balletic quality, he saw a white flash and heard the crump of an explosion. He raised up his head to see the front door gaping on its hinges and five more black shapes clambering through the opening.

'Are you all right?' – Zulu touching his shoulder, barely pausing before he followed the Alpha team into the house.

Cohen sat up as he felt and heard the detonation of stun grenades. Yes, he was all right, he supposed. He unzipped the flak jacket and felt his chest and there were sticky patches of blood, but not much. From inside the house came the intense crackle of automatic fire.

And then there was a lingering silence, as though everyone inside had perished in that bedlam, or were so astonished by its ferocity they could not make a sound. Then Cohen heard the muffled voices of Zulu's men calling to each other and through the shattered windows he saw the searching light of torch beams; life returning.

The house lights started coming on and Zulu appeared in the doorway, pulling off his gloves and his balaclava, signalling to the snipers that the assault was over. Cohen got to his feet and walked slowly towards him knowing and dreading what Zulu would say.

'They're all dead. You better come and take a look.'

Feeling the weight of his failure, Cohen followed Zulu into a large open room where the stench of cordite was almost overwhelming. Broken glass was everywhere, crunching under their feet, and a long dining table lay on its side. In a doorway to his left Cohen saw a lake of blood.

'One of them is in there,' Zulu said.

Cohen braced himself and went to the doorway, watching where he put his feet and looked down on the body of Patrick Shilling. He lay sprawled on his back and there was a small red hole in the middle of his temple and a line of more ragged holes across his chest marked by a row of crimson tears in his shirt. His eyes were wide open giving his face a look of astonishment, as though death had come as a great surprise.

'You know him?'

Not really, Cohen thought. He couldn't begin to count the number of meetings he'd attended at Thames House where Shilling's open sneer had served as his silent commentary on most of Cohen's legal opinions, but they had rarely exchanged more than a formality.

'Yes,' he said. 'His name is – was – Patrick Shilling. He was one of those suspected of organising the bombings.'

'He was already dead when we got here.'

'What! Are you sure?'

Zulu stepped over the blood into the room and squatted down besides Shilling's corpse. 'You see this,' he said, pointing to the temple, 'that's a pistol shot. We don't use handguns. And this' – he took hold of Shilling's hair and lifted his head and Cohen almost gagged at the sight of the gaping wound at the back of the skull – 'is where all the blood came from.' He dropped Shilling's head and stood up and touched the edge of the lake with the toe of his boot. 'It's already started to congeal.'

'So what are those . . .' Cohen began and then shook his head as if to say it didn't matter.

'These?' said Zulu, lifting his foot to point at the chest wounds. 'These are ours. It is our job to make sure. Come on, I'll show you the others.'

He led the way up the stairs to the second floor and to a bedroom where a body lay by the shattered window.

'This is the one that meant to kill you. Is it Harling?'

'How would I know?' Cohen said blanching, for there was nothing left of the face to identify.

'How tall is Harling?'

'My height – no, two or three inches less.'

'Then it's not him. And that means,' Zulu said, 'Harling is not here. There's only one more body – the woman. She was also killed before we got here.'

Now Zulu led Cohen back to the head of the stairs and opened the door on a chamber of obscenity: Naked men and women and even children sprawled about the walls in every form of copulation Cohen could imagine;

Sarah Spenny, also naked, sprawled on the floor, blood on her thighs, a broad crimson ribbon where her throat had once been – until it had been opened from ear to ear.

VII

Grace Flint sat behind the wheel of a Jeep looking down on Nicosia where the street lights still glowed a sodium orange even though it was after dawn. She was less than five miles from where she wanted to be – the UN-controlled 'green line' that slashes through the very heart of the city – and all that stood between it and her was a Turkish army roadblock about five hundred yards beyond the next corkscrew bend.

Driving without lights, coasting down the hill, she had almost run straight into it but some instinct had warned her to pull into a lay-by just short of the bend. She had cut the engine and listened to it cool and then she had climbed the rock through which the road was cut and seen the white helmets of the military police. Six oil drums formed the chicane through which she would have to pass and while she watched no vehicle made it through without being stopped.

There was nothing random about what they were doing – they were searching for something, or someone.

You, Flint, they're searching for you.

Why?

And then a memory had come to her of Mario Silva at his poster board pointing to the right-hand column of his chart. *And here we have The Admiral. We do not know his name but he is – or was – a high official of the NATO Supreme Allied Command.*

Turkey was a member of NATO.

Mario to camera: *So you see, gentlemen, the tentacles of The Enterprise reach far beyond its natural boundaries.*

Oh, holy shit!

Hurrying back to the Jeep, she had turned around and driven back up the hill until she found a track to turn on to. She had followed it on the off-chance that it might lead to another road that would take her to Nicosia but after less than a quarter of a mile it had petered out, together with her hopes.

Hidden from the road, she had decided to stay where she was until daylight came and the traffic built up. Perhaps then they would abandon the block, or the war would start, or something would happen that would allow her to get just five more miles. It had to, she told herself. It would.

Oh, really?

Harling groaned and she turned to look at him. He was stretched out on the back seat, propped against the side wall, covered in a blanket. She had patched him up as best she could but he'd lost a fair amount of blood and even with his tan he looked pallid.

'Don't die on me, Frank,' she said. 'Not now. Not when we're so close.'

To herself – if never, ever to anyone else – she would admit her own hypocrisy. The bullet that had torn through his shoulder – tearing the ligaments, breaking the bone, leaving him incoherent and sweating with pain – had been intended for his heart.

'Come on, for fuck's sake. Do it.'

'Okay, Frank,' squeezing the trigger – and she had wanted to kill him, meant to kill him and, at that range, she had no idea how she missed his heart. The bullet had spun him around and she'd seen him reach for his shoulder as he fell. He'd said, 'Jesus Christ,' and tried to crawl away from her and she'd stood up fully intending to shoot him again. She would have done – very nearly did – if only she could have quieted the voices screaming inside her head.

WHAT ARE YOU DOING?

Shut up!

This is murder. It's worse – it's an execution.

After what he's done? This is justice.

Oh, really? Since when did you get to be judge and jury?

What am I supposed to do?

You're a cop, Flint. You're supposed to arrest him.

And then do what with him – exactly?

That's your problem. That's what you came here to do – or was that a lie? Did you always intend to kill him?

Shut up!

Is that it?

SHUT UP!

Then you're no better than he is, Flint.

She had stood over him, straddling his shoulders, pointing the Ruger at the back of his head, pressure on the trigger, a fraction of an inch to go.

'Harling!'

Pounding on the door, someone trying the handle. 'What the hell's going on in there? Open the door.'

She had recognised that voice. *If you'll all just be quiet for a moment, please* – a phantom surgeon pretending to remove her ovaries.

She had stepped away from Harling and positioned herself five feet from the door and aimed the Ruger as Blade had taught her and said, with all the hysteria she could manage, 'Oh, Frank, don't, please don't.'

The wood around the lock had shattered as he'd kicked open the door and he'd stood there frozen in amazement at the sight of her. Then he'd recovered and lunged for her and tried to bring up the gun he was holding and she had shot him in the head.

You ever fired a weapon in anger, Flint?

Actually, yes, sir. Twice, Mr Cutter. How am I doing?

The shock of it had stilled the voices in her head – no more arguments now. She had felt unnaturally calm and she knew with great clarity what she still had to do.

She had turned off the light and stepped over the dead man's body into the living room. She took in the table, the sofa, the fireplace and – to her right – the front door ajar. She went to it and closed it and found the switches that doused all of the lights on the ground floor. She waited for a moment, getting her bearings, allowing her eyes to adjust to the intermittent light provided by the fire.

When she was ready to hunt, she took off her shoes. Two down, one to go. Stella.

From the supplies Cadessi had fetched her from the kitchen, Flint ate a sparse breakfast: some hard bread, a slice of goat's cheese, sour yogurt, a bitter orange. She wanted Harling to drink at least a little water but he was barely conscious. From the feel of his forehead he was running a fever and he was drifting in and out of delirium. She checked the dressing on the wound and saw that he was leaking blood. The bullet was still in his shoulder and she knew that without treatment he would very probably die. Now he was Prisoner Harling – her prisoner – that was not acceptable.

She made him as comfortable as she could and then she checked her weapons. The clip of Cadessi's Beretta was full and she still had five rounds in the Ruger. It might have been only four rounds but Cadessi had gone to pieces when she'd come up behind him and told him to freeze – though he was still taking in what she'd done to the two men lying on the floor, which, to be fair, was a pretty unnerving sight. She had made him kneel down with his hands on his head before she took a proper look at him. 'Oh, I remember you – Stella's Romeo. So, where is your girlfriend?' Even with the Ruger pressed between his eyes, he'd sworn he didn't know.

She placed the Beretta under the driver's seat and hid the Ruger in the skirt of her dress. She wasn't planning to shoot it out with half the Turkish army. She hoped they would take pity on a highly distressed woman with a livid bruise on her face whose husband had also been injured in the same accident – who had to get to hospital *now*. But if they didn't buy the story and she was forced to show them the gun, the element of surprise might give her the advantage, she thought.

Oh, really?

'Sure as hell beats sitting here,' she said in Cutter's drawl. 'Saddle up, move 'em out.'

She started the engine and drove towards the road at a moderate pace, trying to avoid jolting Harling on the ruts of the track. She stopped short of the junction and assessed the traffic flow: busy in both directions but it was moving steadily – no long tailback of vehicles heading for Nicosia. So, she reasoned, they weren't stopping people passing through the chicane. Maybe there was no chicane any longer? Maybe they'd gone? Holding onto that sprig of hope she nudged the Jeep into the flow.

Wrong, Flint – they hadn't gone.

As she came around the bend she could see the oil drums were no longer in place but the soldiers were, a good two dozen of them, she thought. A mix of military police and rifle-toting soldiers in camouflage gear and red berets, they stood in loose knots on either side of the road peering into every vehicle as it passed. A bus coming from the other direction had been pulled over and they

were checking the passengers – the female passengers –
one by one.

One hundred yards to go and she knew this wasn't
going to work – knew with chilling certainty that they
were looking for her.

*The tentacles of The Enterprise reach far beyond its
natural boundaries.*

She took one hand off the wheel and reached for the
Ruger.

And then her rage came, erupting inside her like
molten lava. She felt a sudden primeval hatred for Buller,
Harling, Shilling, Spenny and the other faceless animals
and acolytes who were part of The Enterprise. She reviled
them for what they'd done to Pete Pendle and Kevin
Hechter and all those others who had died because of
their greed. Most of all she loathed them for what they
had done to her father to make him tell them about
Silva's videotape.

There was a gap in the oncoming traffic because a
truck had paused, unable to get by the bus – not much of
a gap but enough for her purposes. She wrenched the
wheel and pressed the pedal to the floor and put her
hand on the horn, heading for the soldiers. She saw their
startled faces, saw them start to raise their weapons, saw
them leaping for their lives.

Then she was past them, heading directly for the truck
and she wrenched the wheel again, trying to force her
way back into the traffic flow. She was alongside a car
that wouldn't give way until she rammed it, sending it
skewing from the road. The rear window exploded and

she felt the Jeep shudder as it absorbed the impact of a burst of high-velocity rifle fire.

She pulled into the middle of the road to get cover from the truck and she stayed there, her foot still on the floor, butting her way between the two lines of traffic, ricocheting from one side impact to the next, driven on by her rage and the Jeep's unstoppable momentum.

VIII

The manhunt for Harling and Flint now involved hundreds of troops and more, it seemed to Cohen, were arriving by the minute, their trucks cluttering the track and the monastery driveway. Since Harling's Ford was still parked in the barn – the electrical wiring ripped from the ignition by some unknown hand – Zulu assumed they had escaped on foot and, given the ruggedness of the terrain, could not have travelled more than a couple of miles in the dark. Even so, in case he was wrong, he had called for checkpoints on every major road in the republic. His broadcast alert said that both fugitives were armed and extremely dangerous and wanted for murder: two more murders added to the list.

What in God's name had happened here? Watching two detectives collecting forensic evidence from the room where Shilling was killed, Cohen thought that even though the body had been removed, it still looked like a slaughterhouse – and upstairs, where the unknown man and Sarah still lay, was even worse. The pathologist who had arrived from Nicosia to examine the corpses said it was his initial opinion that Sarah had been raped – either just before, or just after, her throat was cut so deeply she had almost been decapitated. Cohen had thought of the last time he'd seen Sarah – kneeling beside him, lifting his head, making him drink a potion intended to kill him – and he'd remembered the terror she had inflicted on him, and he still felt pity for her. Why would Harling do that to her, and – worse – what might such a man now do to Flint?

In Cohen's mind there was little doubt that Harling had shot Shilling and taken the murder weapon with him, for the only handgun in the house was the small black revolver found under Shilling's body, and that had not been fired. But why take Flint – why not just kill her and leave the body here? And who was the man who no longer had a head, and why had Harling left him alive and, having survived, why had he remained in this charnel house?

Every scenario Cohen invented collapsed under one or more implausibility. It did not enter his mind that it was Flint, not Harling, who had shot Shilling; that it was Harling, not Flint, who was now the prisoner – until, that is, Zulu came striding through the front door and said, 'She's broken through a checkpoint on the road to Nicosia.'

And then as Zulu described what few details he had received over the radio, and as he grabbed Cohen's arm and urged him to hurry, and as they ran towards the Rooivalk – its rotor blades already turning – he guessed the gist of what she'd done and what she would do now.

'She's got Harling with her, I know she has,' he said. 'She's going to take him across the line.'

'She can't. It's impossible.'

'Perhaps. But that's what she means to do.'

'Then she's as good as dead,' said Captain Zulū.

In the old walled city of Nicosia, Flint quickly discovered, the 'green line' is not an orderly divide but one that meanders through a maze of thousand-year-old streets. She had looked at the only official crossing point – about a mile west of the old city – and decided it was too substantial, too well guarded, to break through. Better to try here, she thought, where the buffer zone was less than ten yards wide, secured by a hodgepodge of fences, sandbags, oil drums, sentry posts and rusted barbed wire. There were too many Turkish guards for her liking – another symptom of the looming war, she supposed – but if she could just find a street that would allow the Jeep to build up a decent head of speed, she had a chance of getting through. She would risk it because she had no other choice.

And talking of war, the Jeep looked as though it had been in one – the rear window shattered, the wing mirrors and the hubcaps gone, the side panels scratched and dented – and it was drawing some curious looks from the locals. The soldiers at the roadblock would have put out an alert for the vehicle, of course, and it was only a matter of time before some right-minded citizen would call the police to report the suspicious presence of her prowling wreck on wheels. She couldn't abandon the Jeep because that would mean leaving Harling – who was now plunging towards coma – and that she would not do. He was going across the line, he was going to hospital, he was going to be extradited – and he was going to jail. One day soon she was going to tell him, 'Frank Arthur Harling, you're under arrest.'

If you're still alive.

Shut up.

She was following a course that ran roughly parallel to the line. At each junction she paused and looked to her right to assess the suitability of the street and the strength of the barricade at the end of it.

Too narrow, too short, too many parked cars – too many guards.

She was getting near to the eastern edge of the city, running out of options, when she found her escape route – the best she was likely to find. It was perhaps four hundred yards long, empty, relatively wide, with only a chain-link fence at its end for her to breach. There were no guards, as far as she could see.

She turned into the street, drove fifty yards and paused. Like the pilot of an airliner poised for take-off, she scanned the instruments, built up the engine revs, released the handbrake and – leaving more rubber on the cobblestones than she had intended – sent the Jeep hurtling towards the line.

She was no more than two hundred yards from it when they shot out the front tyres.

Zulu on the radio, Zulu instructing the pilot, Zulu telling

his men the news and getting grunts of satisfaction; Alpha
and Lima leaning across Cohen to slap palms.

'We've got her.'

'Alive?' Cohen asked.

'Trapped.'

He showed Cohen a map of the old city and pointed
to the street where he said Flint was now besieged –
where she had taken refuge behind a Jeep that lay on its
side, holding a gun, her back to the wall, refusing to
surrender.

'You have to let me talk to her.'

The Rooivalk banked steeply and Zulu pointed
through the open door to the twin minarets of a mosque
that pointed up at them like missiles in a silo. 'We're
landing there. If she does nothing stupid in the next ten
minutes, you can try.'

She had one last card to play, she thought – not an ace,
more like a three.

Hanging limply in the growing heat, a United Nations
flag marked the presence of an observation post overlooking the buffer zone that had been empty when she
began her run for the line. Now it was crowded with
blue-helmeted peacekeepers watching her through binoculars and she tore off the hem of her soiled dress and
showed it to them: a dirty white symbol of truce, not
surrender. If the Turks shot her at least her death would
provoke questions, even a minor international incident.
Maybe.

To her left an armoured personnel carrier now

guarded the line while to her right a growing barrier of army and police vehicles sealed the street. She was trapped like a rat at the midpoint of a narrow corridor some three hundred yards long with who knew how many pumped-up marksmen waiting to take a shot at her.

'Inspector Flint' – a peremptory English voice coming from behind the barricade – 'I have to speak to you. I'm coming out.'

A man dressed all in black, his hands held in the air, stepped out from behind an army truck. 'I am unarmed,' he shouted, and slowly, as though he was walking on glass, he came towards her.

Crouched behind the underside of the Jeep, Flint could hear Harling's laboured breathing. He was still inside the wreck – the last she'd seen, lying in a crumpled heap in the seat well. If he died, she thought, then none of what was about to happen really mattered.

'That's close enough,' she said when he was about twenty feet from her and able to smell the fumes of the petrol leaking from the gas tank. She wanted him to understand that if the shooting started there was likely to be an explosion in which he would also die.

'I'm going to take this off,' he said awkwardly unzipping his flak jacket with one hand, keeping the other raised. He looked faintly ridiculous in his combat fatigues – a middle-aged Englishman, middleweight, medium height, mid-brown hair a little too long over his collar, sleepy brown eyes.

'My name is Cohen, Harry Cohen, from the Home

Office in London. I'm here to help you – if I can.'

Oh, really?

'He seemed genuine enough,' her father had argued in Amsterdam, puzzled by her insistence that Harry Cohen was not who he had claimed to be. No, he admitted, he had not checked with the Home Office nor asked for credentials – and then it had dawned on him. 'My God, you think he's one of them?'

'I know who you are,' she said flatly.

'No – you only think you do.' She wasn't sure if it was anger or fear that was making him edgy. 'Look, your father told me what you said, what you suspect, and I don't blame you, but—'

He got no further because she pulled back the hammer of the Ruger that was now pointed at his head.

'Where is he? What did you do to him?'

'Do to him? I don't know what you mean.'

She was so close to shooting him.

'I talked to him, Grace. I swear to you that's *all* I did – for hours on end. I met him at the airport and went home with him and sat on the terrace and, knowing what he believed – what you suspected – I told him everything I know. I told him everything I've discovered in the last four weeks, everything we've done to try and find you, to try and save your life.'

'Who's we?'

'Glenning. Cutter. Bourdonnec. The people who are on your side.' She shook her head and he continued, 'Oh, I know what you think about Glenning and Cutter but you're as wrong about them as you are about me. And, as for Gilles: do you really think he would have helped me if he didn't believe I was also on your side? Do you really think Gilles would betray you?'

'Where's my father?'

'He's at home with his patients, Grace. I imagine that at this moment he's worrying himself to death about you.'

Doubts were creeping in, robbing her of her certainty. 'Sit down,' she said. 'Sit down on the ground and keep your hands where I can see them and then tell me what you told him. Everything you say you told him. Make me a believer.'

Cohen glanced towards the barricade. 'I don't think they'll give us enough time.'

'I don't care,' she said. 'Understand something, Mr Cohen – if that really is your name. Right now, I only care about one thing, and so should you: If I believe you're lying about my father, I'll kill you.'

Zulu had said, 'I'll give you thirty minutes' – and that deadline had long passed and Cohen feared that at any minute he would make the final demand for her surrender. For her sake, he tried to hurry through parts of the story but she wouldn't let him.

'How many stairs are there?'

'I'm sorry?'

'You said you stayed with the Bourdonnecs. How many stairs are there up to their apartment?'

He remembered the long climb that had left him breathless. 'A lot. More than one hundred – one hundred and thirty, something like that.'

'Did they give you coffee?'

'No.' He pulled a face. 'Enough Nescafé to last a lifetime.'

'Where did you sleep?'

'In the boys' room. Baptiste and Gaspard had to share with their sister.'

'What's her name?'

'Lucile.'

'What hangs above Gaspard's bed?'

'A helicopter. Fearsome thing.'

'How tall is Dominique?'

Cohen hesitated.

'You said you met her. You must know how tall she is. My height? Shorter? Taller.'

Then he admitted, 'Grace, the only time I saw Dominique she was lying down, covered in a blanket, sedated.'

'What's wrong with her?'

'It's what's wrong with Gilles. He was outside Silva's gallery when the bomb went off.'

There had been more than one moment when Cohen believed that she was ready to shoot him, none closer than this.

'He's still alive,' he said quickly. 'He's in hospital, in intensive care.'

'Go on.'

'His legs were terribly injured. All that glass, you see.

They're doing their best but . . . I'm afraid he may lose his legs.'

From the slight shake of the barrel he could see that she was trembling.

'He saved my life, Grace – twice. I feel as badly as you.'

In a voice so sombre it might have come from the grave she said, 'You have no idea what I feel.'

What finally convinced Flint that Cohen was telling the truth – what saved his life and thus her own – was the revelation that Mario Silva had carried out his threat: that, in the event of his untimely death, a copy of his videotape had indeed been given to the authorities. The alarm caused at FBI headquarters by the unannounced arrival of a man bearing a package demanding to see the director, the calculated gamble Cutter had taken to obtain an intercept warrant, the angry determination of Cutter's pledge to nail 'Jackson Fucking Kurlack' for the murder of Kevin Hechter – it all rang true. She knew all of the pilgrims at the task force meeting Cohen described and she knew Carrie Evanovich; could just hear Carrie's furious objections to Cutter's indiscretion, and his casual reassurance: *Carrie, we're all on the same team. Who's he gonna tell?*

And when Cohen went on to describe Sarah Spenny's discovery of Silva's tape in his study, when he recounted her callous attempt to kill him and admitted the terror and helplessness he had felt, she did not doubt he was telling the truth. She knew she was looking at a fellow survivor. She also knew with a certainty born in her gut that this perspiring Englishman she kept baking in the sun was her cavalry: she was no longer entirely alone.

'There,' he said, 'I've told you everything I can.'

She looked towards the barricade. 'So, what happens now?'

'I have to talk to them.'

'Who are they?'

'Turkish special forces – commandos.'

She lowered the Ruger, pointing it at the ground. 'Go ahead. Tell them I need to get Harling to a hospital.'

Cohen stood up and rubbed the stiffness out of his legs. 'I'm afraid it's more complicated that that. I have to ask you something. Before we came here we were at the house where you were held. What happened?'

'If you mean the body you found, he was one of them. It was Shilling, I suppose. He came at me with a gun. I didn't have any choice.'

'And Sarah?'

'What about her? I locked her in the room at the top of the stairs. You must have found her.'

'Yes,' said Cohen. 'With her throat cut.'

She looked at him in disbelief. 'And they think I did that?'

'Among other things.'

Out of the corner of her eye she could see dark figures emerging from the barricade, crouching men edging down the street towards her. She brought up the Ruger until it was pointing at Cohen's stomach.

'Such as?'

Cohen could not bring himself to tell her what he'd done. 'Grace,' he said. 'Please. There is no more time.' He held out his hand. 'Give me the gun.'

IX

In another UN observation post – this one overlooking the official crossing point between Greek and Turkish Cyprus – A.J. Devereaux trained his binoculars on Grace Flint and watched her intently, as though he was trying to discern what she was thinking. She was on the Greek side of the divide, standing alone by the checkpoint, her face a white mask in the phosphorescent brightness of the full moon. Behind her, preferring the shadows, a Greek army officer in combat fatigues spoke into his radio.

Although it was getting on for midnight it was impossibly warm. There was not a breath of air and the humidity was enervating. Devereaux would have removed his jacket had there been anywhere to hang it. Compromising, he loosened his tie.

'She's not at all what I supposed,' he said.

'I'm sorry?' Cohen had been lost in thoughts of his own.

'I find her something of a disappointment.'

'What are you talking about?'

'Flint. Not the girl I took her to be. No spirit in her, is there?'

'Alan,' Cohen began, 'there are times . . .' He broke off, unwilling to engage Devereaux in yet another pointless squabble.

Like a couple in a tired marriage, they had been bickering ever since he and Flint had arrived at the checkpoint the previous evening escorted by sullen Turkish troops – Flint silent and reserved, Cohen exhausted by his part in the two days of negotiations that had finally achieved her freedom. Devereaux had been waiting for them in the buffer zone, unsmiling, curt with Flint to the point of rudeness. Without troubling to explain his authority, he had ordered Flint to go immediately to the British High Commission and begin writing her report and when Cohen had protested – 'For God's sake, Alan, she's been through a lot' – he had snapped back, 'Haven't we all?' Then he had taken Cohen to one side and dressed him down as though he was a wayward subaltern. 'We are not best pleased with you, Harry Cohen, you are in extremely bad odour. When the minister learned you had been holding back on us about Taggart he went through the roof. Take my word: You will not be quickly forgiven for your sins, not in Whitehall.'

'Frankly, Alan, you're not in any position to complain about "holding back", are you?' Cohen had said.

'Meaning?'

'Harling.'

'What about the wretched Harling?'

'You know full well what I mean.'

Devereaux had pursed his lips and stayed silent and

Cohen had grown tired of the game and turned on his heels.

'And where might you be going, young Cohen?'

'To the High Commission. I also have a report to write.'

'Oh, no you do not – and you will not set foot inside the High Commission. In fact, once Harling is returned to us, you will have nothing more to do with this matter, nothing whatsoever. We are dispensing with your services, with a small gratuity and muted thanks. In due course, if the minister forgives you, you may find your name somewhere on the honour's list – somewhere far down the honour's list – but, frankly, I would not count on it.'

'Go to hell, Alan.'

And Devereaux had smiled. 'If I remember, you've said that to me before.'

Only two guards prowled the Turkish checkpoint but Cohen could hear the voices of many more concealed in slit trenches somewhere behind them. If and when the war started this would be the front line; the most highly militarised line in the world, except for North Korea. That had been Harling's joke, Flint had told him – and his undoing: *Like North Korea but the food's better. So's the climate*.

She had been furiously angry when Cohen had told her that Harling would not be crossing the line – not with her and certainly not in her custody.

'Then I'm not leaving,' she had said.

'Grace, you have to understand you have no status

here – none. You entered the country illegally under a false identity and, officially, you are being deported. You simply don't have any choice in the matter.' Since her only response had been to glare at him and fold her arms in a stubborn set he had continued, 'And, to be blunt, I think you should count yourself extremely fortunate, given everything that's happened. You could have been detained – indeed, but for President Denktash, would have been detained – on any number of charges.'

Still she had not yielded and only Captain Zulu's warning that he would have her gagged and bound and placed aboard the waiting transport had persuaded her to leave. She had barely spoken a word to Cohen since – until, two hours ago, he had told her that she would be the arresting officer.

'And what did shit-face have to say about that?'

'Devereaux? He wanted somebody else sent out from the Yard but Glenning wouldn't hear of it and he got the commissioner on his side, and Devereaux didn't want a messy fight going all the way up to the minister. Nor did he want a public fight – with good reason.'

She had looked at him inquiringly, searching his face with those extraordinary eyes, but he'd shaken his head. 'One day, when it's all over. Meanwhile, you may not be the flavour of the month at Thames House but to Tom Glenning and those who listen to him you are something of a hero.'

'Really?'

'Really. If he has his way – and he will – what you've done will not go unrecognised.'

She had frowned and said, 'That's not the point,' and he had said, 'I know it's not.' And then she'd reached out and touched his arm. 'Thank you.'

'For what?'

'For everything you've done.'

'Oh, God,' Cohen had replied, 'As Cutter might say, Don't go sentimental on me, Flint' – and that had won him a laugh.

Cohen checked his watch and yawned. 'I need some air. I'll be back in a little while.'

Devereaux did not respond until he had started down the stairs. 'Remind her where she is, will you – what she's here for? Representing HMG and all that, not pursuing some personal vendetta. Do that for me, Harry, there's a good chap.'

Detective Inspector Grace Flint of the London Metropolitan Police, duly authorised as the arresting officer, warrant card in the pocket of her smartest summer jacket, waiting for Harling to cross the line. Even then she would have to wait a little longer, until he was transported to the British Sovereign Airbase – a little bit of England left over from Colonial times – where she would get to say: 'Frank Arthur Harling, I am arresting you for the murder of Peter Andrew Pendle.' And then she would caution him – 'You're not obliged to say anything and anything you do say,' and so forth – and then finally it would be over, all bar the shouting.

Shall I tell you how long it has been, Frank? Three

*years, one month and twenty-six days. Shall I tell you
the number of hours . . .*

Not long enough.

She thought of him in the room, standing at the bottom
of the bed. *Before I kill you . . .*

She thought of him gripping the back of the chair. *I'm
going to ram the pieces into places you don't want me to
go.*

She thought of the exquisite pain in her toes.

At the police station in Turkish Nicosia – in a cell
with dirty green walls and the stench of urine coming
from the toilet bowl – they'd asked her why she'd shot
an unarmed man in the shoulder. Was it really necessary
to wound him?

Actually, yes.

Actually, no – and I was aiming for the heart.

She thought of Metin Cadessi on his knees, her gun in
his face, fighting back the tears, frightened for his life –
and rightly so.

'*What did he tell you was going to happen? What was
the plan?*'

'*No plan, no plan.*'

'*I will kill you, Metin. One more makes no difference.*'

'*He said someone would come running out of the
house and I was to shoot them.*'

'*Who would come running out of the house?*'

'*Some fuck with a gun.*'

'*This gun, Metin?*'

'*Yes. I think so.*'

She thought of Cadessi creeping up the stairs, her two

steps behind, calling for Spenny, doing as he was told.

'*Sarah, Sarah, where are you?*'

'*Is that you, Cadessi?*' – Sarah's voice muffled, coming from behind a bedroom door. '*What the hell is going on?*'

'*It's terrible. Frank shot the woman. He shot Mr Shilling. I had to kill Frank.*'

'*You did what?*' – Sarah unlocking the door, flinging it open, coming out onto the landing.

'*Hello, Stella.*'

'*You little fuck*' – Sarah's anger, directed not at Flint but at Cadessi for setting her up. '*You snivelling piece of Turkish shit, you fucking . . .*'

'*Shut her dirty mouth, Metin, and put her in the room.*'

The room with the pictures, dirty pictures. She thought of the pictures the police had shown her of Sarah lying amidst that filth, naked, her thighs bloodied, her throat opened like a can.

It was Cadessi's semen they had found in her vagina. Having been denuded by two women he had reclaimed his manhood from one of them the only way he knew how, apparently.

She saw Cohen coming down the steps of the OP like a tired old man, and she thought of the abject look on his face when he'd come to her cell and confessed what he had done.

'You see, I had to get a proactive search under way – hence the warrant for your arrest. It was the only way I could think of finding you before they did.'

Since, as she saw it, he was then one of the major

obstacles standing between her and Harling she had not spared him. 'Didn't work, did it?' she'd said.

Devereaux's telephone vibrated in his shirt pocket – Glenning calling from England somewhat earlier then expected. Devereaux was not best pleased with Glenning either, and he was cold with him.

'Yes.'

'It's about Taggart. We were too late.'

'Too late for what?'

'He shot himself this afternoon. His wife found him in the library – a real bloody mess. He had the gun in his mouth when he pulled the trigger.'

Devereaux tried to imagine the scene.

Glenning said, 'Hello? Are you there?'

'And are you sure it was suicide?'

'The crime scene lads are still working on it – but, yes, I'd say it's pretty certain. His gun, his prints. His wife says he'd been brooding for days.'

'No note?'

'Not unless he posted it.'

'How thoughtless of him,' said Devereaux.

'You'll tell Harry?'

'What?'

'I know they didn't get on but he was his father-in-law, after all.'

'Yes,' said Devereaux noncommittally. 'Goodbye.'

Harry will be disappointed, Devereaux thought. Cohen had told him that the prospect of confronting his father-in-law with his crimes was what had kept him going – not that there was ever the remotest chance Devereaux would have allowed it.

'You will not go within a hundred miles of the Isle of Wight,' Devereaux would have told him before the night was out.

Now he could go if he wished. Perhaps he might change the name on his wife's gravestone.

Raising the glasses, Devereaux scoured the Turkish checkpoint. Not long now.

Flint said, 'I spoke to Dominique this afternoon. They've told her they think they can save his legs but it will be a long time before he walks again. If ever.'

'And your father?'

For the first time since Cohen had set eyes on her she smiled. 'He's fine. And he said to say hello to you. Actually, he wanted me to be a lot more effusive than that but I'll spare your blushes.'

'Please,' said Cohen. 'And I'll spare yours. I spoke to Cutter. He seems rather pleased with you. They arrested Kurlack this afternoon.' He straightened his back. 'Do you see the lights?'

'Yes.'

'Then it's time.'

Together they ducked under the red and white striped pole that guarded the Greek checkpoint and walked to exactly the midpoint of no-man's land where a UN truck waited with its engine running. By the common consent of the Greeks and the Turks, it was the peacekeepers who would transport Harling and the coffins to the air base, thus avoiding the need for any contact between the two sides. A UN captain, seconded from the Irish Guards, saluted Devereaux as he came to join them.

'Any news?' asked Cohen.

'About?'

'Any word from Glenning?'

Devereaux said, 'It's a little too early, don't you think? Later, I expect.' He nodded to Flint. 'And how are you feeling, Inspector? – oh, no, don't answer that.' He chuckled. 'As I recall from your report, the last person to ask you that question was young Sarah Spenny – and look what happened to her.'

'I'm fine, sir,' said Flint.

The truck that arrived at the checkpoint, passing through without hindrance, bore the markings of the Red Crescent, the Turkish equivalent of the Red Cross – another diplomatic nicety, Cohen supposed. But it was driven by a soldier and it was Zulu who stepped smartly down from the passenger side, still dressed in black. He was in a hurry, apparently – no time for polite formalities.

'Mister Cohen, Miss Flint, I have a delivery for you.' He barked an order and four men jumped from the back of the truck and began unloading simple wooden coffins that they placed side by side on the ground: one coffin, then a second, then a third – and even before the last one emerged, Cohen knew what they had done.

Flint was slower, but not by much.

'Where's Harling?'

'There, Miss Flint,' said Zulu, touching the third coffin with the toe of his boot. 'You're a better shot than Mister

Cohen would have me believe. The injuries you inflicted were fatal.'

'Just a minute,' Flint said but Zulu was already climbing back into the truck.

He slammed the door and leaned out of the window to say, 'I am instructed to tell you, Mister Cohen, that you are welcome in the TRNC at any time. You, on the other hand, Miss Flint, are not. The investigations into the deaths of Shilling and now Harling remain open and there is also the matter of the criminal damage you caused to twenty-three vehicles. Next time – if there is a next time – Mister Cohen will not be permitted to intervene.'

He tipped his fingers to his forehead in a mocking salute and then the truck was reversing back behind the Turkish line.

'Well,' said Devereaux, 'a tidy if not entirely satis-factory conclusion.' He turned to the UN captain and pointed towards the three coffins. 'Shall we get it done?'

'Open it,' said Flint.

Devereaux waved a hand at her as though she had said something ridiculous.

'Captain, will you please get your men to take the lid off that coffin, or get me the tools and I'll do it.'

Devereaux tried to take her arm but she shrugged him away.

'Are you mad?'

'Keep your hands off me, sir.' There was a dangerous edge to her voice that Cohen had heard before.

'Young woman, do not – *do not* – try my patience. You are a police officer, for goodness sake, and you know perfectly well that these are termed 'suspicious deaths' that must be – that will be – investigated by a coroner. The coffins are sealed until the coroner decides otherwise and you will not – *you will not* – tamper with the evidence. Is that clear?' Cohen had never seen Devereaux so agitated. 'Now, captain, if you please.'

'No' – Flint adamant. The coffins would not be moved.

'Harry, talk some sense into this woman.'

Cohen said, 'I can't. I don't have the authority – and neither do you. Captain, we're here merely as observers. Inspector Flint is the arresting officer and if she wants to determine if the man she came to arrest is really in one of those boxes, well . . .'

'I'm going to call London,' Devereaux said, and he turned towards the observation post.

'He worked for you, didn't he, sir?' Flint called after him, stopping him in his tracks. 'Harling, I mean. All along, he was one of yours – off the books but an MI5 asset nonetheless. Isn't that what they call them, Mr Cohen?'

'Sometimes,' said Cohen quietly.

'Captain, if you'll leave us for a moment' – Devereaux coming back fast, a look of thunder on his face.

'Let me guess, sir.'

'Stop this at once.'

'Originally he was legitimate – or as legit as you people get. He was talent spotted – isn't that the term you use? – and you gave him his get-out-of-jail-free card and in return he gave you good information about his crooked clients. Shilling was his handler, wasn't he? Went to the judge to speak up for Frank on your authority? How am I doing?'

'I'm warning you, Flint.'

'Then Maitland leads me to Ellis and you find out that Shilling was playing dirty pool. That's what Mr Cutter would call it – dirty pool: Shilling and his friends using Frank's information – or some of it – to extort money from the crooks. That's bad enough but it gets worse, doesn't it?'

While she was talking Flint walked in small circles that took her ever-nearer the UN truck. Arriving there as if by accident she began rooting in the back of it until she found what she was looking for.

'Because, thanks to Frank's affidavit that I hand you on a plate, you also discover that Shilling had protected Harling after he was involved in the murder of a police officer – not to mention what they did to me – stashed him in one your safe houses, gave him fake ID, got him out of the country on one of your planes. Everybody else thinks that Harling was just part of a rogue operation mounted by Shilling, but you know better. He *was* a rogue operative but he was also one of your assets – a sort of Dr Jekyll and Mr Hyde. When did you work it out, Mr Cohen?'

Cohen said, 'When I was last in Miami.'

Flint had found a crowbar in the back of the truck and she was now moving slowly towards the coffin Zulu had touched with his toe. So, too, was Devereaux.

'Mr Devereaux, sir, if you attempt to obstruct a police officer in the lawful execution of her duty I will use reasonable force to restrain you – meaning I'll hit you with this.'

'She means it, Alan,' Cohen said and Devereaux stopped moving.

'So, when you hired Mr Cohen to get to the bottom of all this – isn't that how he put it, Mr Cohen? – what you really intended was that he should get to the bottom of Shilling's part of it: Shilling, Spenny, Taggart, Kurlack – all those creeps. Oh, excuse my reference to your father-in-law, Mr Cohen.'

'Creep is a very good word,' said Cohen.

'And he was also supposed to find me – but only to stop me getting to Harling. Isn't that right, sir? Arresting Harling was never part of your game, was it?'

'You are out of your depth, young Flint.'

'Why is that, sir?' She had reached the coffin and, crouching down, she was probing the lid with the crowbar, searching for leverage. 'Because I'm just a copper, or just a girl, or both? And if Mr Cohen hadn't found me in time and I'd got hurt in your game – or killed, even – would it have mattered to you? What's one less copper? Plenty more like me.'

'I doubt it,' said Cohen.

'I hope not,' said Devereaux. 'Young Grace Flint, listen to me. It is not too late to redeem yourself – to receive the rewards that you are due. Even you, Cohen, are not yet beyond the pale. Leave that box alone.'

'Why, sir? What do you think I'll find?'

'There are matters that do not concern you. Matters I cannot explain.'

'Yeah,' she said. 'That's what I thought.'

With a strength born from rage she levered off the lid of Frank Harling's coffin and stared down unsurprised at the headless corpse of Metin Cadessi.

Grace Flint and Harry Cohen on a plane heading for London, she apparently asleep, her head resting on his shoulder.

Devereaux had told them that a formal protest would be lodged with the TRNC by Her Majesty's Government demanding that the 'error' be corrected: that Harling's body be returned or – if he was still alive – that his present whereabouts be revealed. Since HMG does not recognise the Turkish Republic of Northern Cyprus, they took no comfort from that.

Flint stirred and said, 'But he can't leave, can he? Frank, I mean: he's got nowhere else to go – not now, not yet.'

Cohen sighed. 'Grace, Zulu wasn't joking. You can't go back.'

She lifted her face and looked at him and Cohen thought that, at least on this, her father was wrong: whatever lay in Grace Flint's eyes it was not resignation.

Afterwards

S ix months on and Flint is spoiling herself in the pretentious coffee shop of the Buccaneer Hotel; Cutter's treat. 'We're running late,' he said, calling her on his cell phone, 'so why don't you divert yourself with some of those fancy strawberries? On me.' To celebrate the fact that this morning the Honorable Judge Walter R. Patterson has rejected the latest clutch of ingenious defence motions with no more than a curt 'denied', she is also diverting herself with a glass of champagne flavoured with peach nectar. 'Make no mistake about it, gentlemen,' the judge had told the assembled lawyers, 'this case *is* going to trial' – viz., Jackson Fucking Kurlack *is* going to trial – and Flint raises her glass in silent tribute to Kevin Hechter.

Now that sufficient time has passed it is the memory of Kevin whole that she holds. It is only in her nightmares that she sees his severed hand.

By calling ahead she has secured the same table where she and Cutter sat watching Aleksei Rykov come apart, Kevin's semi-automatic rock-steady in her hand. Since it was Rykov who led her – indirectly – to Frank Harling, and since Frank is supposedly the subject of this meeting – 'There's some shit about Harling you ought to know,' said Cutter – she thinks it is appropriate that she receives the news here.

She sees Cutter arrive at his customary pace, charging into Le Café at a hundred miles an hour. Though Flint has been back in Miami for almost three months to assist in the prosecution of Kurlack – essentially, to feed Carrie Evanovich's insatiable appetite for more and more incriminating evidence – she has seen Cutter only twice and then only in passing. What he calls the 'spillovers' of the case have taken him to Washington for much of that time, to counter the manoeuvres of those within the intelligence community who would prefer that all 'unnecessary matters' – those not strictly relevant to the destruction of the Lear – go unmentioned at Kurlack's trial.

If, that is, there really has to be a trial. Those in Washington concerned with 'the broader picture' continue to press, to ask if it isn't possible to cut some kind of deal with Kurlack's lawyers – one that would ensure a measure of justice while limiting the collateral damage. 'Not one that I would buy,' has been Cutter's implacable position and so far he has prevailed.

'Why, if it isn't Mrs Breslin,' Cutter says coming to her side, his grin in place, mischief in his eyes.

'Hello, Mr Cutter' – friendly enough but she keeps her smile reserved. Experience has taught her that an amiable Cutter can suck you in like quicksand and before you know it you're up to your neck in trouble. *What do you say, honey? You wanna stay here with Vladimir while we take care of the business? That okay with you, sweetheart?*

No – not okay, actually. Not again.

Sitting down Cutter says, 'Alex is in the john. He'll be here momentarily.'

'Alex?'

'Yeah, Alex Bland, I must have mentioned him. What's that you're drinking – champagne?'

She nods and Cutter continues, 'Carrie told me about the judge's ruling. Good job, Grace.'

'It was Carrie's motion – I'm just her water carrier. You were going to tell me about Mr Bland.'

'Sure. Works out of our embassy in Ankara. And don't give me the modesty bullshit. This is a team game and you're on the team and what I hear from Carrie is that you're more than pulling your weight.'

'Thank you. Is Mr Bland on the team?'

'Sort of,' says Cutter. 'And if you want to know what he does, ask him. Hey, Alex – over here.'

Alex Bland walks with a slight stoop as though apologising for his height. He is as thin as Cutter is stout and, unlike Cutter, he has kept his hair – a thick mop of light-brown hair that flops over his forehead. He has a wide sensuous mouth and dangerous eyes – dangerous for Flint, that is, for she finds herself instantly attracted by them; always a bad sign in a man.

He places on the table a package that is gift-wrapped in silver paper and tied with a scarlet ribbon, and holds out his hand to her. 'I've heard a lot about you,' he says, 'all of it good.'

'Alex was with Harry in Nicosia,' says Cutter, 'leaning on Denktash.'

'So, in part, you have me to thank for Captain Zulu,' says Bland. He has a quick, enriching smile that he can turn on like a light – another warning turn-on for Flint. 'Sorry about that.'

'Wasn't your fault, sir.'

He has still not let go of her hand.

'Oh, please don't call me sir. You make me feel old enough to be your father – which I am not.'

Straight-faced she says, 'Then how old are you, Alex?' and he pulls away his hand in mock alarm.

'None of your business.'

'The same as what you do? At the embassy, I mean.'

Bland laughs and brushes at his forelock and says, 'Well, you did warn me, Aldus.'

Suddenly serious Cutter says, 'He keeps his ear to the ground, Flint. That's why he's here' – he points to the package – 'with that.'

After they have ordered, while Flint stays silent and watches his face, Bland says, 'Initially what we heard is that he was free and clear. There was an infection in the wound and they had to reset the shoulder and he was in hospital for just under three weeks. Then he went back to Kyrenia where he kept a pretty low profile – under orders, I'm told: keep your head down and stay out of trouble until this thing blows over.'

'Never would have blown over,' says Cutter. 'Not so long as she breathes.'

Bland shrugs. 'The Brit protest was simply window-dressing, of course. Denktash's people sent it back across the line and told the high commissioner that if he wanted information he should send a formal request – a letter rogatory; and I quote, "as befits communication between two sovereign governments" – and that was it: end of story.'

'As Devereaux always supposed,' says Cutter.

Mention of Devereaux's name causes Flint to reach for her glass half-filled with champagne.

'Likely so,' says Bland, 'but then about two weeks ago I get word that Harling's growing restless, that he wants to find some way off the island. With the money he's got that's the easy part. The hard part is finding some place to go and what I hear is that he's looking to do a deal – not with the Brits, of course, but with us.'

'Us?' says Flint, breaking her silence.

'Specifically the agency. What he does is get a message to Langley that there were a couple of CIA operations that got compromised by The Enterprise and that he's willing to provide the detail in return for a little help in finding a safe haven. If we – they – give him a *lot* of help then, he says, he'll give up chapter and verse on anything they want to know. Basically, reading between the lines, he was offering to give them every dirty secret he had on Devereaux and MI5 – and MI6, I wouldn't be surprised.'

Catching Flint's startled look Cutter says, 'I didn't know. I wasn't in the loop – not then.'

'Langley was not disinterested,' Bland says carefully, 'but they wanted to know more about the goods on offer. So, they sent a representative to meet Harling. That was ten days ago, at the Dome Hotel – which was Harling's idea. He set the rendezvous. His mistake.'

'Too public,' says Cutter by way of explanation.

'They were due to meet again the next night but Harling never showed.'

'How long did you wait?' asks Flint and Bland replies with a smile.

'As best we know, he was arrested that afternoon – not arrested, exactly, but picked up at a checkpoint on the Nicosia road. It wasn't a routine checkpoint,' says Bland and then he pauses. 'It was Zulu's men. Two days after that – I happened to be in Nicosia – this was delivered to my hotel room.'

By 'this' he means the parcel that now sits on the chair between he and Flint.

'It was intended for you, although I didn't know that until I opened it and found this inside.'

From his pocket Bland takes an unmarked envelope that is not sealed. He hands it to her and she removes the card that is inside on which is typed, 'Give this to Flint – an eye for an eye.'

'You can take it from me,' Bland says, 'that Harling is dead.'

No, I can't, is what she thinks. What she says is, 'How do you know?'

Cutter intervenes. 'Three days ago the TRNC notified the high commissioner that a British tourist name of

Gerald Sutton had been killed in a road accident – so they said. They delivered the body to the checkpoint and it was flown to London. I just got through talking to Glenning – that's why we're late. It's Harling, positively ID'd from his prints. No doubt about it.'

Flint does not reply. She lifts the parcel and feels its weight – and feels in herself the near-certainty that, at least on his final point, they are telling her the truth: Frank Harling is finally beyond her reach.

'You don't believe it was an accident?' she finally says.

'No,' says Cutter. 'Nor will you when you open the package.' She begins pulling at the ribbon but Cutter says sharply, 'Not here.'

'Where, then?'

She stares at them, one to the other, until Bland says with resignation, 'I've got a room upstairs.'

They leave the coffee shop and cross the lobby and take the elevator to the sixth floor and the corridor to Bland's room, he leading the way, Flint in the middle bearing the parcel, Cutter bringing up the rear.

In Bland's room she places the parcel on the bed and unties the ribbon and carefully removes the paper. Now she is looking at a cardboard box with a lid on which has been pasted a garish photograph of a coffin.

'Are you sure about this?' says Bland.

No, actually – but also yes. Nothing – not even her flooding sense of revulsion – can prevent her from lifting the lid.

She does what she must do and finds beneath the lid a mask – a death mask cast from terribly distorted features that tells her Frank Harling did not die peacefully.

An eye for an eye, a mask for a mask – his even more permanent than hers.

'So, what do you feel?'

Good question. Back home in her temporary apartment on Key Biscayne, watching a pair of cigarette boats cutting creamy wakes across the bay, Flint sifted through the maelstrom of emotions that were tugging at her: A sliver of relief that it was finally over but also anger that Devereaux had so neatly closed the books – as he would no doubt put it – and frustration at her inability to do anything about it. There was satisfaction in knowing that Harling had likely experienced something of the terror and the pain he had inflicted on her – but also guilt that she took any comfort from that. She did not know what she really felt until Gilles Bourdonnec forced the issue.

'Grace,' he said, 'are you there?'

'I suppose that most of all I feel cheated.'

'Cheated?' The phone line was extraordinarily clear. 'I don't understand.'

She hesitated – unsure even now if she should tell Gilles what she had not told a living soul.

Why not? She imagined Gilles trapped in his wheelchair, trapped in his small apartment, never able to leave it without the strong back of someone willing to carry him down and back up one hundred and thirty-seven stairs. Because of her, basically – because of her obsession. She owed him the truth.

'Grace.'

'He was mine, Gilles. He belonged to me. I was going back for him.'

'What! What craziness is this? You could never go back.'

'Yes I could,' she said quietly.

'When? How? Grace, I do not believe—'

She cut him off. 'After Kurlack's trial, when I got leave. There is a ferry that runs between the TRNC and Lebanon, which means I didn't have to go anywhere near the Turkish mainland. With luck I could have been in and out in the same day.'

'But there are checks, surely, even on those who come from the Lebanon? There must be a watch list. They would have spotted you the moment you landed.'

'No, they wouldn't,' she said. 'You forget, I'm good at not being me.' Then she brightened. 'I've got new ID: Katia Borville, French national, freelance photographer – what do you think?'

'I think your Captain Zulu did you a very large favour. *Merde!*'

'It wasn't right, Gilles. I couldn't just let him go.'

'So . . .' She could hear the irritation building in his voice. 'So, let us assume – just for one crazy moment – that you had succeeded, that you had got there. Then what? Then what would you have done?'

Then what? – that same old question they always asked; the one she asked herself.

'He would have been protected,' Gilles said.

'No he wouldn't – watched, more like it, rather than protected. They would never have assumed I would be stupid enough to go back.' She laughed. 'Like you, darling Gilles.'

'Oh, no, Grace, not like me,' he said firmly. 'I know better. I know you are a mule. Dominique told me, "She will never stop, never give up." I argued with her but of course I knew she was right. I just did not believe you would be *this* crazy. Tell me,' he said, 'you think – you really believe – he would have gone with you, back on your ferry to the Lebanon?'

She thought about her answer and then she said, 'Yes.'

'Why? Why would he do that?'

'Because he knew – he's the only one who really knew – that when I shot him I meant to kill him. I missed, Gilles. I was aiming for his heart.'

'And?'

'I wouldn't have missed a second time.'

Now he knew what she meant to do – why she felt cheated. She let the silence hang. Eventually, as though the subject of Harling had ceased to interest him, Gilles said, 'So, the Kurlack matter goes well?'

'Better than well. I've got a strong lead on the three assholes Kurlack sent down to the island to take us out – the ones who planted the bomb. I'm going down there tomorrow to see if Peggy Pringle can identify them from their mug shots. They all match her descriptions – I'm pretty sure she'll ID them. And, if she does, one or more of them will turn. That's the kind of assholes they are.'

'*Bien*. Then it will be over.'

'No,' she said. 'There's those other assholes to find – the ones who killed Mario and hurt you. Somebody knows who they are. That's next.'

'Then I am even more pleased that Harling is no longer around to distract you. I would like them found, Grace.'

'Count on it,' she said, using Cutter's drawl.

Now Gilles laughed and said, 'Dominique wants to speak with you. Take care, *gros bisous*.'

While she waited for Dominique to come to the phone, she wandered out onto the balcony from where she could see the whole sweep of the bay; where, so too, could Harling – in a manner of speaking – for she had mounted his mask on the wall.

For fuck's sake get it done, he seemed to be saying, his mouth set in an eternal scream.

Well, it is done now, Frank.

'Did he tell you?' Dominique's voice bursting with excitement on the phone.

'Tell me what?'

'He walked.'

'*What!* When?'

'Today! He walked five steps! Tomorrow, they say, it will be six.'

Now she was in tears, Flint not far behind.

'Oh, Dominique.'

'He's going to get better, Grace. It's going to be okay.'

Now it is, she thought. Now, at last, it could be.

Thanks

Despite the circumstances of her recollection, Grace Flint is a stand-up, front-row fan of Annie Lennox. She – and I – are grateful for Annie's permission to use lyrics from her masterfully enigmatic 'Why'.

Three remarkable women – Special Agent Wendy Lovato of the Drug Enforcement Administration, Detective Superintendent Suzanne Williams of the London Metropolitan Police and Commissaire Mireille Ballestrazzi of the Police Judiciaire – were the unwitting inspiration for Flint.

Sarah Spankie, Gwen Clark, Sue Bastable, Pat and John Barry, Ros and Richard Baronio, Bob Cardona, Louise Chinn, Françoise Doucet, Laurence Miller-Franiatte, Len Gowland, John Malkovich, David Miller, Alan Samson, Christopher Morgan, Janet de Botton, Marina Voikhanskaya, Nicky Dingwall-Main and Stephen Moorby provided encouragement and help.

Robert Ducas, having given me twenty-five years of friendship and superb representation, gave me support and understanding when it really mattered.

Kate and Bob Gavron shared with us a pizza supper, went home to read the first draft – and changed my life.

Ed Victor did what no other literary agent could have done. He is simply the best not least because he values the strength of his team. So, too, does Andrew Nurnberg. To them and all of theirs, thank you.

Phyllis Grann of Penguin-Putnam and Amanda Ridout of Headline Publishing were the first publishers to make the huge leap of faith. Phyllis also gave me the sage advice to listen to my editors – Neil Nyren and Bill Massey – and, because I did, this is a far better book than it might have been.

Sara Walden, who is Flint's soul sister, was the first and last reader of every draft and made the difference a thousand times. For her belief in Grace – and me – and constant support, I owe her more than I can ever repay.

Finally, Gilles and Dominique Bourdonnec allowed me to borrow their names, their home and much else of their lives. For all that they have given me, and for all that we have shared, this book is dedicated to them.

When the Wind Blows

James Patterson

In his best book yet, James Patterson has written a riveting adventure-thriller that no reader will ever forget. Never has it been truer of a Patterson novel – the pages fly.

Frannie O'Neill, a young and talented veterinarian whose husband was recently murdered, comes across an amazing discovery in the woods near her animal hospital. Soon after, Kit Harrison, a troubled and unconventional FBI agent, arrives on Frannie's doorstep. And then there is eleven-year-old Max – Frannie's amazing discovery – and one of the most unforgettable creations in thriller fiction.

WHEN THE WIND BLOWS will not just thrill readers. It will make their imaginations and hearts soar. In the most brilliant and original 'what if' suspense novel to come along in a decade, James Patterson has surpassed the page-turning chills of his megabestsellers CAT AND MOUSE and KISS THE GIRLS.

'Patterson, among the best novelists of crime stories ever, has reached his pinnacle' *USA Today*

'Packed with white-knuckled twists' *Daily Mail*

'Patterson's action-packed story keeps the pages flicking by' *The Sunday Times*

0 7472 5789 2

Nemesis

Bill Napier

According to a shock CIA report, Russian cosmonauts have deflected a giant asteroid onto a collision course with the United States – presenting the President with an impossible moral dilemma: either he must wait passively for almost certain annihilation, or retaliate first with a massive nuclear strike.

The only hope of averting catastrophe lies with an elite team of the world's top astronomers and astrophysicists, gathered secretly at Eagle Peak Observatory, Arizona. They have five days to identify the asteroid – codename Nemesis – and stop it. If they can't, the President will have to assume the asteroid is going to hit and make his appalling choice.

But as time begins to run out and the search for Nemesis becomes increasingly desperate, British asteroid expert Oliver Webb has an extraordinary idea – that the key lies in the dusty pages of an obscure seventeenth-century Latin manuscript, a manuscript which has just gone mysteriously missing . . .

'The most exciting book I have ever read' Arthur C. Clarke

'Napier has put a lifetime's knowledge into a stomach-churning thriller . . . a gripping read' *Scotsman*

0 7472 5993 3

HEADLINE
FEATURE

If you enjoyed this book here is a selection of other bestselling titles from Headline